John Adams Library, Jethro Tull, John Adams

Horse-Hoeing Husbandry

An essay on the principles of vegetation and tillage. Designed to introduce a new

method of culture - whereby the produce of land will be increased, and the usual

expence lessened

John Adams Library, Jethro Tull, John Adams

Horse-Hoeing Husbandry
An essay on the principles of vegetation and tillage. Designed to introduce a new method of culture - whereby the produce of land will be increased, and the usual expence lessened

ISBN/EAN: 9783337381387

Printed in Europe, USA, Canada, Australia, Japan

Cover: Foto ©Andreas Hilbeck / pixelio.de

More available books at **www.hansebooks.com**

Horfe-Hoeing Husbandry:

OR,

An ESSAY on the PRINCIPLES

OF

Vegetation *and* Tillage.

Defigned to introduce

A New Method of Culture;

WHEREBY

The Produce of Land will be increafed, and the
ufual Expence leffened.

Together with

Accurate DESCRIPTIONS and CUTS of the Inftruments
employed in it.

By JETHRO TULL, *Efq;*
Of Shalborne *in* Berkfhire.

The FOURTH EDITION, very carefully Corrected.

To which is prefixed,

A New PREFACE by the EDITORS, addreffed to all
concerned in AGRICULTURE.

LONDON:

Printed for A. MILLAR, oppofite to *Catharine-ftreet*
in the *Strand.*

M.DCC.LXII.

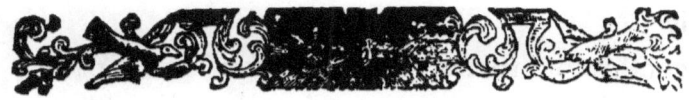

THE
P R E F A C E.

A S Mr. *Tull*'s Eſſay on *Horſe-hoeing Huſbandry* has been publiſhed ſome Years, it may be preſumed that the World hath by this time formed ſome Judgment of his Performance; which renders it the leſs neceſſary for the Editors of this Impreſſion to ſay much concerning it. For every Man who has attended to the Subject, and duly conſidered the Principles upon which our Author's Method of Culture is founded, is an equal Judge how far his Theory is agreeable to Nature: Though it is but too true, that few have made ſufficient Experiments to be fully informed of its Worth.

How it has happened, that a Method of Culture, which propoſes ſuch Advantages to thoſe who ſhall duly proſecute it, hath been ſo long neglected in this Country, may be matter of Surprize to ſuch as are not acquainted with the Characters of the Men on whom the Practice thereof depends; but to thoſe who know them thoroughly it can be none. For it is certain that very few of them can be prevailed on to alter their uſual Methods upon any Conſideration; though they are convinced that their

con-

continuing therein difables them from paying
their Rents, and maintaining their Families.

And, what is ftill more to be lamented,
thefe People are fo much attached to their old
Cuftoms, that they are not only averfe to alter
them themfelves, but are moreover induftrious
to prevent others from fucceeding, who attempt to introduce any thing new; and indeed
have it too generally in their Power, to defeat
any Scheme which is not agreeable to their
own Notions; feeing it muft be executed by
the fame Sort of Hands.

This naturally accounts for Mr. *Tull*'s Hufbandry having been fo little practifed.   But as
the Methods commonly ufed, together with
the mean Price of Grain for fome Years paft,
have brought the Farmers every-where fo low,
that they pay their Rents very ill, and in many
Places have thrown up their Farms; the Cure
of thefe Evils is certainly an Object worthy of
the public Attention : For if the Proprietor
muft be reduced to cultivate his own Lands,
which cannot be done but by the Hands of
thefe indocile People, it is eafy to guefs on
which Side his Balance of Profit and Lofs will
turn.

This Confideration, together with many
others which might be enumerated, hath in-
duced the Editors to recommend this Treatife
once more to the ferious Attention of every one
who wifhes well to his Country; in hopes that
                                                    fome

fome may be prevailed upon, by regard either to the public Good or their own private Intereft, to give the Method here propofed a fair and impartial Trial : For could it be introduced into feveral Parts of this Country by Men of generous Principles, their Example might, in time, eftablifh the Practice thereof, and bring it into general Ufe; which is not to be expected by any other means.

It is therefore to fuch only, as are qualified to judge of a Theory from the Principles on which it is founded, that the Editors addrefs themfelves, defiring they will give this Effay another Reading with due Attention : and at the fame time they beg leave to remind them how unfit the common Practifers of Hufbandry are to pafs Judgment, either on the Theory or Practice of this Method; for which Reafon it is hoped that none will be influenced by fuch, but try the Experiment themfelves with proper Care.

As a Motive to this, it is to be obferved that, although the Method of Culture here propofed has made little Progrefs in *England*, it is not like to meet with the fame Neglect abroad, efpecially in *France*; where a Tranflation of Mr. *Tull's* Book was undertaken, at one and the fame time, by three different Perfons of Confideration, without the Privity of each other : But afterwards, Two of them put their Papers into the Hands of the Third, Mr. *Du Hamel du Manceau*, of the *Royal Academy of Sciences* at *Paris*, and of

the

the *Royal Society* at *London*; who has publifhed
a Book, intituled, *A Treatife of Tillage on the
Principles of Mr.* Tull. The ingenious Author
has indeed altered the Method obferved by Mr.
Tull in his Book; yet has very exactly given his
Principles and Rules: But as he had only feen
the Firft Edition of the *Horfe-hoeing Hufbandry*,
fo he is very defective in his Defcriptions of the
Ploughs and Drills, which in that were very
imperfect, and were afterwards amended by Mr.
Tull in his Additions to that Effay.

One of our principal Reafons for taking Notice of this Book is, to fhew the Comparifon this
Author has made between the Old Method of
Hufbandry and the New. By his Calculation
the Profits arifing from the New, are confiderably more than double thofe of the Old. For,
according to him, the Profits of Twenty Acres
of Land for Ten Years, amount, at 10*d.* $\frac{1}{4}$ *per*
Livre,

	l.	*s.*	*d.*	
By the Old Method, to 3000 Livres, or	131	5	0	} *Sterling.*
By the New Method, to 7650 Livres, or	334	13	9	

which makes a prodigious Difference in favour
of the latter. As this Computation was made
by one who cannot be fuppofed to have any
Prejudice in favour of Mr. *Tull*'s Scheme, it
will naturally find more Credit with the Public
than any Comparifon made by Mr. *Tull* himfelf, or by fuch as may have an Attachment to
his Principles.

It

It may probably be expected, that the Editors fhould take Notice of fuch Objections as have been made, either to Mr. *Tull*'s Theory or Practice; but we do not know any that in the leaft affect his Principles : They ftand uncontroverted : Nor are there any to the Practice, which may not be equally urged againft every Sort of Improvement. One of the principal which have come to our Knowlege is, its being impracticable in common Fields, which make a great Part of this Country, without the Concurrence of every one who occupies Land in the fame Field. But doth not this equally affect the Old Hufbandry ? For every fuch Perfon is obliged to keep the Turns of plowing, fallowing, &c. with the other Occupiers ; fo that if any of them were inclinable to improve their Lands, by fowing Grafs-feeds, or any other Method of Culture, they are now under the fame Difficulties as they would be, were they to practife Mr. *Tull*'s Method. Therefore this is rather to be lamented as a public Misfortune, than to be brought as an Objection to the Practicablenefs of that Method. Others object, that the introducing this Sort of Hufbandry is unneceffary, feeing the Improvements which are made by Grafs-feeds are fo confiderable ; befides, that the Returns made by the Fold and the Dairy, being much quicker than thofe of Grain, engage the Farmer to mix Plowing and Grazing together. But when this is duly confidered it

can

can have no fort of Weight : for is it not well known that, in thofe Farms where the greateft Improvements have been made by Grafs-feeds, the Quantity of Dreffing required for the Arable Land often runs away with moft of the Profit of the whole Farm? efpecially when the Price of Grain is low. And if this be the Situation of the moft improved Farms, what muft be the Cafe of thofe which chiefly confift of Arable Land; where moft of the Dreffing muft be purchafed at a great Price, and often fetched from a confiderable Diftance? Add to this the great Expence of Servants and Horfes, unavoidable in Arable Farms; and it will appear how great the Advantages are which the Grafier hath over the plowing Farmer. So that it is much to be wifhed, the Practice of mixing the Two Sorts of Hufbandry were more generally ufed in every Part of the Kingdom; which would be far from rendering Mr. *Tull*'s Method of Culture ufelefs; feeing that, when it is well underftood, it will be found the fureft Method to improve both.

For although Mr. *Tull* chiefly confined the Practice of his Method to the Production of Grain (which is a great Pity), yet it may be extended to every Vegetable which is the Object of Culture in the Fields, Gardens, Woods, &c. and perhaps may be applied to many other Crops, to equal, if not greater Advantage, than to Corn.

In

In the Vineyard it has been long practised with Succefs ; and may be ufed in the Hop-Ground with no lefs Advantage. For the Culture of Beans, Peas, Woad, Madder, and other large-growing Vegetables ; as alfo for Lucern, Saintfoin, and the larger Graffes; we dare venture to pronounce it the only Method of Culture for Profit to the Farmer ; feeing that, in all thefe Crops, one Sixth Part of the Seeds now commonly fown will be fufficient for the fame Quantity of Land, and the Crop in Return will be much greater; which, when the Expence of Seeds is duly confidered, will be found no fmall Saving to the Farmer.

Nor fhould this Method of Culture be confined to *Europe :* for it may be practifed to as great Advantage in the *Britifh* Colonies in *America,* where, in the Culture of the Sugar-Cane, Indigo, Cotton, Rice, and almoft all the Crops of that Country, it will certainly fave a great Expence of Labour, and improve the Growth of every Plant, more than can be imagined by fuch as are ignorant of the Benefit arifing from this Culture. And fhould the Subjects of *Great Britain* neglect to introduce this Method into her Colonies, it may be prefumed our Neighbours will take care not to *be blameable on this Head*; for they feem to be as intent upon extending every Branch of Trade, and making the greateft Improvements of their Land, as we are indifferent to both : So that, unlefs a contrary Spirit be foon exerted, the Balance of

Trade, Power, and every other Advantage, muft
be againft us.

There have been Objections made by fome to
Mr. *Tull*'s Method, as if it were practicable only
on fuch Lands as are foft and light, and not at
all on ftiff and ftony Ground. That it hath not
been practifed on either of thefe Lands in *England* we are willing to grant; but we muft not
from thence infer that it is impoffible to apply it
to them. For the Hoe-Plough has been very
long ufed in the Vineyards in many Countries,
where the Soil is ftronger, and abounds with
Stones full as much as any Part of this Country.
However, though the Ufe of this Plough may
be attended with fome Difficulties upon fuch
Land, for Wheat, or Plants of low Growth,
whofe Roots may be in Danger of being turned
out of the Ground, or their Tops buried by the
Clods or Stones; yet none of the larger-grow-
ing Plants are fubject to the fame Inconveniencies.
Befides, the ftronger the Soil is, the more Benefit
will it receive from this Method of Culture, if
the Land be thereby more pulverized; which
will certainly be the Confequence, where the
Method laid down by Mr. *Tull* is duly obferved.

But as moft Inftruments, in their Firft Ufe,
are attended with fome Difficulty, efpecially in
the Hands of fuch as are indocile, the Hoe-plough
has been complained of, as cumberfome and un-
wieldy to the Horfe and Ploughman. But perhaps this arifes chiefly from the Unwillingnefs of
the

the Workmen to introduce any new Inftrument: Indeed, feeing little is to be expected from thofe who have been long attached to different Methods, the fureft Way to promote the Ufe of it, is to engage young Perfons, who may probably be better difpofed, to make the Trial at their firft entering into Bufinefs; and then a little Ufe will make it eafy. It is proper to obferve here, that the Swing-plough, which is commonly ufed in the deep Land about *London*, will do the Bufinefs of the Hoe-plough in all Ground that is not very ftrong, or very ftony; and that where it is fo, the Foot-plough, made proportionably ftrong, will completely anfwer all Purpofes. But it muft be remembered, that when thefe are ufed to hoe Corn, the Board on the Left Hand of the Plough, anfwering the Mould-Board, muft be taken off; otherwife fo much Earth will run to the Left Side, as to injure the Crop when it is low.

The *Drills* are excellent Inftruments; yet we imagine them capable of fome farther Improvement. Parallel Grooves, at about an Inch afunder, round the Infide of the Hopper, would fhew the Man who follows the Drill, whether or no both Boxes vent the Seed equally. By an Hitch from the Plank to the Harrow, the latter may be lifted to a proper Height, fo as not to be in the Way when the Ploughman turns at the Headland. Two light Handles on the Plank, like thofe of the common Plough, would

3 enable

enable the Perfon who follows the Drill to keep
it from falling off the Middle of the Ridge.   It
may alfo be ufeful, in wet Weather, to double
the Drills ; by which means Two Ridges may
be fown at the fame time, the Horfe going between them : For the Planks of Two Drills,
each Plank having one of the Shafts fixed to it,
may be joined End for End by Two flat Bars of
Iron, one on each Side, well fecured by Iron
Pins and Screws ; and, by correfponding Holes
in the Planks and Bars, the Diftance between
the Drills may be altered, according to the different Spaces between the Ridges.

    The Alterations made by the Editors of this
Impreffion are little more than omitting the con-
troverfial Parts of the Book, which were judged
of no Service to the Reader, as they no-ways af-
fected the Merits of Mr. *Tull*'s Principles.

    But as he endeavoured to recommend his
Theory by drawing a Comparifon between the
Old Method of Culture and the New, fo we
beg leave to annex a Computation of the Expence and Profit of each ; for which we are
obliged to a Gentleman, who for fome Years
practifed both in a Country where the Soil was
of the fame Nature with that from whence
Mr. *Tull* drew his Obfervations, *viz.* light and
chalky.   And we chufe to give this the rather,
as it comes from one who has no Attachment
to Mr. *Tull*'s Method, farther than that he
found it anfwer in his Trials.   We appeal to
                                    Experience,

Experience, whether every Article in this Calculation is not eftimated in favour of the Common Hufbandry ; whether the Expence be not rated lower than moft Farmers find it, and the Crop fuch as they would rejoice to fee, but feldom do, in the Country where this Computation was made.

In the New Hufbandry every Article is put at its full Value, and the Crop of each Year is Four Bufhels fhort of the other ; tho', in feveral Years Experience, it has equalled, and generally exceeded, thofe of the Neighbourhood in the Old Way.

An Eftimate of the Expence and Profit of Ten Acres of Land in Twenty Years.

I. *In the Old Way.*

First Year, for Wheat, cofts
33 *l.* 5 *s. viz.*

	l.	*s.*	*d.*	*l.*	*s.*	*d.*
Firft Plowing, at 6 *s. per* Acre - - - -	3	0	0			
Second and Third Ditto, at 8 *s. per* Acre - -	4	0	0			
Manure, 30 *s. per* Acre	15	0	0			
				22	0	0
Two Harrowings, and Sowing, at 2 *s.* 6 *d. per* Acre - - -	1	5	0			
Seed, three Bufhels *per* Acre, at 4 *s. per* Bufh.	6	0	0			
Weeding, at 2 *s. per* Acre	1	0	0			
Reaping, Binding, and Carrying, at 6 *s. per* Acre - - - -	3	0	0			
				11	5	0

	l.	s.	d.
Brought over - - - - - -	33	5	0

Second Year, for Barley, costs 11 *l.* 6 *s.* 8 *d. viz.*

	l.	s.	d.
Once Plowing, at 6 *s. per* Acre - - - - -	3	0	0
Harrowing and Sowing, at 1 *s.* 6 *d. per* Acre,	0	15	0
Weeding, at 1 *s. per* Acre	0	10	0
Seed, 4 Bushels *per* Acre, at 2 *s. per* Bushel -	4	0	0
Cutting, Raking, and Carrying, at 3 *s.* 2 *d. per* Acre - - -	1	11	8
Grass-Seeds, at 3 *s. per* Acre - - - - -	1	10	0

	l.	s.	d.
	11	6	8
	44	11	8

	l.	s.	d.
Third and Fourth Years, lying in Grass, cost nothing: So that the Expence of Ten Acres in Four Years comes to 44 *l.* 11 *s.* 8 *d.* and in Twenty Years to - -	222	18	4

	l.	s.	d.
First Year's Produce is half a Load of Wheat *per* Acre, at 7 *l.* - -	35	0	0
Second Years Produce is Two Quarters of Barley *per* Acre, at 1 *l.*	20	0	0
Third and Fourth Years Grass is valued at 1 *l.* 10 *s. per* Acre - -	15	0	0
So that the Produce of Ten Acres in Four Years is - - - -	70	0	0

And in Twenty Years it will be - 350 0 0
Deduct the Expence, and there re-⎫
  mains clear Profit on Ten Acres ⎬ 127 1 8
  in 20 Years by the Old Way - ⎭

II. *In the New Way.*

First Year's extraordinary Expence⎫
  is, for plowing and manuring ⎪
  the Land, the same as in Old ⎬ 22 0 0
  Way - - - - - - ⎭

Plowing once more, at⎫
  4 s. *per* Acre   - ⎬ 2 0 0

Seed, 9 Gallons *per* Acre,⎫
  at 4 s. *per* Bushel - ⎬ 2 5 0

Drilling, at 7 d. *per* Acre   0 5 10

Hand-hoeing and Weed-⎫
  ing, at 2 s. 6 d. *per* Acre ⎬ 1 5 0

Horse-hoeing Six times,⎫
  at 10 s. *per* Acre - ⎬ 5 0 0

Reaping, Binding, and⎫
  Carrying, at 6 s. *per* ⎬ 3 0 0
  Acre - - - - -⎭

The standing annual⎫
Charge on Ten Acres is - ⎬ 13 15 10

  Therefore the Expence on Ten⎫ 275 16 8
Acres in Twenty Years is - - ⎭

  Add the Extraordinaries of the⎫ 297 16 8
First Year, and the Sum is - - ⎭

  The yearly Produce is at least⎫
Two Quarters of Wheat *per* Acre, ⎪
at 1 l. 8 s. *per* Quarter; which, on ⎬ 560 0 0
Ten Acres in Twenty Years, a-⎪
mounts to - - - - - ⎭

  Therefore, all things paid, there⎫
remains clear Profit on Ten Acres ⎬ 262 3 4
in Twenty Years by the New Way ⎭

So that the Profit on Ten Acres of Land in Twenty Years, in the New Way, exceeds that in the Old by 135 *l.* 1 *s.* 8 *d.* and consequently is considerably more than double thereof: an ample Encouragement to practise a Scheme, whereby so great Advantage will arise from so small a Quantity of Land, in the Compass of a Twenty-one Years Lease; One Year being allowed, both in the Old and New Way, for preparing the Ground.

It ought withal to be observed, that Mr. *Tull's* Husbandry requires no Manure at all, tho' we have here, to prevent Objections, allowed the Charge thereof for the first Year; and moreover, that tho' the Crop of Wheat from the *Drill-plough* is here put only at Two Quarters on an Acre, yet Mr. *Tull* himself, by actual Experiment and Measure, found the Produce of his drilled Wheat-crop amounted to almost Four Quarters on an Acre: And, as he has delivered this Fact upon his own Knowlege, so there is no Reason to doubt of his Veracity, which has never yet been called in question. But that we might not be supposed to have any Prejudice in favour of his Scheme, we have chosen to take the Calculations of others rather than his, having no other View in what we have said, than to promote the Cause of Truth, and the public Welfare.

The Wheat and Turnep Drill-Boxes, or the Drill Plough complete, mentioned in this Treatise, may be had at Mr. *Mulford's* in *Cursitor-street, Chancery-lane, London.*

C H A P.

CHAP. I.

Of Roots *and* Leaves.

SINCE the moſt immediate Uſe of *Agriculture*, in feeding Plants, relates to their *Roots*, they ought to be treated of in the firſt Place.

Roots are very different in different Plants: But 'tis not neceſſary here to take notice of all the nice Diſtinctions of them; therefore I ſhall only divide them in general into two Sorts, *viz.* *Horizontal-Roots*, and *Tap-Roots*, which may include them all.

All have Branchings and Fibres going all manner of ways, ready to fill the Earth that is open.

But ſuch *Roots* as I call Horizontal (except of Trees) have ſeldom any of their Branchings deeper than the Surface or Staple of the Earth, that is commonly mov'd by the Plough or Spade.

The Tap-Root commonly runs down Single and Perpendicular *(a)*, reaching ſometimes many Fathoms below.

This (tho' it goes never ſo deep) has horizontal ones paſſing out all round the Sides; and extend to ſeveral Yards Diſtance from it, after they are by their

---

(a) In this manner deſcends the firſt Root of every Seed ; but of Corn very little, if at all, deeper than the Earth is tilled.

Theſe firſt Seed Roots of Corn die as ſoon as the other Roots come out near the Surface, above the Grain : and therefore this firſt is not called a Tap Root ; but yet ſome of the next Roots that come out near the Surface of the Ground, always reach down to the Bottom of the pulveriz'd Staple ; as may be ſeen, if you carefully examine it in the Spring time ; but this firſt Root in Saint-foin becomes a Tap Root.

Minute-

Minutenefs, and earthly Tincture, become invifible to the naked Eye.

A Method how to find the Diftance to which Roots *extend Horizontally.*

Pl. 6. *Fig.* 7. Is a Piece or Plot dug and made fine in whole hard Ground, the End *A* 2 Feet, the End *B* 12 Feet, the Length of the Piece 20 Yards ; the Figures in the middle of it are 20 *Turneps,* fown early, and well ho'd.

The manner of this Hoing muft be at firft near the Plants, with a Spade, and each time afterwards, a Foot farther Diftance, till all the Earth be once well dug ; and if Weeds appear where it has been fo dug, hoe them out fhallow with the Hand-Hoe. But dig all the Piece next the out Lines deep every time, that it may be the finer for the *Roots* to enter, when they are permitted to come thither.

If thefe *Turneps* are all gradually bigger, as they ftand nearer to the End *B,* 'tis a Proof they all extend to the Outfide of the Piece ; and the *Turnep* 20 will appear to draw Nourifhment from fix Feet Diftance from its Centre.

But if the *Turneps* 16, 17, 18, 19, 20, acquire no greater Bulk than the *Turnep* 15, it will be clear, that their *Roots* extend no farther than thofe of the *Turnep* 15 does; which is but about 4 Feet.

By this Method the Diftance of the Extent of *Roots* of any Plant may be difcover'd.

What put me upon this Method was an Obfervation of two Lands (or Ridges) drill'd with *Turneps* in Rows, a Foot afunder, and very even in them ; the Ground, at both Ends, and one Side, was hard and unplow'd ; the *Turneps* not being ho'd, were very poor, fmall, and yellow, except the Three outfide Rows, *B, C, D,* which ftood next to the Land (or Ridge) *E,* which Land being plow'd and harrow'd, at the time the Land *A* ought to have been ho'd,

gave

gave a dark flourishing Colour to these three Rows; and the *Turneps* in the Row *D*, which stood farthest off from the new-plow'd Land *E*, received so much Benefit from it, as to grow twice as big as any of the more distant Rows. The Row *C*, being a Foot nearer to the new-plow'd Land, became twice as large as those in *D*; but the Row *B*, which was next to the Land *E*, grew much larger yet (a).

F Plate 6. is a Piece of hard whole Ground, of about two Perch in Length, and about two or three Feet broad, lying betwixt those two Lands, which had not been plow'd that Year; 'twas remarkable, that during the Length of this interjacent hard Ground, the Rows *B*, *C*, *D*, were as small and yellow as any in the Land.

The *Turneps* in the Row *D*, about three Feet distant from the Land *E*, receiving a double Increase, proves they had as much Nourishment from the Land *E*, as from the Land *A*, wherein they stood; which Nourishment was brought by less than half the Number of *Roots* of each of these *Turneps*.

In their own Land they must have extended a Yard all round, else they could not have reach'd the Land *E*, wherein 'tis probable these few Roots went

(a) A like Observation to this on the Land E, has been made in several Turnep Fields of divers Farmers, where Lands adjoining to the Turneps have been well tilled; all the Turneps of the contiguous Lands that were within three or four Feet, or more, of the newly pulveriz'd Earth, received as great, or greater Increase, in the Manner as my Rows B C D did: and what is yet a greater Proof of the Length of Roots, and of the Benefit of deep Hoing, all these Turneps have been well Hand-ho'd; which is a good Reason why the Benefit of the deep Pulveration should be perceivable at a greater Distance from it than mine, because my Turneps, not being hoed at all, had not Strength to send out their Roots through so many Feet of unpulveriz'd Earth, as these can through their Earth pulveriz'd by the Hoe, tho' but shallowly.

This Observation, as 'tis related to me (I being unable to go far enough to see it myself) sufficiently demonstrates the mighty Difference there is between Hand-hoing and Horse-hoing.

more

more than another Yard, to give each *Turnep* as much Increaſe as all the Roots had done in their own Land.

Except that it will hereafter appear, that the new Nouriſhment taken at the Extremities of the Roots in the Land *E*, might enable the Plants to ſend out more new Roots in their own Land, and receive ſome-thing more from thence.

The Row *C* being twice as big as the Row *D*, muſt be ſuppos'd to extend twice as far ; and the Row *B*, four times as far, in proportion as it was of a Bulk quadruple to the Row *D*.

A *Turnep* has a Tap-Root, from whence all theſe Horizontal Roots are deriv'd.

And 'tis obſervable ; that betwixt theſe two Lands there was a Trench, or Furrow, of about the Depth of nine or ten Inches, where theſe Roots muſt de-ſcend firſt, and then aſcend into the Land *E* : But it muſt be noted, that ſome ſmall Quantity of Earth was, by the Harrowing, fall'n into this Furrow, elſe the Roots could not have paſs'd thro' it.

Roots will follow the open Mould *(a)*, by deſcend-ing

(a) A Chalk-Pit, contiguous to a Barn, the Area of which being about 40 Perch of Ground, was made clean and ſwept ; ſo that there was not the Appearance of any Part of a Vegetable, more than in the Barn's Floor: Straw was thrown from thence into the Pit, for Cattle to lie on ; the Dung made thereby was haled away about three Years after the Pit had been cleanſed ; when, at the Bottom of it, and upon the Top of the Chalk, the Pit was cover'd all over with Roots, which came from a Witch-Elm, not more than Five or Six Yards in Length, from Top to Bottom, and which was about Five Yards above, and Eleven Yards from the Area of the Pit ; ſo that in three Years the Roots of this Tree extended themſelves Eight times the Length of the Tree, beyond the Extremities of the old Roots, at Eleven Yards Diſtance from the Body: The annual-increaſed Length of the Roots was near Three times as much as the Height of the Tree. I'm told an Objection hath been made from hence againſt the Growth of a Plant's being in proportion to the Length of its Roots; but when the Caſe is fully ſtated, the Objection may vaniſh. This Witch-

ing perpendicularly, and mounting again in the same manner : As I have obferv'd the Roots of a Hedge to do, that have pafs'd a fteep Ditch two Feet deep, and reach'd the Mould on the other fide, and there fill it; and digging Five Feet diftant from the Ditch, found the Roots large, tho' this Mould was very fhallow, and no Roots below the good Mould.

So in an Orchard, where the Trees are planted too deep, below the Staple or good Mould, the Roots, at a little Diftance from the Stem, are all as near the upper Superficies of the Ground, as of thofe Trees, which are planted higher than the Level of the Earth's Surface.

But the Damage of planting a Tree too low in moift Ground is, that in pafling thro' this low Part, ftanding in Water, the Sap is chill'd, and its Circulation thereby retarded.

One Caufe of Peoples not fufpecting Roots to extend to the Twentieth Part of the Diftance which in reality they do, was from obferving thefe Horizontal-Roots, near the Plant, to be pretty taper; and if they did diminifh on, in proportion to what they do

Witch-Elm is a very old decay'd Stump, which is here called a *Staggar*, appearing by its Crookednefs to have been formerly a *Plafher* in an old White-thorn Hedge wherein it ftands: It had been lopped many Years before that accidental Increafe of Roots happened ; it was ftunted, and fent out poor Shoots ; but in the third Year of thefe Roots, its Boughs being moft of them horizontally inclined, were obferved to grow vigoroufly, and the Leaves were broad, and of a flourifhing Colour ; at the End of the third Year all thefe Roots were taken away, and the *Area* being a Chalk-Rock lying uncovered, round the Place where the Single Root, that produced all thefe, came out of the Bank, no more Roots could run out on the bare Chalk, and the Growth of the Boughs has been but little fince.

Wheat, drill'd in double Rows in *November*, in a Field well till'd before Planting, look'd yellow, when about Eighteen Inches high ; at Two Feet Diftance from the Plants, the Earth was Ho-plow'd, which gave fuch Nourifhment to 'em, that they recover'd their Health, and changed their fickly Yellow, to a lively Green Colour.

there,

there, they muft foon come to an End. But the
Truth is, that after a few Inches, they are not dif-
cernibly taper, but pafs on to their Ends very nearly
of the fame Bignefs ; this may be feen in *Roots* growing in Water, and in fome other, tho' with much
Care and Difficulty.

In pulling up the aforemention'd *Turneps,* their
Roots feem'd to end at few Inches Diftance from the
Plants, they being, farther off, too fine to be per-
ceiv'd by ordinary Obfervation.

I found an extreme fmall Fibre on the Side of a
Carrot, much lefs than a Hair ; but thro' a Microfcope it appear'd a large Root, not taper, but broken off fhort at the End, which it is probable might
have (before broken off) extended near as far as the
Turnep Roots did.   It had many Fibres going out of
it, and I have feen that a *Carrot* will draw Nourifhment from a great Diftance, tho' the Roots are almoft invifible, where they come out of the *Carrot*
itfelf.

By the Piece *F* Plate 6. may be feen, that thofe
Roots cannot penetrate, unlefs the Land be open'd
by Tillage, *&c.*

As Animals of different Species have their Guts
bearing different Proportions to the Length of their
Bodies ; fo 'tis probable, different Species of Plants
may have their Roots as different. But if thofe which
have fhorter Roots have more in Number, and having fet down the means how to know the Length of
them in the Earth, I leave the different Lengths of
different Species to be examin'd by thofe who will
take the Pains of more Trials.   This is enough for
me, that there is no Plant commonly propagated, but
what will fend out its Roots far enough, to have the
Benefit of all the ho'd Spaces or Intervals I in the
following Chapters allot them, even tho' they fhould
not have Roots fo long as their Stalks or Stems.

And

And this great Length of Roots will appear very reafonable, if we compare the Largenefs of the Leaves (which are the Parts ordain'd for Excretion) with the Smalnefs of the Capillary Roots, which muft make up in Length or Number what they want in Bignefs, being deftin'd to range far in the Earth, to find out a Supply of Matter to maintain the whole Plant; whereas the chief Office of the Stalks and Leaves is only to receive the fame, and to difcharge into the Atmofphere fuch Part thereof as is found unfit for Nutrition; a much eafier Tafk than the other, and confequently fewer Paffages fuffice, thefe ending in an obtufe Form; for otherwife the Air would not be able to fuftain the Stalks and Leaves in their upright Pofture: but the Roots, tho' very weak and flender, are eafily fupported by the Earth, notwithftanding their Length, Smalnefs, and Flexibility.

Plants have no Stomach, nor *Oefophagus,* which are neceffary to convey the Mafs of Food to an Animal: Which Mafs, being exhaufted by the Lacteals, is eliminated by way of Execrements, but the Earth itfelf being that Mafs to the Guts (or Roots) of Plants, they have only fine Recrements, which are thrown off by the Leaves.

In this, Animal and Vegetable Bodies agree, that Guts and Roots are both injured by the open Air; and Nature has taken an equal Care, that both may be fupply'd with Nourifhment, without being expos'd to it. Guts are fupply'd from their Infides, and Roots from their Outfides.

All the Nutriment (or *Pabulum*) which Guts receive for the Ufe of an Animal, is brought to them; but Roots muft fearch out and fetch themfelves all the *Pabulum* of a Plant; therefore a greater Quantity of Roots, in Length or Number, is neceffary to a Plant, than of Guts to an Animal.

All *Roots* are as the Inteftines of Animals, and have their Mouths or Lacteal Veffels opening on their outer

B 4   fpongy

fpongy Superficies, as the Guts of Animals have theirs opening in their inner fpongy Superficies.

The Animal Lacteals take in their Food by the Preffure that is made from the Periftaltic Motion, and that Motion caus'd by the Action of Refpiration, both which Motions prefs the Mouths of the Lacteals againft the Mafs or Soil which is within the Guts, and bring them into clofer Contact with it.

Both thefe Motions are fupply'd in Roots by the Preffure occafion'd by the Increafe of their Diameters in the Earth, which preffes their Lacteal Mouths againft the Soil without. But in fuch Roots as live in Water, a Preffure is conftantly made againft the Roots by the Weight and Fluidity of the Water; this preffes fuch fine Particles of Earth it contains, and which come into Contact with their Mouths, the clofer to them.

And when *Roots* are in a till'd Soil, a great Preffure is made againft them by the Earth, which conftantly fubfides, and preffes their Food clofer and clofer, even into their Mouths; until itfelf becomes fo hard and clofe, that the weak Sorts of Roots can penetrate no farther into it, unlefs re-open'd by new Tillage, which is call'd Hoing.

When a good Number of Single-Mint Stalks had ftood in Water, until they were well ftock'd with Roots from their two lower Joints, and fome of them from three Joints, I fet one in a Mint-Glafs full of Salt Water; this Mint became perfectly dead within three Days.

Another Mint I put into a Glafs of fair Water; but I immers'd one String of its Roots (being brought over the Top of that Glafs into another Glafs of Salt-water, contiguous to the Top of the other Glafs: This *Mint* dy'd alfo very foon.

Of another (ftanding in a Glafs of Water and Earth till it grew vigoroufly) I ty'd one fingle Root into a Bag, which held a Spoonful of dry Salt, adjoining to
the

the Top of the Glaſs, which kill'd this ſtrong Mint alſo. I found that this Salt was ſoon diſſolv'd, tho' on the Outſide of the Glaſs; and tho' no Water reach'd ſo high, as to be within Two Inches of the Joint which produc'd this Root: The Leaves of all theſe were ſalt as Brine to the Taſte.

Of another, I put an upper Root into a ſmall Glaſs of Ink, inſtead of a Bag of Salt, in the Manner above-mention'd; this Plant was alſo kill'd by ſome of the Ink Ingredients. The Blackneſs was not com-municated to the Stalk, or Leaves, which inclin'd rather to a yellowiſh Colour as they died, which ſeem'd owing to the *Copperas*.

I made a very ſtrong Liquor with Water, and bruiſed Seeds of *Wild-Garlick*, and, filling a Glaſs therewith, plac'd the Top of it cloſe to the Top of another Glaſs, having in it a Mint, two or three of whoſe upper Roots, put into this ſtinking Liquor, full of the bruiſed Seeds, and there remaining, it kill'd the Mint in ſome time; but it was much longer in dying than the others were with Salt and Ink. It might be, becauſe theſe Roots in the *Garlick* were very ſmall, and did not bear ſo great a Proportion to their whole Syſtem of Roots, as the Roots, by which the other Mints were poiſon'd, did to theirs.

When the Edges of the Leaves began to change Colour, I chew'd many of them in my Mouth, and found at firſt the ſtrong aromatic Flavour of Mint, but that was ſoon over; and then the nauſeous Taſte of *Garlick* was very perceptible to my Palate.

I obſerv'd, that when the *Mint* had ſtood in a Glaſs of Water, until it ſeem'd to have finiſh'd its Growth, the Roots being about a Foot long, and of an earthy Colour, after putting in ſome fine Earth, which ſunk down to the Bottom, there came from the upper Joint a new Set of white Roots, taking their Courſe on the Outſide of the Heap of old Roots downwards, until they reach'd the Earth at the Bottom; and then, after ſome

some time, came to be of the same earthy Colour
with the old ones.

Another *Mint* being well rooted from Two Joints,
about Four Inches asunder; I plac'd the Roots of the
lower Joint in a deep Mint-Glass, having Water at
the Bottom, and the Roots of the upper Joint into a
square Box, contriv'd for the Purpose, standing over
the Glass, and having a Bottom, that open'd in the
Middle, with a Hole, that shut together close to the
Stalk, just below the upper Joint; then laying all these
upper Roots to one Corner of the Box, I fill'd it with
Sand, dry'd in a Fire-shovel, and found, that in one
Night's time, the Roots of the lower Joint, which
reach'd the Water at the Bottom of the Glass, had
drawn it up, and imparted so much thereof to those
Roots in the Box above, that the Sand, at that Corner
where they lay, was very wet, and the other three
Corners dry. This Experiment I repeated very often,
and it always succeeded as that did.

And for the same Purpose I prepar'd a small Trough,
about two Foot long, and plac'd a Mint-Glass under
each End of the Trough; over each Glass I plac'd a
Mint, with half its Roots in the Glass, the other half
in the Trough: The Mints stood just upon the Ends
of the Trough. Then I cover'd these Roots with pulveriz'd Earth, and kept the Glasses supply'd with
Water; and as oft as the white fibrous Roots shot
thro' the Earth, I threw on more Earth, till the
Trough would hold no more; and still the white Fibres came thro', and appear'd above it; but all seem'd
(as I saw by the Help of a coarse Microscope) to turn,
and when they came above-ground, their Ends enter'd into it again.   These two *Mints* grew thrice as
large as any other *Mint* I had, which were many,
that stood in Water, and much larger than those which
stood in Water with Earth in it: They being all of
an equal Bigness when set in, and set at the same time.
Tho' these two, standing in my Chamber, never had
                                                        any

any Water in their Earth, but what thofe Roots. which reach'd the Water in the Glaffes, fent up to the Roots, which grew in the Trough. The vaft Quantity of Water thefe Roots fent up, being fufficient to keep all the Earth in the Troughs moift, tho' of a thoufand times greater Quantity than the Roots which water'd it, makes it probable, that the Water pafs'd out of the Roots into the Earth, without mixing at all with the Sap, or being alter'd to any Degree. The Earth kept always moift, and in the hot Weather there would not remain a Drop of Water in the Glaffes, when they had not been frefh fupply'd in two Days and one Night ; and yet thefe Roots in the Glaffes were not dry'd, tho' they ftood fometimes a whole Day and Night thus in the empty Glaffes. Thefe two Mints have thus liv'd all one Summer.

Remarks on the Mints, *&c.*

Tho' the Veffels of Marine Plants be fome ways fortify'd againft the Acrimony of Salt, as Sea-fifh are, yet the Mints all fhew, that Salt is poifon to other Plants.

The Reafon why the Salts in Dung, Brine, or Urine, do not kill Plants in the Field or Garden, is, that their Force is fpent in acting upon, and dividing the Parts of Earth; neither do thefe Salts, or at leaft any confiderable Quantity of them, reach the Roots.

I try'd Salt to many Potatoes in the Ground being undermin'd, and a few of their Roots put into a Difh of Salt-water, they all died fooner or later, according to their Bignefs, and to the Proportions the Quantity of Salt apply'd did bear to them.

By the Mints it appears, that Roots make no Diftinctions in the Liquor they imbibe, whether it be for their Nourifhment or Deftruction; and that they do not infume what is difagreeable, or Poifon to them, for lack of other Suftenance ; fince they were very vigorous, and well fed in the Glaffes, at the time when the moft inconfiderable Part of their Number

ber

ber had the Salt, Garlick, and Ink offer'd to
them.

The sixth *Mint* shews, that when new Earth is
apply'd to the old Roots, a Plant sends out new Roots
on Purpose to feed on it: And that the more Earth is
given it, the more Roots will be form'd, by the new
Vigour the Plant takes from the Addition of Earth.
This correſponds with the Action of Hoing; for
every time the Earth is mov'd about Roots, they
have a Change of Earth, which is new to them.

The seventh *Mint* proves, that there is such a
Communication betwixt all the Roots, that when any
of them have Water, they do impart a Share thereof
to all the rest: And that the Root of the lower Joint
of this Mint had Paſſages (or Veſſels) leading from
them, through the Stalk, to the Roots of the upper
Joint; tho' the clear Stalk (through which it muſt
have paſs'd) that was betwixt theſe two Joints, was
ſeveral Inches in Length.

This accounts for the great Produce of long tap-
rooted Plants, ſuch as *Luſern* and *St. Foin*, in very
dry Weather: for the Earth at a great Depth is always
moiſt.   It accounts alſo for the good Crops we have
in dry Summers, upon Land that has a Clay Bottom;
for there the Water is retain'd a long time, and the
lower Roots of Plants which reach it, do, like thoſe
of this Mint, ſend up a Share to all the higher Roots.

If thoſe Roots of a Plant, which lie at the Surface
of the Ground, did not receive Moiſture from other
Roots, which lie deeper, they could be of no Uſe in
dry Weather. But 'tis certain, that if this dry Surface
be mov'd or dung'd, the Plant will be found to grow
the faſter, tho' no Rain falls; which ſeems to prove,
both that the deep Roots communicate to the ſhallow
a Share of their Water, and receive in Return from
them a Share of Food, in common with all the reſt
of the Plant, as in the Mints they did.

The

The two laft *Mints* fhew, that when the upper Roots have Moifture (as they had in the Earth in the Trough, carried thither firft by the lower Roots) they impart fome of it to the lower, elfe thefe could not have continu'd plump and frefh, as they did for 24 Hours in the empty Glafs. And I have fince ob-ferved them to do fo, in the cooler Seafon of the Year, for feveral Weeks together, without any other Water, than what the upper Roots convey'd to them, from the moift Earth above in the Trough (*a*). I know not what Time thefe Roots might continue to be fupply'd thus in the hot Weather, becaufe I did not try any longer, for fear of killing them.

But it muft be noted, that the Depth of the Glafs protected the Roots therein from the Injury of the Motion of the free Air, which would have dry'd them, if they had been out of the Glafs.

In this Trough is fhewn moft of the Hoing Effects; *viz.* That Roots, by being broken off near the Ends, increafe their Number, and fend out feveral where one is broken off.

That the Roots increafe their Fibres every time the Earth is ftirr'd about them.

That the ftirring the Earth makes the Plants grow the fafter.

LEAVES are the Parts or Bowels of a Plant, which perform the fame Office to Sap, as the Lungs of an Animal do to Blood ; that is, they purify or cleanfe it of the Recrements, or fuliginous Steams, received in the Circulation, being the unfit Parts of the Food ; and perhaps fome decay'd Particles, which fly off the

---

(*a*) 'Tis certain, that Roots and other Chyle Veffels of a Plant have a free Communication throughout all their Cavities, and the Liquor in them will run towards that Part where there is leaft Refiftance; and fuch isthat which is the moft empty, whether it be above or below ; for there are no *Valves* that can hinder the Defcent or Afcent of Liquor in thefe Veffels, as appears by the growing of a Plant in an inverted Pofture.

Veffels,

Veffels, through which Blood and Sap do pafs refpec-
tively.

Befides which Ufe, the Nitro-aerous Particles may
there enter, to keep up the vital Ferment or Flame.

Mr. *Papin* fhews, that Air will pafs in at the
Leaves, and out thro' the Plant at the Roots, but
Water will not pafs in at the Leaves ; and that if the
Leaves have no Air, a Plant will die ; but if the
Leaves have Air, tho' the Root remain in Water *in
vacuo*, the Plant will live and grow.

Dr. *Grew*, in his Anatomy of Plants, mentions
Veffels, which he calls, Net-work, Cobweb, Skeins
of Silk, *&c.* but above all, the Multitude of Air-
Bladders in them, which I take to be of the fame
Ufe in Leaves, as the Veficulæ are in Lungs. Leaves
being as Lungs inverted, and of a broad and thin
Form ; their Veficulæ are in Contaٌt with the free
open Air, and therefore have no need of Trachea, or
Bronchia, nor of Refpiration.

C H A P. II.

Of FOOD *of* PLANTS.

THE chief Art of an Hufbandman is to feed
Plants to the beft Advantage ; but how fhall
he do that, unlefs he knows what is their Food ? By
Food is meant that Matter, which, being added and
united to the firft *Stamina* of Plants, or *Plantulæ*,
which were made in little at the Creation, gives them,
or rather is their Increafe.

'Tis agreed, that all the following Materials contribute, in fome manner, to the Increafe of Plants ;
but 'tis difputed which of them is that very Increafe
or Food.   1. *Nitre.*   2. *Water.*   3. *Air.*   4. *Fire.*
5. *Earth.*

I will

I will not mention, as a Food, that acid Spirit of the Air, so much talk'd of; since by its eating asunder Iron Bars it appears too much of the Nature of *Aqua Fortis*, to be a welcome Guest alone to the tender Vessels of the Roots of Plants.

Nitre is useful to divide and prepare the Food, and may be said to nourish Vegetables in much the same Manner as my Knife nourishes me, by cutting and dividing my Meat: But when *Nitre* is apply'd to the Root of a Plant, it will kill it as certainly as a Knife misapply'd will kill a Man: Which proves, that *Nitre* is, in respect of Nourishment, just as much the Food of Plants, as *White Arsenick* is the Food of Rats. And the same may be said of Salts.

Water, from *Van-Helmont*'s Experiment, was by some great Philosophers thought to be it. But these were deceived, in not observing, that Water has always in its Intervals a Charge of Earth, from which no Art can free it. This Hypothesis having been fully confuted by Dr. *Woodward*, no body has, that I know of, maintain'd it since: And to the Doctor's Arguments I shall add more in the Article of Air.

Air, because its Spring, &c. is as necessary to the Life of Vegetables, as the Vehicle of Water is; some modern Virtuosi have affirm'd, from the same and worse Arguments than those of the Water-Philosophers, that Air is the Food of Plants. Mr. *Bradley* being the chief, if not only Author, who has publish'd this Phantasy, which at present seems to get Ground, 'tis fit he should be answer'd: And this will be easily done, if I can shew, that he has answer'd this his own Opinion, by some or all of his own Arguments.

His first is, that of *Helmont*, and is thus related in Mr. *Bradley*'s general Treatise of *Husbandry and Gardening*, Vol. I. *p.* 36. , Who dry'd Two hun-
‘ dred Pounds of Earth, and planted a Willow of
‘ Five Pounds Weight in it, which he water'd with
‘ Rain,

‘ Rain, or diftill’d Water; and to fecure it from any
‘ other Earth getting in, he covered it with a perfo-
‘ rated Tin Cover. Five Years after, weighing the
‘ Tree, with all the Leaves it had borne in that Time,
‘ he found it to weigh One hundred Sixty-nine
‘ Pounds Three Ounces ; but the Earth was only di-
‘ minifh’d about two Ounces in its Weight.’

On this Experiment Mr. *Bradley* grounds his Airy
Hypothefis.   But let it be but examined fairly, and
fee what may be thence inferr’d.

The Tin Cover was to prevent any other Earth
from getting in.   This muft alfo prevent any Earth
from getting out, except what enter’d the Roots,
and by them pafs’d into the Tree.

A Willow is a very thirfty Tree, and muft have
drank in Five Years time feveral Tuns of Water,
which muft neceffarily carry in its Interftices a great
Quantity of Earth (probably many times more than
the Tree’s (*a*) Weight, which could not get out,
but by the Roots of the Willow.

Therefore the Two hundred Pounds of Earth not
being increafed, proves that fo much Earth as was
poured in with the Water, did enter the Tree.

Whether the Earth did enter to nourifh the Tree,
or whether only in order to pafs through it (by way
of Vehicle to the Air), and leave the Air behind for
the Augment of the Willow, may appear by examin-
ing the Matter of which the Tree did confift.

If the Matter remaining after the Corruption or
Putrefaction of the Tree be Earth, will it not be a
Proof, that the Earth remained in it, to nourifh and
augment it ? for it could not leave what it did not firft
take, nor be augmented by what pafs’d through it.
According to *Ariftotle*’s Doctrine, and Mr. *Bradley*’s

(*a*) The Body of an Animal receives a much lefs Increafe in
Weight than its Perfpirations amount to, as *Sanctorius*’s *Static-
Chair* demonftrates.

too,

too, in Vol. I. *pag.* 72. " Putrefaction refolves it
" again into Earth, its firft Principle."

The Weight of the Tree, even when green, muft
confift of Earth and Water. Air could be no Part of
it, becaufe Air being of no greater fpecific Gravity
than the incumbent Atmofphere, could not be of any
Weight in it; therefore was no Part of the One
hundred Sixty-nine Pounds Three Ounces.

Nature has directed Animals and Vegetables to
feek what is moft neceffary to them. At the Time
when the *Fœtus* has a Neceffity of Refpiration, 'tis
brought forth into the open Air, and then the Lungs
are filled with Air. As foon as a Calf, Lamb, &c.
is able to ftand, it applies to the Teat for Food, without any Teaching. In like manner Mr. *Bradley* re-
marks, in his Vol. I. *pag.* 10. ' That almoft every
' Stem and every Root are formed in a bending man-
' ner under Ground; and yet all thefe Stems become
' ftrait and upright when they come above-ground,
' and meet the Air; and moft Roots run as directly
' downwards, and fhun the Air as much as poffible.'

Can any thing more plainly fhew the Intent of
Nature, than this his Remark does? *viz.* That the Air
is moft neceffary to the Tree above ground, to purify
the Sap by the Leaves, as the Blood of Animals is
depurated by their Lungs: And that Roots feek the
Earth for their Food, and fhun the Air, which would
dry up and deftroy them.

No one Truth can poffibly contradict or interfere
with any other Truth; but one Error may contradict and interfere with another Error, *viz.*

Mr. *Bradley*, and all Authors, I think, are of Opinion, that Plants of different Natures are fed by a
different Sort of Nourifhment; from whence they
aver, that a Crop of Wheat takes up all that is peculiar to that Grain; then a Crop of Barley all that is
proper to it; next a Crop of Peafe, and fo on, 'till
each has drawn off all thofe Particles which are proper

C   to

to it ; and then no more of thefe Grains will grow in
that Land, till by Fallow, Dung, and Influences of
the Heavens, the Earth will be again replenifh'd with
new Nourifhment, to fupply the fame Sorts of Corn
over again.   This, if true (as they all affirm it to
be), would prove, that the Air is not the Food of Vegetables.   For the Air being in itfelf fo homogeneous as it is, could never afford fuch different Matter
as they imagine ; neither is it probable, that the Air
fhould afford the Wheat Nourifhment more one
Year, than the enfuing Year ; or that the fame Year
it fhould nourifh Barley in one Field, Wheat in another, Peafe in a Third; but that if Barley were fown
in the Third, Wheat in the Firft, Peafe in the Second, all would fail : Therefore this Hypothefis of
Air for Food interferes with, and contradicts this
Doctrine of Neceffity of changing Sorts.

I fuppofe, by Air, they do not mean dry Particles
of Earth, and the Effluvia which float in the Air: The
Quantity of thefe is too fmall to augment Vegetables
to that Bulk they arrive at.   By that way of fpeaking they might more truly affirm this of Water, becaufe it muft be like to carry a greater Quantity of
Earth than Air doth, in proportion to the Difference
of their different fpecific Weight; Water, being about
800 times heavier than Air, is likely to have 800
times more of that terreftrial Matter in it; and we fee
this is fufficient to maintain fome Sort of Vegetables,
as Aquatics ; but the Air, by its Charge of Effluvia,
&c. is never able to maintain or nourifh any Plant ;
for as to the Sedums, Aloes, and all others, that are
fuppofed to grow fufpended in the Air, 'tis a mere Fal-
lacy ; they feem to grow, but do not ; fince they conftantly grow lighter; and tho' their Veffels may be
fomewhat diftended by the Ferment of their own
Juices which they received in the Earth, yet fufpended
in Air, they continually diminifh in Weight (which
is the true Argument of a Plant) until they grow to
nothing.

nothing.   So that this Inftance of Sedums, &c. which they pretend to bring for Proof of this their Hypothefis, is alone a full Confutation of it.

Yet if granted, that Air could nourifh fome Vegetables by the earthy Effluvia, &c. which it carry'd with it (*a*), even that would be againft them, not for them.

They might as well believe, that *Martins* and *Swallows* are nourifh'd by the Air, becaufe they live on Flies and Gnats, which they catch therein; this being the fame Food, which is found in the Stomach of the Chameleon.

If, as they fay, the Earth is of little other Ufe to Plants, but to keep them fix'd and fteady, there would be little or no Difference in the Value of rich and poor Land, dung'd or undung'd; for one would ferve to keep Plants fix'd and fteady, very near, if not quite as well as the other.

If Water or Air was the Food of Plants, I cannot fee what Neceffity there fhould be of Dung or Tillage.

4. *Fire.*   No Plant can live without Heat, tho' different Degrees of it be neceffary to different Sorts of Plants.   Some are almoft able to keep Company with the *Salamander*, and do live in the hotteft Expofures of the hot Countries.   Others have their Abode with Fifhes under Water, in cold Climates: for the Sun has his Influence, tho' weaker, upon the Earth cover'd with Water, at a confiderable Depth; which appears by the Effect the Viciffitudes of Winter and Summer have upon fubterraqueous Vegetables.

Tho' every Heat is faid to be a different Degree of Fire; yet we may diftinguifh the Degrees by their different Effects. Heat warms; but Fire burns: The firft helps to cherifh, the latter deftroys Plants.

(*a*) This is meant of dry Earth, by its Lightnefs (when pulveriz'd extremely fine) carried in the Air without Vapour: For the Atmofphere, confifting of all the Elements, has Earth in it in confiderable Quantity, mix'd with Water; but a very little Earth is fo minutely divided, as to fly therein pure from Water, which is its Vehicle there for the moft Part.

C 2

5. Earth.

5. *Earth.* That which nourifhes and augments a Plant is the true Food of it.

Every Plant is Earth, and the Growth and true Increafe of a Plant is the Addition of more Earth.

Nitre (or other Salts) prepares the Earth, Water and Air move it, by conveying and fermenting it in the Juices; and this Motion is called Heat.

When this additional Earth is affimilated to the Plant, it becomes an abfolute Part of it.

Suppofe Water, Air, and Heat, could be taken away, would it not remain to be a Plant, tho' a dead one?

But fuppofe the Earth of it taken away, what would then become of the Plant? Mr. *Bradley* might look long enough after it, before he found it in the Air among his fpecific or certain Qualities.

Befides, too much *Nitre* (or other Salts) corrodes a Plant; too much Water drowns it; too much Air dries the Roots of it; too much Heat (or Fire) burns it; but too much Earth a Plant never can have, unlefs it be therein wholly buried; and in that Cafe it would be equally mifapply'd to the Body, as Air or Nitre would be to the Roots.

Too much Earth, or too fine, can never poffibly be given to Roots; for they never receive fo much of it as to furfeit the Plants, unlefs it be depriv'd of Leaves, which, as Lungs, fhould purify it.

And Earth is fo furely the Food of all Plants, that with the proper Share of the other Elements, which each Species of Plants requires, I do not find but that any common Earth will nourifh any Plant.

The only Difference of Soil *(a)* (except the Richnefs) feems to be the different Heat and Moifture it has;

(a) As I have faid in my *Effay,* 'That *a Soil being once proter to a Species of Vegetables, it will always continue to be fo*; it muft be fuppofed, that there be no Alteration of the *Heat* and *Moifture* of it; and that this Difference I mean, is of its Quality
of

has ; for if thofe be rightly adjufted, any Soil will
nourifh any Sort of Plant ; for let *Thyme* and *Rufhes*
change Places, and both will die ; but let them change
their Soil, by removing the Earth wherein the *Thyme*
grew, from the dry Hill down into the watry Bottom,
and plant *Rufhes* therein ; and carry the moift Earth,
wherein the *Rufhes* grew, up to the Hill ; and there
Thyme will grow in the Earth that was taken from the
Rufhes ; and fo will the *Rufhes* grow in the Earth that
was taken from the *Thyme* ; fo that 'tis only more or
lefs Water that makes the fame Earth fit either for the
Growth of *Thyme* or *Rufhes*.

So for Heat ; our Earth, when it has in the Stove
the juft Degree of Heat that each Sort of Plants requires, will maintain Plants brought from both the
Indies.

Plants differ as much from one another in the Degrees of Heat and Moifture they require, as a Fifh
differs from a Salamander.

Indeed *Mifletoe*, and fome other Plants, will not
live upon Earth, until it be firft alter'd by the Veffels
of another Plant or Tree, upon which they grow,
and therein are as nice in Food as an Animal.

There is no need to have Recourfe to Tranfmuta-
tation ; for whether Air or Water, or both, are tranf-
form'd into Earth or not, the thing is the fame, if it
be Earth when the Roots take it ; and we are convinced that neither Air nor Water alone, as fuch, will
maintain Plants.

Thefe kind of Metamorphofes may properly enough
be confider'd in Differtations purely concerning Matter, and to difcover what the component Particles of
Earth are ; but not at all neceffary to be known, in
relation to the maintaining of Vegetables.

of nourifhing different Species of Vegetables, not of the Quantity
of it ; which Quantity may be alter'd by Diminution or Super-
induction.

CHAP.

C H A P.   III.

Of PASTURE *of* PLANTS.

CATTLE feed on Vegetables that grow upon the Earth's external Surface; but Vegetables themselves first receive, from within the Earth, the Nourishment they give to Animals.

The Pasture of Cattle has been known and understood in all Ages of the World, it being liable to Inspection; but the Pasture of Plants, being out of the Observation of the Senses, is only to be known by Disquisitions of Reason; and has (for ought I can find) pass'd undiscover'd by the Writers of Husbandry (a).

The Ignorance of this seems to be one principal Cause, that Agriculture, the most necessary of all Arts, has been treated of by Authors more superficially than any other Art whatever. The Food or *Pabulum* of Plants being prov'd to be Earth, where and whence (b) they take that, may properly be called their Pasture.

This Pasture I shall endeavour to describe.

(a) When Writers of Husbandry, in discoursing of Earth and Vegetation, come nearest to the Thing, that is, the *Pasture* of *Plants*, they are lost in the Shadow of it, and wander in a Wilderness of obscure Expressions, such as *Magnetism, Virtue, Power, Specific Quality, Certain Quality,* and the like; wherein there is no manner of Light for discovering the real Substance, but we are left by them more in the Dark to find it, than Roots are when they feed on it: And when a Man, no less sagacious than Mr. *Evelyn,* has trac'd it thro' all the *Mazes* of the *Occult Qualities,* and even up to the *Metaphysics,* he declares he cannot determine, whether the Thing he pursues be *Corporeal* or *Spiritual.*

(b) By the *Pasture* is not meant the *Pabulum* itself; but the *Superficies* from whence the *Pabulum* is taken by Roots.

'Tis

'Tis the inner or (internal) Superficies *(a)* of the Earth; or which is the same thing, 'tis the Superficies of the Pores, Cavities, or Interstices of the divided Parts of the Earth, which are of two Sorts, viz. *Natural* and *Artificial.*

By Nature, the whole Earth (or Soil) is compofed of Parts; and, if thefe had been in every Place abfolutely joined, it would have been without Interstices or Pores, and would have had no internal Superficies, or Pafture for Plants: but fince it is not fo ftrictly denfe *(b)*, there muft be Interstices at all thofe Places where the Parts remain feparate and divided.

Thefe Interstices, by their Number and Largenefs, determine the fpecific Gravity (or true Quantity) of every Soil: The larger they are, the lighter is the Soil; and the inner Superficies is commonly the lefs.

. The Mouths, or Lacteals, being fituate, and opening, in the convex Superficies of Roots, they take their *Pabulum*, being fine Particles of Earth, from the Superficies of the Pores, or Cavities, wherein the Roots are included.

(a) This Pafture of Plants never having been mentioned or defcribed by any Author that I know of, I am at a lofs to find any other Term to defcribe it by, that may be fynonymous, or equipollent to it: Therefore, for want of a better, I call it the inner, or internal Superficies of the Earth, to diftinguifh it from the outer or external Superficies, or Surface, whereon we tread.

Inner or internal Superficies may be thought an abfurd Expreffion, the Adjective expreffing fomething within, and the Subftantive feeming to exprefs only what is without it; and indeed the Senfe of the Expreffion is fo; for the Vegetable Pafture is within the Earth, but without (or on the Outfides of) the divided Parts of the Earth.

And, befides, Superficies muft be joined with the Adjective Inner (or Internal) when 'tis ufed to defcribe the Infide of a thing that is hollow, as the Pores and Interstices of the Earth are.

The Superficies, which is the Pafture of Plants, is not a bare Mathematical Superficies; for that is only imaginary.

(b) For were the Soil as denfe as Glafs, the Roots or Vegetables (fuch as our Earth produces) would never be able to enter its Pores.

And

And 'tis certain, that the Earth is not divested or robb'd of this *Pabulum*, by any other Means, than by actual Fire, or the Roots of Plants.

For, when no Vegetables are suffer'd to grow in a Soil, it will always grow richer. Plow it, harrow it, as often as you please, expose it to the Sun in Horse-Paths all the Summer, and to the Frost of the Winter; let it be cover'd by Water at the Bottom of Ponds, or Ditches; or if you grind dry Earth to Powder, the longer 'tis kept expofed, or treated by these or any other Method possible (except actual Burning by Fire); instead of losing, it will gain the more Fertility.

These Particles, which are the *Pabulum* of Plants, are so very minute (*a*) and light, as not to be singly attracted to the Earth, if separated from those Parts to which they adhere (*b*), or with which they are in Contact (like Dust to a Looking-Glass, turn it upwards, or downwards, it will remain affixt to it), as these Particles do to those Parts, until from thence remov'd by some Agent.

(*a*) As to the Fineness of the *Pabulum* of Plants, 'tis not unlikely, that Roots may infume no grosser Particles, than those on which the Colours of Bodies depend; but to difcover the greatest of those Corpufcles, Sir *Ifaac Newton* think, it will require a Microfcope, that with sufficient Diftinctnefs can reprefent Objects Five or Six hundred times bigger, than at a Foot Diftance they appear to the naked Eye.

My Microfcope indeed is but a very ordinary one, and when I view with it the Liquor newly imbibed by a fibrous Root of a Mint, it feems more limpid than the cleareft common Water, not ing at all appearing in it.

(*b*) Either Roots muft infume the Earth, that is their *Pabulum*, as they find it in whole Pieces. having intire Superficies of their own, or elfe fuch Particles as have not intire Superficies of their own, but want fome Part of it, which adheres to, or is Part of the Superficies of larger Particles, before they are feparated by Roots. The former they cannot infume (unlefs contained in Water); becaufe they would fly away at the firft Pores that were open: *Ergo* they muft infume the latter.

A

A Plant cannot separate these Particles from the Parts to which they adhere, without the Assistance of Water, which helps to loosen them.

And 'tis also probable, that the Nitre of the Air may be necessary to relax this Superficies, to render the prolific Particles capable of being thence disjoin'd; and this Action of the Nitre seems to be what is call'd, Impregnating the Earth.

Since the grosser Vegetable Particles, when they have pass'd thro' a Plant, together with their moist Vehicle, do fly up into the Air invisibly; 'tis not likely they should, in the Earth, fall off from the Superficies of the Pores, by their own Gravity: And if they did fall off, they might fly away as easily before they enter'd Plants, as they do after they have pass'd thro' them; and then a Soil might become the poorer (a) for all the Culture and Stirring we bestow upon it; tho' no Plants were in it; contrary to Experience.

It must be own'd, that Water does ever carry, in its Interstices, Particles of Earth fine enough to enter Roots; because I have seen, that a great Quantity of Earth (in my Experiments) will pass out of Roots set in Rain-water; and tis found that Water can never be, by any Art, wholly freed from its earthy Charge; therefore it must have carry'd in some Particles of Earth along with it: But yet I cannot hence conclude, that the Water did first take these fine Particles from the aforesaid Superficies: I rather think, that they are exhal'd, together with very small Pieces to which they adhere, and in the Vapour divided by the Aereal Nitre; and, when the Vapour is condens'd, they descend with it to replenish

(a) But we see it is always the richer by being frequently turned and exposed to the Atmosphere: Therefore Plants must take all their *Pabulum* from a Superficies of Parts of Earth; except what may perhaps be contained in Water fine enough to enter Roots intire with the Water.

the Pasture of Plants; and that these do not enter intire into Roots, neither does any other of the earthy Charge that any Water contains; except such fine Particles which have already pass'd thro' the Vegetable Vessels, and been thence exhal'd.

This Conjecture is the more probable, for that Rain-Water is as nourishing to Plants set therein as Spring-Water, tho' the latter have more Earth in it; and tho' Spring-water have some Particles in it that will enter intire into Roots, yet we must consider, that even that Water may have been many times exhal'd into the Air, and may have still retain'd a great Quantity of Vegetable Particles, which it received from Vegetable Exhalations in the Atmosphere; tho' not so great a Quantity as Rain-water, that comes immediately thence.

These, I have to do with, are the Particles which Plants have from the Earth, or Soil; but they have also fine Particles of Earth from Water, which may impart some of its finest Charge to the Superficies of Roots, as well as to the Superficies of the Parts of the Earth *(a)* which makes the Pasture of Plants.

Yet it seems, that much of the Earth, contain'd in the clearest Water, is there in too large Parts to enter a Root; since we see, that in a short time the Root's Superficies will, in the purest Water, be cover'd with Earth, which is then form'd into a terrene Pasture, which may nourish Roots; but very few Plants will live long in so thin a Pasture, as any Water affords them. I cannot find one as yet that has liv'd a Year, without some Earth have been added to it.

And all Aquatics, that I know, have their Roots in the Earth, tho' cover'd with Water.

The Pores, Cavities, or Interstices of the Earth, being of two Sorts, viz. *Natural* and *Artificial*; the

(a) If Water does separate, and take any of the mere *Pabulum* of Plants from the Soil, it gives much more to it.

one

one affords the Natural, the other the Artificial Pasture of Plants.

The natural Pasture alone will suffice, to furnish a Country with Vegetables, for the Maintenance of a few Inhabitants; but if Agriculture were taken out of the World, 'tis much to be fear'd, that those of all populous Countries, especially towards the Confines of the frigid Zones (for there the Trees often fail of producing Fruit), would be oblig'd to turn *Anthropophagi*, as in many uncultivated Regions they do, very probably for that Reason.

The artificial Pasture of Plants is that inner Superficies which is made from dividing the Soil by Art.

This does, on all Parts of the Globe, where used, maintain many more People than the natural Pasture (*a*); and in the colder Climates, I believe, it will not be

(*a*) The extraordinary Increase of St. Foin, Clover, and natural Grass, when their Roots reach into pulveriz'd Earth, exceeding the Increase of all those other Plants of the same Species (that stand out of the Reach of it) above One hundred Times, shew how vastly the artificial Pasture of Plants exceeds the natural. A full Proof of this Difference, (besides very many I have had before) was seen by two Intervals in the middle of a poor Field of worn-out St. Foin, pulveriz'd in the precedent Summer, in the manner describ'd in a Note on the latter Part of Chap. XII. relating to *St. Foin*. Here not only the *St. Foin* adjoining to these Intervals recover'd its Strength, blossom'd, and seeded well, but also the natural Grass amongst it was as strong, and had as flourishing a Colour, as if a Dung-heap had been laid in the Intervals; also many other Weeds came out from the Edges of the unplow'd Ground, which must have lain dormant a great many Years, grew higher and larger than ever were seen before in that Field; but above all, there was a Weed amongst the St. *Foin*, which generally accompanies it, bearing a white Flower; some call it *White Weed*, others *Lady's Bedstraw:* Some Plants of this that stood near the Intervals, were, in the Opinion of all that saw them, increased to a thousand Times the Bulk of those of the same Species, that stood in the Field three Feet distant from such pulveriz'd Earth.

Note, These Intervals were each an Hundred Perch long, and had each in them a treble Row of Barley very good. The Reason I take to be this, That the Land had lain still several Years after

be extravagant to fay, ten times as many : Or that, in Cafe Agriculture were a little improved (as I hope to fhew is not difficult to be done), it might maintain twice as many more yet, or the fame Number, better.

The natural Pafture is not only lefs than the artificial, in an equal Quantity of Earth; but alfo, that little confifting in the Superficies of Pores, or Cavities, not having a free Communication (*a*) with one another, being lefs pervious to the Roots of all Vegetables, and requiring a greater Force to break thro' their Partitions; by that Means, Roots, efpecially of weak Plants, are excluded from many of thofe Cavities, and fo lofe the Benefit of them.

But the artificial Pafture confifts in Superficies of Cavities, that are pervious to all Manner of Roots, and that afford them free Paffage and Entertainment in and thro' all their Receffes. Roots may here extend to the utmoft, without meeting with any Barricadoes in their Way.

The internal Superficies, which is the natural Pafture of Plants, is like the external Superficies or

after its artificial Pafture was loft ; whereby all the Plants in it having only the natural Pafture to fubfift on, became fo extremely *fmall* and *weak*, that they were not able to exhauft the Land of fo great a Quantity of the (vegetable) nourifhing Particles as the Atmofphere brought down to it.

And when by Pulveration the artificial Pafture came to be added to this natural Pafture (not much exhaufted), and nothing at all fuffered to grow out of it for above Three Quarters of a Year, it became rich enough, without any Manure, to produce this extraordinary Effect upon the Vegetables, whofe Roots reached into it. How long this Effect may continue, is uncertain: but I may venture to fay, it will continue until the Exhauftion by Vegetables doth over-balance the Defcent of the Atmofphere, and the Pulveration.

And what I have faid of any one Species of Plants in this Refpect may be generally apply'd to the reft.

(*a*) None of the natural Vegetable Pafture is loft or injured by the artificial; but on the contrary, 'tis mended by being mix'd with it, and by having a greater Communication betwixt Pore and Pore.

Surface

Surface of the Earth, whereon is the Pasture of Cattle; in that it cannot be inlarg'd without Addition of more Surface taken from Land adjoining to it, by inlarging its Bounds or Limits.

But the artificial Pasture of Plants may be inlarg'd, without any Addition of more Land, or inlarging of Bounds, and this by Division only of the same Earth.

And this artificial Pasture may be increas'd in proportion to the Division of the Parts of Earth, whereof it is the Superficies, which Division may be mathematically infinite; for an Atom is nothing; neither is there a more plain Impossibility in Nature, than to reduce Matter to nothing, by Division or Separation of its Parts.

A Cube of Earth of One Foot has but Six Feet of Superficies. Divide this Cube into Cubical Inches, and then its Superficies will be increas'd Twelve times, *viz.* to Seventy-two Superficial Feet. Divide these again in like Manner and Proportion; that is, Divide them into Parts that bear the same Proportion to the Inches, as the Inches do to the Feet, and then the same Earth, which had at first no more than Six Superficial Feet, will have Eight hundred Sixty-four Superficial Feet of artificial Pasture; and so is the Soil divisible, and this Pasture increasable *ad Infinitum.*

The common Methods of dividing the Soil are these; *viz.* by *Dung,* by *Tillage,* or by both *(a).*

C H A P. IV.

Of D U N G.

ALL Sorts of Dung and Compost contain some Matter, which, when mixt with the Soil, ferments therein; and by such Ferment dissolves, crum-

(a) For *Vis Unita Fortior.*

5   bles,

bles, and divides the Earth very much: This is the chief, and almoſt only Uſe of Dung: For, as to the pure earthy Part, the Quantity is ſo very ſmall, that, after a perfect Putrefaction, it appears to bear a moſt inconſiderable Proportion to the Soil it is deſign'd to manure: and therefore, in that reſpect, is next to nothing.

Its fermenting Quality is chiefly owing to the Salts wherewith it abounds; but a very little of this Salt applied alone to a few Roots of almoſt any Plant, will (as, in my Mint Experiments, it is evident common Salt does) kill it.

This proves, that its Uſe is not to nouriſh, but to diſſolve; *i. e.* Divide the terreſtrial Matter, which affords Nutriment to the Mouths of Vegetable Roots.

It is, I ſuppoſe, upon the Account of the acrimonious fiery Nature of theſe Salts, that the Floriſts have baniſh'd Dung from their Flower-Gardens.

And there is, I'm ſure, much more Reaſon to prohibit the Uſe of Dung in the Kitchen-Garden, on Account of the ill Taſte it gives to eſculent Roots and Plants, eſpecially ſuch Dung as is made in great Towns.

'Tis a Wonder how delicate Palates can diſpenſe with eating their own and their Beaſts Ordure, but a little more putrefied and evaporated; together with all Sorts of Filth and Naſtineſs, a Tincture of which thoſe Roots muſt unavoidably receive, that grow amongſt it.

Indeed I do not admire, that learned Palates, accuſtom'd to the *Goût* of *Silphium, Garlick, la Chair venee,* and mortify'd Veniſon, equalling the Stench and Rankneſs of this Sort of City-Muck, ſhould reliſh and approve of Plants that are fed and fatted by its immediate Contact.

People who are ſo vulgarly nice, as to nauſeate theſe modiſh Dainties, and whoſe ſqueamiſh Stomachs

even

even abhor to receive the Food of Nobles, fo little different from that wherewith they regale their richeft Gardens, fay that even the very Water, wherein a rich Garden Cabbage is boil'd, ftinks ; but that the Water, wherein a Cabbage from a poor undung'd Field is boil'd, has no Manner of unpleafant Savour; and that a Carrot, bred in a Dunghill, has none of that fweet Relifh, which a Field-Carrot affords.

There is a like Difference in all Roots, nourifh'd with fuch different Diet.

Dung not only fpoils the fine Flavour of thefe our Eatables, but inquinates good Liquor. The dung'd Vineyards in *Languedoc* produce naufeous Wine; from whence there is a Proverb in that Country, That poor People's Wine is beft, becaufe they carry no Dung to their Vineyards.

Dung is obferv'd to give great Encouragement to the Production of Worms; and Carrots in the Garden are much worm-eaten, when thofe in the Field are free from Worms.

Dung is the Putrefaction of Earth, after it has been alter'd by Vegetable or Animal Veffels. But if Dung be thoroughly ventilated and putrefy'd before it be fpread on the Field (as I think all the Authors I have read direct) fo much of its Salts will be fpent in fermenting the Dung itfelf, that little of them will remain to ferment the Soil; and the Farmer who might dung One Acre in Twenty, by laying on his Dung whilft fully replete with vigorous Salts, may (if he follows thefe Writers Advice to a Nicety) be forced to content himfelf with dunging one Acre in an Hundred.

This indeed is good Advice for Gardeners, for making their Stuff more palatable and wholefome; but would ruin the Farmer who could have no more Dung than what he could make upon his Arable Farm.

For

For every Sort of Dung, the longer Time it ferments without the Ground, the lesser Time it has to ferment in it, and the weaker its Ferment will be.

The Reason given for this great Diminution of Dung is, that the Seeds of Weeds may be rotted, and lose their vegetating Faculty; but this I am certain of by Demonstration, that let a Dunghil remain Three Years unmov'd, though its Bulk be vastly diminish'd in that Time, and its best Quality lost, Charlock-seed will remain found in it, and stock the Land whereon it is laid: For that Ferment which is sufficient to consume the Virtue of the stercoreous Salts, is not sufficient to destroy the vegative Virtue of Charlock-seeds, nor (I believe) of many other Sorts of Weeds.

The very Effluvia of animal Bodies, sent off by Perspiration, are so noxious as to kill the Animal that emits them, if confin'd to receive them back in great Quantity, by breathing in an Air replete with them; which appears from the soon dying of an Animal shut up in a Receiver full of Air. Yet this seems to be the most harmless of all sorts of animal Excrements the Air can be infected with. How noxious then must be the more fetid Steams of Ordure!

If a Catalogue were publish'd of all Instances from Charnel-houses (or Cœmeteries) and of the pestiferous Effects, which have happen'd from the Putrefaction of dead Bodies, after great Battles, even in the open Air, no body, I believe, would have a good Opinion of the Wholsomeness of Animal Dung; for if a great Quantity do so infect the Air, 'tis likely a less may infect it in proportion to that less Quantity.

In great Cities the Air is full of these Effluvia, which in hot Climes often produce the Pestilence; and in cold Climes People are generally observ'd to live a less time, and less healthfully, in Cities, than in the Country; to which Difference, 'tis likely, that the eating unwholsome Gardenage may contribute.

This

This Dung is a fitter Food for venomous Creatures *(a)* than for edible Plants ; and 'tis (no doubt) upon Account of this, that dung'd Gardens are so much frequented by Toads, which are seldom or never seen in the open undung'd Fields.

What can we say then to the Salubrity of those Roots themselves, bred up and fatten'd among these Toads and Corruption ? The Leaves indeed are only discharging some of the Filth, when we eat them ; but the Roots have that unsavoury infected Food in their very Mouths, when we take them for our Nourishment.

But tho' *Dung* be, upon these and other Accounts, injurious to the Garden, yet a considerable Quantity of it is so necessary to most Corn-fields, that without it little Good can be done by the old Husbandry.

Dung is not injurious to the Fields *(b)* being there in less Proportion : And the Produce of Corn is the Grain.   When the Leaves have done their utmost to purify the Sap, the most refin'd Part is secern'd to be yet further elaborated by peculiar Organs ; then, by the Vessels of the Blossoms, 'tis become double-refin'd, for the Nourishment of the Grain ; which is therefore more pure from Dung, and more wholsome, than any other Part of the Plant that bears it.

And common Tillage alone is not sufficient for many Sorts of Corn, especially Wheat, which is the King of Grains.

Very few Fields can have the Conveniency of a sufficient Supply of Dung, to enable them to produce half the Wheat those will do near Cities, where they have Plenty of it.

(a) Mr. *Evelyn* says, that Dung is the Nurse of Vermin.

(b) Such Plants as *Cabbages*, *Turneps*, *Carrots*, and *Potatoes*, when they are designed only for fatting of Cattle, will not be injured by Dung, Tillage, and Hoeing all together, which will make the Crops the greater, and the Cattle will like them never the worse.

The Crop of 20 Acres will fcarce make Dung fufficient for one Acre, in the common Way of laying it on.

The Action of the Dung's Ferment affords a Warmth (*a*) to the Infant-plants, in their moft tender State, and the moft rigorous Seafon.

But 'tis hard to know how long the Warmth of this Ferment lafteth, by reafon of the great Difficulty to diftinguifh the very leaft Degree of Heat from the very leaft Degree of Cold.

Under the Name of Dung we may alfo underftand whatever ferments with the Earth (except Fire); fuch as green Vegetables cover'd in the Ground, &c.

As to the Difference of the Quantity of artificial Pafture made by *Dung* without Tillage, and that made by Tillage without *Dung*; the latter is many Times greater, of which I had the following Proof. An unplow'd Land, wherein a Dunghil had lain for two or three Years, and being taken away, was planted with *Turneps*; at the fame time a till'd Land, contiguous thereto, was drill'd with *Turneps*, and Horfe-ho'd; the other, being Hand-ho'd, profpered beft at the firft; but at laft did not amount to the Fifth Part of the Till'd and Horfe-ho'd, in Bignefs, nor in Crop. The Benefit of the Dung and Hand-hoe was fo inconfiderable, in comparifon of the Plough and Hoe-plough; the little Quantity of artificial Pafture raifed to the other, was only near the Surface, and did not reach deep enough to maintain the *Turneps*, till they arrived at the Fifth Part of the Growth of

(*a*) But though Dung in fermenting may have a little Warmth, yet it may fometimes, by letting more Water enter its Hollow-nefs, be in a Froft much colder than undung'd pulveriz'd Earth; for I have feen Wheat-plants in the Winter die in the very Spits of Dung, when undung'd drill'd Wheat, adjoining to it, planted at the fame Time, has flourifh'd all the fame Winter; and I could not find any other Reafon for this, but the Hollownefs of the Dung; and yet it feemed to be well rotted.

thofe

thofe, whofe artificial Pafture reach'd to the Bottom of the Staple of the Land.

A like Proof is; that feveral Lands of *Turneps*, drill'd on the Level, at three Foot Rows, plow'd, and doubly dung'd, and alfo Horfe-ho'd, did not produce near fo good a Crop of *Turneps*, as Six Foot Ridges adjoining, Horfe-ho'd, tho' no Dung had been laid thereon for many Years: There was no other Difference, than that the three Foot Rows did not admit the Hoe-plough to raife half the artificial Pafture, as the Six Foot Rows did. The Dung plow'd into the narrow Intervals, before drilling, could operate no further, with any great Effect, than the Hoe-plough could turn it up, and help in its Pulveration.

Dung, without Tillage, can do very little; with fome Tillage doth fomething; with much Tillage pulverizes the Soil in lefs Time, than Tillage alone can do; but the Tillage alone, with more Time, can pulverize as well: This the Experiments of *artificially* pulverizing of the pooreft Land, as they are related by Mr. *Evelyn*, fully prove.

And thefe Experiments are the more to be depended on, as they are made both in *England* and *Holland* by Perfons of known Integrity.

This Truth is alfo further confirmed by thofe Authors who have found, that High-way Duft alone is a Manure preferable to Dung: And all thefe Pulverations being made by Attrition or Contufion, why fhould not our Inftruments of Pulveration, in Time, reduce a fufficient Part of the Staple of a dry friable Soil, to a Duft equal to that of a Highway?

The common Proportion of Dung ufed in the Field pulverizes only a fmall Part of the Staple: but how long a time may be required for our Inftruments to pulverize an equal Part, it depending much upon the Weather, and the Degree of Friability of the Soil, is uncertain.

I have feen furprifing Effects from Ground, after being kept unexhaufted, by plowing with common Ploughs for Two whole Years running: And I am confident, that the Expence of this extraordinary Tillage and Fallow will not, in many Places, amount to above half the Expence of a dreffing with Dung; and if the Land be all the Time kept in our Sort of little Ridges of the Size moft proper for that Purpofe, the Expence of plowing will be diminifhed one half; befides the Advantage the Earth of fuch Ridges hath, of being friable in Weather which is too moift for plowing the fame Land on the Level.

I have made many Trials of fine *Dung* on the Rows; and, notwithftanding the Benefit of it, I have, for thefe feveral Years laft paft, left it off, finding that a little more Hoeing will fupply it at a much lefs Expence, than that of fo fmall a Quantity of Manure, and of the Hands neceffary to lay it on, and of the Carriage.

C H A P. V.

Of TILLAGE.

TIllage is breaking and dividing the Ground by Spade, Plough, Hoe, or other Inftruments, which divide by a Sort of Attrition (or Contufion) as Dung does by Fermentation *(a)*.

(a) *Neque enim aliud eft Colere quam Refolvere, & Fermentare Terram.* Columella.

And fince the artificial Pafture of Plants is made and increas'd by Pulveration, 'tis no Matter whether it be by the Ferment of *Dung*, the Attrition of the *Plough*, the Contufion of the *Roller*, or by any other Inftrument or Means whatfoever, except by Fire, which carries away all the Cement of that which is burnt.

By

By Dung we are limited to the Quantity of it we can procure, which in moſt Places is too ſcanty: But by Tillage, we can inlarge our Field of ſubterranean Paſture without Limitation, tho' the external Surface of it be confin'd within narrow Bounds: Tillage may extend the Earth's internal Superficies, in proportion to the Diviſion of its Parts; and as Diviſion is infinite, ſo may that Superficies be.

Every Time the Earth is broken by any Sort of Tillage, or Diviſion, there muſt ariſe ſome new Superficies of the broken Parts, which never has been open before. For when the Parts of Earth are once united and incorporated together, 'tis morally impoſſible, that they, or any of them, ſhould be broken again, only in the ſame Places; for to do that, ſuch Parts muſt have again the ſame numerical Figures and Dimenſions they had before ſuch Breaking, which even by an infinite Diviſion could never be likely to happen: As the Letters of a Diſtichon, cut out and mixt, if they ſhould be thrown up never ſo often, would never be likely to fall into the ſame Order and Poſition with one another, ſo as to recompoſe the ſame Diſtich.

Although the internal Superficies may have been drain'd by a preceding Crop, and the next Plowing may move many of the before divided Parts, without new-breaking them; yet ſuch as are new-broken, have, at ſuch Places where they are ſo broken, a new Superficies, which never was, or did exiſt before; becauſe we cannot reaſonably ſuppoſe, that any of thoſe Parts can have in all places (if in any Places) the ſame Figure and Dimenſions twice.

For as Matter is diviſible *ad infinitum,* the Places or Lines whereat 'tis ſo diviſible, muſt be, in relation to Number, infinite, that is to ſay, without Number; and muſt have at every Diviſion Super-

ficies

ficies of Parts of infinite Variety *(b)* in Figure and Dimenfions.

And becaufe 'tis morally impoffible, the fame Figure and Dimenfions fhould happen twice to any one Part, we need not wonder, how the Earth, every time of Tilling, fhould afford a new internal Superficies (or artificial Pafture); and that the till'd Soil has in it an inexhauftible Fund, which by a fufficient Divifion (being capable of an infinite one) may be produc'd.

Tillage (as well as Dung) is beneficial to all Sorts of Land *(c)*. Light Land, being naturally hollow, has larger Pores, which are the Caufe of its Lightnefs: This, when it is by any Means fufficiently divided,

---

(b) Their Variety is fuch, that 'tis next to impoffible, any two Pieces, or Clods, in a Thoufand Acres of till'd Ground, fhould have the fame Figure, and equal Dimenfions, or that any Piece fhould exactly tally with any other, except with that from whence it was broken off.

(c) 'Tis of late fully prov'd, by the Experience of many Farmers, that two or three additional Plowings will fupply the Place of Dung, even in the old Hufbandry, if they be perform'd at proper Seafons : and the hiring Price of three Plowings, after Land has been thrice plow'd before, is but Twelve Shillings, whereas a Dunging will coft three Pounds : This was accidentally difcovered in my Neighbourhood, by the Practice of a poor Farmer, who, when he had prepar'd his Land for Barley, and could not procure Seed to fow it, plow'd it on till Wheat Seed-Time, and (by means of fuch additional Plowing) without Dung, had fo good a Crop of Wheat, that it was judg'd to be more than the Inheritance of the Land it grew on.

The fame Effect follows when they prepare Land for Turneps, fince they are come in Fafhion, and fow them feveral Times upon feveral Plowings, the Fly as often taking them off; they have from fuch extraordinary Tillage a good Crop of Wheat, inftead of the loft Turneps, without the Help of Dung ; hence double-plowing is now become frequent in this Country.

The Reafon why Land is enrich'd by lying long unplow'd, is that fo very few Vegetables are carried off it, very little being produc'd ; the Exhauftion is lefs than what is added by the Atmofphere, Cattle, &c. But when 'tis plow'd, a vaftly greater Quantity of Vegetables is produc'd, and carried off, more than by the old Hufbandry is return'd to it.

the

the Parts being brought nearer together, becomes, for a time, Bulk for Bulk, heavier; *i. e.* The same Quantity will be contain'd in less Room, and so is, made to partake of the Nature and Benefits of strong Land, *viz.* to keep out too much Heat and Cold, and the like.

But strong Land, being naturally less porous, is made for a Time lighter (as well as richer) by a good Division; the Separation of its Parts makes it more porous, and causes it to take up more Room than it does in its natural State; and then it partakes of all the Benefits of lighter Land.

When strong Land is plow'd, and not sufficiently, so that the Parts remain gross, 'tis said to be rough, and it has not the Benefit of Tillage; because most of the artificial Pores (or Interstices) are too large; and then it partakes of the Inconveniences of the hollow Land untill'd.

For when the light Land is plow'd but once, that is not sufficient to diminish its natural Hollowness (or Pores;) and, for Want of more Tillage, the Parts into which 'tis divided by that once (or perhaps twice) Plowing, remain too large; and consequently the artificial Pores are large also, and, in that respect, are like the ill-till'd strong Land.

Light-land, having naturally less internal Superficies, seems to require the more Tillage *(d)* or Dung

to

(d) As for puffy Land, which naturally swells up, instead of subsiding, tho' its Hollowness is much abated by Tillage, yet it is thought little better than barren Land, and unprofitable for Corn: But what we usually call Light-land, is only comparatively so, in Respect of that which is heavier and stronger. And this Sort of Light land becomes much lighter by being ill-till'd; the unbroken Pieces of Turf underneath undissolved, forming large Cavities, increase its Hollowness, and consequently its Lightness: I have often known this Sort of Land despis'd by its Owners, who fear'd to give it due Tillage, which they thought would make it so light, that the Wind would blow it away; but whenever such has been thoroughly till'd, it never fail'd to become

much

to enrich it ; as when the poor, hollow, thin Downs have their upper Part (which is the beſt) burnt, whereby all. (except a *Caput Mortuum*) is carried away ; yet the Salts of this ſpread upon that barren Part of the Staple, which is unburnt, divide it into ſo very minute Particles, that their Paſture will nouriſh two or three good Crops of Corn : But then the Plough, even with a conſiderable Quantity of Dung, is never able afterwards to make a Diviſion equal to what thoſe Salts have done ; and therefore ſuch burnt Land remains barren.

Artificial Pores cannot be too ſmall, becauſe Roots may the more eaſily enter the Soil that has them, quite contrary to natural Pores ; for theſe may be, and generally are, too ſmall, and too hard for the Entrance of all weak Roots, and for the free Entrance of ſtrong Roots.

Inſufficient Tillage leaves ſtrong Land with its natural Pores too ſmall, and its artificial ones too large. It leaves Light-land, with its natural and artificial Pores both too large.

Pores that are too ſmall in hard Ground, will not eaſily permit Roots to enter them.

Pores that are too large in any Sort of Land, can be of little other Uſe to Roots, but only to give them Paſſage to other Cavities more proper for them ; and if in any Place they lie open to the Air, they are dry'd up, and ſpoil'd, before they reach them.

much ſtronger than before ; and conſidering that 'tis till'd with leſs Expence than very ſtrong Land, it is, for ſeveral Sorts of Corn, found to be more profitable than Land of greater Strength and Richneſs, that is more difficult to be till'd.

And I am apt to think, that this Sort of Light-land acquires more Cement, by having its *external* Superficies often changed, and expoſed to the Dews, and other Benefits of the Atmoſphere, as well as by the Increaſe of (its *internal* Superficies, which is the Surfaces of all the divided Parts of Earth, or) the Paſture of Plants ; the one being augmented by the other ; *i. e*, that into the more Parts the Earth is broken, the more Cement will it attain, from the Sulphur, which is brought by the Dews.

For

For fibrous Roots (which alone maintain the Plant; the other Roots ferve for receiving the Chyle from them, and convey it to the Stem) can take in no Nourifhment from any Cavity, unlefs they come into Contact with *(e)*, and prefs againft, all the Superficies of that Cavity, which includes them ; for it difpenfes the Food to their Lacteals by fuch Preffure only : But a fibrous Root is not fo prefs'd by the Superficies of a Cavity whofe Diameter is greater than that of the Root.

The Surfaces of great Clods form Declivities on every Side of them, and large Cavities, which are as Sinks to convey, what Rain and Dew bring, too quickly downwards to below the plow'd Part.

The firft and fecond Plowings with common Ploughs fcarce deferve the Name of Tillage ; they rather ferve to prepare the Land for Tillage.

The third, fourth, and every fubfequent Plowing, may be of more Benefit, and lefs Expence, than any of the preceding ones.

(e) Roots cannot have any Nourifhment from Cavities of the Earth that are too large to prefs againft them, except what Water, when 'tis in great Quantity, brings to them, which is imbibed by the gentle Preffure of the Water; but when the Water is gone, thofe large Cavities being empty, the Preffure ceafes ; and this is the Reafon, that when Land has few other but fuch large Cavities, the Plants in it always fuffer more by dry Weather, than in Land which by Dung or Tillage has more minute and fewer large Cavities.

There may be fome Moifture on the Superficies of large Cavities ; but without Preffure the fibrous Roots cannot reach it ; and very little or no Preffure can be made to one Part of the Root's Superficies, unlefs the Whole that is included be preffed.

If it be objected that a Charlock-Plant, when pulled up, and thrown upon the Ground, will grow thereon ; this proves nothing againft the Neceffity of Preffure, &c. for the Weight of that Plant preffes fome of its Roots fo clofely againft the Ground, that they fend out (unlefs the Weather be very dry) new Fibres into the Earth ; and there they are preffed in all their Superficies ; without which Fibres the Plant doth not grow.

But

But the laſt Plowings will be more advantageouſly perform'd by Way of Hoeing, as in the following Chapters will appear.

For the finer Land is made by Tillage, the richer will it become, and the more Plants it will maintain.

It has been often obſerv'd, that when Part of a Ground has been better till'd than the reſt, and the whole Ground conſtantly manag'd alike afterwards for ſix or ſeven Years ſucceſſively; this Part that was but once better till'd, always produc'd a better Crop than the reſt, and the Difference remain'd very viſible every Harveſt.

One Part being once made finer, the Dews did more enrich it; for they penetrate within and beyond the Superficies, whereto the Roots are able to enter: The fine Parts of the Earth are impregnate, throughout their whole Subſtance, with ſome of the Riches carried in by the Dews, and there repoſited; until, by new Tillage, the Inſides of thoſe fine Parts become Superficies; and as the Corn drains them, they are again ſupply'd as before; but the rough large Parts cannot have that Benefit; the Dews not penetrating to their Centres, they remain poorer.

I think nothing can be ſaid more ſtrongly to confirm the Truth of this, than what is related by the Authors quoted by Mr. *Evelyn* (*f*), to this Effect, *viz.*

‘ Take of the moſt barren Earth you can find,
‘ pulverize it well, and expoſe it abroad for a Year,
‘ inceſſantly agitated (*g*); it will become ſo fertile as
‘ to receive an exotic Plant from the furtheſt *Indies*;
‘ and to cauſe all Vegetables to proſper in the moſt
‘ exalted Degree, and to bear their Fruit as kindly
‘ with us as in their natural Climates.’

(*f*) In Pag. 17, 18, and 19, of his *Phil. Diſcourſe of Earth*.
(*g*) *i. e.* Stirr'd often.

This

. This artificial Duſt (*h*), he ſays, will entertain Plants which refuſe Dung, and other violent Applications ; and that it has a more nutritive Power than any artificial Dungs or Compoſt whatſoever : And further, that by this Toil of pulverizing, " 'tis found, that " Soil may be ſo ſtrangely alter'd from its former " Nature, as to render the harſh and moſt uncivil " Clay (*i*) obſequious to the Huſbandmen, and to " bring forth Roots and Plants, which otherwiſe re- " quire the lighteſt and holloweſt Mould (*k*)."

'Tis to be ſuppos'd, that the *Indian* Plants had their due Degrees of Heat and Moiſture given them; and I ſhould not chuſe to beſtow this Toil upon the pooreſt of Earth in a Field or Garden, tho' that be the moſt ſure wherein to make the Experiment (*l*).

I never myſelf try'd this way of pounding or grinding, becauſe impracticable in the Fields.

But I have had the Experience of a Multitude of Inſtances, which confirm it ſo far, that I am in no

(*h*) Tho' it may be impoſſible for the Plough to reduce the whole Staple into ſo fine Powder, yet the more internal Superficies it makes, the more Duſt will be made by the Atmoſphere in Proportion ; and great Clods perhaps are of no Uſe to Plants, but by that Duſt they let fall, being thence extricated by the inſenſible Ferment of the nitrous Air; and the Surfaces of this artificial Duſt muſt receive ſuch Operations from the Air, before the utmoſt Fertility be obtain'd.

(*i*) But I take harſh uncivil Clay to be the leaſt profitable of any to keep in Tillage.

(*k*) To this Duſt, *Namque hoc imitamur arando* ought to be apply'd, and not to *Putre Solum*, which itſelf needs Tillage, as well as ſtrong Land : But it ſeems the Antients did not obſerve the Difference between natural Pores (or Hollowneſs) and artificial ones, tho' it is very great ; as is ſhewn in Chap. of *Paſture of Plants*: Tis eaſier indeed to imitate this artificial Duſt in *hollow* than in *ſtrong* Land.

(*l*) This is the moſt proper Trial of the Effect of Pulveration by *pounding* and *grinding* ; but Land may be ſo barren, that Plough or Spade may not be ſufficient to pulverize it to that Degree, which is neceſſary to give it the ſame Fertility, that Pounding in a Mortar, or grinding betwixt Marbles (as Colours are ground), can.

Doubt,

Doubt, that any Soil (*m*) (be it rich or poor) can ever be made too fine by Tillage (*n*).

For 'tis without Difpute, that one cubical Foot of this minute Powder may have more internal Superficies, than a thoufand cubical Feet of the fame, or any other Earth till'd in the common Manner; and, I believe no two arable Earths in the World do exceed one another in their natural Richnefs Twenty Times; that is, one cubical Foot of the richeft is not able to produce an equal Quantity of Vegetables, *cæteris paribus*, to Twenty cubical Feet of the pooreft;

(*m*) Land that is too hollow and light, having no Cement to join its Parts together, tho' in Nature they are capable of infinite Divifion, yet in Practice the Plough cannot divide them to any Purpofe, unlefs they were firft join'd, but glides through without breaking them; being more like to the primary Particles of Water againft the Plough, which are broken by no Force, than to Earth; it may be moved, but not broken by Tillage, and therefore ought not to be reputed arable; nor does it indeed deferve the Name of Land, but as the defart Sands of *Lybia*, to diftinguifh it from Sea.

(*n*) According to fome, this Rule is only general, and not univerfal; for, fay they, there's a Sort of binding Gravel, that, when it is made *fine*, will, by a fudden Dafh of Rain, run together like a Metal; and I have feen the fame Accident in a particular Sort of *white* Land; but this very rarely happens to the latter: I never knew it above once, and that was after Barley was fown on it; the Hardnefs was only like a very thin Ice upon the Surface, which was fome Hindrance to the coming up of the Barley, until the Harrow's going over it once or twice broke that Ice or Cruft, and then it came up very well.

I never had any other Sort of Land liable to this Misfortune: therefore can fay nothing to the Gravel in that Cafe, nor how deep the *Conftipation* may reach in it, nor what Remedy is moft proper to prevent the ill Confequence of it: But if there fhould be two or three Exceptions out of *One thoufand Seventy-nine Millions One thoufand and Sixty different Sorts of* Earth (*fee Mr. Evelyn's Terra*, p. 2), 'twill be no great Matter.

But I think thefe are no real Exceptions againft any Degree of *Pulverizing*; for it only fhews, that fome Sorts of Land, tho' very few, are fubject by Accident to lofe too foon their Pulveration: And if the Finenefs were no Benefit to that Land, fuch Lofs of it would be no Injury to it.

therefore

therefore 'tis not ſtrange, that the pooreſt, when by pulverizing it has obtain'd One hundred Times the internal Superficies of the rich untill'd Land, it ſhould exceed it in Fertility ; or, if a Foot of the pooreſt was made to have Twenty Times the Superficies of a Foot of ſuch rich Land, the pooreſt might produce an equal Quantity of Vegetables with the rich (*o*). Beſides, there is another extraordinary Advantage, when a Soil has a larger internal Superficies in a very little Compaſs ; for then the Roots of Plants in it are better ſupply'd with Nouriſhment, being nearer to them on all Sides within Reach, than it can be when the Soil is leſs fine, as in common Tillage ; and the Roots in the one muſt extend much further than in the other, to reach an equal Quantity of Nouriſhment : They muſt range and fill perhaps above twenty Times more Space to collect the ſame Quantity of Food.

But in this fine Soil, the moſt weak and tender Roots have free Paſſage to the utmoſt of their Extent, and have alſo an eaſy, due, and equal Preſſure every-where, as in Water.

(*o*) And very poor Land, well pulveriz'd, will produce better Corn than very rich will do, without Manure or Tillage. The Experiment may be made by paring off the Turf, and ſetting Corn in the whole Ground that is very rich ; and that will ſhew how much the natural Paſture of the rich is inferior to the artificial Paſture of the poor Land ; but then the *poor* muſt have this Proportion of Exceſs of internal Superficies continued to it, during the whole Time of their Growth, which cannot be done without frequently repeated Diviſions of the Soil by Hoeing or Manure ; elſe it might require forty Times the internal Superficies at the Time of Sowing, to keep twenty Times the internal Superficies of the *rich* till Harveſt : For although the rich is continually loſing ſome of its artificial Paſture, as well as the *poor*, yet by loſing this equally, they ſtill draw nearer and nearer to the firſt Inequality of their natural Paſture.

But *poor* Land, being lighter, has this Advantage, that it being more *friable* than the ſtrong, requires leſs Labour to pulverize it ; and therefore the Expence of it is much leſs, than in proportion to the Exceſs of Poorneſs of its internal Superficies.

Hard

Hard Ground makes a too great Refiftance, as Air makes a too little Refiftance, to the Superficies of Roots.

Farmers, juft when they have brought their Land into a Condition fit to be further till'd to much greater Advantage, leave off, fuppofing the Soil to be fine enough, when, with the Help of Harrows, they can cover the Seed; and afterwards with a Roller they break the Clods; to the End that, if a Crop fucceed, they may be able to mow it, without being hinder'd by thofe Clods: By what I could ever find, this Inftrument, call'd a Roller, is feldom beneficial to good Hufbands; it rather untills the Land, and anticipates the fubfiding of the Ground, which in ftrong Land happens too foon of itfelf *(p)*.

But more to blame are they, who neglect to give their Land due Plowing, trufting to the Harrow to make it fine; and when they have thrown in their Seed, go over it twenty Times with the Harrows *(q)* till the Horfes have trodden it almoft as hard as a Highway, which in moift Weather fpoils the Crop; but on the contrary, the very Horfes, when the Earth is moift, ought all to tread in the Furrows only, as in plowing with a Hoe-Plough they always do, when they ufe it inftead of a common Plough.

(p) This Injury the Roller does, is only when tis ufed to prefs down the Earth after the Seed is fown; and is the greater, if Land be moift; but the Rolling of it in dry Weather, when 'tis to be immediately plow'd up again, is the moft fpeedy Way to pulverize the Soil; and the Harrow is then very ufeful in pulling up the Clods, to the End that the Roller may the better come at them to crufh them.

(q) Nam veteres Romani dixerunt male fubactum Agrum, qui fatis Frugibus occandus fit.

Sed ut compluribus Iterationibus fic refolvatur vervactum in Pulverem, ut nullam vel exiguam defideret Occationem, cum feminaverimus. Col. Lib. 2. Cap. 4.

CHAP.

CHAP. VI.

Of HOEING.

HOEING is the breaking or dividing the Soil by Tillage, whilst the Corn or other Plants are growing thereon.

It differs from common Tillage (which is always perform'd before the Corn or Plants are sown or planted) in the Times of performing it; 'tis much more beneficial; and 'tis perform'd by different Instruments.

Land that is before Sowing tilled never so much (tho' the more 'tis till'd the more it will produce) will have some Weeds, and they will come in along with the Crop for a Share of the Benefit of the Tillage, greater or less, according to their Number, and what Species they are of.

But what is most to be regarded is, that as soon as the Ploughman has done his Work of plowing and harrowing, the Soil begins to undo it, inclining towards, and endeavouring to regain, its natural specific Gravity; the broken Parts by little and little coalesce, unite, and lose some of their Surfaces; many of their Pores and Interstices close up during the Seed's Incubation and Hatching in the Ground; and, as the Plants grow up, they require an Increase of Food proportionable to their increasing Bulk; but on the contrary, instead thereof, that internal Superficies, which is their artificial Pasture, gradually decreases.

The Earth is so unjust to Plants, her own Off-spring, as to shut up her Stores in proportion to their Wants; that is, to give them less Nourishment when they have need of more: Therefore Man, for whose Use they are chiefly design'd, ought to bring in his reasonable

fonable Aid for their Relief, and force open her Magazines with the Hoe, which will thence procure them at all times Provifions in Abundance, and alfo free them from Intruders; I mean, their fpurious Kindred, the Weeds, that robb'd them of their too fcanty Allowance.

There's no Doubt, but that one third Part of the Nourifhment raifed by Dung and Tillage, given to Plants or Corn at many proper Seafons, and apportion'd to the different Times of their Exigencies, will be of more Benefit to a Crop, than the Whole apply'd, as it commoniy is, only at the time of Sowing. This old Method is almoft as unreafonable as if Treble the full Stock of Leaves, neceffary to maintain Silk-worms till they had finifhed their Spinning, fhould be given them before they are hatched, and no more afterwards.

Next to Hoeing, and fomething like it, is Tranfplanting, but much inferior; both becaufe it requires a fo much greater Number of Hands, that by no Contrivance can it ever become general, nor does it fucceed, if often repeated; but Hoeing will maintain any Plant in the greateft Vigour 'tis capable of, even unto the utmoft Period of Age. Befides, there is Danger in removing a whole Plant, and Lofs of Time before the Plant can take Root again, all the former Roots being broken off at the Ends in taking up (for 'tis impoffible to do it without), and fo muft wait until by the Strength and Virtue of its own Sap (which by a continual Perfpiration is daily enfeebled) new Roots are form'd, which, unlefs the Earth continue moift *(a)*, are fo long in forming, that they not only

(*a*) But when the Earth doth continue moift, many tranfplanted Vegetables thrive better than the fame Species planted in Seeds, becaufe the former, ftriking Root fooner, have a greater Advantage of the frefh-pulveriz'd Mould, which lofes fome of its artificial Pafture before the Seeds have Roots to reach it. The fame Advantage alfo have Seeds by foaking till ready to fprout before they are planted. To both thefe the Moifture of the Earth is neceffary.

find

find a more difficult Reception into the clofing Pores; but many Times the Plant languifhes and dies of an Atrophy, being ftarv'd in the midft of Plenty; but whilft this is thus decaying, the hoed Plant obtains a more. flourifhing State than ever, without removing from the fame Soil that produc'd it.

'Tis obferv'd that fome Plants are the worfe for Tranfplanting (*a*). *Fenochia* removed is never fo good and tender as that which is not, it receives fuch a Check in Tranfplanting in its Infancy; which, like the Rickets, leaves Knots that indurate the Parts of the Fennel, and fpoil it from being a Dainty.

Hoeing has moft of the Benefits without any Inconveniences of Tranfplanting; becaufe it removes the Roots by little and little, and at different Times; fome of the Roots remaining undifturb'd, always fupply the moved Roots with Moifture, and the whole Plant with Nourifhment fufficient to keep it from fainting, until the moved Roots can enjoy the Benefit of their new Pafture, which is very foon.

Another extraordinary Benefit of the new Hoeing (*b*) Hufbandry is, that it keeps Plants moift in dry Weather, and this upon a double Account.

(*a*) As moft long Tap-rooted Plants are; for I have often try'd the Tranfplanting of Plants, of *St. Foin* and *Luferne*; and could never find, that any ever came near to the Perfection that thofe will do which are not removed, being equally fingle.

Tap-rooted Graffes and Turneps are always injur'd by Tranfplanting; their long Root once broken off never arrives at the Depth it would have arriv'd unbroken; as for this Reafon they cut off the Tap-root of an Apple-tree, to prevent its running downward, by which it would have too much Moifture.

(*b*) Hoeing may be divided into Deep, which is our Horfe-hoeing, and Shallow, which is the Englifh Hand-hoeing; and alfo the Shallow Horfe-hoeing, ufed in fome Places betwixt Rows, where the Intervals are very narrow, as fixteen or eighteen Inches; this is but an Imitation of the Hand-hoe, or a *Succedaneum* to it; and can neither fupply the Ufe of Dung, nor of Fallow, and may be properly called Scratch-hoeing.

E   Firft,

Firſt, as they are better nouriſhed by Hoeing, they require leſs Moiſture, as appears by Dr. *Woodward*'s Experiment, that thoſe Plants which receive the greateſt Increaſe, having moſt terreſtrial Nouriſhment, carry off the leaſt Water in Proportion to their Augment: So Barley or Oats, being ſown on a Part of a Ground very well divided by Dung and Tillage, will come up and grow vigorouſly without Rain, when the ſame Grains, ſown at the ſame Time, on the other Part, not thus enriched, will ſcarce come up; or, if they do, will not thrive till Rain comes.

Secondly, The Hoe, I mean the Horſe-hoe (the other goes not deep enough), procures Moiſture to the Roots from the Dews, which fall moſt in dry Weather; and thoſe Dews (by what Mr. *Thomas Henſhaw* has obſerv'd) ſeem to be the richeſt Preſent the Atmoſphere gives to the Earth; having, when putrefy'd in a Veſſel, a black Sediment like Mud at the Bottom. This ſeems to cauſe the darkiſh Colour to the upper Part of the Ground. And the Sulphur, which is found in the Sediment of the Dew, may be the chief Ingredient of the Cement of the Earth; Sulphur being very glutinous, as Nitre is diſſolvent. Dew has both theſe.

Theſe enter in proportion to the Fineneſs and Freſhneſs of the Soil, and to the Quantity that is ſo made fine and freſh by the Hoe. How this comes to paſs, and the Reaſon of it, are ſhewn in the Chapter of Tillage.

To demonſtrate that Dews moiſten the Land when fine, dig a Hole in the hard dry Ground, in the drieſt Weather, as deep as the Plough ought to reach: Beat the Earth very fine, and fill the Hole therewith; and, after a few Nights Dews, you'll find this fine Earth become moiſt at the Bottom, and the hard Ground all round will continue dry.

Till

Till a Field in Lands; make one Land very fin
by frequent deep Plowings; and let another be rough
by infufficient Tillage, alternately; then plow the
whole Field crofs-ways in the drieft Weather, which
has continued long; and you will perceive, by the
Colour of the Earth, that every fine Land will be
turn'd up moift; but every rough Land will be dry
as Powder, from Top to Bottom.

Altho' hard Ground, when thoroughly foak'd with
Rain, will continue wet longer than fine till'd Land
adjoining to it; yet this Water ferves rather to chill,
than nourifh the Plants ftanding therein, and to keep
out the other Benefits of the Atmofphere, leaving
the Ground ftill harder when 'tis thence exhaled;
and being at laft once become dry, it can admit no
more Moifture, unlefs from a long-continued Deluge
of Rain, which feldom falls till Winter, which is not
the Seafon for Vegetation.

As fine hoed Ground is not fo long foaked by
Rain, fo the Dews never fuffer it to become perfectly
dry: This appears by the Plants, which flourifh and
grow fat in this, whilft thofe in the hard Ground are
ftarved, except fuch of them, which ftand near enough
to the hoed (*a*) Earth, for the Roots to borrow
Moifture and Nourifhment from it.

And

(*a*) As when Wheat is drill'd late in very poor Land, fo that
in the Spring the young Plants look all very yellow; let your
Hoe-plough, making a crooked Line, like an Indenture, on one
Side of a ftrait Row of this poor Wheat in the Spring, turn a
Furrow from it; and in a fhort time you will fee all thofe yellow
Plants, that are contiguous to this Furrow, change their yellow
Colour to a deep Green; whilft thofe Plants of the fame Row,
which ftand fartheft off from this indented Furrow, change not
their Colour till afterwards; and all the Plants change or retain their
Colour fooner or later gradually, as they ftand nearer to, or farther from it; and the other Rows, which have no Furrow near
them, continue their yellow, after all this Row is become green
and flourifhing: But this Experiment is beft to be made in poor
fandy Ground, when the Mould is friable; elfe perhaps the differ-

ent

And I have been informed by some Persons, that they have often made the like Observations; that, in the driest of Weather, good Hoeing *(a)* procures Moisture to Roots; tho' the Ignorant and Incurious fansy, it lets in the Drought; and therefore are afraid to hoe their Plants at such Times, when, unless they water them, they are spoil'd for Want of it.

There is yet one more Benefit Hoeing gives to Plants, which by no Art can possibly be given to Animals: For all that can be done in feeding an Animal is, what has been here already said of Hoeing; that is, to give it sufficient Food, Meat and Drink, at the times it has occasion for them; if you give an Animal any more, 'tis to no manner of Purpose, unless you could give it more Mouths, which is impossi-

ent Colour may not appear until the Furrow be turn'd back to the Row, having lain some time to be somewhat pulveriz'd (or impregnated) by the Weather, &c.

This Experiment I often made on Wheat drill'd on the Level before I drill'd any on Ridges.

The plowing one Furrow in sandy or mellow Ground makes a Pulveration, which is enjoy'd first by those Plants that are the nearest to it; and also delivers them from the Weeds, which, though there may be very few, yet there is a vast difference between their robbing the Wheat of its Pasture in the Row, and the Wheat's enjoying both that and the whole Pasture of the Furrow also.

I never remember to have seen a Plant poor, that was contiguous to a well-hoed Interval, unless overpower'd by a too great Multitude of other Plants; and the same Exception must be made, if it were a Plant that required more or less Heat or Moisture, than the Soil or Climate afforded.

(a) When Land is become hard by lying too long unho'd, the Plough in turning a deep Furrow from each Side of a single Row of young Plants (suppose of Turneps) may crack the Earth quite through the Row, and expose the Roots to the open Air and Sun in very dry Weather; but if the Earth wherein the Plants stand be fine, there will be no Cracks in it: 'Tis therefore the delaying the Hoeing too long that occasions the Injury. But to hoe with Advantage against dry Weather, the Ground must have been well tilled or hoed before, that the Hoe may go deep, else the Dews, that fall in the Night, will be exhal'd back in the Heat of the Day.

ble;

ble; but in hoeing a Plant the additional Nourishment thereby given, enables it to send out innumerable
additional Fibres and Roots, as in one of the Glasses
with a Mint in it, is seen ; which fully demonstrates,
that a Plant increaseth its Mouths, in some Proportion to the Increase of Food given to it: So that
Hoeing, by the new Pasture it raises, furnishes both
Food and Mouths to Plants; and 'tis for Want of
Hoeing, that so few are brought to their Growth and
Perfection *(a)*

In what Manner the Sarrition of the Antients was
performed in their Corn, is not very clear: This
seems to have been their Method ; *viz.* When the
Plants were some time come up, they harrowed the
Ground, and pull'd out the Weeds by Hand.   The
Process of this appears in *Columella,* where he directs
the Planting of *Medica* to be but a Sort of Harrow-
ing or Raking amongst the young Plants, that the
Weeds might come out the more easily: *Ligneis
Rastris statim jacta Semina obruantur.   Post Sationem
Ligneis Rastris Jarriendus, & identidem runcandus est
Ager, ne alterius generis Herba invalidam Medicam
perimat.*

(*a*) A Ground was drill'd with Ray-grass and Barley, in Rows
at Five Inches Distance from each other ; it produced a pretty
good Crop of Ray-grass the second Year as is usual; there was
adjoining to it a Ground of Turneps, that were in Rows, with
wide Intervals Horse-ho'd ; they stood for Seed; and amongst
them there was, in Room of a Turnep, a single Plant of Ray-grass,
which, being hoed as the Turneps were, had (in every one's Opinion that saw it) acquired a Bulk at least equal to a Thousand
Plants of the same Species in the other Ground ; tho' that vast
Plant had no other Advantage above the other, except its Singleness, and the deep Hoeing.

I have seen a Chickweed, by the same means, as much increas'd
beyond its common Size; and a Plant of Mustard-seed, whose
collateral Branches were much bigger than ever I saw a whole
Plant of that Sort ; it was higher than I could reach its Top, and
indeed more like a Tree than an Herb; many other sorts of Plants
have I seen thus increas'd beyond what I had ever observ'd before,
but none so much as those.

They

They harrowed and hoed *Raftris*; fo that their *Occatio* and *Sarritio* were performed with much the fame Sort of Inftrument, and differed chiefly in the Time: The firft was at Seed-time, to cover the Seed, or level the Ground; the other was to move the Ground after the Plants were up.

One Sort of their Sarrition was, *Segetes permota Terra debere adobrui, ut fruticare poffint.* Another Sort was thus: *In Locis autem frigidis farriri nec adobrui, fed Plana Sarritione Terram permoveri.*

For the better Underftanding of thefe two Sorts of Sarrition, we muft confider, that the Antients fowed their Corn under Furrow; that is, when they had harrowed the Ground, to break the Clods, and make it level, they fowed the Seed, and then plowed it in: This left the Ground very uneven, and the Corn came up (as we fee it does here in the fame Cafe) moftly in the loweft Places betwixt the Furrows, which always lay higher: This appears by *Virgil*'s *Cum Sulcos æquant Sata.* Now, when they ufed *Plana Sarritio*, they harrowed Length-ways of the Furrows, which being fomewhat harden'd, there could be little Earth thrown down thence upon the young Corn.

But the other Sort of Sarrition, whereby the Corn is faid *Adobrui*, to be cover'd, feems to be perform'd by Harrowing crofs the Furrows; which muft needs throw down much Earth from the Furrows, which neceffarily fell upon the Corn.

How this did contribute to make the Corn *fruticare*, is another Queftion: I am in no doubt to fay, it was not from covering any Part of it (for I fee that has a contrary Effect), but from moving much Ground, which gave a new Pafture to the Roots: This appears by the Obfervation of the extraordinary Frutication of Wheat ho'd without being cover'd; and by the Injury it receives by not being uncover'd when any Earth falls on the Rows.

The fame Author faith, *Faba, & cætera Legumina, cum quatuor Digitis à Terra extiterint, recte farrientur,*
excepto

*excepto tamen Lupino, cujus Semini contraria eſt Sarritio;
quoniam unam Radicem habet, quæ ſive Ferro ſucciſa
ſeu vulnerata eſt, totus Frutex emoritur.*

If they had ho'd it only betwixt Rows, there had
been no Danger of killing the Lupine, which is a
Plant moſt proper for Hoeing. What he ſays of the
Lupine's having no need of Sarrition, becauſe it is
able of itſelf to kill Weeds, ſhews the Antients were
ignorant of the chief Uſe of Hoeing; *viz.* to raiſe
new Nouriſhment by dividing the Earth, and making
a new Internal Superficies in it.

Sarrition ſcratched and broke ſo ſmall a Part of the
Earth's Surface, amongſt the Corn and Weeds, without Diſtinction, or favouring one any more than the
other, that it was a Diſpute, whether the Good it did
in facilitating the Runcation (or Hand-weeding) was
greater, than the Injury it did by bruiſing and tearing
the Corn : And many of the Antients choſe rather
to content themſelves with the Uſe of Runcation only,
and totally to omit all Sarrition of their Corn.

But Hoeing is an Action very different from that
of Sarrition, and is every Way beneficial, no-way injurious to Corn, tho' deſtructive to Weeds. Therefore ſome modern Authors ſhew a profound Ignorance, in tranſlating *Sarritio,* Hoeing : They give
an Idea very different from the true one : For the
Antients truly hoed their Vineyards, but not their
Corn ; neither did they plant their Corn in Rows,
without which they could not give it the Vineyard-
hoeing : Their Sarculation was uſed but amongſt
ſmall Quantities of ſown Corn, and is yet in Uſe for
Flax ; for I have ſeen the *Sarculum* (which is a Sort
of a very narrow Hoe) uſed amongſt the Plants of
Flax ſtanding irregularly : But this Operation is too
tedious and too chargeable, to be apply'd to great
Quantities of irregular Corn.

If they ho'd their Crops ſown at Random, one
would think they ſhould have made mad Work of

E 4   it;

it; since they were not at the Pains to plant in Rows, and hoe betwixt them with their Bidens; being the Instrument with which they tilled many of their Vineyards, and enters as deep as the Plough, and is much better than the *English* Hoe, which indeed seems, at the first Invention of it, to be designed rather to scrape Chimneys, than to till the Ground.

The highest and lowest Vineyards are ho'd by the Plough; first the high Vineyards, where the Vines grow (almost like Ivy) upon great Trees, such as Elms, Maples, Cherry-trees, &c. These are constantly kept in Tillage, and produce good Crops of Corn, besides what the Trees do yield; and also these great and constant Products of the Vines are owing to this Sort of Hoe-tillage; because neither in Meadow or Pasture Grounds can Vines be made to prosper; tho' the Land be much richer, and yet have a less Quantity of Grass taken off it, than the Arable has Corn carried from that.

The Vines of low Vineyards *(a)*, ho'd by the

(a) From these I took my Vineyard Scheme, observing that indifferent Land produces an annual Crop of Grapes and Wood without Dung; and though there is annually carried off from an Acre of Vineyard, as much in Substance as is carried off in the Crop of an Acre of Corn produced on Land of equal Goodness; and yet the Vineyard Soil is never impoverished, unless the hoeing Culture be denied it: But a few annual Crops of Wheat, without Dung in the common Management, will impoverish and emaciate the Soil.

The Vine indeed has the Advantage of being a large perennial Plant, and of receiving some Part of its Nourishment below the Staple; but it has also Disadvantages: The Soil of the Vineyard never can have a true Summer Fallow, tho' it has much Summer Hoeing; for the Vines live in it, and all over it all the Year: neither can that Soil have Benefit from Dung, because though by increasing the Pulveration, it increases the Crop, yet it spoils the Taste of the Wine; the Exhaustion of that Soil is therefore supply'd by no artificial Help but Hoeing: And by all the Experience I have had of it, the same Cause will have the same Effect upon a Soil for the Production of Corn, and other Vegetables, as well as upon the Vineyard.

Plough,

Plough, have their Heads juſt above the Ground, ſtanding all in a moſt regular Order, and are conſtantly plowed in the proper Seaſon : Theſe have no other Aſſiſtance, but by Hoeing; becauſe their Head and Roots are ſo near together, that Dung would ſpoil the Taſte of the Wine they produce, in hot Countries.

All Vineyards muſt be ho'd one Way or other (*a*), or elſe they will produce nothing of Value ; but Corn-Fields without Hoeing do produce ſomething, tho' nothing in Compariſon to what they would do with it.

Mr. *Evelyn* ſays, that when the Soil, wherein Fruit-Trees are planted, is conſtantly kept in Tillage, they grow up to be an Orchard in half the Time they would do, if the Soil were not till'd ; and this keeping an Orchard-Soil in Arable, is Horſe-hoeing it.

In ſome Places in *Berkſhire* they have uſed, for a long time to Hand-hoe moſt Sorts of Corn, with very great Succeſs ; and I may ſay this, that I myſelf never knew, or heard, that ever any Crop of Corn was properly ſo ho'd, but what very well anſwer'd the Expence, even of this Hand-work ; but be this never ſo profitable, there are not a Number of Hands to uſe it in great Quantities ; which poſſibly was one Reaſon the Antients were not able to introduce it into their Corn-Fields to any Purpoſe ; tho' they ſhould not have been ignorant of the Effect of it, from what they ſaw it do in their Vineyards and Gardens.

In the next Place I ſhall give ſome general Directions, which by Experience I have found neceſſary to be known, in order to the Practice of this Hoeing-Huſbandry.

I. *Concerning the Depth to plant at.*
II. *The Quantity of Seed to plant.*
III. *And the Diſtance of the Rows.*

(*a*) Vines, that cannot be ho'd by the Ploughs, are ho'd by the Bidens.

I. 'Tis

I. 'Tis neceſſary to know how deep we may plant our Seed, without Danger of burying it; for ſo 'tis ſaid to be, when laid at a Depth below what 'tis able to come up at.

Different Sorts of Seeds come up at different Depths; ſome at ſix Inches, or more; ſome at not more than half an Inch: The Way to know for certain the Depth any Sort will come up at is, to make Gauges in this Manner: Saw off 12 Sticks of about 3 Inches Diameter: Bore a Hole in the End of each Stick, and drive into it a taper Peg; let the firſt Peg be half an Inch long, the next an Inch, and ſo on; every Peg to be half an Inch longer than the former, till the laſt Peg be ſix Inches long; then in that ſort of Ground where you intend to plant, make a Row of Twenty Holes with the half-Inch Gauge; put therein Twenty good Seeds; cover them up, and ſtick the Gauge at the End of that Row; then do the like with all the other Eleven Gauges: This will determine the Depth, at which the moſt Seeds will come up *(a)*.

When the Depth is known, wherein the Seed is ſure to come up, we may eaſily diſcover, whether the Seed be good or not, by obſerving how many will fail: For in ſome Sorts of Seeds the Goodneſs cannot be known by the Eye; and there has been often great Loſs by bad Seed, as well as by burying good Seed; both which Misfortunes might be prevented by this little Trouble; beſides 'tis not convenient to plant ſome ſorts of Seed at the utmoſt Depth they

---

(a) In the common way of Sowing tis hard to know the proper Depth, becauſe ſome Seeds lying deep, and others ſhallow, it is not eaſy to diſcover the Depth of thoſe that are buried: But I have found in drilling of black Oats, that when the Drill-Plough was ſet a little deeper for Trial, very few came up: Therefore 'tis proper for the Driller to uſe the Gauges for all Sorts of Seeds; for, if he drills them too deep, he may loſe his Crop; or, if too ſhallow, in dry Weather, he may injure it, eſpecially in Summer Seeds; but for thoſe planted againſt Winter, there is the moſt Damage by planting too deep.

will come up at ; for it may be fo deep, as that the
Wet may rot or chill the firft Root, as in Wheat in
moift Land.

The Nature of the Land, the Manner how it is
laid, either flat, or in Ridges, and the Seafon of
Planting, with the Experience of the Planter, acquired
by fuch Trials, muft determine the proper Depths
for different Sorts of Seeds.

II. The proper Quantity of Seed to be drill'd on
an Acre, is much lefs than muft be fown in the common Way ; not becaufe Hoeing will not maintain as
many Plants as the other ; for, on the contrary, Experience fhews it will, *cæteris paribus*, maintain more ;
but the Difference is upon many other Accounts :
As that 'tis impoffible to fow it fo even by Hand, as
the Drill will do ; for let the Hand fpread it never
fo exactly (which is difficult to do fome Seeds, efpecially in windy Weather), yet the Unevennefs of
the Ground will alter the Situation of the Seed ; the
greateft Part rebounding into the Holes, and loweft
Places ; or elfe the Harrows, in Covering, draw it
down thither ; and tho' thefe low Places may have
Ten Times too much, the high Places may have
little or none of it : This Inequality leffens, in Effect,
the Quantity of the Seed ; becaufe Fifty Seeds, in
Room of One, will not produce fo much as One will
do ; and where they are too thick, they cannot be
well nourifhed, their Roots not fpreading to near
their natural Extent, for Want of Hoeing to open
the Earth.   Some Seed is buried (by which is meant
the laying them fo deep, that they are never able to
come up, as *Columella* cautions, *Ut abfque ulla Refur-
rectionis Spe fepeliantur*) : Some lies naked above the
Ground ; which, with more uncovered by the firft
Rain, feeds the Birds and Vermin.

Farmers know not the Depth that is enough to
bury their Seed, neither do they make much Difference in the Quantity they fow on a rough, or a
                                                      fine

fine Acre; tho' the fame that is too little for the one, is too much for the other; tis all mere Chance-work, and they put their whole Truft in good Ground, and much Dung, to cover their Errors.

The greateft Quantity of Seed I ever heard of to be ufually fown, is in *Wiltfhire*, where I am inform- ed by the Owners themfelves, that on fome Sorts of Land they fow Eight Bufhels of Barley to an Acre; fo that if it produce four Quarters to an Acre, there are but four Grains for one that is fown, and is a very poor Increafe, tho' a good Crop; this is on Land plowed once, and then double-dung'd, the Seed only harrow'd into the ftale and hard Ground (a), 'tis like not two Bufhels of' the eight will enter it to grow; and I have heard, that in a dry Summer an Acre of this fcarce produces four Bufhels at Harveft.

But, in Drilling, Seed lies all the fame juft Depth, none deeper, nor fhallower, than the reft; here's no Danger of the Accidents of burying, or being un- cover'd, and therefore no Allowance muft be made for them; but Allowance muft be made for other Accidents, where the Sort of Seed is liable to them; fuch as Grub, Fly, Worm, Froft, &c.

Next, when a Man unexperienc'd in this Method has proved the Goodnefs of his Seed, and Depth to plant at it, he ought to calculate what Number of Seeds a Bufhel, or other Meafure or Weight, con- tains: For one Bufhel or one Pound of fmall Seed, may contain double the Number of Seeds, of a Bufhel, or a Pound, of large Seed of the fame Species.

This Calculation is made by weighing an Ounce, and counting the Number of Seeds therein; then weighing a Bufhel of it, and multiplying the Num- ber of Seeds of the Ounce, by the Number of Ounces

(a) Stale Ground is that which has lain fome confiderable time after Plowing, before it is fown, contrary to that which is fown immediately after plow'd; for this laft is generally not fo hard as the former.

of

of the Bushel's Weight ; the Product will shew the Number of Seeds of a Bushel near enough : Then, by the Rule of Three, apportion them to the Square Feet of an Acre; or else it may be done, by divideing the Seeds of the Bushel by the Square Feet of an Acre ; the Quotient will give the Number of Seeds for every Foot : Also consider how near you intend to plant the Rows, and whether Single, Double, Treble, or Quadruple ; for the more Rows, the more Seed will be required (*a*).

Examine what is the Produce of one middle-siz'd Plant of the Annual, but the Produce of the best and largest of the perennial Sort ; because that by Hoeing will be brought to its utmost Perfection : Proportion the Seed of both to the reasonable Product ; and, when 'tis worth while, adjust the Plants to their competent Number with the Hand-hoe, after they are up ; and plant Perennials generally in single Rows: Lastly, Plant some Rows of the Annual thicker than others, which will soon give you Experience (better than any other Rule) to know the exact Quantity of Seed to drill.

III. The Distances of the Rows are one of the most material Points, wherein we shall find many apparent Objections against the Truth; of which, tho' full Experience be the most infallible Proof, yet the World is by false Notions so prejudiced against wide Spaces between Rows, that unless these common (and I wish I could say, only vulgar) Objections be first answer'd, perhaps no-body will venture so far out of the old Road, as is necessary to gain the Experience ; without it be such as have seen it.

(*a*) The narrow Spaces (suppose seven Inches) betwixt Double, Treble, or Quadruple Rows, the Double having One, the Treble Two, and the Quadruple Three of them, are called *Partitions*.

The wide Space (suppose of near five Feet) betwixt any Two of these Double, Treble, or Quadruple Rows, is call'd an *Interval*.

I for-

I formerly was at much Pains, and at some Charge, in improving my Drills, for planting the Rows at very near Distances; and had brought them to such Perfection, that One Horse would draw a Drill with Eleven Shares, making the Rows at three Inches and half Distance from one another; and at the same Time sow in them Three very different Sorts of Seeds, which did not mix; and these too, at different Depths; as the Barley-Rows were seven Inches asunder, the Barley lay four Inches deep; a little more than three Inches above that, in the same Chanels, was Clover; betwixt every Two of these Rows was a Row of St. Foin, cover'd half an Inch deep.

I had a good Crop of Barley the first Year; the next Year, Two Crops of Broad-Clover, where that was sown; and where Hop-Clover was sown, a mix'd Crop of That and St. Foin, and every Year afterwards a Crop of St. Foin; but I am since, by Experience, so fully convinced of the Folly of these, or any other such mix'd Crops, and more especially of narrow Spaces, that I have demolish'd these Instruments (in their full Perfection) as a vain Curiosity, the Drift and Use of them being contrary to the true Principles and Practice of Horse-Hoeing.

Altho' I am satisfied, that every one, who shall have seen as much of it as I have, will be of my Mind in this Matter; yet I am aware, that what I am going to advance, will seem shocking to them, before they have made Trials.

I lay it down as a Rule (to myself) that every Row of Vegetables, to be Horse-ho'd, ought to have an empty Space or Interval of thirty Inches on one Side of it (a) at least, and of near five Feet in all Sorts of Corn.

In

(a) *Note,* We call it one Row, tho' it be a Double, Treble, or Quadruple Row; because when they unite in the Spring, they seem to be all single; even the Quadruple then is but as one single Row.   Observ.

In Hand-hoeing there is always lefs Seed, fewer Plants, and a greater Crop, *cæteris paribus*, than in the common Sowing : Yet there, the Rows muft be much nearer together, than in Horfe-hoeing; becaufe as the Hand moves many times lefs Earth than the Horfe, the Roots will be fent out in like Proportion ; and if the Spaces or Intervals, where the Hand-hoe only fcratches a little of the upper Surface of them, fhould be wide, they would be fo hard and ftale underneath, that the Roots of perennial Plants would be long in running thro' them; and the Roots of many annual Plants would never be able to do it.

An Inftance which fhews fomething of the Difference between Hand-hoeing and Deep-hoeing is, That a certain poor Man is obferv'd to have his Cabbages vaftly bigger than any-body's elfe, tho' their Ground be richer, and better dung'd : His Neighbours were amaz'd at it, till the Secret at length came out, and was only this :   As other People ho'd their Cab-

Obferve, that as wide Intervals are neceffary for perfect Horfe-hoeing, fo the largeft Vegetables have generally the greateft Benefit by them; tho' fmall Plants may have confiderable Benefit from much narrower Intervals than Five Feet.

The Intervals may be fomewhat narrower for conftant annual Crops of Barley, than of Wheat; becaufe Barley does not fhut out the Hoe-Plough fo foon, nor require fo much Room for Hoeing, nor fo much Earth in the Intervals, it being a leffer Plant, and growing but about a Third-part of the Time on the Ground ; but he that drills Barley, muft refolve to reap it, and bind it up in Sheaves; for if he mows it, or does not bind it, a great Part will be loft among the Earth in the Intervals : But 'tis now found, that in a wet Harveft the beft Way is not to bind up drill'd Barley or Oats ; but inftead thereof, to make up the Grips into little Heaps by Hands, laying the Ears upon one another inwards, and the Stubble-ones outwards; fo that with a Fork that hath Two Fingers, and a Thumb, 'tis very eafy to pitch fuch Heaps up the Waggons without fcattering, or wafting any of the Corn.

'Tis alfo feen, that when the Reapers take Care to fet their Grips with the But-ends in the Bottoms of the Intervals, and the Ears properly on the Stubble, they will fo ftand up from the Ground, as to efcape much better from fprouting, than mow'd Corn.

bages

bages with a Hand-hoe, he inftead thereof dug his
with a Spade : And nothing can more nearly equal
(*a*) the Ufe of the Horfe-hoe than the Spade does.

And when the Plants have never fo much *Pabulum*
near them, their fibrous Roots cannot reach it all,
before the Earth naturally excludes them from it; for,
to reach it all, they muft fill all the Pores (*b*), which
is impoffible : So far otherwife it is, that we fhall find
it probable, that they can only reach the leaft Part of
it, unlefs the Roots could remove themfelves from
Place to Place, to leave fuch Pores as they had exhaufted, and apply themfelves to fuch as were unexhaufted ;
but they not being endow'd with Parts neceffary for
local Motion (as Animals are), the Hoe-Plough fup-
lies their Want of Feet ; and both conveys them to
their Food, and their Food to them, as well as pro-
vides it for them ; for by tranfplanting the Roots, it
gives them Change of the Pafture, which it increafes
by the very Act of changing them from one Situation
to another, if the Intervals be wide enough for this
Hoeing Operation to be properly perform'd.

The Objections moft likely to prepoffefs Peoples
Minds, and prevent their making Trials of this Hufbandry, are thefe :

Firft, they will be apt to think, that thefe wide,
naked Spaces, not being cover'd by the Plants, will
not be fufficient to make a good Crop.

For Anfwer, we muft confider, that tho' Corn,
ftanding irregular and *fparfim*, may feem to cover

(*a*) The Hoe-plough exceeds the Spade in this Refpect, that it
removes more of the Roots, and cuts off fewer ; which is an Advantage when we till near to the Bodies of Plants that are grown
large.

(*b*) The Roots of a Mint, fet a whole Summer in a Glafs,
kept conftantly replenifhed with Water, will, in Appearance, fill
the whole Cavity of the Glafs ; but by compreffing the Roots, or
by obferving how much Water the Glafs will hold when the
Roots are in it, we are convinc'd, that they do not fill a Fourth-
part of its Cavity ; tho' they are not ftopp'd by Water, as they
are by Earth.   the

the Ground better than when it ftands regular in
Rows ; this Appearance *(a)* is a mere *Deceptio vifus* ;
for Stalks are never fo thick on any Part of the
Ground as where many come out of one Plant, or
as when they ftand in a Row ; and a ho'd Plant of
Corn will have Twenty or Thirty Stalks *(b)*, in the
fame Quantity of Ground where an unho'd Plant,
being equally fingle, will have only Two or Three
Stalks. Thefe tillered ho'd Stalks, if they were
planted *fparfim* all over the Interval, it might feem
well cover'd, and perhaps thicker than the fown Crop
commonly is ; fo that tho' thefe ho'd Rows feem to
contain a lefs Crop, they may contain, in reality, a
greater Crop than the fown, that feems to exceed it ;
and 'tis only the different Placing that makes one
feem greater, and the other lefs, than it really is ; and
this is only when both Crops are young.

The next Objection is, That the Space or Interval
not being *planted*, much of the Benefit of that Ground
will be loft ; and therefore the Crop muft be lefs than
if it were planted all over.

I anfwer, It might be fo, if not Horfe-ho'd ; but
if well Horfe-ho'd, the Roots can run through the
Intervals ; and, having more Nourifhment, make a
greater Crop.

The too great Number of Plants, plac'd all over
the Ground in common fowing, have, whilft it is
open, an Opportunity of *wafting*, when they are very
young, that Stock of Provifion, for Want of which
the greateft Part of them are afterwards ftarv'd ; for

(a) For the Eye to make a Comparifon betwixt a fown Crop
and fuch a ho'd Crop, it ought, when 'tis half grown, to look
on the ho'd Crop acrofs the Rows ; becaufe in the other it does
fo, in Effect, which way foever it looks ; but whatever Appearance the ho'd Crop of Vegetables (of as large a Species as Wheat)
makes when young, it furely, if well managed, appears more
beautiful at Harveft than a fown Crop.

(b) I have counted Fifty large Ears on one fingle ho'd Plant
of Barley.

F   their

their irregular Standing prevents their being relieved with fresh Supplies from the Hoe: Hence it is, that the old Method exhausting the Earth to no Purpose, produces a less Crop; and yet leaves less *Pabulum* behind for a succeeding one, contrary to the Hoeing-Husbandry, wherein Plants are manag'd in all Respects by a quite different Oeconomy.

In a large Ground of Wheat it was prov'd, that the widest ho'd Intervals brought the greatest Crop of all: Dung without Hoeing did not equal Hoeing without Dung. And what was most remarkable, amongst Twelve Differences of wider and narrower Spaces, more and less ho'd, dung'd and undung'd, the Hand-sow'd was considerably the worst of all; tho' all the Winter and Beginning of the Spring, that made infinitely the most promising Appearance; but at Harvest yielded but about One-fifth Part of Wheat of that which was most hoed; there was some of the most hoed, which yielded Eighteen Ounces of clean Wheat in a Yard in Length of a double Row, the Intervals being thirty Inches, and the Partition Six Inches *(a)*.

A Third Objection like the two former is, that so small a Part of the Ground, as that whereon the Row stands, cannot contain Plants or Stalks sufficient for a full Crop.

This some Authors endeavour to support by Arguments taken from the perpendicular Growth of Vegetables, and the Room they require to stand on; both which having answer'd elsewhere, I need not say much of them here; only I may add, that if Plants could be brought to as great Perfection, and so to

(a) The same Harvest, a Yard in Length of a double Row of Barley, having Six Inches Partition, produc'd Eight hundred and Eighty Ears in a Garden; but the Grains happen'd to be eaten by Poultry before 'twas ripe, so that their Produce of Grains could not be known: One like Yard of a ho'd Row of Wheat, in an undung'd Field, produc'd Four hundred Ears of Lammas-Wheat.

stand

ſtand as thick all over the Land, as they do in the ho'd Rows, there might be produc'd, at once, many of the greateſt Crops of Corn that ever grew.

But ſince Plants thrive, and make their Produce, in Proportion to the Nouriſhment they have within the Ground, not to the Room they have to ſtand upon it, one very narrow Row may contain more Plants than a wide Interval can nouriſh, and bring to their full Perfection, by all the Art that can be uſed; and 'tis impoſſible a Crop ſhould be loſt for want of room to ſtand above the Ground, tho' it were leſs than a Tenth-part of the Surface (*a*).

In wide Intervals there is another Advantage of Hoeing, I mean Horſe-hoeing (the other being more like Scratching and Scraping than Hoeing) : There is room for many Hoeings (*b*), which muſt not come
very

(*a*) Mr. *Houghton* calculates, that a Crop of Wheat of Thirty Quarters to an Acre, each Ear has two Inches and a Half of Surface; by which 'tis evident, that there would be Room for many ſuch prodigious Crops to ſtand on.

And a Quick-hedge, ſtanding between two Arable Grounds, one Foot broad at Bottom, and Eighteen Feet in Length, will, at fourteen Years Growth, produce more of the ſame Sort of Wood, than eighteen Feet ſquare of a Coppice will produce in the ſame Time, the Soil of both being of equal Goodneſs.

This ſeems to be the ſame Caſe with our ho'd Rows; the Coppice, if it were to be cut in the firſt Years, would yield perhaps ten Times as much Wood, as the Hedge; but many of the Shoots of the Coppice conſtantly die every Year, for Want of ſufficient Nouriſhment, until the Coppice is fit to be cut; and then its Product is much leſs than that of the Hedge, whoſe Paſture has not been over-ſtock'd to ſuch a Degree as the Coppice-Paſture has been; and therefore brings its Crop of Wood to greater Perfection than the Coppice-Wood, which has Eighteen Times the Surface of Ground to ſtand on : The Hedge has the Benefit of Hoeing, as oft as the Land on either Side of it is till'd; but the Coppice, like the ſown Corn, wants that Benefit.

(*b*) Many Hoeings; but if it ſhould be aſked how many, we may take *Columella*'s Rule in hoeing the Vines, *viz. Numerus autem vertendi Soli (bidentibus) definiendus non eſt, cum quanto cre-*

brier

very near the Bodies of some annual Plants, except whilst they are young ; but in narrow Intervals, this cannot be avoided at every Hoeing : 'Tis true, that in the last Hoeings, even in the middle of a large Interval, many of the Roots may be broken off by the Hoe-plough, at some considerable Distance from the Bodies ; but yet this is no Damage, for they send out a greater Number of Roots than before ; as in Chap. I. appears.

In wide Intervals, those Roots are broken off only where they are small ; for tho' they are capable of running out to more than the Length of the external Parts of a Plant ; yet 'tis not necessary they should always do so ; if they can have sufficient Food nearer to the Bodies (*a*) of the Plants.

And these new, young, multiply'd Roots are fuller of Lacteal Mouths than the older ones ; which makes it no Wonder, that Plants should thrive faster by having some of their Roots broken off by the Hoe ; for as Roots do not enter every Pore of the Earth, but miss great Part of the Pasture, which is left unexhausted, so when new Roots strike out from the broken Parts of the old, they meet with that Pasture, which their Predecessors miss'd, besides that new Pasture which the Hoe raises for them ; and those Roots which the Hoe pulls out without breaking,

---

brior sit, plus prodesse fossionem conveniat.   Sed imperfarum Ratio modum postulat.   Lib. 4. Cap. 5.

Neither is it altogether the Number of Hoeings that determines the Degrees of Pulveration : For, Once well done, is Twice done ; and the oftener the better, if the Expence be not excessive.

Poor Land, be it never so light, should have the most Hoeings ; because Plants, receiving but very little Nourishment from the natural Pasture of such Land, require the more artificial Pasture to subsist on.

(*a*) All the Mould is never so near to the Bodies of Plants, as 'tis when the Row stands on a high Six-feet Ridge, when the middle of the Interval is left bare of Earth, at the last Hoeing ; for then all the Mould may be but about a Foot, or a Foot and half, distant from the Body of each Plant of a Treble Row.

and

and covers again, are turn'd into a fresh Pasture; some broken, and some unbroken : All together invigorate the Plants.

Besides, the Plants of sown Corn, being treble in Number to those of the drill'd, and of equal Strength and Bulk, whilst they are very young, must exhaust the Earth whilst it is open, thrice as much as the drill'd Plants do; and before the sown Plants grow large, the Pores of the Earth are shut against them, and against the Benefit of the Atmosphere; but for the drill'd, the Hoe gives constant Admission to that Benefit; and if the Hoe procures them (by dividing the Earth) Four Times the Pasture of the sown during their Lives, and the Roots devour but one half of that, then tho' the ho'd Crop should be double to the sown, yet it might leave twice as much *Pabulum* for a succeeding Crop. 'Tis impossible to bring these Calculations to Mathematical Rules; but this is certain in Practice, that a sown Crop, succeeding a large undung'd ho'd Crop, is much better than a sown Crop, that succeeds a small dung'd sown Crop. And I have the Experience of poor, worn out Heathground, that, having produc'd Four successive good ho'd Crops of Potatoes (the last still best), is become tolerable good Ground.

In a very poor Field were planted Potatoes, and, in the very worst Part of it, several Lands had them in Squares a Yard asunder; these were plowed four ways at different times : Some other Lands adjoining to them, of the very same Ground, were very well dung'd and till'd; but the Potatoes came irregularly, in some Places thicker, and in others thinner : These were not ho'd, and yet, at first coming up, looked blacker and stronger than those in Squares not dung'd, either that Year, or ever, that I know of; yet these Lands brought a good Crop of the largest Potatoes, and very few small ones amongst them; but in the dung'd Lands, for Want of Hoeing, the Potatoes

were

were not worth the taking up; which proves, that in
thofe Plants that are planted fo as to leave Spaces
wide enough for Repetitions of Hoeing, that Inftrument can raife more Nourifhment to them, than a
good Coat of Dung with common Tillage.

Another Thing I have more particularly obferv'd,
viz. That the more fucceffive Crops are planted in
wide Intervals, and often ho'd, the better the Ground
does maintain them; the laft Crop is ftill the beft,
without Dung, or changing the Sort of Plant; and
this is vifible in Parts of the fame Field, where fome
Part has a firft, fome other Part a fecond, the reft
a third Crop growing all together at the fame time;
which feems to prove, that as the Earth is made by
this Operation to difpenfe or diftribute her Wealth to
Plants, in Proportion to the Increafe of her inner
Superficies (which is the Pafture of Plants); fo the
Atmofphere, by the Riches in Rain and Dews, does
annually reimburfe her in Proportion to the fame
Superficies, with an Overplus for Intereft: But if that
Superficies be not increafed to a competent Degree,
and, by frequent Repetitions of Hoeing, kept increafing (which never happens in common Hufbandry)
this Advantage is loft; and, without often repeated
Stercoration, every Year's Crop grows worfe; and it
has been made evident by Trials, which admit of no
Difpute, that Hoeing, without Dung or Fallow, can
make fuch Plants as ftand in wide Intervals, more
vigorous in the fame Ground, than both common
Dunging and Fallowing can do without Hoeing.

This Sort of Hoeing has in Truth every Year the
Effect of a Summer-fallow; tho' it yearly produce a
good Crop.

This is one Reafon of the different Effects Plants
have upon the Soil; fome are faid to enrich it, others
to burn it, *i. e.* to impoverifh it; but I think it
may be obferved, that all thofe Plants, which are
ufually ho'd, are reckoned among the Enrichers;

and

and tho' it be certain that some Species of Plants are, by the Heat of their Conſtitution, greater Devourers than thoſe of another Species of equal Bulk ; yet there is Reaſon to believe, that were the moſt cormorant Plant of them all to be commonly ho'd, it would gain *(a)* the Reputation of an Enricher or

(a) But this muſt be intended of the deep Horſe-hoeing; for Turneps that ſtand for Seed, are ſuch Devourers, and feed ſo long on the Soil, that tho' they are Hand-ho'd, ſuch a ſhallow Operation doth not ſupply the uſual Thickneſs of thoſe Plants with Paſture ſufficient to raiſe their Stems to half their natural Bulk ; and they leave ſo little of that Paſture behind them, that the Soil is obſerv'd to be extremely impoveriſhed for a Year or two, and ſometimes three Years after them ; but 'tis otherwiſe with my Horſe-ho'd Turnep-Seed ; for I never fail'd of a good Crop of Barley after it, ſown on the Level in the following Spring, tho' no Dung hath been uſed on the Land where the Turnep-Seed grew for many Years. And alſo my Barley Crops thus ſown after two ſucceſſive Crops of Turnep-Seed without a Fallow between them, are as good as thoſe ſown after a ſingle Crop of it. For I have ſeveral Times made theſe Turnep-Seed Crops annual, that is, to have Two Crops of it in Two Years, which would in the old Way require three Years, becauſe this Crop ſtands about a Year on the Ground, and is not ripe till Midſummer, which is too late to get that Land into a Tilth proper to plant another Seed Crop on it the ſame Summer; neither can the Soil be able to bear ſuch another Crop immediately after being ſo much exhauſted, and unplowed for a whole Year, except it be extraordinary rich, or much dunged : However, Two Crops of Turnep-Seed immediately ſucceeding one another, is what I never knew, or heard of, except my own that were Horſe-ho d ; and of theſe the ſecond Crop was as good as the firſt ; their Stalks grew much higher than they uſually do in the common Way; and tho' the Number of Plants was much leſs, their Produce was ſo valuable, that the *Vicar's Agent* declared, he made Twenty Shillings *per* Acre of his Tythe of a whole Field which he tythed in Kind. The Expence of theſe Crops was judg'd to be anſwered by the Fuel of the threſh'd Stalks. It muſt be noted, that the extraordinary Value of theſe Crops aroſe, not from a greater Quantity of Seed than ſome common Crops; but from their Quality, Experience having brought this Seed into great Eſteem, on account of its being perfectly clean, and produced by large Turneps of a good Sort, and of a proper Shape; for thoſe that are not well cultivated are very apt to degenerate, and then their Seed will produce Turneps of a ſmall Size, and of a long rapy ill Shape.

Improver

Improver of the Soil ; except it fhould be fuch, as might occafion Trouble, by filling it full of its fhatter'd Seeds, which might do the Injury of Weeds to the next Crop ; and except fuch Plants, which have a vaft Bulk to be maintained a long Time, as Turnep-Seed (*a*).

The wider the Intervals are, the more Earth may be divided ; for the Row takes up the fame Room with a wide, or a narrow Interval ; and therefore with the wide, the unho'd Part bears a lefs Proportion to the ho'd Part than in the narrow.

And 'tis no Purpofe to hoe, where there is not Earth to be ho'd, or Room to hoe it in.

There are many Ways of Hoeing with the Hoe-Plough ; but there is not Room to turn Two deep clean Furrows in an Interval that is narrower than Four Feet Eight Inches ; for if it want much of this Breadth, one, at leaft, of thefe Furrows, will reach, and fall upon the next Row, which will be very injurious to the Plants; except of grown St. Foin, and fuch other Plants, that can bear to have the Earth pull'd off them by Harrows.

Thus much of Hoeing in general may fuffice : And different Sorts of Plants requiring different Management; that may more properly be defcribed in the Chapter, where particular Vegetables are treated of.

It may not be amifs to add, that all Sorts of Land are not equally proper for Hoeing : I take it, that a dry friable Soil is the beft. Intractable wet Clays, and fuch Hills as are too fteep for Cattle to draw a Plough up and down them, are the moft improper (*b*).

(*a*) Turneps run to Seed, not till the fecond Summer.

(*b*) For by hoeing crofs the Hill, the Furrow turn'd againft the Declivity cannot be thrown up near enough to the Row above it ; and the Furrow that is turn'd downwards will bury the Row below it.

That 'tis not fo beneficial to hoe in Common-fields, is not in Refpect of the Soil, but to the old Principles, which have bound the Owners to unreafonable Cuftoms of changing the Species of Corn, and make it neceffary to fallow every Second, Third, or Fourth Year at fartheft.

C H A P. VII.

Of WEEDS.

PLANTS, that come up in any Land, of a different Kind from the fown or planted Crop, are Weeds.

That there are in Nature any fuch things as *inutiles Herbæ*, the Botanifts deny ; and juftly too, according to their Meaning.

But the Farmer, who expects to make Profit of his Land from what he fows or plants in it, finds not only *Herbæ inutiles*, but alfo *noxiæ*, unprofitable and hurtful Weeds ; which come like *Muficæ*, or uninvited Guefts, that always hurt, and often fpoil his Crop, by devouring what he has, by his Labour in Dunging and Tilling, provided for its Suftenance.

All Weeds, as fuch, are pernicious ; but fome much more than others ; fome do more Injury, and are more eafily deftroy'd ; fome do lefs Injury, and are harder to kill ; others there are, which have both thefe bad Qualities. The hardeft to kill are fuch as will grow and propagate by their Seed, and alfo by every Piece of their Roots, as Couch-grafs, Coltsfoot, Melilot, Fern, and fuch-like. Some are hurtful only by robbing legitimate (or fown) Plants of their Nourifhment, as all Weeds do ; others both leffen a legitimate Crop by robbing it, and alfo fpoil that Crop, which efcapes their Rapine, when they infect

it

it with their naufeous Scent and Relifh, as Melilot, wild Garlick, &c.

Weeds ftarve the fown Plants, by robbing them of their Provifion of Food *(a)*, not of their Room (as fome Authors vainly imagine); which will appear by the following Experiment.

Let three Beds of the fame Soil, equal, and equally prepared, be fown with the fame Sort of Corn. Let the firft of thefe Beds be kept clean from Weeds: In the Second, let a Quantity of Weeds grow along with the Corn; and in the Third, ftick up a Quantity of dead Sticks, greater in Bulk than the Weeds.

It will be found, that the Produce of the Corn in the Firft will not exceed that of the Third Bed; but in the Second, where the Weeds are, the Corn will be diminifh'd in Proportion to the Quantity of Weeds amongft it.

The Sticks, having done no Injury to the Corn, fhew there was room enough in the Bed for Company to lodge, would they forbear to eat; or elfe (like Travellers in *Spain*) bring their Provifion with them to their Inn, or (which would be the fame thing) if Weeds could find there fome Difh fo difagreeable to the Palate of the Corn, and agreeable to their own, that they might feed on it without robbing; and then they would be as innocent as the Sticks, which take up the fame Room with the Weeds.

The Quantity of Nourifhment Weeds rob the Corn of, is not in Proportion only to their Number and Bulk, but to the Degrees of Heat in their Con-

(a) A Tree of any Sort will fpoil Corn all round it, in a large Circle; half an Acre of Turneps has been fpoil'd by one: Hereby 'tis plain, that Trees rob as Weeds; becaufe 'tis not by their Shadow, there being as much Damage done by them on the South-Side, where their Shadow never comes, as on their North-Side: Nor can it be by their dropping; for 'tis the fame on the Side where a Tree has no Boughs to drop over the Plants, when they are alfo at a very great Diftance from all Parts of the Tree, except its Roots.

ftitution;

ftitution; as'appears by the Inftance of Charlock and Turneps, mention'd in the Chapter *Of Change of Species.*

'Tis needlefs to go about to compute the Value of the Damage Weeds do, fince all experienc'd Hufband-men know it to be very great, and would unani-moufly agree to extirpate their whole Race as intirely, as in *England* they have done the Wolves, tho' much more innocent, and lefs rapacious than Weeds *(a).*

But alas! they find it impoffible to be done, or even to be hoped for, by the common Hufbandry; and the Reafons I take to be thefe.

The Seeds of moft Sorts of Weeds are fo hardy, as to lie found and uncorrupt for many Years *(b),* or perhaps Ages in the Earth; and are not kill'd until they begin to grow or fprout, which very few of them do, unlefs the Land be plow'd; and then enough of them will ripen amongft the fown Crop, to propa-gate and continue their Species, by fhedding their Off-fpring in the Ground (for 'tis obferv'd they are generally ripe before the Corn); and the Seeds of thefe do the fame in the next fown Crop; and thus perpetuate their favage, wicked *(c)* Brood, from Generation to Generation.

Befides, their Seeds never all come up in one Year, unlefs the Land be very often plow'd; for they muft have their exact Depth, and Degrees of Moifture and

---

(a) If we confider the Crops they utterly deftroy, and thofe they extremely diminifh; and that very few Crops efcape without receiving Injury from them; it may be a Queftion, whether the Mifchief Weeds do to our Corn, is not as great as the Value of the Rent of all the Arable Lands in *England.*

(b) The Seeds of *Lethean Poppy* (call'd *Red-weed*) have lain dormant 24 Years 'the Land being, during that time, in *St. Foin)* and then at firft Plowing the; came up very thick; this I have feen, and fo will many other Sorts of Weeds, when the Ground has lain untill'd for an Age.

(c) The *French* call them, *les Herbes Sauvages, & les mechan-tes Herbes.*

Heat,

Heat, to make them grow; and such as have not these, will lie in the Ground, and retain their vegetative Virtue for Ages; and the common usual Plowings, not being sufficient to make them all, or the greatest Part, grow, almost every Crop that ripens increases the Stock of Seed, until it make a considerable Part of the Staple of such Land as is sown without good Tillage and Fallowing.

The best Defence against these Enemies, which the Farmer has hitherto found, is to endeavour their Destruction by a good Summer-fallow: This indeed, if the Weather be propitious, does make Havock of them; but still some will escape one Year's Prosecution. Either by being sometimes situate so high, that the Sun's Heat dries them, or sometimes lying so deep, that it cannot reach them; either way their Germination, which would have proved their Death, is prevented.

Another Faculty secures abundance of them, and that is, their being able to endure the Heat and Moisture of one Year without growing; as (*a*) wild Oats, and innumerable other Sorts of Weeds, will do; for gather these when ripe, sow them in the richest Bed, water them, and do all that is possible to make them grow the First Year, it will be vain Labour; they will resist all Enticements till the Second; that is, if you gather them in Autumn, you cannot force them to grow until the next Spring come Twelvemonth; and many of them will remain dormant even to the next Year after that, and some of them longer.

By this Means, One Year's Summer-Fallow can have no Effect upon them, but to prepare the Soil

---

(*a*) I have not try'd wild Oats by sowing them in a Bed myself, but have been so inform'd by others; and my own Experience hath frequently shewn me, that they will come up, after lying many Years in the Ground; and that very few Sorts of Weeds will come all up the first Year, as Corn doth: If they did, the Tillage of one Year's Summer-fallow might extirpate them.

for their more vigorous Growth and plentiful Increase the next Year after; and very rarely will the Farmer fallow his Land Two Years succeffively ; and often the Dung, which is made of the Straw of fown Corn, being full of the Seeds of Weeds, when fpread on the Fallows, incumbers the Soil with another Stock of Weeds, as ample as that the Fallowing has deftroy'd ; and tho' perhaps many of thefe may not grow the next Year, they will be fure to come up afterwards.

The other old Remedy is what often proves worfe than the Difeafe ; that is, what they call Weeding among fown Corn ; for if by the Hook or Hand they cut fome Sorts (as Thiftles) while they are young, they will fprout up again, like *Hydras*, with more Heads than before ; and if they are cut when full-grown, after they have done almoft their utmoft in robbing the Crop, 'tis like fhutting the Stable-Door after the Steed is ftolen.

Hand-weeders often do more Harm to the Corn with their Feet, than they do Good by cutting or pulling out the Weeds with their Hands ; and yet I have known this Operation fometimes coft the Farmer Twelve Shillings an Acre ; befides the Damage done by treading down his Wheat ; and, after all, a fuffi-cient Quantity of them have efcaped, to make a too plentiful Increafe in the next Crop of Corn.

The new Hoeing-Hufbandry in Time will pro-bably make fuch an utter Riddance (*a*) of all Sorts of Weeds (*b*), except fuch as come in the Air, that

---

(*a*) A very pernicious, large, perennial Weed, like *Barrage*, with a blue Flower, infefted a Piece of Land, for Time out of Mind: Hoeing has deftroyed it utterly ; not one of the Species has been feen in the Field thefe Seven Years, tho' conftantly till'd and ho'd.

(*b*) I have now a Piece of Wheat drill'd early the laft Autumn upon an Hill, fallowed and well pulveriz'd : Part of it was drill'd with Wheat in double Rows upon the Level Nine Years ago, Horfe-

that (c) as long as this Management is properly
continued, there is no Danger to be apprehended
from them; which is enough to confute the old Error

Horfe-ho'd, and the Partitions thoroughly Hand-ho'd to cleanfe
out the Poppies, of which the Land was very full; the other
Part of this Piece was never drilled till this Year: The whole
Piece hath not been before this Winter Horfe-ho'd. Now the Partitions of the Part that was never any Way Ho'd, are fo ftock'd
with Poppies matted together, that unlefs they are taken out
early in the Spring, they will totally devour the Rows of Wheat;
but in the other Part that was ho'd fo long fince, there are now
very few Poppies to be feen. Both thefe Parts have had feveral
fown Crops of Barley together fince, and have lain with *St. Foin*
thefe laft Five or Six Years.

(c) And except alfo fuch Weeds, whofe Seed is carried by
Birds, which is the moft common Manner of tranfporting the
Seeds of Vegetables from Field to Field, againft the Confent of
the Owner: For Birds, whether great or fmall, do not care to eat
their Prey where they take it, but generally chufe fome open
Place for that Purpofe. 'Tis, I am perfuaded, by this Means
chiefly, that a Vineyard or Field, made ever fo clean from Grafs,
will, in lying untilled a few Years, be replenifhed with a Turf of
that neighbouring Species of Grafs, which beft fuits the Heat
and Moifture of the Soil: Yet there are fome Species of Seeds
that Birds (at leaft fuch as frequent this Place) do not affect; elfe
the Burrage-weed (mentioned in *p. 77.*) would have appeared
again in my Field in fome of the many Years fince the Hoeing
has extirpated it there; for it grows plentifully in the unplowed
Way adjoining thereto.

The Seeds of fome Weeds may be fufpected to come in the
Air; as the Seed of the Grafs that grew in the *Cheapfide*, in the
Time of the Plague; but it might come from Seeds in the Dirt,
brought thither by the Feet of People and Cattle, and by the
Wheels of Coaches, Carts carrying Hay: Or otherwife continual Treading might keep it from Growing; and when the Treading ceafed, 'tis no Wonder the Seeds fhould furnifh the Streets
with Grafs.

And I have obferv'd on the Floors, two Stories high, of a lone,
ruinous, uninhabited Houfe, being long uncover'd, a fort of Herb
growing very thick; I think it was *Pimpernel*, and believe that
its Seeds did not come thither in the Air; but in the Sand which
was mix'd with the Mortar that had fallen from the Cielings; and
'tis like there were few Seeds at firft: Yet, thefe, ripening for
feveral Years, fhed their Seeds annually, until the Floors became
all over very thick planted: Befides, Hay-feeds and Pimpernel
are too heavy to be carry'd far by the Air.

of

of equivocal Generation, had it not been already
fufficiently exploded, ever fince that Demonftration
of *Malpighius's* Experiment.   For if Weeds were
brought forth without their proper Seeds, the Hoeing
could not hinder their Production, where the Soil
was inclined naturally to produce them.   The Belief
of that blind Doctrine might probably be one of the
Caufes that made the Antients defpair of finding fo
great Succefs in Hoeing, as now appears ; or elfe, if
they had had true Principles, they might perhaps have
invented and improved that Hufbandry, and the Inftruments neceffary to put it in Practice.

C H A P.   VIII.

Of T U R N E P S.

A S far as I can be inform'd, 'tis but of late Years
that Turneps have been introduc'd as an Improvement in the Field.

All Sorts of Land, when made fine by Tillage, or
by Manure and Tillage, will ferve to produce Turneps, but not equally ; for chalky Land is generally
too dry (a Turnep being a thirfty Plant); and they
are fo long in fuch dry poor Land before they get
into rough Leaf, that the Fly is very apt to deftroy
them there ; yet I have known them fucceed on fuch
Land, tho' rarely.

Sand and Gravel are the moft proper Soil for Turneps, becaufe that is moft eafily pulveriz'd, and its
Warmth caufeth the Turneps to grow fafter, and fo
they get the fooner out of the Danger of the Fly ; and
fuch a Soil, when well-till'd, and Horfe-ho'd, never
wants a fufficient Moifture, even in the drieft Weather; and the Turneps being drill'd will come up
without Rain, and profper very well with the fole
Moifture

Moifture of the Dews, which are admitted as deep as the Pulveration reacheth ; and if that be to Five or fix Inches, the hotteft Sun cannot exhale the Dews thence in the Climate of *England :* I have known Turneps thrive well in a very dry Summer by repeated Horfe-hoeings, both in Sand and in Land which is neither fandy nor gravelly.

When I fow'd Turneps by Hand, and ho'd them with a Hand-hoe, the Expence was great, and the Operation not half perform'd, by the Deceitfulnefs of the Hoers, who left half the Land unho'd, and cover'd it with the Earth from the Part they did hoe, and then the Grafs and Weeds grew the fafter : Befides, in this Manner a great Quantity of Land could not be managed in the proper Seafon.

When I drill'd upon the Level *(a)*, at Three Feet Intervals, a Trial was made between thofe Turneps and a Field of the next Neighbour's, fown at the fame Time, whereof the Hand-hoeing coft Ten Shillings *per* Acre, and had not quite half the Crop of the drill'd, both being meafur'd by the Bufhel, on Purpofe to find the Difference *(b)*.

In the new Method they are more certain to come up quickly ; becaufe in every Row, half the Seed is planted about Four Inches deep *(c)* ; and the other Half is planted exactly over that, at the Depth of half an Inch, falling in after the Earth has cover'd

---

(a) 'Tis impoffible to hoe-plow them fo well when planted upon the Level, as when they are planted upon Ridges; for if we plow deep near the Row, the Earth will come over on the Left-Side of the Plough, and bury the younger Turneps; but when they ftand on Ridges, the Earth will almoft all fall down on the Right Side into the Furrow in the Middle of the Interval.

(b) And I have fince found, that Turneps on the fame Land, planted on Ridges, with Six-feet Intervals, make a Crop double to thofe that are planted on the Level, or even on Ridges with Three-feet Intervals.

(c) Turnep-feed will come up from a greater Depth than moft other Sorts of Seeds.

the firft Half : Thus planted, let the Weather be never fo dry, the deepeft Seed will come up; but if it
raineth (immediately after planting), the Shallow will
come up firft : We alfo make it come up at Four *(d)*
Times, by mixing our Seed, half new and half old
(the new coming up a Day quicker than the old) : Thefe
four Comings up give it fo many Chances for efcaping
the Fly, it being often feen, that the Seed fown over
Night will be deftroy'd by the Fly, when that fown
the next Morning will efcape, and *vice verfa* *(e)* ; or
you may hoe-plow them, when you the Fly is like
to devour them ; this will bury the greateft Part of
thofe Enemies ; or elfe you may drill in another Row,
without new-plowing the Land.

This Method has alfo another Advantage of efcaping the Fly, the moft certain of any other, and infallible, if the Land be made fine, as it ought to be :
This is to roll it with a heavy Roller acrofs the
Ridges, after 'tis drill'd, which clofing up the Cavities
of the Earth, prevents the Fly's Entrance and Exit,
to lay the Eggs, hatch, or bring forth the young
ones to prey upon the Turneps ; which they might
intirely devour, if the Fly came before they had more
than the firft two Leaves, which, being form'd of the
very Seed itfelf, are very fweet; but the next Leaves
are rough and bitter, which the Fly does not love : I
have always found the Rolling difappoint the Fly ; but
very often it difappoints the Owner alfo, who fows
at Random ; for it makes the Ground fo hard, that
the Turneps cannot thrive, but look yellow, dwindle,
and grow to no Perfection, unlefs they have a good
Hoeing foon after the rough Leaves appear ; for

(d) I have feen drill'd Turnep-feed come up daily for a Fortnight together, when it has not been mixt thus, the old with the
new.

(e) I have had the firft Turneps that came up all deftroy'd by
the Fly ; and about a Fortnight afterwards more have come up,
and been ho'd time enough, and made a good Crop.

G when

when they ftand long without it, they will be fo poor
and ftinted, that the Hand-hoe does not go deep
enough to recover them; and 'tis feldom that thefe
rolled Turneps can be Hand-ho'd at the critical Time,
becaufe the Earth is then become fo hard, that the
Hoe cannot enter it without great Difficulty, unlefs it
be very moift; and very often the Rain does not come
to foak it, until it be too late; but the drill'd Turneps being in fingle Rows with Six-feet Intervals,
may be roll'd without Danger: For be the Ground
ever fo hard, the Hand-hoe will eafily fingle them
out, at the Price of Six-pence per Acre, or lefs (if
not in Harveft); and the Horfe-hoe will, in thofe wide
Intervals, plow at any Time, wet or dry; and, tho'
the Turneps fhould have been neglected till ftinted,
will go deep enough to recover them to a flourifhing
Condition.

Drill'd Turneps, by being no-where but in the
Rows (*f*), may be more eafily feen than thofe which
come up at Random; and may therefore be fooner (*g*)

(f) Drill'd Turneps coming all up nearly in a *Mathematical
Line*, 'tis very nearly that a Charlock, or other like Weed, comes
up in the fame Line amongft them, unlefs it be drill'd in with the
Turnep-feed, of which Weeds our Horfe-ho'd Seed never has
any; there being no Charlock in the Rows, nor any Turnep in
the Intervals: We know, that whatever comes up in the Interval
is not a Turnep, though fo like to it, that, at firft coming up, if
promifcuoufly, it cannot eafily be diftinguifhed by the Eye, until
after the Turneps, &c. attain the rough Leaf; and even then,
before they are of a confiderable Bignefs, they are fo hard to be
diftinguifhed by thofe People, who are not well experienced, that
a Company of *Hand-hoers* cut out the Turneps by Miftake, and
left the Charlock for a Crop of a large Field of fown Turneps.
Such a Misfortune can never happen to drill'd Turneps, unlefs
wilfully done, be they fet out ever fo young.

(g) The fooner they are made fingle, the better; but yet,
when they are not very thick, they may ftand till we have the beft
Conveniencе of fingling them without much Damage; but, when
they come up extraordinary thick, 'twill be much more difficult
to make them fingle, if they are neglected at their very firft coming
into rough Leaf.

fingled

fingled out by the Hand-hoe; which is another Advantage; becaufe the fooner they are fo fet out, the better they will thrive (*h*).

Three or Four Ounces of Seed is the ufual Quantity to drill; but, at random, Three or Four Pounds are commonly fown, which, coming thick all over the Ground, muft exhauft the Land more than the other, efpecially fince the fown muft ftand longer, before the Hoers can fee to fet them out.

The Six-feet Ridges, whereon Turneps are drill'd in fingle Rows, may be left higher than for double-row'd Crops; becaufe there will be more Earth in the Intervals, as the fingle Row takes up lefs.

There is no prefix'd Time for planting Turneps, becaufe that muft be according to the Richnefs of the Land; for fome Land will bring them as forward, and make them as good, when planted the beginning of *Auguft*, as other Land will, when planted in *May*; but the moft general Time is, a little before, and a little after *Midfummer*.

Between thefe Rows of Turneps (*i*), I have planted Wheat in this Manner; *viz.* About *Michaelmas*, the

Turneps

(*h*) Becaufe fuch young Turneps will enjoy the more of the Pafture made by the Plowing, and by that little Pulveration of the Hand-hoe, without being robb'd of any Pafture by their own fupernumerary Plants.

(*i*) As I have formerly drilled Wheat between Rows of Turneps, fo I have fince had the Experience of drilling Tnrneps between Rows of Barley and Rows of Oats: I have had them in the Intervals between Six-feet Ridges, and between Four-feet Ridges, and between thofe of feveral intermediate Diftances; but which of them all is the beft, I leave at prefent undetermined. I fhall only add, that the poorer the Land is, the wider the Intervals ought to be; and that, in the narrow, 'tis convenient at the Hoeing, to leave more Earth on that Side of each Interval whereon the Turneps are to be drill'd; and this is done by going round feveral Intervals with the Hoe-Plough, without going forwards and backwards in each immediately: But in the wide Intervals the Earth may be equal on both Sides of them.

I will

Turneps being full grown, I plow'd a Ridge in the
Middle of each of their Intervals, taking moſt of the
Earth

I will propoſe another Method of Drilling, which may be very
advantageous to thoſe who ſow their Barley upon the Level, and
ſow Turnep-ſeed amongſt it. at Random, as they do Clover;
which is, of late, a common Practice in ſome Places. The Barley
keeps the Turneps under it, and ſtints them ſo much, that they
are uſeful in the Winter or Spring, chiefly by the Food their
Leaves afford to Sheep, their Roots being exceeding ſmall; and
for this ſmall Profit they loſe the Time of tilling the Ground,
until after the Turneps are eaten off; which is a Damage we
think greater than the Profit of ſuch Turneps: To prevent
which Damage, they may drill them in Rows at competent
Diſtances, and Horſe-hoe them, and ſet them out as ſoon as the
Barley is off: This will both keep the Ground in Tilth, fit for
another Crop of Spring Corn, and cauſe the Turneps to grow
great enough (eſpecially if Harveſt be early, and the Winter prove
favourable) for feeding of Sheep in a moveable Fold to dung the
Ground into the Bargain.

What induces me to propoſe this Improvement is, that a Gentleman plows up his Barley-Stubble, and tranſplants Turneps
therein, and Hand-hoes them with Succeſs. By the propoſed
Way all the Expence of tranſplanting (which muſt be conſiderable)
will be ſaved; and the ſetting out cannot be more than an Eighth
of the Labour of *Hand hoeings*; and I conjecture the Horſe-hoed
Turneps may be as good; for they (though ſtinted) having their
Tap-roots remaining unmoved below the Staple of the Land,
their horizontal Roots, being ſupply'd with Moiſture from the
Tap-roots, immediately take hold of the freſh-plowed Earth, as
ſoon as 'tis turned back to them; whereas the tranſplanted, having
their Tap-roots broken off, and their Horizontal Roots crumpled
in the Holes wherein they are ſet, muſt loſe Time, and be in
Danger of dying with Thirſt, if the Weather proves dry.

Alſo this Way ſeems better than the common Practice of ſowing
Turneps upon once plowing after Wheat; becauſe the Wheat-
land commonly lies longer unplow'd by Six or Eight Months than
Barley-land; and therefore cannot be in ſo good Tilth for Tur-
neps as Barley-land may, unleſs the former be of a more friable
Nature, or much more dunged, than the latter. Beſides, theſe
Wheat-Turneps are uncertain, in Reſpect of the Fly that often
deſtroys them at their firſt coming up; which Misfortune hap-
pened the Autumn 1734. to almoſt all that were ſown in that
Manner.

I have obſerv'd, that Barley ſown on the Level, and not hoed,
overcomes the Turneps that come up amongſt it; but that Turneps

Earth from the Turneps, leaving only juft enough to keep them alive; and on this Ridge drill'd my Crop of Wheat (*k*), and towards the Spring pull'd up my Turneps, and carried them off for Cattle.

When Turneps are planted too late, to have Time and Sun for attaining to their full Bulk, fome drill a double Row on each Six-feet Ridge, with a Partition of Fourteen Inches; but I am told, that in this double Row the Turneps do not, even at that late Seafon, grow fo large, as thofe planted at the fame time in fingle Rows; tho' the double Row requires

neps, which come up in the Partitions of Treble Rows of my Ridges of Horfe-hoed Barley, grew fo vigoroufly as to overcome the Barley. And this was demonftrated at Harveft in a long Field, one Side of which had borne Turnep-feed, and the drilled Ridges of Barley crofting the Middle of it; and both Ends of the Field having Barley fown on the Level, one End of every Ridge crofs'd the Turnep-feed Part of the Field for about Ten Perches of their Length.

I obferved alfo, that the Turneps near the Edges of the Lands of fown Barley, adjoining to the hoed Intervals, grew large, but not fo large as thofe in the Partitions on the Ridges, their Intervals being hoed on each Side of them.

But different from this have I feen fhattered Turnep-feed coming up in the like Partitions of drilled Wheat, on the very fame Sort of Land, fo miferably poor and ftinted, that they fcarce grew a Hand's Breadth high, when thofe Turneps which the Hoe left in the Sides of the Intervals, and at the narrow Edges of the unhoed Earth of the Interval Sides of the Rows of Wheat, grew large; and the Wheat was good alfo: But I do not remember how the middle Row of it fucceeded.

This laft Experience of the Turneps among the Wheat was got by this Accident: The Wheat was drilled after drilled Turneps on Ridges of a different Size. The Turneps were all pulled up before the Ground was plowed for the Wheat; but as Turnep-feed never comes *all* up the firft Year, enough remained of this to come up (though thinly) in the Wheat, to fhew exactly where every Row had been drilled; whereupon the Obfervation was made.

(*k*) This Wheat, being thus drill'd on the new Ridges made in the Intervals, betwixt the Rows of Turneps, being well Horfe-ho'd in the Spring, prov'd a very good Crop; it was drill'd in treble Rows, the Partitions Seven Inches each.

G 3 double

double the Expence in setting out ; and there will be less Earth ho'd by the Breadth of fourteen Inches of the deepest Part of the Ridge, and consequently the Land will be the less improv'd for the next Crop. We need not to be very exact, in the Number (*l*) or Distance (*m*) we set them out at ; we contrive to leave the Master-turneps (when there is much Difference in them), and spare such when near one another, and leave the more Space before and behind them ; but if they be Three Master-turneps too near together, we take out the middlemost.

Turneps that were so thick as to touch one another when half-grown, by means of well Hoeing their wide Intervals, have afterwards grown to a good Bigness, and by thrusting against one another became oval, instead of round.

'Tis beneficial to hoe Turneps (especially the first Time) alternately; *viz.* to hoe every other Interval, and throw the Earth back again before we hoe the other Intervals; for by this Means the Turneps are kept from being (*n*) stinted: 'Tis better to have Nourishment given them moderately at twice, than to have it all once, and be twice as long before a Repetition (*o*).

(*l*) The least Number will be the largest Turneps ; yet we should have a competent Stock, which I think is not less than Thirty on a square Perch.

(*m*) The Distance need not to be regular ; for when a Turnep has Six Inches of Room on one Side, and Eighteen Inches on the other Side, 'tis almost as well as if there was one Foot on each Side : tho' then it would be equally distant from the Two Turneps betwixt which it stood.

(*n*) Because this alternate Hoeing doth not at all endanger the Roots by being dried by the Sun ; for whilst one half of the Roots have Moisture, 'tis sufficient; the other Half will be supplied from those ; so that they will soon take hold of the Earth again after being moved by the Hoe.

(*o*) Sometimes, when Turneps are planted late, this alternate Hoeing suffices without any Repetition ; but when they are planted early, 'twill be necessary to hoe them again ; especially if Weeds appear.

Tho'

Tho' the Earth on each Side the Row be left as narrow as poſſible (*p*) ; yet 'tis very profitable to hoe that little with a *Bidens* (*q*), called here a Prong-hoe (*r*); for this will be ſure to let out all the Roots into the Intervals; even ſuch as run very nearly parallel to the Rows.

This alternate Way of Hoeing Plants that grow in ſingle Rows, is of ſuch vaſt Advantage, that four of theſe, which are but equal to Two of the *whole* Hoeings in Labour, are near equal to four *whole* Hoeings in Benefit; for when one Side is well nouriſhed, the other Side cannot be ſtarv'd (*s*).

Beſides, where a great Quantity of Turneps are to be ho'd, the laſt ho'd may be ſtinted, before the firſt are finiſh'd by *whole* Hoeings.

In this alternate Hoeing, the Hoe-plough may go deeper (*t*) and nearer to the Row, without Danger of thruſting it down on the Left Side, whilſt the Plants are very ſmall; becauſe the Earth on the other Side of the Row always bears againſt it for its Support : But in the *whole* Hoeing, there is an open Furrow left the firſt Time on both Sides of the Row, and there is Danger of throwing it into one Furrow in

(*p*) I do not think that we can go nearer to the Plants with the Hoe-plough, than within Three Inches of their Bodies.

(*q*) We ought not to uſe the *Bidens* for this Purpoſe, before the perpendicular Roots are as big as one's litle Finger.

(*r*) Some of theſe Prong-hoes have Three Teeth, and are reckoned better as a *Tridens* than a *Bidens*; but this is only in mellow Ground.

(*s*) But yet ſometimes the Weeds, or other Circumſtances, may make it proper to give them a *whole* Hoeing at firſt.

(*t*) This deep Plowing ſo near to the Row is very beneficial at firſt; but afterwards, when the Plants are grown large, and have ſent their Roots far into the Intervals, it would almoſt totally diſroot them; and they, being Annuals, might not live long enough for a new Stock of Roots to extend ſo far as is neceſſary to bring the Turneps to their full Bigneſs.

Note, At the laſt Hoeing we generally leave a broad, deep Trench in the middle of each Interval.

plowing

plowing the other; or, if the Row is not thrown down, it may be too much dry'd in hot Weather, by the Two Furrows lying too long open : Yet, when the Turneps are large before Hoeing, we need not fear either of thefe Dangers in giving them a *whole* Hoeing; as I have found by Experience, even when there has been left on each Side of the Row only about Three Inches Breadth of Earth; tho' it is not beft to fuffer it to lie long open *(u)*.

Dry Weather does not injure Turneps when Horfe-ho'd, as it does fown Turneps ; the Hand-hoe does not go deep enough to keep the Earth moift, and fecure the Plants againft the Drought ; and that is the beft Seafon for Horfe-hoeing, which always can keep the Roots moift *(x)*.

Dung and Tillage together will attain the neceffary Degree of Pulveration, in lefs time than Plowing can do alone : Therefore Dung is more ufeful for Tur-neps, becaufe they have commonly lefs time to grow than other Plants.

Turneps of Nineteen Pounds Weight I have feve-ral Times heard of, and of Sixteen Pounds Weight often known ; and Twelve Pounds may be reckon'd the middle Size of great Turneps : And I can fee no Reafon, why every Turnep fhould not arrive to the full Bignefs of its Species, if it did not want Part of its due Nourifhment.

(u) But, if the Weather prove wet, we always fuffer thofe Furrows to lie open, until the Earth be dry enough to be turn'd back again to the Row, without fmearing or fticking together ; unlefs fuch Weather continue fo long that the Weeds begin to come up, and then we throw back the Furrows to ftifle the Weeds, before they grow large, tho' the Earth be wet.

(x) But if fome Sorts of Earth have lain fo long unmoved as to become very hard before the firft Hoeing, the Hoe, going very near to the Rows on each Side, may caufe fuch hard Earth where-on the Rows ftand, to crack and open enough to let in the Drought *(i. e.* the Sun and Air) to the Roots in very dry Weather. In this Cafe 'tis beft to *Horfe-hoe* alternately, as is directed in *Page* 86.

The

The greateft Inconvenience, which has been obferv'd in the Turnep-hufbandry, is, when they are fed
off late in the Spring (which is in many Places the
greateft Ufe of them), there is not time to bring the
Land in Tilth for Barley; the Lofs of which Crop
is fometimes more than the Gain of the Turneps:
This is intirely remedied by the drilling Method;
for, by that, the Land may be almoft as well till'd
before the Turneps are eaten, or taken off, as it can
afterwards.

If Turneps be fown in *June*, or the Beginning of
July, the moft experienced Turnep-Farmers will have
no more than Thirty to a fquare Perch left in Hand-
hoeing; and find that when more are left, the Crop
will be lefs; but, in drilling the Rows at Six Feet
Intervals, there may be Sixty to a Perch; and the
Horfe-hoe, by breaking fo much more Earth than
the Hand-hoe does, can nourifh Sixty drill'd, as well
as Thirty are by the fowing Method, which has been
made appear upon Trial; but, I think, about Forty
or Forty-five better than Sixty on a Perch; and the
Number of Plants fhould always be proportion'd to
the natural and artificial Pafture which is to maintain
them; and fixty Turneps on a fquare Perch, at Five
Pounds each (which is but a Third of the Weight of
the large Size of Sheep-Turneps), make a Crop of
above Eighty Quarters to an Acre (y).

When

(y) I have had Turneps upon poor undung'd Land, that weigh'd
Fourteen Pounds a-piece; but thefe were only fuch as had more
Room than the reft. I have feen a whole Waggon-load of
drill'd Turneps fpread on the Ground, wherein I believe one
could not have found one that weighed fo little as fix Pounds; or
if the Rows had been fearched before they had been pull'd up,
they would have weighed Seven or Eight Pounds apiece one with
another; we weighed fome of them that were Thirteen, fome
Fourteen Pounds each, and yet they ftood pretty thick: There
might be, as I guefs, about Fifty on a fquare Perch; but this
Crop was on fandy Land, not poor; and was dung'd the Third
or

When Turneps are planted late (especially upon poor Ground), they may be a greater Number than when planted early ; because they will not have time enough of Heat to enjoy the full Benefit of Hoeing, which would otherwise cause them to grow larger.

The greatest Turnep-Improvement used by the Farmer, is for his Cattle in the Winter; one Acre of Turneps will then maintain more than Fifty of Meadow or Pasture-ground.

'Tis now so well known, that most Cattle will eat them, and how much they breed Milk, &c. that I need say nothing about it.

Sheep always refuse them at first, and, unless they have eaten them whilst they were Lambs, must be ready to starve before they will feed on them ; tho', when they have tasted them, they will be fatted by them; and I have seen Lambs of Three Weeks old scoop them prettily, when those of a Year old (which are called Tegs) have been ready to die with Hunger amongst them; and for Three or Four Days would not touch them, but at last eat them very well.

In some Places, the greatest Use of Turneps (except for fatting Oxen and Sheep) is for Ewes and Lambs in the Spring, when natural Grass is not grown on poor Ground; and if the artificial Grass be then fed by the common Manner, the Crop will be spoil'd, and it will yield the less Pasture all the Summer : I have known Farmers, for that Reason, oblig'd to keep their Ewes and Lambs upon Turneps (tho' run up to Seed) even until the Middle of *April*.

There are now three Manners of spending Turneps with Sheep, amongst which I do not reckon the Way of putting a Flock of Sheep into a large Ground of Turneps without dividing it ; for in that Case the

or Fourth Year before ; and had every Year a ho'd Crop of Potatoes, or Wheat, until the Year wherein the Turneps were planted.

Flock

Flock will deftroy as many Turneps in a Fortnight, as fhould keep them well a whole Winter.

The Firft Manner now in Ufe is, to divide the Ground of Turneps by Hurdles, giving them leave to come upon no more at a Time than they can eat in one Day, and fo advance the Hurdles farther into the Ground daily, until all be fpent; but we muft obferve, that they never eat them clean this Way, but leave the Bottoms and Outfides of the Turneps they have fcoop'd in the Ground. Thefe Bottoms People pull up with Iron Crooks, made for that Pur-pofe; but their Cavities being tainted with Urine, Dung, and Dirt from their Feet, tho' the Sheep do eat fome of the Pieces, they wafte more, and many the Crooks leave behind in the Earth; and even what they do eat of this tainted Food, can't nourifh them fo well as that which is frefh and cleanly.

The fecond Manner is, to move the Hurdles every Day, as in the Firft; but that the Sheep may not tread upon the Turneps, they pull them up firft, and then advance the Hurdles as far daily as the Turneps are pull'd up, and no farther: By this Means there is not that Wafte made as in the other Way; the Food is eaten frefh and clean; and the Turneps are pull'd up with lefs Labour than their Pieces can be (z).

The Third Manner is, to pull them up, and to carry them into fome other Ground in a Cart, or Waggon, and there fpread them every Day on a new

---

(z) I have feen Three Labourers work every Day with their Crooks, to pull up thefe Pieces, which was done with much Difficulty, the Ground being trodden very hard by the Sheep; when one Perfon, in Two Hours time, would have pull'd up all the *whole* Turneps daily, and the Sheep would have eaten them clean; but fo many of thofe Pieces were dry'd and fpoil'd, that, after the Land was fown with Barley, they appear'd very thick ppon the Surface, and there could not be much lefs than half the Crep of Turneps wafted, notwithftanding the Contrivance of thefe Crooks.

Place,

Place, where the Sheep will eat them up clean, both Leaf and Root : This is done when there is Land not far off, which has more Need of Dung, than that where the Turneps grow, which perhaps is alfo too wet for Sheep in the Winter; and then the Turneps will, by the too great Moifture and Dirt of the Soil, fpoil the Sheep, and in fome Soils give them the Rot, yet fuch Ground will bring forth more and larger Turneps than dry Land; and when they are carry'd off, and eaten on plow'd Ground in dry Weather, and on Green-fwerd in wet Weather, the Sheep will thrive much better; and that moift Soil, not being trodden by the Sheep, will be in much the better Order for a Crop of Corn. And generally the Expence of Hurdles, and removing them, being faved, will more than countervail the Labour of carrying off the Turneps.

Thefe Three Ways of fpending Turneps with Sheep are common to.thofe drill'd, and to thofe fown in the random Manner ; but they muft always be carry'd off for Cows and Oxen; both which will be well fatted by them, and fome Hay in the Winter : The Management of thefe is the Bufinefs of a Grazier.

C H A P. IX.

Of W H E A T.

THO' all Sorts of Vegetables may have great Benefit from the Hoe, becaufe it fupplies them with Plenty of Food, at the Time of their greateft Need, yet they do not all equally require Hoeing ; but the Plant that is to live the longeft, fhould have the largeft Stock of Suftenance provided for it : Generally

nerally Wheat lives, or ought to live, longer than
other Sorts of Corn; for if it be not fown before
Spring, its Grain will be thin, and have but little
Flour in it, which is the only ufeful Part for making
Bread. And when fown late in the Winter, 'tis in
great Danger of Death from the Froft, whilft weak
and tender, being maintain'd (as a *Fœtus*) by the um-
bilical Veffels, until the Warmth of the Sun enables
it to fend out fufficient Roots of its own to fubfift on,
without Help of the *Ovum*.

To prevent thefe Inconveniences, Wheat is ufually
fown in Autumn: Hence, having about thrice the
Time to be maintain'd that Spring Corn hath, it requires a larger Supply of Nourifhment, in proportion
to that longer Time; not becaufe the Wheat in its Infancy confumes the Stock of Food, during the Winter,
proportionably to what it does afterwards; but becaufe, during that long Interval betwixt Autumn and
Spring Seed-times, moft of the artificial Pafture is
naturally loft, both in light and in ftrong Land.

For this very Reafon is that extraordinary Pains of
fallowing and dunging the Soil, neceffary to Wheat;
tho', notwithftanding all that Labour and Expence,
the Ground is generally grown fo ftale by the Spring,
and fo little of the Benefit of that chargeable Culture
remains, that, if Part of the fame Field be fown in
the Beginning of *April*, upon frefh Plowing, without
the Dung, or Year's Fallow, it will be as great or a
greater Crop, in all Refpects, except the Flour, which
fails only for want of Time to fill the Grain.

Poor light Land, by the common Hufbandry,
muft be very well cultivated and manur'd, to maintain Wheat for a whole Year, which is the ufual Time
it grows thereon; and if it be fown late, the greateft
Part of it will feldom furvive the Winter, on fuch
Land; and if it be fown very early on ftrong Land,
tho' rich, well till'd, and dung'd, the Crop will be
worfe than on the poor light Land fown early. So
much

much do the long Winter's Rains cause the Earth to subside, and the divided Parts to coalesce, and lock out the Roots from the Stock of Provision, which, tho' it was laid in abundantly at Autumn, the Wheat has no great Occasion of until the Spring; and then the Soil is become too hard for the Roots to penetrate; and therefore must starve (like *Tantalus*) amidst Dainties, which may tempt the Roots, but cannot be attain'd by them.

But the new Method of Hoeing gives, to strong and to light Land, all the Advantages, and takes away all the Disadvantages, of both; as appears in the Chapters of *Tillage* and *Hoeing*. By this Method the strong Land may be planted with Wheat as early as the light (if plow'd dry); and the Hoe-Plough can, if rightly apply'd, raise a Pasture to it *(a)*, equal to that of Dung in both Sorts of Land.

About the Year 1701, when I had contrived my Drill for planting St. Foin, I made use of it also for Wheat. Drilling many Rows at once, which made the Work much more compendious, and perform'd it much better than Hands could do, making the Channels of a Foot Distance, drilling in the Seed, and covering it, did not in all amount to more than Six-pence *per* Acre Expence, which was above ten Times over-paid by the Seed that was saved; for One Bushel to an Acre was the Quantity drill'd; there remain'd then no need of Hand-work, but for the Hoeing; and this did cost from Half a Crown to Four Shillings *per* Acre. This way turn'd to a very good Account, and in considerable Quantities; it has brought as good a Crop of Wheat on Barley-stubble, as that sown the common Way on Summer-fallow;

(a) Because the Hoe may go in it all the Year, and the Soil being *infinitely divisible*, the Division which the Hoe may make whilst the Crop is growing, added to the common Tillage, may equal, or even exceed, a common Dressing with Dung, as I have often experienced.

and

and when that fown the old Way, on the fame Field, on Barley-ftubble, intirely fail'd, tho' there was no other Difference but the Drilling and Hoeing : It was alfo fuch an Improvement to the Land, that when one Part of a ftrong whitifh Ground, all of equal Goodnefs, and equally fallow'd and till'd, was dung'd and fown in the common Manner, and the other Part was thus drill'd and hand-ho'd without Dung, the ho'd Part was not only the beft Crop, but the whole Piece being fallow'd the next Year, and fown all alike by a Tenant, the ho'd Part produc'd fo much a better Crop of Wheat than the dung'd Part, that a Stranger would have believ'd by looking on it, that that Part had been dung'd which was not (*a*), and that Part not to have been dung'd which really was.

Scarce any Land is fo unfit, and ill prepar'd, for Wheat, as that where the natural Grafs (*b*) abounds. Moft other forts of Weeds may be dealt withal when they come among drill'd Wheat; but 'tis impoffible to extract Grafs from the Rows : Therefore let that be kill'd before the Wheat be planted.

The Six-feet Ridges being Eleven, on Sixty-fix Feet, which is an Acre's Breadth, ought to be made Lengthways of the Field, if there be no Impediment againft it ; as if it be an Hill of any confiderable Steepnefs, then they muft be made to run up and down, whether that be the Length or Breadth of the Piece; for if the Ridges fhould go crofs fuch a Hill, they could not be well Horfe-ho'd ; becaufe it would be very difficult to turn a Furrow upwards, clofe to the Row above it, or to turn a Furrow downwards, without burying the Row below it ; and even

(*a*) If the Dung did pulverize as much as the Hoeing, the Caufe muft be from the different Exhauftion.

(*b*) One Bunch of natural Grafs, tranfplanted by the Plough into a treble Row of Wheat, will deftroy almoft a whole Yard of it.

when

when a Furrow is turn'd from the lower Row, enough of the Earth to bury that Row will be apt to run over on the Left-fide of the Plough; unlefs it goes at fuch a Diftance from the Row, as to give it no Benefit of Hoeing.

Thefe Ridges fhould be made ftrait and equal: And to make them ftrait (c) all good Ploughmen know how; and they will, by fetting up Marks to look at, plow in a Line like the Path of an Arrow: But to make the Ridges equal, 'tis neceffary to mark out a Number of them, before you begin to plow, by fhort Sticks fet up at each End of the Piece; and then if one Ridge happen to be a little too broad, the next may be made the narrower; for if the Plough comes not out exactly at the fecond Stick, the Two Ridges may be made equal by the next Plowing, or by the Drilling; but if many contiguous Ridges fhould be too wide, or too narrow, 'twill be difficult to bring them all to an Equality afterwards, without levelling the whole Piece, and laying out the Ridges all anew.

The exact Height of Ridges, which is beft, I cannot determine (d): A different Soil may require a different Height, according to the Depth, Richnefs, and Pulveration of the Mould. As Wheat covets always to lie dry in the Winter, fo there is no other way to keep it fo dry as thefe Ridges; for when they are, after the firft Hoeing, about Eighteen Inches

---

(c) But if the Piece be of fuch a crooked or ferpentine Form, that the Ridges cannot well be plow'd ftrait the firft Time, 'tis beft to drill it upon the Level; and then the marking Wheels may direct for making the Row all parallel and equidiftant; which will guide the Plough to make all the Ridges for the next and all the fubfequent Crops, as equal.

(d) I find by meafuring my Wheat Ridges in the Spring, that none of them are quite a Foot high; and fome of them only Six Inches; but I know not how much they have fubfided in the Winter; for they were certainly higher when firft made.

broad,

broad *(a)*, with a Ditch on each Side, of almoſt a
Foot deep, the Rain-water runs off ſuch narrow
Ridges as faſt it falls, and much ſooner *(b)* than
'tis poſſible for it to do from broad Ridges.

And the deeper the Soil, the more occaſion there
commonly is of this high Situation; becauſe ſuch
Land is wetter for the moſt Part than ſhallow Land,
where we cannot make the Furrows ſo deep, nor the
Ridges ſo high *(c)*, as in deep Land; for we muſt
never plow below the Staple. I ſee the Wheat on
theſe ho'd Ridges flouriſh, and grow vigorouſly, in
wet Weather, when other Wheat looks yellow and
ſickly.

The ſame wide Interval, which is ho'd betwixt
Ridges the Firſt time, with Two Furrows, muſt have
had Four Furrows, to hoe it on the Level; or elſe
the Furrow, that is turn'd from the Row, would
riſe up, and a great Part of it fall over to the Left-
hand, and bury the Row; but when turn'd from a
Ridge, it will all fall down to the Right-hand.

You muſt not leave the Tops of the Ridges quite
ſo narrow and ſharp for Drilling of Wheat, as you
may for drilling Turneps; Wheat being in treble
Rows, but Turneps generally in ſingle Rows *(d)*.
This is our Method of making Ridges for the Firſt
Crop of drill'd Wheat.

(a) This is the Breadth the Ridges are generally left at, when
the Furrows are hoed from them, and thrown into the Intervals.

(b) Water, when it runs off very ſoon, is beneficial, as is ſeen
in water'd Meadows; but where it remains long on, or very near
the Bodies of terreſtrial Plants, it kills them, or at leaſt is very
injurious to them.

(c) If we ſhould make our Ridges as high on a ſhallow Soil,
as we may on a deep Soil, there would be a Deficiency of Mould
in the Intervals of equal Breadth with thoſe of a deep Soil.

(d) A ſingle Row taking up leſs of the Breadth, may be afforded to have more of the Ridge's Depth; becauſe it leaves the Interval wider.

But the Method of making Ridges for a fucceeding Crop, after the former is harvefted, is beft perform'd as follows: In making Ridges for Wheat after
Wheat, you muft raife them to their full Height,
before you plow the old Partitions, with their Stubble, up to them; for if you go about to make the
Ridges higher afterwards, the Stubble will fo mix
with the Mould of their Tops, that it may not only
be an Hindrance to the Drill, but alfo to the Firft
Hoeing; becaufe if the Hoe-plough goes fo near to
the Rows as it ought, it would be apt to tear out the
Wheat-plants along with the Stubble.

In Reaping, we cut as near as we can to the Ground
(a); which is eafily done, becaufe the Stalks ftand
all clofe together at Bottom, contrary to thofe of
fown Wheat.

I find this Stubble, when 'tis only mixt with the
Intervals, very beneficial to the Hoeing of my Wheat;
but I know not whether it may be fo in rich miry
Land.

As foon as conveniently you can, after the Crop
of Wheat is carried off (if the Trench in the Middle
of each wide Interval be left deep enough by the laft
Hoeing), go as near as you can to the Stubble with a
common Plough, and turn Two large Furrows into
the Middle of the Intervals, which will *(b)* make a
Ridge

(a) When Wheat is reap'd very low, the Stubble is no great
Impediment; and I do this when I am forc'd to inlarge the
Breadth of my Ridges, or to change their Bearing, as I do when
I find it convenient for them to point Crofs-ways of the Field inftead of Length ways; as if one End of it be wetter than the
other: For 'tis inconvenient, that one End of a Ridge fhould be
in the wet Part, and the other in the dry; becaufe, in that Cafe,
we cannot hoe the dry End without hoeing the wet at the fame
time; and whilft we attend for the wet Part to become dry, it
may happen, that the Seafon for hoeing the whole (if the Quantity be great) may be loft.

(b) 'Tis the Depth and Finenefs of this Ridge that the Succefs of
our Crop depends on; the Plants having nothing elfe to maintain
them.

Ridge over the Place where the Trench was: But if the Trench be not deep enough, go firſt in the Middle of it with one Furrow; which with Two more

them during the Firſt Six Months; and if, for want of Suſtenance, they are weak in the Spring, 'twill be more difficult to make them recover their Strength afterwards ſo fully as to bring them to their due Perfection.   But Ploughmen have found a Trick to diſappoint us in this fundamental Part of our Huſbandry, if they are not narrowly watched: They do it in the following Manner; *viz.* They contrive to leave the Trench very ſhallow; and then, in turning the Two Firſt Furrows of the Ridge, they hold the Plough towards the Left, which raiſes up the Fin of the Share, and leaves ſo much of the Earth whereon the Rows are to ſtand whole and unplowed, that after once Harrowing there doth not remain above Two or Three Inches in Depth of fine Earth underneath the Rows when drilled, inſtead of Ten or Twelve Inches.

On a Time, when my Diſeaſes permitted me to go into the Wheat-field, where my Ploughs were at Work, I diſcovered this Trick, and ventured to aſk my chief Ploughman his Reaſon for doing this in my Abſence, contrary to my Direction.   He magiſterially anſwer'd, according to his own Theory, which Servants judge ought to be follow'd before that of him they call Maſter, ſaying, That as the Roots of Wheat never reached more than Two or Three Inches deep, there was no need that the fine Mould ſhould be any deeper.   But thoſe ſhallow Ridges, which were indeed too many, producing a Crop very much inferior to the contiguous deep Ridges, ſhewed, at my Coſt, the Miſtake of my cunning Ploughman.

'Tis true, that People who examine Wheat-roots when dead, are apt to fall into this miſtake; for then they are ſhrivell'd up, and ſo rotten, that they break off very near to the Stalk in pulling up; but if they are examined in their Vigour at Summer with Care, in a friable Soil, they may be ſeen to deſcend as deep as the fine pulveriz'd Mould reacheth, though that ſhould be a Foot in Thickneſs.

I took up a Wheat-ear in Harveſt that had lain on the Graſs in wet Weather, where the Wind could not come to dry it, which had ſent out white Roots like the Teeth of a Comb, ſome of them Three Inches long: None having reached the Ground, they could not be nouriſhed from any thing but the Grains, which remained faſt to the Ear, and had not as yet ſent out any Blade. 'Tis unreaſonable to imagine, that ſuch a ſingle Root as one of theſe, when in the Earth, from whence it muſt maintain a pretty large Plant all or moſt Part of the Winter, ſhould deſcend no farther than when it was itſelf maintained from the Flour of the Grain only.

H 2   taken

taken from the Ridges, will be three Furrows in each Interval; continue this Plowing as long as the dry Weather lafteth; and then finifh, by turning the Partitions (whereon the laft Wheat grew) up to the new Ridges, which is ufually done at Two great Furrows. You may plow thefe laft Furrows, which complete the Ridges, in wet Weather.

To make a Six-feet Ridge very high, will fome-times require more Furrows; as when the Middle of the Intervals are open very wide and deep, then Six Furrows to the whole Ridge may be neceffary, and they not little ones; and the Seafon makes a Difference, as well as the Size of the Furrows; for when the fine Mould is very dry (which is beft), it will much of it run to the Left-hand before the Plough, and alfo more will run back again to the Left after the Plough is gone paft it.

But when fuch Ridges have been made for Wheat, and the Seafon continues long too dry for planting it, and the Stubble not thrown up, we then plow one deep Furrow on the Middle of each Ridge, and then plow the whole Ridge at Four Furrows more, which will raife it very high. This Way of replowing the Ridges moves all the Earth of them, and yet is done at Five Furrows.

The Furrows, neceffary for raifing up the Ridges, muft be more, or fewer, in regard to the Bignefs of them; becaufe Six fmall Furrows may be lefs than Four great ones. 'Tis not beft to plow the Stub-ble up to the Ridges, until juft before Planting (efpecially in the early Plowing); becaufe that will hinder the Re-plowing of the Firft Furrows, which, if the Seafon continues dry, may be neceffary: Sometimes we do this by opening One Furrow in the Middle of the Ridge, fometimes Two, and after-wards raife up the Ridges again; and when they are become moift enough at Top (the old Partitions being plow'd up to them), we harrow them

once

once (*a*) (and that only Lengthways); and then drill them.

There is a Neceſſity of plowing the old Partitions up to the new Ridges, to ſupport their other Earth from falling down by the Harrowing and Drilling, which would elſe make them level.

Our Ridges, after the Firſt Time of Plowing, excel common Ridges of the ſame Height; becauſe theſe, tho' as deep in Mould at the Tops, have little of it till'd at the laſt Plowing; but ours, being made upon the open Trenches, conſiſt of new-till'd pulveriz'd Mould, from Top to Bottom.

'Tis a general Rule, that all Sorts of Grain and Seeds proſper beſt, ſown when the Ground is ſo dry, as to be broken into the moſt Parts by the Plough. The Reaſon why Wheat is an Exception to that Rule is, becauſe it muſt endure the Rigours of Winter, which 'tis the better able to do, by the Earth's being

(*a*) But if once be not ſufficient to level the Tops of the Ridges fit for the Drill to paſs thereon, as it always will, unleſs the Two hard Furrows lie ſo high, that all the Three Shares of the Drill cannot reach to make their Channels, in this Caſe you muſt harrow again until they can all reach deep enough. Alſo in ſome Sort of Land, that when drilled late, and very moiſt, will ſtick to · the Shares like Pitch or Bird-lime, whereby the Channels are in Part left open by the Drill-harrow, it muſt be harrowed after 'tis drilled, becauſe 'tis neceſſary in ſuch Land to take off the common Drill-harrow, in order for a Man to follow the Drill with a Paddle, or elſe a forked Stick, with which he frees the Sheats of the adhering Dirt; this Harrow being gone, much of the Seed will lie uncovered, and then muſt be covered with common Harrows; unleſs a Drill-harrow, which was not in Uſe when my Plates were made, be placed inſtead of that taken off: This, with its two Iron *Tines*, will cover the Seed in this Caſe much better than common Harrows, and will be no Hindrance to cleanſing of the Sheats, the Legs by which this Harrow is drawn, being remote from them, placed at near the End of the Plank; and *note*, that the moſt proper Drill for this Purpoſe is one that has only Two Shares, ſtanding a Foot or fourteen Inches aſunder: This Harrow ſerves for taking up the Drill to turn it.

　　　　　　　　preſs'd

prefs'd or trodden harder, and clofer.to it (*a*), as it is when moved wet.

If Wheat were as hardy as Rye, and its Roots as patient of Cold, it might, no doubt, be fown in as dry a Seafon as Rye is, and profper the better for it, as Rye doth. This will appear, if Wheat and Rye be both fown in the fame dry Seafon, after the Winter is over.

But as Wheat requires to have the Earth lie harder on and about it, in the Winter; fo it alfo requires more Dung (or fomewhat elfe) to diffolve the Earth about its Roots, after the cold Winter is paft, than Rye doth, whofe Roots never were fo much confined.

'Tis another general Rule, that all Sorts of Vegetables thrive beft, when fown on frefh till'd Ground, immediately after 'tis plow'd.

Wheat is an Exception to this Rule alfo; for 'tis better to plow the Ground dry, and let it lie till the Weather moiftens it (tho' it be feveral Weeks), and then drill the Wheat: The Harrows and the Drill will move a fufficient Part of the Ground, which will ftick together for Defence of the fmall Roots, during the Winter, the reft of the Mould, lying open, and divided underneath until Spring, to nourifh them.

There is a Sort of binding Sand, that requires not only to be plow'd dry, but fow'd dry alfo; or elfe the Wheat will dwindle in the Spring, and fail of being a tolerable Crop.

But what I mean by dry Plowing is, not that the Land fhould always be fo void of Moifture, as that the Duft fhould fly; but it muft not be fo wet, as to ftick together (*b*). Neither fhould we drill when

(*a*) 'Tis for that Reafon, that Farmers drive their Sheep over very light Land, as foon as 'tis fown with Wheat, to tread the (Top or) Surface of it hard; and then the Cold of the Winter cannot fo eafily penetrate, to kill the Roots of the tender Plants.
(*b*) But the drier 'tis plow'd the better

the

thè Earth is wet as Pap ; it fuffices that it be moift, but moifter in light Land than in ftrong Land, when we drill.

If the Two Furrows, whereon the treble Row is to ftand, be plow'd wet, the Earth of the Partitions may grow fo hard by the Spring, that the Roots cannot run freely therein, unlefs there be Dung to ferment and keep it open.

So we fee, that a fteep Bank, made of wet Earth, will lie faft for feveral Years, when another, made of the fame Earth dry, will moulder, and run down very foon; becaufe its Parts have not the Cohefion that holds the other together, it continues open, and more porous, and crumbles continually down.

I have feen Trials of this Difference betwixt plowing Dry, and plowing Wet, for planting of Wheat, both in the Old Way, and in the Drilling Way, but moft in the latter ; and never faw an Inftance where the Dry-Plowing did not outdo the Wet; if the Wheat was not planted thereon before the Earth was become moift enough at Top.

And ftrong Land, plow'd wet in *November*, will be harder in the Spring, than if plow'd dry in *Auguft* ; tho' it would then have Three Months longer to lie.

After Rain, when the Top of the Ground is of a fit Moifture for Drilling, harrow it with Two light Harrows, drawn by a Horfe going in the Furrow betwixt Two Ridges (*a*); once will be enough, the Furrow being juft broken to level, or rather fmooth it for the Drill.

If the Veerings (*b*) whereon the next Drop is to ftand, be plow'd dry, we may drill at any Time
during

(*a*) Once Harrowing is generally enough, but not always.
(*b*) The Word veering is, I believe, taken from the Seamen, and fignifies to turn : It is the Ploughman's Term for turning Two Furrows toward each other, as they muft do to begin a Ridge :

and

during the common and ufual Wheat-feed time, that is proper for the fort of Wheat to be drill'd, and the fort of Land, whether that be early or late, we may drill earlier, but not later than the fowing Farmers. But I have had good Crops of Wheat drill'd at all Times betwixt Harveft and the Beginning of *November*.

For the Benefit of the middle Rows, 'tis better not to drill Wheat on ftrong Land before the ufual Seafon; becaufe the later 'tis planted, the more open the Partitions will be for the Roots of thofe Rows to run through them in the Spring: and yet, if the Earth of the Partitions be plow'd very wet, tho' late, they may be harder at the Spring, than thofe which are plow'd early and dry.

There is a Sort of Wheat call'd by fome (a) *Smyrna Wheat*: It has a prodigious large Ear, with many lefs (or collateral) Ears, coming all round the Bottom of this Ear; as it is the largeft of all Sorts of Wheat, fo it will difpenfe with the Nourifh-ment of a Garden, without being over-fed, and re-quires more Nourifhment than the common Hufban-

---

and therefore they call the Top of a Ridge a Veering; they call the Two Furrows that are turn'd from each other at the Bottom, between Two Ridges, a Henting, *i. e.* an Ending: becaufe it makes an End of plowing Ridges.

Our Intervals wholly confift of Veerings or Hentings; when Two Furrows are turn'd from the Rows, they make a Veering; when turn'd towards the Rows, they are a Henting, which is the deep wide Trench in the Middle of an Interval.

(a) 'Tis faid to grow moftly in fome Iflands of the *Archipelago*, and fome Author defcribes it *Triticum fpica multiplici*: There is another Sort of Wheat that has many little Ears coming out of Two Sides of the main Ear, but this is very late ripe, and doth not fucceed well here, nor is it liked by them who have fown it; yet I have had fome Ears of it by chance among my drill'd Wheat, which have been larger than thofe of any common Sort. I have not as yet been able to procure any of the *Smyrna Wheat*, which I look on as a great Misfortune; but I had fome of it above Forty Years ago.

dry

dry will afford it; for there its Ears grow not much bigger than thofe of common Wheat: This I believe to be, for that Reafon, the very beft Sort for the Hoeing Hufbandry; next to this I efteem the White-cone Wheat, then the Grey-cone. I have had very good Crops from other Sorts; but look upon thefe to be the beft.

When Wheat is planted early, lefs Seed is required than when late; becaufe lefs of it will die in the Winter than of that planted late, and it has more Time to tiller *(a)*.

Poor Land fhould have more Seed than rich Land, becaufe a lefs Number of the Plants will furvive the Winter on poor Land.

The leaft Quantity of Seed may fuffice for rich Land that is planted early; for thereon very few Plants will die; and the Hoe will caufe a fmall Number of Plants to fend out a vaft Number of Stalks, which will have large Ears; and in thefe, more than in the Number of Plants, confifts the Goodnefs of a Crop *(b)*.

Another thing muft be confider'd, in order to find the juft Proportion of Seed to plant; and that is, that fome Wheat has its Grains twice as big as other Wheat of the fame Sort; and then a Bufhel *(c)* will contain but half the Number of Grains; and one Bufhel of Small-grain'd Wheat will plant as much Ground as Two Bufhels of the Large-grain'd; for, in Truth, 'tis not the Meafure of the Seed, but the Number of the Grains, to which refpect ought to be had in apportioning the Quantity of it to the Land.

(a) To *tiller* is to branch out into many Stalks, and is the Country Word, that fignifies the fame with *fruticare*.

(b) A too great Number of Plants do neither tiller, nor produce fo large Ears, nor make half fo good a Crop, as a bare competent Number of Plants will.

(c) Our Bufhel contains Seventy Pounds of the beft Wheat.

Some

Some have thought, that a large Grain of Wheat would produce a larger Plant than a small Grain; but I have full Experience to the contrary. The small Grain, indeed, sends up its first single Blade in Proportion to its own Bulk, but afterwards becomes as large a Plant, as the largest Grain can produce (*a*), *cæteris paribus.*

Six Gallons of middle-siz'd Seed we most commonly drill on an Acre; yet, on rich Land planted early, Four Gallons may suffice; because then the Wheat will have Roots at the Top of the Ground before Winter, and tiller very much, without Danger of the Worms, and other Accidents, that late-planted Wheat is liable to.

If it is drill'd too thick, 'twill be in Danger of falling; if too thin, it may happen to tiller so late in the Spring, that some of the Ears may be blighted; yet a little thicker or thinner does not matter.

As to the Depth, we may plant from half an Inch, to three Inches deep; if planted too deep, there is more Danger of its being eaten off by Worms, betwixt the Grain and the Blade (*b*); for as that

---

(*a*) Farmers in general know this, and choose the thinnest, smallest-grained Wheat for Seed; and therefore prefer that which is blighted and lodged, and that which grows on new-broken Ground, and is not fit for Bread; not only because this thin Wheat has more Grains in a Bushel; but also because such Seed is least liable to produce a smutty Crop, and yet brings Grains as large as any.

I myself have had as full Proofs of this as can possibly be made in both Respects.

'Twas from such small Seed that my drill'd *Lammas* Wheat produced the Ears of that monstrous Length described in this Chapter. I never saw the like, except in that one Year; and the Grains were large also.

And as full Proofs have I seen of thin Seed-wheat escaping the Smut, when plump large grain'd Seed of the same Sort have been smutty.

(*b*) A Wheat plant, that is not planted early, sends out no Root above the Grain before the Spring; and is nourish'd all the Winter by a single Thread, proceeding from the Grain up to the Surface of the Ground. 'Thread

Thread is the Thread of Life during the Winter (if not planted early), fo the longer the Thread is, the more Danger will there be of the Worms (*a*).

'Tis a neceffary Caution to beware of the Rooks (*b*), juft as the Wheat begins to peep ; for before

(*a*) Becaufe the Worms can more eafily find a Thread, that extends by its Length to five or fix Inches Depth, than one which reaches but One Inch ; and befides, the Worms in Winter do not inhabit very near the Surface of the Ground ; and therefore alfo mifs the fhort Threads, and meet with the long ones.

(*b*) 'Tis true, that Wheat which is planted early enough for its Grain to be unfit for the Rooks, before the Corn that is left on the Ground at Harveft is either all eaten by them, or by Swine, or elfe grow'd, plowed in, or otherwife fpoiled, is in no Danger : but as this fometimes happens foon after Harveft, the Time of which is uncertain, a timely Care is neceffary.

Many are the Contrivances to fright the Rooks ; *viz*. To dig an Hole in the Ground, and ftick Feathers therein ; to tear a Rook to Pieces, and lay them on divers Parts of the Field : This is fometimes effectual ; but Kites or other Vermin foon carry away thofe Pieces. Hanging up of dead Rooks is of little Ufe ; for the living will dig up the Wheat under the dead ones. A Gun is alfo of great Ufe for the Purpofe ; but unlefs the Field in Time of Danger be conftantly attended the Rooks will at one Time or other of the Day do their Work, and you may attend often, and yet to no Purpofe ; for they will do great Damage in your Abfence.

The only Remedy that I have found infallible is a Keeper (a Boy may ferve very well) to attend from Morning until Night ; when he fees Rooks either flying over the Field, or alighted in it, he halloos, and throws up his Hat, or a dead Rook, into the Air : upon which they immediately go off ; and 'tis feldom that any one will alight there : They, finding there is no Reft for them, feek other Places for their Prey, wherein they can feed more undifturbed.

This was the Expedient I made ufe of for preferving my prefent Crop : It fucceeded fo well, that in Sixfcore Acres, I believe there is not Two-pence Damage done by the Rooks ; but I had two Boys (one at Four-pence, and the other at Three-pence a Day) to attend them ; becaufe my Wheat is on Two Sides of my Farm ; the whole Expence was about Twenty Shillings. The Damage I received by Rooks the laft Year in a Field of Seventeen Acres, was more than would have, in this manner, preferved my whole Crops for Twenty Years running. I wifh I could as eafily defend my Wheat againft Sheep, which are to me a more pernicious Vermin than the Rooks.

you

you can perceive it to be coming up, they will find it, and dig it up to eat the Grain; therefore you muft keep them off for a Week or Ten Days; and in that time the Blade will become green, and the Grain fo much exhaufted of its Flour, that the Rooks think it not worth while to dig after it.

But the Rooks do not moleft Wheat that is planted before or a little after St. *Michael*; for then there remains Corn enough in the Fields, which is left at Harveft above-ground, that Rooks prefer always before Corn which muft coft them the Labour of digging to find it.

Of Partitions.

I have now intirely left out the middle Row for Wheat, and keep only to the double Row, for the following Reafons.

It makes the cleanfing from Weeds more difficult, than when there is only a double Row.

The Hand-hoe cannot give near fo much Nourifhment (*i. e.* pulverize fo much Earth) in Two Seven-inch Partitions, as it can in One Ten-inch Partition.

There is Four Inches lefs Earth to be pulveriz'd by the Horfe-hoe from the Surface of a Ridge that has Two Seven-inch Partitions, than from a Ridge that hath One Ten-inch Partition.

The Ridge muft be almoft twice as deep in Mould for the treble as for the double Row, or elfe the middle Row will be very weak and poor; and then, according to the Principles, the whole Ridge will be more exhaufted, than by an equal Product produced by ftrong Plants.

As the Ridges may be much lower that have only the one Partition, fo the Intervals may be narrower, and yet have as much Earth in them to be pulveriz'd, as in wide ones that are betwixt treble Rows; becaufe the Four Inches that are in the two Partitions more than in the fingle Partition, being on the Top of

the

the Ridge, may have more Mould under them than Eight Inches on the Side of a Ridge ; and the Four Inches, being in the Partitions, lose the Benefit of Horse-hoeing.

Instead of using the middle Row as an Alloy, 'tis better to plant such Sorts of Wheat as do not require any Alloy to the double Row ; and these are the *White-cone*, and above all other Sorts the right *Smyrna*.

The *White-cone* Wheat must not be reaped so green as the *Lammas* Wheat may ; for if it is not full-ripe, it will be difficult to thresh it clean out of the Straw.

It happened once that my *White-cone* being planted early, and being very high, the Blade and Stalk were kill'd in the Winter ; and yet it grew high again in the Spring, and had then the same Fortune a Second time ; it lay on the Ridges like Straw, but sprung out anew from the Root, and made a very good Crop at Harvest : Therefore, if the like Accident should happen, the Owner needs not be frighted at it.

One thing that made Six-feet Ridges seem at first necessary, was the great Breadth of the Two Partitions (which were Eight Inches apiece), which, together with the Earth left on each Side of the treble Row not well cleansed by Hand-work, made Two large whole Furrows, at the first Plowing for the next Crop, that could not be broken by Harrows : These Two strong Furrows, being turned to the Two Furrows that are in the middle of a narrow Interval, for making a new Ridge, would cover almost all the pulveriz'd Earth, not leaving room betwixt the Two whole Furrows for the Drill to go in.   But now the single Partition, and the Earth left by the Hoe-Plough, on the Outsides of the double Row, making Two narrow Furrows, and the one Partition being cleansed, and deeper Hand-ho'd than those of the treble Row were, or could be, are easily broken by the

Harrows ;

Harrows; for, befides their Narrownefs, they have no Roots to hold their Mould together, except the Wheat-roots, which, being fmall and dead, have not Strength enough to hold it; and therefore that Neceffity of fuch broad Ridges now ceafes along with the treble Row.

When the Two narrow fragile Furrows are harrowed, and mixed with the pulveriz'd Earth of the Intervals, the Roots of the Wheat will reach it; and it is no Matter whether the Crop be drill'd after Two Plowings, in which Cafe the Row will ftand on the very fame Place whereon the Row ftood the precedent Year, or whether it be drill'd after One or Three Plowings; and then the Rows will ftand on the Middle of the laft Year's Intervals.

I cannot prefcribe precifely the moft proper Width of all Intervals; becaufe they fhould be different in different Circumftances. In deep rich Land they may be a little narrower than in fhallow Land.

There muft be (as has been faid) a competent Quantity of Earth in them to be pulveriz'd; and, when the Soil is rich, the lefs will fuffice.

Never let the Intervals be too wide to be Horfehoed at Two Furrows, without leaving any Part unplowed in the Middle of them, when the Furrows are turned towards the Rows.

Some Ploughmen can plow a wider Furrow than others, that do not underftand the fetting of the Hoe-Plough fo well, can.

By making the Plank of the Hoe-plough fhorter, and the Limbers more crooked, we can now hoe in narrower Intervals than formerly, without doing any Damage to the Wheat.

I now choofe to have Fourteen Ridges on an Acre, and one only Partition of Ten Inches on each of them. This I find anfwers all the Ends I purpofe. If the Partitions are narrower, there is not fufficient room in them for the Hand-hoe to do its work effectu-

ally;

ally; if wider, too much Earth will lose the Benefit of the Horse-hoe.

The poorer the Soil is, the more Pulveration will be neceffary to it.

When a great Seafon of Wheat is drill'd, it cannot be expected that much of it can be plowed dry, tho' it is advantageous when there happens an Opportunity for doing it; but by long Experience I find, that in moft of my Lands it does very well, when plowed in a moderate Temper of Moifture.

It may not be amifs to harrow it once after it is drill'd, which will, in fome Meafure, difappoint the Rooks; befides covering the Wheat, if, perchance, any fhould mifs being covered by the Drill-harrow.

But thefe, and all Harrows that go on a Ridge, both before and after it is drill'd, fhould be very light, and faftened together in the common Manner; except that the Pole muft be faftened to each Harrow in two Places; which keeps them both as level as if they were One fingle Harrow: Otherwife the Ridges would be too fharp at the Top, and the Partitions would lie higher than the Rows, and fome of their Earth would be apt to fall on the Rows when it is Hand-hoed.

By Means of this level Harrowing, there is left an open Furrow in the Middle of the Interval, which much facilitates the Firft Horfe-hoeing.

But when, after a Crop is taken off, the Ridges are plowed twice, as they may be where the one Partition hath been well Hand-ho'd; 'tis better to harrow the firft-made Ridges in the common Manner; becaufe then fome of the fine Earth, that is harrow'd down, will reach to the middle of the Intervals whereon the Ridges are to be made for Drilling: Or if there fhould be time for plowing thrice, the Ridges of the Firft and Second Plowings are to be harrow'd in the common Manner alfo.

The

The Harrowing of Ridges muft never be crofs-ways, unlefs they are to be made level for Crofs-plow-ing, in order to lay out the Ridges of a Breadth different to what they were of before.

When you perceive the Ridges are too high, harrow them lower by the defcribed manner of Harrowing ; firft with the heavy Harrows for harrowing out the Stubble, and then with light ones, which may be often, for making the Earth on the Ridges the finer for Drilling, without throwing much of it down; frequent Harrowings in this manner, not being injurious like too much Harrowing on level Ground, which is fometimes trodden as hard as the Highway by the Cattle that draw the Harrows; for in harrowing thefe Ridges, the Beaft draws the Two Harrows, and always treads in the Furrow between them where there is none or very little Mould to tread on.

The Price of Hand-hoeing of thefe double Rows is a Peny for thirty Perches in Length of Row, which amounts to between Eighteen and Nineteen Pence for an Acre.

I fhould fay, that in Hand-hoeing the Earth muft never be turned towards the Wheat; for, if it were, it might crufh it when young; neither could the Partition be clean hoed.

The Hand-hoes for hoeing the Ten-inch Partition have their Edges Seven Inches lcng; they are about Four Inches deep from the Handle; if they were deeper, they would be too weak ; for they muft be thin, and well fteeled. The Labourers pay for them, and keep them in Order, for their own Ufe.

Thefe Hoes muft not cut out any Part of the Two Rows, nor be drawn through them, as the Four-inch Hoes fometimes may through the treble Rows.

If I am taxed with Levity in changing my treble Rows for double ones, it will not appear to be done of a fudden. In *p.* 132. I adviffed the Trial of both

Sorts :

Sorts : And now, upon fuller Experience, I find the double Rows much preferable to the treble, efpecially for Wheat.

When Gentlemen faw the middle Row on low Ridges fo much inferior to the outfide Rows, they were convinced of the Effect of deep Hoeing ; for they faid, there was no other Reafon for this fo vifible a Difference, except the outfide Rows ftanding nearer to the pulveriz'd Intervals than the middle Row did.

And when on high Ridges the middle Row was nearly or quite as good as one of the outfide Rows, I was not convinced, that they were not diminifhed by the middle Row, as much as the Produce of it amounted to : And this I now find to be the Cafe ; for Four Rows of Oats, without a middle Row, produced fomewhat more than the fame Number that had a middle Row ; Two of which treble Rows were taken on one Side, and Two on the other Side of the double Rows, purpofely to make an unexceptionable Trial. And it is, as far as I can judge, the fame in Wheat.

'Tis true, I began my Horfe-hoeing *Scheme* firft with double Rows ; but then they were different to what they are now ; for the firft had their Partition uneven, being the parting Space, whereby it was lefs proper for Hand-hoeing, which I then feldom ufed, except for abfolute Neceffity, as to cleanfe our Poppies, and the like. The Intervals alfo were too narrow for conftant annual Crops.

By all thefe Three Methods I have had very good Crops ; but as this I now defcribe is the lateft, and is (as it ought to be) the beft ; I publifh it as fuch, without Partiality to my own Opinions; for I think it lefs difhonourable to expofe my Errors, when I chance to detect them, than to conceal them : And as I aim at nothing but Truth, I cannot, with any Satisfaction to myfelf, fuffer any thing of my own

I   know-

knowingly to efcape, that is in the leaft contrary to it.

I have a Piece of Five or Six Acres of Land which I annually plant with boiling Peafe, in the very fame manner as Wheat; except that the Second Horfe-hoeing (which is the laft) throws the Earth fo far upon the Peafe as to make the Two Rows become One. Thefe Peafe cannot be planted until after the 25th of *March*; elfe Two Horfe-hoeings might not be fufficient. The fame Drill that plants Wheat plants Peafe; only fometimes we change the Spindle for one that has its Notches a little bigger.

I drill no more Barley, becaufe 'tis not proper to be followed by a Crop of Wheat without a Fallow; for fome of the fhattered Barley will live over the Winter, and mix with the Wheat in the Rows, and can fcarce poffibly be thence timely taken out, its firft Stalk and Blade being difficult to diftinguifh from the Wheat; and this is a great Damage to the Sale in the Market; and for the fame Reafon I plant no more Oats.

The Firft Hoeing is performed by turning a Furrow from the Row.

We are not fo exact as to the Weather in the Firft Hoeing; for if the Earth be wet, the Hoe-plough may go nearer to the Row, without burying the Wheat; and the Froft of the Winter will pulverize that Part of the *(a)* Furrow, which is to be thrown to the Wheat in the Spring, altho' it was hoed wet.

Neither is it neceffary to be very exact as to Time; but it muft never be till the Wheat has more than One Blade; and it may be foon enough, when it has Four or Five Leaves, fo that it is done before *(b)*, or in the Beginning of Winter.

The

(a) The Word Furrow fignifies the Earth that is thrown out, as well as the Trench from whence it is thrown by the Plough.

(b) But if the Wheat is planted very late, it may not be *hoeable* before the Winter is paft; nor is there fuch a Neceffity of hoeing

The greateft Fault you can commit in Hoeing, is the Firft Time, when the Furrow is turned from the Row, not to go near enough to it, nor deep enough. You cannot then go too near it, unlefs you plow it out, or bury it with Mould, and do not uncover it; nor too deep, unlefs you go below the Staple of the Ground.

Servants are apt to hoe too far from the Rows, going backwards and forwards, in the Middle of the Intervals, without coming near the Rows: This lofes moft of the Benefit of Hoeing, and is very injurious to the prefent Crop, and alfo to the Two fucceeding Crops; for then there will be a Deficiency of pulverized Earth; and nobody can fuppofe, that the hoed Earth can be of any Benefit to the Rows, before the Roots reach into it; and when 'tis far off, few of the Roots reach it at all; and thofe that do reach, come there too late to bring the Plants to their full Perfection: Therefore, if the Firft Furrow was not near enough, nor deep enough, plow a Second Furrow at the Bottom of the former, which will go deeper than the Firft, and break the Earth more; befides taking away from the Rows fuch unmoved Ground, which the Firft Plowing may poffibly have miffed. If this can't be conveniently done foon after the Firft Hoeing, do it before the Ridge is turned back in the Spring.

Always leave the Furrows turned up, to make (*a*) Ridges in the Middle of the Intervals during the Winter;

---

hoeing the late planted before the great Frofts are over, as there is of the early-planted; for the later 'tis planted, the lefs time the Earth has to fubfide, and grow hard.

Note, By Winter we do not mean only thofe Months that are properly fo reckoned, but alfo fuch other Months as have hard Frofts in them, as *January*, *February*, and fometimes the Beginning of *March*.

(*a*) Tho' the Ridge in the Middle of the Interval fhould, for Want of fufficient Mould, or otherwife, be too low to give Shelter,

ter,

Winter; and then the hollow Furrows, or Trenches next the Rows, being enriched by the Froft *(b)* and Rains *(c)*, the Wheat will have the Benefit of them earlier in the Spring, than if the Trenches had been left open in the Middle of the Intervals.

The outfide Rows of Wheat, from which the Earth is hoed off before or in the Beginning of Winter,

ter, yet there is generally fome Earth falls to the Left of the Hoe-plough, and lodges upon that Part which is left on the Outfide of the Row; which, notwithftanding that Part be very narrow (as fuppofe Two or Three Inches), yet a fmall Quantity of Earth lying thereon, fo near to the outfide Row, gives an extraordinary Shelter to the young Wheat plants that grow in it.

Shelter is a great Benefit to Wheat; but yet Nourifhment is more: for in the Winter I fee the Wheat-plants upon the moft expofed Part of the Ridge flourifh, when fingle Plants in the Bottom of the Furrow are in a very poor languifhing Condition, without any Annoyance of Water, they being upon a Chalk Bottom.

(b) Froft, if it does not kill the Wheat, is of great Benefit to it; Water or Moifture, when it is frozen in the Earth, takes up more Room than in its natural State; this Swelling of the Ice (which is Water congealed) muft move and break the Earth wherewith it is mixt; and when it thaws, the Earth is left hollow and open, which is a kind of Hoeing to it. This Benefit is done chiefly to and near the Surface; confequently the more Surface there is, by the Unevennefs of the Land, the more Advantage the Soil has from the Froft.

This is another very great Ufe of the Ridge left in the Middle of the Interval during the Winter; becaufe that Ridge, and its Two Furrows, contain Four Times as much Surface as when level. This thus pulverized Surface, turned in in the Spring hoeing, enriches the Earth, in proportion to its Increafe of internal Superficies, and likewife proportionably nourifhes the Plants, whofe Roots enter it; and that Part of it wherein they do not enter, muft remain more enriched for the next Crop, than if the Soil had remained level all the Winter.

(c) It is a vulgar Error that the Winter Rains do not enrich the Earth; and is only thought fo, becaufe we do not fee the Effect of them upon Vegetables, for lack of Heat in that Seafon. But fome Farmers have frequently obferved, that one half of a Ground plowed up juft before Winter has produced a Crop of Barley as much better than the other Part plowed up at the End of Winter, as is the Difference of a Dunging, even when there has been very little Froft.

and

and left almoft bare till the Spring, one would think fhould fuffer by the Froft coming fo near them *(d)*, or for want of Pafture: But it appears to be quite contrary ; for where the Hoe has gone neareft to a Row, its Plants thrive beft : The Earth, which the Froft hath pulverized, being within the Reach of the young fhort Roots, on that Side of the Row, from the Top to the Bottom of the Trench, nourifhes them at firft ; and before the Plants have much exhaufted this, as they grow larger in the Spring, the Ridge from the Middle of the Interval is thrown to them, having a perfectly unexhaufted Pafture, to fupply their increafing Bulk with more Nourifhment.

The Row ftanding as it were on the Brink of this almoft perpendicular Ditch, the Water runs off quickly, or doth not enter but a very little Way into this fteep Side; fo that, the Earth at the Plants being dry, the Froft doth not reach quite to all their Roots to hurt them, tho' the Diftance from the Air to the Roots be very fhort ; and dry Earth doth not freeze as wet doth, neither is this Ditch much expofed to the cold Winds.

The Spring-hoeing is performed after the great Frofts are paft, and when the Weather will allow it; and then turn *(e)* the Ridge from *(f)* the Middle of the

(d) In very light Land, perhaps, we muft not hoe quite fo near to the Rows of Wheat, as in ftrong Land, for fear the Winter fhould lay the Roots bare, and expofe them too much to the Cold; but then we may be fure, that, in this Cafe, the Roots will reach the Interval at a greater Diftance than in ftrong Land ; yet fuch very light Land is not proper for Wheat.

(e) 'Tis an errant Miftake of the Vulgar, when they imagine that the immediate Benefit of frefh Earth to Plants is from that Part which remains uppermoft; for 'tis from turning the impregnated pulverized Side downwards, to be fed on by the Roots, that gives the *Pabulum* or Nourifhment of the frefh Earth to Plants : The other Side, being turned upwards, becomes impregnate alfo in a little time.

(f) But note, that when we fee Weeds coming up near the Row in the Spring, we plow again from the Rows (and fome-

the Interval, to the Rows on each Side by Two Furrows as near as can be, without covering the Wheat; in doing which have regard to the Row only, without looking at the Middle of the Interval; for 'tis no matter if a little Earth be left there; the next Hoeing, or the next fave one *(g)*, will move it.

As to how many times Wheat is to be hoed in the Summer, after this Spring Operation, it depends upon the Circumftances *(h)* and Condition of the Land *(i)* and Weather *(k)*; but be the Seafon as it will, never fuffer the Weeds to grow high, nor let any unmoved Earth lie in the Middle of the Intervals long enough to grow hard; neither plow deep near the Rows in the Summer, when the Plants are large *(l)*, but as deep in the Middle of the Intervals

times can plow within one Inch of the Row) before we turn down the Mould from the Middle of the Interval.

(*g*) If at the next Hoeing we turn another Furrow towards the Row (which is feldom done), then 'tis the next that moves the remaining Earth, left in the Middle of the Interval: But if the next Hoeing be from the Row (as it generally is), then that covers the Middle of the Interval; and then 'tis the next Hoeing after that, that turns all the Earth clean out of the Middle of the Interval toward the Rows.

(*h*) If the Land was not fufficiently tilled or hoed in the precedent Year, it will require the more Hoeings in the following Year.

(*i*) The poorer the Land is, the more Hoeings it fhould have.

(*k*) A wet Summer may prevent fome of the Hoeings that we fhould perform in a dry Summer.

(*l*) Our Hoeing deep near the Plants, when fmall, breaks off only the Ends of the Roots; but after the Roots are fpread far in the Interval, the greateft Part of them, being then on the Right-hand Side of the Hoe plough, might hold faft on that Side, and not be drawn out; and then the whole Roots would be broken off clofe to the Bodies of the Plants: Therefore at the Second deep Hoeing, that turns a Furrow from the Row in the Summer, we go about Four or Six Inches farther off from the Roots than the time before; but we go nearer or farther off, according to the Diftance of Time between thofe Two Hoeings: Yet we may hoe *fhallow* near to the Plants at any time, without Injury to their Roots, but, on the contrary, it will be advantageous to them.

as

as the Staple will allow ; turning the Earth towards
the Wheat, especially at the last Hoeing, so as to
leave a deep, wide Trench in the Middle of each Interval.

We augment our Wheat-crops Four Ways; not in
Number of Plants, but in Stalks, Ears, and Grains.

The First is, by increasing the Number of Stalks
from One, Two, or Three, to Thirty or Forty to a
Plant, in ordinary Field-land.

And we augment the Crop, by bringing up all the
Stalks into Ears, which is the Second Way ; for, if it
be diligently observed, we shall find, that not half (*m*)
the Stalks of sown Wheat come into Ear.

I saw an Experiment of this in Rows of Wheat
that were equally poor : One of these Rows was increased (*n*) so much, as to produce more Grains than
Ten of the other, by bringing up more of its Stalks
into Ears, and also by augmenting its Ears to a much
greater Bigness; which is the Third Way : For, whatever *Varro* means by saying, that the Ears remain
Fifteen Days *in Vaginis*, 'tis pretty plain, that the
Ears are formed together with the Stalks, and will
be very large, or very small, in proportion to the
Nourishment given them (*o*).

The last and Fourth Way of augmenting the Produce of Wheat-plants, is by causing them to have
large and plump Grains in the Ears; and this can no
way be so effectually done as by late Hoeing, especi-

(*m*) If a square Yard of sown Wheat be marked out, and the
Stalks thereon numbered in the Spring, it will be found, that
Nine parts in Ten are missing at Harvest.

(*n*) These Rows were drilled a Foot asunder, not hoed; and
were, by the Shallowness and Wetness of the Soil, very poor in
the Spring; and then, by pouring Urine to the Bottom of this
Row, it was so vastly increased above the rest.

(*o*) Like as the Vines, if well nourished, bring large Bunches
of Grapes ; but if ill nourished, they produce few Bunches, and
those small ones ; and many Claspers are formed, which would
have been Bunches, if they had had sufficient Nourishment given
them at the proper time.

ally

ally juſt after the Wheat is gone out of the Bloſſom; and when ſuch hoed Grains weigh double the Weight of the ſame Number of unhoed (which they frequently will) tho' the Number of Grains in the hoed are only equal, yet the hoed Crop muſt be double.

Thus, by increaſing the Number of Stalks (*p*), bringing more of them up into Ear (*q*), making the Ears larger (*r*), and the Grain plumper, and fuller of Flour (*s*), the Hoeing Method makes a greater Crop from

(*p*) The ſame Plant that, when poor, ſends out but Two or Three Tillers, would, if well nouriſhed by the Hoe, or other-wiſe, ſend up a Multitude of Tillers, as is ſeen in hoed Wheat, and ſown Wheat.

(*q*) Mr. *Houghton* relates Eighty Ears on one ſingle Plant of Wheat, and a greater Number has been counted lately in a Garden: Thoſe Eighty, reckoned to have Fifty Grains apiece, make an Increaſe of Four thouſand Grains for one; but I have never found above Forty Ears from a ſingle Plant in my Fields; yet there is no doubt, but that every Plant would produce as many as Mr. *Houghton*'s, of the ſame Sort, with the ſame Nouriſhment: But I ſhould not deſire any to be ſo prolific in Stalks, leſt they ſhould fail of bringing ſuch a Multitude of Ears to Perfection. The Four hundred Ears, that I numbered in a Yard, were not weighed, becauſe they were told before ripe; and the greateſt Weight of Wheat that ever I had from a Yard, was the Product of about Two hundred and Fifty Ears, and ſome of them were ſmall.

(*r*) I have numbered One hundred and Nine Grains in One Ear of my hoed Cone-wheat of the grey Sort; and One Ear of my hoed Lammas-wheat has been meaſured to be Eight Inches long, which is double to thoſe of ſown Wheat. I have ſome of theſe Ears now by me almoſt as long, the longeſt being given away as a Rarity; and indeed 'tis not every Year that they grow to that Length, and 'tis always where the Plants are pretty ſingle. But there is no Year wherein One Ear of my hoed does not more than weigh Two of the ſown Ears, taking a whole Sheaf of each together without chooſing. The Sheaves of the hoed are of a different Shape from the other; almoſt all the Ears of the hoed are at the Top of the Sheaf; but moſt of the other are ſituate at the lower Part, or near the Middle of the Sheaf.

(*s*) Seed Cone wheat coming all out at the ſame Heap, planted all at the ſame Time, and on Land of the ſame Sort adjoining near together, the Wheat that was ſown produced Grains ſo ſmall, and

from a Tenth Part of the Plants (*t*) that the fowing Method can.

All

and that which was drilled fo very large, that no Farmer or Wheat-buyer would believe them to be of the fame Sort of Wheat, except thofe who knew it, which were many. One Grain of the drilled weighed Two of the fown, and there was twice the Chaff in an equal Weight of the fown, being both weighed before and after the Wheat was feparated from the Chaff.

(*t*) The Fact of this nobody can doubt, who has obferved the different Products of ftrong and of weak Plants, how the one exceeds the other.

The greateft Difference of having an equal Crop from a fmall Number of ftrong Plants, and from a great Number of weak ones, is, that the Soil is vaftly lefs exhaufted by the former than by the latter, not only from the latter's exhaufting more in proportion to their Number when young, and whilft each of them confumes as much Nourifhment as each of the fmall Number; but alfo from the different Increafe that a ftrong Plant makes by receiving the fame Proportion of Food with a weak one: For it appears from Dr. *Woodward*'s Experiments, that the Plant which receives the *leaft* Increafe carries off the *greateft* Quantity of Nourifhment in proportion to that Increafe; and that 'tis the fame with an Animal, all who are acquainted with fatting of Swine know; for they eat much more Food daily for the firft Two Weeks of their being put into the Sty, than they do afterwards, when they thrive fafter; the fatter they grow, the lefs they eat.

Hence, I think, it may be inferred, that a Plant, which, by never having been robbed or ftinted by other Plants, is ftrong, receives a much greater Increafe from an equal Quantity of Food, than a Number of weak Plants (as thick ones are), equalling the Bulk of the fingle ftrong Plant, do.

And this of the Doctor's have I feen by my own Obfervations confirmed in the Field in Potatoes, Turneps, Wheat, and Barley; a following Crop fucceeds better after an equal Crop, confifting of a bare competent Number of ftrong Plants, than after a Crop of thick weak ones, *cæteris paribus.*

Thus the hoed Crops, if well managed, confifting of fewer and ftronger Plants than the fown Crops of equal Produce, exhauft the Ground lefs; whereby, and by the much (I had almoft faid infinitely) greater Pulveration of the Soil, indifferent good Land may, for any thing I have yet feen to the contrary, produce profitable Crops always without Manure, or Change of *Species,* if the Soil be proper for it in refpect of Heat and Moifture; and alfo as Crops of fome *Species,* by their living longer, by their

greater

All thefe Advantages will be loft by thofe Drillers, who do not overcome the unreafonnble Prejudices of the unexperienced, concerning the Width of Intervals.

.In wide Intervals, we can raife a good Crop with lefs Labour, lefs Seed, no Dung, no Fallow, but not without a competent Quantity of Earth, which is the leaft expenfive of any thing given to Corn; the Earth of a whole good Acre being but about the Tenth Part of the common Expence; and of indifferent Land, a Twentieth; and fuch I count that of Five Shillings and Six-pence *per* Acre.

The Crop enjoys all the Earth; for betwixt the laft Hoeing, and the Harveft, there remains nothing but Space empty of Mould in the Middle of the Intervals.

'Tis an Objection, that great Part of thofe wide Intervals muft be loft *(u)*, becaufe the Wheat-roots do

not

greater Bulk, or different Conftitution, exhauft more than others, refpect ought to be had to the Degree of Richnefs of the Soil, that is to produce each *Species*: The Sowing and the Hoeing Hufbandry differ fo much both in Pulveration and Exhauftion, that no good Argument can be drawn from the former againft the latter: But tho' a too great Number of Plants be, upon many Accounts, very injurious to the Crop, yet 'tis beft to have a competent Number; which yet needs not be fo exact, but that we may expect a great Crop from Twenty, Forty, or Fifty Plants in a Yard of the treble Row, if well managed.

(*u*) They do reach through all the Mould (as fhall be proved by-and-by); and yet may leave fufficient Pafture behind; becaufe it is impoffible for them to come into Contact with all the Mould in One Year; no more than when Ten Horfes are put into an Hundred Acres of good Pafture, their Mouths come into Contact with all the Grafs to eat it in one Summer, though they will go all over it, as the Vine-roots go all over the Soil of a Vineyard without exhaufting it all; becaufe thofe Roots feed only fuch a bare competent Quantity of Plants, which do not overflock their Pafture.

The Superficies of the fibrous Roots of a proper Number of Wheat-plants bear a very fmall Proportion to the Superficies of the fine Parts of the pulverized Earth they feed on in thefe Intervals; for one cubical Foot of this Earth may, as is fhewn in

p. 29.

nor reach it; but as we generally turn the Mould towards the Row at the laft Hoeings, there is no Part of

p. 29. have many thoufand Feet of internal Superficies : But this is in proportion to the Degree of its Pulveration : and that Degree may be fuch as is fufficient to maintain a competent Number of Wheat-plants, without over-exhaufting the vegetable Pafture, but not fufficient to maintain thofe, and a great Stock of Weeds befides, without over-exhaufting it.   And this was plainly feen in a Field of Wheat drilled on *Six-feet* Ridges, when the South Ends of fome of the Ridges, and the North Ends of others, had their Partitions Hand-hoed, and cleanfed of Weeds, early in the Spring, the oppofite Ends remaining full of a fmall *Species* of Weeds, called *Crow-needles,* which fo exhaufted the whole Intervals of the weedy Part of the Ridges, that the next Year the whole Field being drilled again with Wheat exactly in the Middle of the laft Intervals, the following Crop very plainly diftinguifhed how far each Ridge had its Partitions made clean of thofe fmall Weeds in the Spring, from the other End where the Weeds remained till full-grown; the Crop of the former was twice as good as that of the latter, even where both were cleanfed of Weeds the next *Spring.*   This Crop ftanding only upon that Part of the Mould, which was fartheft from the Rows of the precedent Crop, proves that the Roots, both of the Wheat and Weeds, did enter all the Earth of the former Intervals.

It was alfo obfervable, that where the Partitions of Two of the Six-feet Ridges had been in the precedent Year cleanfed of Weeds, and thofe of the adjoining Ridges on each Side of them not cleanfed, the Row that was the next Year planted exactly in the Middle of the Interval between thofe two Ridges, was perceivably better than either of the Two Rows planted in the Intervals on the other Side of each of them : The Reafon of which Difference muft be, that the Midde of the Interval, that was between the Two cleanfed Ridges, was fed on by the Wheat only, and by no Weeds; but the other Two Intervals were fed on by the Wheat on one Side, and by both the Wheat and Weeds on the other Side of each.

There were, in the fame Field, feveral Ridges together, that had the Ends of their Rows of Wheat plowed out by the Hoeplough, and their other Ends cleanfed of Weeds: This was done on purpofe, to fee what Effect a Fallow would have on the next Crop, which was indeed extraordinary; for thefe fallowed Ends of the Ridges, being Horfe-hoed in the Summer, as the other Ends were, and the Intervals of them made into Ridges, the following Year produced the largeft Crop of all; this Crop was received in 1734.

Thefe

of it above Two Feet diſtant from even the middle Row, and Seventeen Inches from either of the outſide Rows.

And I have plainly proved, that the Roots of Cone-wheat have reached Mould at Two Feet Diſtance, after paſſing through another Row at a Foot Diſtance from it, the Plants being then but Eighteen Inches high, and but half-grown.

Farmers do not grudge to beſtow Three or Four Pounds in the Buying and Carriage of Dung for an Acre; but think themſelves undone, if they afford an extraordinary Eighteen-penyworth of Earth to the wide Intervals of an Acre; not conſidering that Earth is not only the beſt, but alſo the cheapeſt Entertain-

Theſe ſeveral different Managements performed in this Field, ſhewed by the different Succeſs of the Crops in each Sort, what ought to be done, and which is the beſt Sort of Management.

This Field indeed is ſome of my beſt Land; and by all the Experiments I have ſeen on it, I do not find but that, by the beſt Management, never omitted in any Year, it might produce good annual Crops of Wheat always, without Aſſiſtance of Dung or Fallow; but it would be very difficult for me to get Hands to do this to the greateſt Perfection, unleſs I were able conſtantly to attend them.

The whole pulverized Earth of the Interval being pretty equally fed on by the former Crop, 'tis no great Matter in what Part of it the following Crop is drill'd: I never drill it but on the Middle of the laſt Year's Interval, becauſe there is the Trench whereon the next Year's Ridge is made with the greateſt Conveniency: But there may be ſome Reaſon to ſuſpect, that the Plants of the Rows exhauſt more Houriſhment from that Earth of the Intervals which is fartheſt from their Bodies, than from that which is neareſt to them: Since their fibrous Roots, at the greateſt Diſtance from the Rows, are moſt numerous, &c. by theſe the Plants, when they are at their greateſt Bulk, are chiefly maintained.

It muſt be *noted*, that the above Experiments would not have been a full Proof, if Weeds had been ſuffered to grow in the Partitions of the Ends of thoſe Ridges, in the Year wherein the Difference appeared. It may alſo be *noted*, that a Mixture and Variety of bad Huſbandry are uſeful for a Diſcovery of the *Theory* and *Practice* of good Huſbandry.

ment

ment that can be given to Plants ; for at Five Shillings and Six-pence Rent, the whole Earth belonging
to each of our Rows cofts only Six-pence, *i. e.* a Peny
for a Foot broad, and Six hundred and Sixty Feet
long; that being the Sixty-fixth Part of an Acre (*x*).

And if for conftant annual Wheat-crops you make
fewer than Eleven Rows on Four Perches Breadth, you
will always increafe the Expence of Hoeing; becaufe
then Two Furrows will not Hoe One of thofe Intervals, and you will alfo thereby leffen the Crops, but
improve the Land more : And if you increafe that
Number of Rows, you will thereby increafe every
Expence ; for there muft be Two Furrows to hoe a
narrow Interval, and an Increafe of the Quantity of
Seed, and the Labour in uncovering, weeding, and
reaping; and alfo you will lefs improve the Land, and
leffen the Crops after the Firft Year.

If the Intervals are narrower in deep Land, tho'
there might be Mould enough in them, yet there
would not be Room to pulverize it.

If narrower in fhallow Land, tho' there were
Room, yet there would not be Mould enough in
them to be pulverized.

The Horfe-hoe, well applied, doth fupply the Ufe
of Dung and Fallow; but it cannot fupply the Ufe of
Earth, tho' it can infinitely increafe the vegetable Pafture of it, by pulverizing it, where it is in a reafonable
Quantity: Yet if the Intervals be fo narrow, that near
all the Earth of them goes to make the Partitions
raifed at the Top of the Ridges, there will be fo little
to be pulverized, that you muft return to Fallowing,

(*x*) But the Vulgar compute this Expence of a Foot Breadth
of Ground, not only as of the Rent, as they ought, but as an
Eleventh Part of their own ufual Charges added to the Rent.

And there is Land enough in *England* to be had, at the Rent
of Five Shillings and Six-pence the Acre, that is very proper for
Wheat in the Hoeing-Hufbandry.

and to the Dung-cart, and to all the old exorbitant Charges (*y*).

Eight Acres, Part of a Ground of Twenty Acres, drilled with Intervals of Three Feet and an half, brought a good Crop ; but the Second Year, not being hoed, the Crop was poor ; and the Third Crop made that Land fo foul and turfy, that 'twas forced to lie for a Fallow, there being no way to bring it into Tilth without a Summer-plowing (*z*), when the reft of the fame Piece, in wider Intervals, being conftantly hoed, continued in good Tilth, and never failed to yield a good Crop, without miffing one Year.

In another Field, there is now a Sixth Crop of Wheat, in wide Intervals, very promifing, tho' this Ground has had no fort of Dung to any of thefe Crops, or in feveral Years before them : The laft Year's Crop was the Fifth, and was the beft of the Five, tho' a Yard of the Row yielded but Eighteen Ounces and Three Quarters; and the Third Crop yielded Twenty Ounces Weight (*a*) of clean Wheat
in

(*y*) The Objections againft thefe wide Intervals are only for faving a Penyworth or Two of Earth in each Row, or a few Groats-worth of it in an Acre ; by faving of which Earth they may lofe, in the prefent and fucceeding Crops, more Pounds.

(*z*) This Narrownefs of the Intervals, if the Damage of it be rightly computed, would amount to half the Inheritance of the Land ; and was occafioned by the Wilfulnefs of my Bailiff, who, drilling it upon the Level, ordered the Horfe to be guided half a Yard within the Mark, becaufe he fanfied the Intervals would be too wide, if he followed my Directions.

(*a*) Wheat, before Harveft, ftanding in Rows with wide Intervals betwixt them, may not feem, to the Eye, to equal a Crop of half the Bignefs difperfed all over the Land, when fown in the common Manner ; and yet there is more Deceit in the Appearance of thofe different Crops, whilft they are young, and in Grafs : We fhould therefore not judge of them then by our Imagination, but as we do of the Sun and Moon nigh the Horizon, *viz.* by our Reafon.

Imain the fame Spot; but 'twas becaufe the Spot where the Twenty grew, was then a little higher than the reft, which in Two Years became more equal; and the thin Land was more deficient in that Third Crop, than the thick Land exceeded the thin in the Fifth Crop.

In the thick the Hoe-plough went deeper, and confequently raifed more Pafture there; but then it went the fhallower in the thin; and when the Land became of a more equal Depth the Fifth Year, the Plough and the Hoe-plough went deeper, all the Piece being taken together; for the Crop could be but in proportion to the different Pafture, allowing fomewhat for the more or lefs Seafonablenefs of the Year.

The Soil, in this our Cafe, cannot be fupplied in Subftance, but from the Atmofphere. The Earth which the Rain brings can do it alone, if it fall in great Quantity; for by Water, 'tis plain, the Earth which nourifhed *Helmont*'s Tree was fupplied; for the Tin-cover of the Box wherein it ftood, prevented the Dews from entering.

Dews muft add very much to the Land, thus continually tilled and hoed; for they are more heavily charged with terreftrial Matter than Rain is, which appears from their forcing a Defcent through the Air, when 'tis ftrong enough to buoy up the Clouds from falling into Rain : And Dew, when kept in a Veffel long enough to putrefy, leaves a greater Quantity of black Matter at the Bottom of the

Imagination often deceives us by Arguments falfe or precarious; but Reafon leads us to Demonftration, by Weights and Meafures : Yet this Prejudice will vanifh at Harveft before weighing; for then all thofe wide Intervals that were bare, will be covered with large Ears interfering to hide them quite, and make a finer Appearance than a fown Crop. But 'tis obferved, that the Cone-wheat makes the fineft Shew, when you look on it length ways of the Rows, both at Harveft, and a confiderable time before Harveft.

Veffel,

Veſſel, than Rain-water does in a Veſſel of the ſame Bigneſs, filled with it till putrefied.

Dews at Land, I ſuppoſe, are firſt exhaled from Rivers, and moiſt Lands, and from the Expirations of Vegetables; moſt of the Dew which falls on it is exhaled from untilled Land; but moſt of that which falls on well tilled or well hoed Land, remains therein unexhaled; ſo that the untilled Ground helps, by that means, to enrich and augment the tilled: For if an Acre be tilled for Two Years together without ſowing, it will become richer by that Tillage, than by lying unplowed Four Years, which may be eaſily proved by Experience (*b*).

But then, as to Rain, the Sea being larger than all the Land (and its Waters, by their Motion, becoming replete with terreſtrial Matter), 'tis not unlikely, that more Vapour is raiſed from One Acre of Sea, than from One hundred Acres of Land.

Some have been ſo curious as to compute the Quantity of Rain, that falls yearly in ſome Places in *England*, by a Contrivance of a Veſſel to receive it; and 'tis found, in one of the drieſt Places, far from the Sea, to be Fourteen Inches deep, in the Compaſs of a Year; in ſome Places much more; *viz.* at *Paris*, Nineteen Inches; in *Lancaſhire*, Mr. *Townley* found, by a long-continued Series of Obſervations, that there falls above Forty Inches of Water in a Year's time.

Could we as eaſily compute the true Quantity of Earth in Rain-water, as the Quantity of Water is computed, we might perhaps find it to anſwer the Quantity of Earth taken off from our hoed Soil annually by the Wheat.

But if Land ſown with Wheat be not hoed, its Surface is ſoon incruſtate; and then much of this Water, with its Contents, runs off, and returns to

(*b*) *Non igitur Fatigatione, quemadmodum plurimi crediderunt, nec Senio, ſed noſtra ſcilicet* Inertia; *minus benigne nobis Arva reſpondent.* Colum. *lib.* xi. *cap.* 1.

the

the Sea, without entering the Ground; and in Summer a great deal of what remains is exhaled by the Sun, and raifed by the Wind, both in Summer and Winter.

Some there are who think it a fatal Objection, that the more an Interval is hoed, the more Weeds will grow in it; and that the Hoe can produce, or (as they fay) breed in it as many Weeds in one Summer, as would have come thereon in Ten Years by the old Hufbandry. But by this Objection they only maintain, that the Hoe can deftroy as many Weeds in One Summer, as the old Hufbandry can in Ten Years.

And they might add, that fince all Weeds that grow where the Hoe comes, are killed before they feed, and that few of thofe which grow in the old Hufbandry, are killed (c) before their Seed be ripe and fhed; thefe Objectors will be forced to allow, that our Hufbandry will leffen a Stock of Weeds more in one Summer, than theirs can do to the World's End; unlefs they believe the equivocal Generation of Weeds, than which Opinion nothing can be more abfurd.

Some object againft my Method of (d) weighing a Yard, or a Perch in Length of a Row, faying, this does not determine the Produce of a whole Field.

I an-

(c) Weeds cannot be killed before they grow, but will lie dormant, as they do in our Partitions, and in their fown Land; and while Seeds are in the Ground, they are always ready to grow at the firft Opportunity, and will certainly break out at one time or other; fo that preventing their coming, is only like healing up a Wound before it be cured.

(d) I did not weigh this Yard, as different from the other Yards round about it, for I had much Difficulty to determine which Row I fhould chufe it in; when I was going to cut in one Row, it ftill feemed that another was better, and I queftion whether I did chufe the beft at laft.

Note, Whereas I often mention the Wheat of this Field to be without Dung or Fallow, it muft be underftood of that Part of the Field wherein my *Weighings* and other Trials were made:

K   becaufe

I anfwer, that they judge right, if the Produce of the whole Field be not of equal Goodnefs; but if it be not, it muft be becaufe one Part of the Field is richer, or differently managed from the other Part: For the fame Caufes that produce Twenty Ounces of clean Wheat upon one Yard, muft produce the fame Quantity upon every Yard, of a Million of Acres.

When the Crop of half a Field is fpoiled by Sheep, not hoed at all, or improperly, it would be ridiculous to compute the whole Field together for an Experiment: We might indeed weigh the pooreft, to prove the Difference of the one from the other, to try (as they fometimes feem to do) how poor a Crop we can raife; but my Defign was, to try how good a Crop I could raife with a Tenth Part of the common Expence.

And I have often weighed the Produce of the fame Quantity of Ground (*e*), of all Sorts of fown Wheat, both the beft and the worft; but never have found any of the fown equal to the beft of my drilled. Indeed we have none of the richeft Land (*f*) in our

becaufe there was a fmall Part once fallowed Eight or Nine Years ago, and a little Dung laid on another Part about the laft *Michaelmas*, after the Crop of Oats was taken off. But this being a Year in which Dung is obferved to have little or no Effect on *fown* Wheat (my Dung being weak and laid thin), 'tis the fame here; for thofe Rows which are in the dunged Part, can hardly be diftinguifhed from the reft of the Rows which had not been dunged: And yet the Ends of the Rows which were cleanfed of Weeds, are very diftinguifhable by the Colour of the Wheat, though fome are the Third, and fome the Fourth Crop fince the Difference was made; and the *whole* Rows manag'd alike every Year, from that time to this; fo that *here* Un-exhauftion is more effectual than Dung. This is certain, that neither Dung nor Fallow hath been near the Part wherein my Experiments were made.

(*e*) I allow Two fquare Yards of their Crops to One Yard in Length of my Treble Row.

(*f*) I am forry that this Farm, whereon I have practifed Horfehoeing, being fituate on an Hill, that confifts of Chalk on one Side, and Heath ground on the other, has been ufually noted for the pooreft and fhalloweft Soil in the Neighbourhood.

Country

Country within my Reach, that being not above One Mile.

As a Yard in Length of my treble Row of the Third fucceffive Crop of Wheat, without Dung or Fallow, produced Twenty Ounces of Wheat; which, allowing Six Feet to the Ridge, is about Six Quarters (*a*) to an Acre ; and, allowing Seven Inches to each Partition, and Two Inches on each Outfide, is in all Eighteen Inches of Ground to each treble Row, and but juft One-fourth Part of the Ridge. Now, if, in the old Hufbandry, the Crop was as good all over the Ground, as it was in thefe Eighteen Inches of the treble Row, they muft have Twenty-four Quarters to an Acre; but let them dung whilft they can, they will fcarce raife Twenty-four Gallons of Wheat the Third Year, on an Acre of Land of equal Goodnefs; and let them leave out their Dung, and add no more Tillage in lieu of it, and I believe they will not expect Three Quarters to an Acre, in all the Three Years put together.

The mean Price of Wheat, betwixt Dear and Cheap, is reckoned Five Shillings a Bufhel (*b*) ; and

there-

(*a*) Eight Bufhels make a Quarter.

(*b*) 'Tis commonly faid, that a Farmer cannot thrive, who for want of Money is obliged to fell his Wheat under Five Shillings a Bufhel ; but if he will fell it dear, he muft keep it when 'tis cheap : And his Way of keeping it is in the Straw, ufing his beft Contrivances to preferve it from the Mice.

The moft fecure Way of keeping a great Quantity of Wheat, that ever I heard of, is by drying it. When I lived in *Oxfordfhire*, one of my neareft Neighbours was very expert in this, having practifed it for great Part of his Life: When Wheat was under Three Shillings a Bufhel, he bought in the Markets as much of the middle Sort of Wheat as his Money would reach to purchafe: He has often told me, that his Method was to dry it upon an Hair-cloth, in a Malt-kiln, with no other Fuel than clean Wheat-Straw ; never fuffering it to have any ftronger Heat than that of the Sun. The longeft time he ever let it remain in this Heat was Twelve Hours, and the fhorteft time about Four Hours; the damper the Wheat was, and the longer intended to be kept,

the

therefore an Acre that would produce every Year, without any Expence, Eight Bushels, would be thought

the more Drying it requires: But how to diftinguish nicely the Degrees of Dampnefs, and the Number of Hours proper for its Continuance upon the Kiln, he faid was an Art impofible to be learned by any other Means than by Practice. About Three or Four and Twenty Years ago, Wheat being at Twelve Shillings a Bufhel, he had in his Granaries, as I was informed, Five thoufand Quarters of dried Wheat; none of which coft him above Three Shillings a Bufhel.

This dried Wheat was efteemed by the *London* Bakers to work better than any new Wheat that the Markets afforded. His Speculation, which put him upon this Project, was, that 'twas only the fuperfluous Moifture of the Grain that caufed its Corruption, and made it liable to be eaten by the Wevil; and that when this Moifture was dried out, it might be kept fweet and good for many Years; and that the Effect of all Heat of the fame Degree was the fame, whether of the Straw, or of the Sun.

As a Proof, he would fhew, that every Grain of his Wheat would grow after being kept Seven Years.

He was a moft fincere honeft Yeoman, who from a fmall Subftance he began with, left behind him about Forty thoufand Pounds; the greateft Part whereof was acquired by this Drying Method.

For the Hand-hoeing they ufe Hoes of Four Inches Breadth, very thin, and well fteeled: Their Thinnefs keeps them from wearing to a thick Edge, and prevents the Neceffity of often grinding them. Such Hoes are in Ufe with fome Gardeners near *London*. They need not be afraid of drawing thefe little Hoes acrofs the Rows of young Wheat to take out the few Weeds that come therein at the early Hoeing; for whilft the Wheat-plants are fmall, it may be an Advantage to cut out fome of the weakeft, as they do of Turneps; for I perceive there are oftener too many Plants than too few. But the thing that caufes the greateft Trouble in cleanfing the Rows, is when the Seed is foul (*i. e.* full of Seeds of Weeds): Therefore I cleanfe my Seed-wheat by drawing it on a Cloth on a Table, which makes it perfectly clean.

This Hand-hoeing fhould be performed about the End of *March*, or Beginning of *April*, before the Wheat is fpindled (*i. e.* run up to Stalks); and if the Weather be dry enough, you may go lengthways of the Ridges with a very light Roller to break the Clods of the Partitions, whereby the Hoe will work the better.

If there fhould afterwards more Weeds come up, they muft not be fuffered to ripen; and then the Soil will be every Year freer from Weeds.

This

thought an extraordinary profitable Acre; but yet
a drilled Acre, that produces Sixteen Bushels of
Wheat,

This Hand-hoeing of the Rows should be done at the proper
time, though it happen, by late Planting, that the Horse-hoe
has not gone before it; for it may be, that the Weather has kept
out the Horse-hoe : and the Earth may not be dry deep enough
in the Intervals for the Hoe-plough, but deep enough in the Partitions for the Hand-hoe.

And the Expence of this Hand-work on the Rows would be
well answered, though there should not be one Weed in them ;
and so it would be, if a second Hand hoeing were bestowed on
the Partitions of every Crop of Wheat not suspected of being too
luxuriant.

If after the last Horse-hoeing there should be Occasion for another Hoeing of the Intervals, where the Narrowness of them,
and the Leaning of tall Wheat, make it difficult or dangerous to
be performed by the Hoe-plough ; a slight shallow Hoeing may
be performed therein by the Hand-hoe with Ease and Safety, at
a very small Expence, which would be more than doubly repaid
in the following Crops.

IF any one doubts of the Efficacy of thus managing Wheat,
it can't cost much to make proper Trials. But then Care must
be taken, that the Trials be proper. I do not advise any one to
be at the Expence of my Instruments for that Purpose, but to
imitate them in pulverizing, and all other directed Operations
by the Spade and common Hoes. His Ridges of Experiment
need be no longer than Six Feet. Instead of a Drill, make use
of a triangular Piece of Wood, Seven Feet long, and Four or
Five Inches thick, with one Edge of which make Channels, and
place the Seed regularly even into them by Hand, and cover it
with the same Piece of Wood; but if the Earth be so wet, as to
cling to the Piece, then make use of it only as a Ruler, whereby
to make the Channels strait with a Stick.

Let some of the Ridges have double Rows, others treble ; and
let some have treble Rows half-way, and leave out the middle
Row in the other Half, to shew whether the double Row or the
treble Row produce a better Crop.

Then for the First time of Hoeing, the Spade must work with
its Back towards the Row. The Second time, in turning the
Earth to the Row, the Spade's Face must be towards it. These
Two, and several other Hoeings should be deep ; but when the
Roots are large (and the Hoeing is near the Plants), the Spade
must go shallow ; and neither the Face nor the Back of it must

be

Wheat, with the Expence of Ten or Fifteen Shillings, is above a Third Part more profitable.

I don't

be towards the Row, except when the Earth is turned towards it; and then the Face must be always towards it; but for the rest of the last Hoeings, the Spade should work with its Face towards one or other of the Ends of the Intervals, that the fewer of the Roots may be cut off, and the more of them removed, and covered again.   Let the Spits be thin for the better pulverizing of the Mould.   The Hand-hoe will sometimes be useful in the Intervals, as well as in the Partitions.

Four or Five Perches of Land may suffice for making proper Trials.

The Expence of this will be little, though perhaps Ten times more than that which is done by the proper Instruments for the same Proportion of Land.

But I must give this Caution, that no Part of it be done out of the Reach of the Master's Eye; for if it should, he may expect to be disappointed.

The richer the Land, the thinner it must be planted to prevent the lodging of Corn.

The Master ought to compute the Quantity of Seed, due to each Perch, at the Rate of Five or Six Gallons to an Acre, by Weighing, &c. as I have shewn in my Essay.

I cannot commend more than Two Partitions in a Row, or more than One, when the Intervals are narrow; because the broader the Row is, the more Earth will remain unpulverized, under the Partitions; too much of which Earth being whole, will disappoint, at least, one of the Differences mentioned in my xviith Chapter.

Indifferent Land I think most proper whereon to make the Experiment, and the most improper for Corn is barren Land, as the best brings the largest Crops.

To ascertain the Quantity of the Crop, take a Yard in the Middle of a Ridge, and weigh its Produce.

Every Year leave one Interval unhoed, to prove the Difference of that Side of a double or treble Row next to it, from the other Side next to the hoed Interval.

But it must be *noted*, that the Spade doth not always pulverize so much as the Plough, or Hoe plough; therefore there may be occasion for more Diggings than there would be of Horse-hoeings.

One of the Observations that put me upon Trials of wide Intervals, and Horse work for Corn, was the following; *viz.* One Half of a poorish Field was sown with Barley; the other Half drilled with Turneps, the Rows Thirty Inches asunder, at the proper Season, and twice hoed with a Sort of Horse-hoe contrived

trived for that Purpose (but nothing like that I have deſcribed); the Drill, beginning next to the Barley, left an Interval of the ſame (30 Inches) Breadth between the Firſt Row of Turneps and the Barley, which, being ſown on large Furrows, came up in a ſort of Rows, as is common for Barley to come when ſown on ſuch wide Furrows. This Interval between the Barley and the Turneps had the ſame Hoeings as the reſt, and had this Effect on the broad Row of Barley next to it; *viz.* Each Plant had many Stalks; it was of a very deep flouriſhing Colour, grew high, the Ears very long, and, in all reſpects, the Barley was as good as if it had been produced by the richeſt Land. The next Row of Barley had ſome little Benefit on the Side next to the ſtrong Row; but all the reſt of the Barley, either by the too late Sowing of it, the Poverty of the Soil (not being in any manner dunged), or elſe by the Coldneſs of the Land, or Coldneſs of the Summer, or by all of theſe Cauſes, though pretty free from Weeds, was exceeding poor, yellow, low, thin, and the Ears were very ſhort and ſmall

I intended to have taken the exact Difference there was between the Produce of this outſide Row, and one of thoſe that ſtood out of the Reach of the hoed Interval: But I was diſappointed by my Neighbour's Herd of Cows, that in the Night broke in juſt before Harveſt, and eat off almoſt all the Ears of the rich Row, doing very little Damage to the reſt, except by treading it. It muſt be from the different Taſtes, the one being ſweet, and the other bitter, that they make their Election to eat the one, and re-fuſe the other.

This accidental Obſervation was ſufficient to demonſtrate the Efficacy of deep Hoeing, which I look upon as ſynonymous to Horſe-hoeing.

I immediately ſet about contriving my limbered Hoe, finding all other Sorts inſufficient for the Exactneſs required in this hoe-ing Operation: Thoſe drawn in any other manner, when they went too far from the Row, and the Holder went to lift the Plough nearer, it would fly back again, like the Sally of a Bell, and go at no Certainty not being ſubject to the Guidance of the Holder, as the limber Hoe-plough is. The *Michaelmas* follow-ing I began my preſent Horſe-hoeing Scheme; which has never yet deceived my Expectations, when performed according to the Directions I have given my Readers. And the Practice of this Scheme proves the Advantage of deep Hoeing, by the Ends of the Ridges and Intervals; for there, whilſt the drawing Cattle go on the Headland that is higher, the Furrows are ſhallower, and the Corn of the Rows is always there viſibly poorer in proportion to that Shallowneſs.

Another Proof of the Difference there is between deep Hoeing and ſhallow, is in the Garden, where a ſquare Perch of Cabbages, the Rows of which are Three Feet aſunder; the middle Row of

them

them having the Intervals on each Side of it deeply and well dug by the Spade at the same proper time, when the rest of the Intervals are Hand-hoed; this middle Row will shew the Difference of those Two Operations: But in this must be observed what I have here before-mentioned, of turning the Back of the Spade to the Plants, to avoid the total removing them, especially in very dry Weather.

This Experiment hath been tried, and always succeeds with every one that has made the Trials.

But before any one makes his Trials of my Field-scheme, I would advise him to be Master of the Treatise, by making an *Index* himself to it: This will both direct him in his Proceedings, and shew him the Rashness of those, who go into the Practice of my Husbandry, without the necessary Preparation; for they that do so now, seem to act as rashly, as they that went into it before the Treatise was published. 'Tis reasonable to presume, that such their Practice must be either different from, or contrary to mine.

This *Index* may be also useful for discovering Pretenders by an Examination, without which, Gentlemen are liable to be imposed on by them, as I am afraid too many have been; for amongst all those who have undertaken the Management of my Scheme for Noblemen, or others, I declare I do do not know one Person that sufficiently understands it: There may be some who have seen, or perhaps performed, some of the mechanical Part; but I don't think it can be properly performed without a thorough Knowlege of the Principles, which cannot be expected of such illiterate Persons; and yet is necessary for the proper Applications in different Cases, which cannot be distinguished by Pretenders: Therefore, until the Scheme becomes common, the Management must be under the Direction of the Master himself, or of one who has past his Examination, and is faithful.

To the above Trials, I here add the following, together with some Alterations of the former.

Gentlemen who can get the *Smyrna* Wheat, I advise to make Trials of it in single Rows, of between 17 and 18 to an Acre, in this Method; there being no Partitions, the Intervals will be of the same Width as in the Ridges of 14 to an Acre, that have Partitions of Ten Inches. Thus almost all the Earth of the Ridges may be pulverized by the Hoe-plough in the Field, or by the Spade in this Trial; and very little Hand-work will be necessary for cleansing out the Weeds that come in the Rows, and on each side of them. The Land will be the fitter for a succeeding Crop of Wheat with less Harrowing. But this must be observed, that, in regard to hard Frosts in Winter, and very dry Weather in Summer, the alternate Hoeing described in the Chapter of Turneps may be proper; lest the little Earth that may be left for the Row to stand on, when the Furrows are turned from both Sides
of

of it, fhould not be fufficient to fecure the Roots from the Injuries that may happen to them by being expofed either to Froft or Drought on both Sides of the Row at the fame time.

In the Field, when the Ridges are all of an equal Breadth, the beft Way is to plant Two of the fingle Rows at once, by fetting the Two Beams of the Drill at the fame Diftance afunder, as each of the Ridges is broad ; and the Beaft that draws it muft go in the Middle of the Interval, planting a Row on each Side of it; but if the Ridges are very unequal, the Beaft (a little Horfe is beft) that draws the Drill muft go on the Top ot a Ridge, planting one Row thereon; and the Drill for this Purpofe is the fame as the Turnep-drill, except that the Beam-fhare, Seed-box, and Spindle, are the fame as thofe of the Wheat-drill; and 'tis but to take off from the Wheat-drill one of its Beams, and place it in the room of the Beam of the Turnep-drill, and placing the Crofs-piece of the Turnep-beam (fee Plate 5.) on this Beam, and alfo a fhort Wheat-hopper to be drawn by the Turnep-ftandards, fetting the Wheels near enough together ; *i. e.* as near as the Wheels of the Wheat-drill are, I mean thofe which plant Two Rows.

Two Gallons of *Smyrna* Wheat I judge will be Seed fufficient for an Acre, efpecially if planted early.

Planting one Row upon a Ridge, I think is the moft advantageous Method of all ; but, not being able to get any *Smyrna* Wheat (tho' I have been often promifed it), I have made no Trial of it; and I do not believe the Plants of any other Sort of Wheat are large enough for fuch fingle Rows.

I am not quite a Stranger to this Wheat; for I have feen the Product of it, both in the Garden, and in the Field, above Forty Years ago.

I am now making Trials, in order to know how much a fingle Row of White-cone Wheat will exceed half a double one : For this Purpofe, I caufe one Row of the double, with the Partition, to be dug out with a Spade, in Part of every Field, Two or Three Yards in a Place: Thefe I intend fhall be hoed as the double Rows are; and where the Hoe-plough doth not reach, the Spade fhall fupply its Ufe.

I do not expect this fingle Row will equal the double Row ; but I am in no doubt but that it will produce more Grain than half a double Row.

I cannot tell whether the Sort of Cone-wheat that fends out little Branches on each Side of the Ear, might not fucceed tolerably well in fingle Rows; for its Ear is, when well nourifhed, larger than the Ear of the White-cone ; tho' not near fo large as that of the *Smyrna*.

Another Experiment I propofe to be made as a Trial for the Satisfaction of fuch fceptical Gentlemen who may doubt the
Truth.

I don't know that I ever had an Acre yet, that was tolerably well managed in this Manner, but what produced much more.

C H A P.

Truth of what I have related in p. 27, 28. concerning the wonderful Effect of deep Hoeing. In a Field of very poor old decayed St. Foin, let Two or Three Perches be hedged in, in a square Piece, and Two, Three, or more Intervals, of Three or Four Feet wide each, be well pulverized by the Spade, leaving between every Two of them, Two or Three Feet of the St. Foin unmoved. Begin this Work in Summer, and repeat the Hoeing pretty often, obferving the Rules I have laid down for Hoeing the Intervals of Wheat. Let not the Back of the Spade be turned towards the unmoved St. Foin, from which it throws the Earth at the Firft time of Hoeing; which is contrary to the Firft Hoeing of Wheat with a Spade; becaufe there would otherwife be Danger of moving Wheat-roots; but there is no Danger of moving the St. Foin Roots, unlefs you wholly dig them out: Therefore the beft Way for this Hoeing is to dig with the Back of the Spade towards one or the other End of the Interval: This cuts off the feweft Roots, and covers the moft of them, and may perhaps be fometimes beft for Wheat alfo. When the Earth is turned towards the St. Foin Rows, the Spade's Face will be towards them of courfe.

Be fure to leave Four or more Feet untouched next to the Hedge that bounds the Piece, to the End that the Increafe of the hoed St. Foin may the more plainly appear by comparing its Plants with thofe that are not hoed.

If the Plants are very thick, make them thinner on one fide of an Interval; and, on the other fide, let them remain thick. You will certainly find the thin Plants moft wonderfully increafed in a Year or two, and the thick ones in proportion; and alfo the natural Grafs, and all other Vegetables that grow near to the Intervals when they are well pulverized. I am confident mine, thus managed by Ploughs, increafed fome to an Hundred, fome to a Thoufand times the Size they were of before that Pulveration.

All the Methods I have here and elfewhere defcribed for the Field, I advife to be tried in thefe few Perches for Experiments.

I think fome of thofe Ridges whereon one End is to be managed differently from the other End, fhould be longer than Six Feet; elfe the Roots of the Wheat and Weeds may fo mix, and draw Nourifhment from one another in the Middle of the Ridge, that the Difference of the Managements may not fo plainly be feen as when the Ridge is longer.

The few Perches of Land whereon any of the propofed Experiments are to be made, fhould be bounded in with dead Hedges;
and

CHAP. X.

Of SMUTTINESS.

SMUTTINESS is when the Grains of Wheat
instead of Flour, are full of a black, stinking
Powder: 'Tis a Disease of Wheat, which I don't know
is usual any-where but in cold Northern Countries;
for if it had been common in *Greece* or *Italy*, there
would probably have been some Word to express it
by, in those Languages, as well as there is for the
Blight.

I take it to be caused by cold wet Summers; and
I was confirmed in this by several Plants of Wheat,
taken up when they were in Grass in the Spring, and
placed in Troughs in my Chamber-window, with
some of the Roots in Water. These Wheat-plants
sent up several Ears each; but at Harvest, every
Grain was smutty; and I observed, none of the Ears
ever sent out any Blossom: This Smuttiness could
not be from any Moisture that descended upon it,
but from the Earth, which always kept very moist,
as in the aforesaid Mint Experiment. The Wheat-
plants in the Field, from whence these were taken,
brought very few smutty Grains, but brought much
larger Ears than these.

Whatsoever the Cause (d) be, there are but Two
Remedies proposed; and those are Brining, and
Change of Seed.

Brining of Wheat, to cure or prevent Smuttiness
(as I have been credibly informed), was accidentally

and should not be situate within Three or Four Poles of a live
Hedge or Tree.

The Three Instruments to be used in these unexpensive Trials,
are, the Spade, to supply the Use of the Plough and Hoe plough;
the Hand-hoe; and a Rake, instead of Harrows.

(d) The largest grained, plump, fat Wheat, is more liable to
Smuttiness, than small-grained thin Wheat.

discovered

diſcovered about Seventy Years ago, in the following Manner ; *viz.* A Ship-load of Wheat was ſunk near *Briſtol* in Autumn, and afterwards at Ebbs all taken up, after it had been ſoaked in Sea-water; but it being unfit for making of Bread, a Farmer ſowed ſome of it in a Field ; and when it was found to grow very well, the whole Cargo was bought at a low Price by many Farmers, and all of it ſown in different Places. At the following Harveſt, all the Wheat in *England* happened to be ſmutty, except the Produce of this brined Seed, and that was all clean from Smuttineſs. This Accident has been ſufficient to juſtify the Practice of Brining ever ſince in all the adjacent Parts, and in moſt Places in *England.*

I knew Two Farmers, whoſe Farms lay intermixed ; they bought the ſame Seed together, from a very good Change of Land, and parted every Load betwixt them in the Field. The oldeſt Farmer believed Brining to be but a Fancy, and ſowed his Seed unbrined ; the other brined all his Part of Seed, and had not a ſmutty Ear in his Crop; but the old Farmer's Crop was very ſmutty.

Wheat for Drilling muſt have no other Brine, than what is made of pure Salt; for if there be any Brine of Meat amongſt it (*e*), the Greaſe will not ſuffer the Wheat to be dry enough to be drilled.

If Seed-wheat be ſoaked in Urine, it will not grow ; or if only ſprinkled with it, it will moſt of it die, unleſs planted preſently.

The moſt expeditious Way of brining Wheat for the Drill, is to make a very ſtrong Brine ; and when the Wheat is laid on an Heap, ſprinkle or lave it therewith ; then turn it with a Shovel, and lave on more Brine ; turn it again with a Shovel, until, by many Repetitions of this, the Wheat be all equally

---

(*e*) Urine alſo makes the Wheat ſo greaſy, that it will not be dry time enough to be drilled.

wet.

wet. Next, fift on Quick-lime through a Sieve ; turn the Wheat with a Shovel, and fift on more Lime ; repeat this Sifting and Turning many times, which will make it dry enough to be drilled immediately ; and this has been found fufficient to preferve uninfected Wheat from the Smut in a bad Year, the Seed being changed.

To dry it, we ufe *(f)* Quick-lime (that is, unflacked), which, beaten to Powder, and fifted thereon, confines the Brine to the Surfaces of the Grains, and fuffers none of it to be exhaled by the Air : But when Lime has been long flacked, and is grown weak, 'tis unfit for this Purpofe.

Smutty Seed-wheat, tho' brined, will produce a fmutty Crop, unlefs the Year prove very favourable.

For 'tis to be known, that favourable Years will cure the Smut, as unkind ones will caufe it : Elfe, before Brining was ufed, and the bad Years had caufed all the Wheat in *England* to be fmutty, they muft have brought their Seed from Foreign Countries, or never have had any clean Wheat : Therefore 'tis certain, that kind Years will cure the Smut : 'Tis therefore to prevent the Injury of a bad Year, that we plant clean Seed, and well brined.

But of the Two Remedies againft Smuttinefs, a proper Change of Seed fome think the moft certain.

A very worthy Gentleman affures me, that fince he has found out a Place that affords a Change of Seed proper to his Land, which is for thefe Ten

---

(f) But if this doth not afford Powder enough, the Pieces muft be flacked immediately before ufing ; for if the Lime lie long after it is flacked (efpecially that made of Chalk), it will become weak, and lofe moft of its drying Quality.

Some Farmers ufe only to boil the ftrongeft Quick-lime in Water, with which, inftead of Brine, they fprinkle their Wheat, affirming it to be as effectual as that for preventing the Smut : But this not being within the Compafs of my own Experience, I am doubtful of it ; yet I wifh it may be found effectual, becaufe it would fave Trouble to the fower, and more to the Driller.

Years paft, he never had a Smutty Ear in any of his Crops (and he never brines nor limes it), tho' all other Wheat have been often fmutty throughout his Neighbourhood every wet Year, tho' brined and limed. He fays, the Perfon who furnifhes him with this Seed, is very curious in changing his Seed alfo every Year.

This gives a Sufpicion, that our drowned Wheat at *Briftol* might poffibly be Foreign; and then might not have been fmutty the next Year, tho' it had not been foaked in the Sea-water.

The Wheat fown by the Two Farmers aforementioned might be from a good Change of Land, but the Seed not changed the precedent Year; and then it might be no more infected, than what the Brine and Lime did cure.

To know what Changes are beft to prevent Smuttinefs of Wheat, we muft confult the moft Experienced; and they tell us, that the ftrong Clay Land is beft to be fent to for Seed-wheat, whatever Sort of Land it be to be fowed upon; a White-clay is a good Change for a Red-clay, and a Red for a White. That from any ftrong Land is better than from a light Land; and the old Rhyme is, that Sand is a Change for no Land. But from whatever Land the Seed be taken, if it was not changed the preceding Year, it may poffibly be infected; and then there may be Danger, tho' we have it immediately from never fo proper a Soil.

The ftrongeft Objection that has been yet made againft conftant annual Crops of Wheat, is, that thofe Grains of the precedent Crop which happen to fhed, and grow in the following Crop, will be in Danger of Smuttinefs, for want of changing thofe individual Seeds.

All I can fay in Anfwer is, that during thefe Five Years, which is all the time I have had thefe annual Crops, this objected Inconvenience never has hap-

pened to me, even when a precedent Crop has been
fmutty.

The Reafon I take to be, that a Crop very early
planted is not fo apt to be fmutty ; and if it be not
planted early, the Grains that are fhed grow, and
are killed before, or at the time of planting the
next Crop.   This faves a Crop following a fmutty
one (which is always occafioned by bad Seed, or bad
Ordering) ; and when the former Crop was planted
with good Seed well ordered, the fhattered Grains of
that may produce clean Wheat the Second Year ;
and 'tis very unlikely, that any Breed of thefe
Grains fhould remain to grow in the Crop the
Third Year.

C H A P. XI.

Of BLIGHT.

WHEAT is blighted at Two Seafons ; Firft,
when in the Bloffom ; and then its Generation is prevented and many of the Hufks are empty
in the Ear, the Grains not being impregnated.

Secondly, Wheat is blighted, when the Grains are
brought to the time of their Maturity, but are light,
and of little Value for making of Bread ; becaufe
they are not well filled with Flour.

The Firft cannot happen in *England* by the Froft
becaufe the Winters do not fuffer it to grow fo
much, as to come into Bloffom before the Month
of *June* ; but they are long continual Rains that rot
or chill the Bloffoms, and prevent their Fertility.
Yet this is what feldom happens to any great Degree.   Wheat that grows in open Fields has fome
Advantage from the Wind, that diflodges the Water
fooner

sooner from the Ears, than it can do in sheltry Places; and Lammas Wheat does not hold the Drops of Rain so long as the Bearded (or Cone) Wheat, which received very great Damage by this sort of Blight in the Year 1725, the like never having been heard of before.

The Second sort of Blight, *viz.* from light Ears, is that which is most frequent, and more general: This brings the greatest Scarcity of Wheat. The Cause is plainly Want of Nourishment to perfect the Grain, by whatever means that Want is occasioned.

Several Accidents kill the Plants, or injure their Health, and then the Grains are not filled; as Lightning, the Effects whereof may be observed by the blackish Spots and Patches in Fields of Wheat, especially in such Years as have more of it than usual. Against this there is no Defence.

The other Causes of the Blight, which are most general, and do the most Damage, may, in some measure, be prevented.

One Cause is the lodging or falling of Corn; for then the Stalks are broken near the Ground, whereby many of the Vessels are so pressed, that the Juices cannot pass them; and then the free Circulation is hindered; the Chyle cannot mount in sufficient Quantity to be purified, and turned into Sap; the Defect whereof makes the Plants become languid, and only just able to live; they have Strength enough to linger on to the time of their Period, as in very old Age, but not to bring their Fruit, which is the Grain, to its natural Bulk, nor to fill it with Flour: and the sooner the Stalks fall, the less and thinner the Grain will be.

Hence it often happens, that when Tillage, Dung, and good Land have brought a Crop of Wheat, that in the Months of *April* and *May* promise to yield the Owner Five or Six Quarters on an Acre, then in *June* it falls down, and scarce

affords

affords Five or Six Bushels ; and that perhaps is so thin and lank, that the Expence of reaping and threshing it may overbalance its Value.

That the falling down of Wheat does cause the Ruin of the Crop, is well known ; but what causes it to fall, is not so plain.

And, without knowing the true Causes, 'tis not likely that a Remedy should be found against the Disease.

I take this Weakness of the Stalks, which occasions their falling, to proceed from want of Nourishment, want of Air, want of the Sun's Rays, or of all Three.

One Argument, that it lodges for want of Nourishment, is, that a rich Acre has maintain'd a Crop of Five Quarters standing, when another poorer Acre was not able to support a Crop from falling, which was but large enough to have brought Three Quarters, if it had stood : and this in the same Year, and on the same Situation.   And 'tis very plain, that if one Acre was twice as rich as the other, it must be able to nourish Five Quarters better than the other could nourish Three Quarters.

Air is necessary to the Life and Health of all Plants, tho' in very different Degrees : Aquatics, which live under Water, are content with as little Air, as their Companions the Fishes.

But Wheat, being a terrestrial Plant, (tho' in Winter it will live many Days under Water, whilst the slow Motion of its Sap gives it litle or no Increase), requires a free open Air, and does not succeed so well in low sheltery Places, as upon higher and opener Situations ; where the Air has has a greater Motion, and can more easily carry off the Recrements from the Leaves, after it has shaken off the Dews and Rains, which would otherwise suffocate the Plants ; and therefore the Leaves are made so susceptible of Motion from the Air, which frees them from

L   the

the Dews, that would ftop in the Recrements at the *Veficulæ* of the Leaves, but fhaken down will nourifh the Plants at the Roots: The want of this Motion weakening the Wheat, 'tis (as Animals in the like fickly Cafe are) the more unable to ftand, and the more liable to be prefs'd down by the Weight of Rain-water, and more unable to rife up again when down: All which Evils are remov'd by the free Motion of the Air, which fhakes off both Dews and Rains, and thus contributes to prevent the falling (or lodging) of Wheat.

A great Quantity alfo of the Sun's Rays is necef-fary to keep Wheat ftrong, and in Health; and in *Egypt*, and other hot Countries, it is not fo apt to fall, as it is when fown in Northern Climates, tho' the Produce of the South be the greateft (*a*).

It may be obferv'd, that every Leaf is inferted into a Sort of Knot, which probably delivers the Sap to be depurated at the *Veficulæ* of the Leaves, and then receives it back again for the Nourifhment of the Plant, doing for that Purpofe the Office of an Heart: But the Sun with his Rays fupplies the Part of Pulfe, to keep the Sap in Motion, and carry on its Circulation, inftead of the Heart's *Syftole* and *Diaftole*. Wheat, being doubtlefs originally a Native of a hot Country, requires by its Conftitution a con-fiderable Degree of Heat to bring it to Perfection; and if much of that Degree be wanting, the Wheat will be the weaker; and when the Solar Rays cannot reach the lower Parts of the Stalks, the loweft Leaves and Knots cannot do their Office; for which Reafon the Chyle muft mount higher before it be made into Sap, and there muft be then a greater Mixture of crude Chyle next to the Ground, as by the white

(*a*) This proves that the Crop doth not lodge on account of its Bignefs.

Colour

Colour it appears *(b)*. By this Means that Part, which, if it had a due Share of the Sun's Influence, would be harden'd like a Bone or Spring, for the Support of the Stalks, for lack of that, becomes more like to a Cartilage, soft and weak, unable to sustain the Weight of the bending Ear, which, having its greatest *Impetus* against this Part, which is most feeble to resist it, it yields, and lets it fall to the Ground; and then the Grain will be blighted.

There is also another Cause of the Blight; and that is, the Wheat's coming too late into Blossom.   The usual Time is the Beginning of *June*; and if it be later, the Days shorten so fast after the Solstice, that the Autumn of the Year hastening the Autumn of the Wheat's Life, the full Time of its Pregnancy *(c)* is not accomplish'd; and then its Fruit, which is the Grain, becomes as it were abortive, and not full-grown. This Time betwixt the Generation, Blossoming, and the Maturity of the Grain, is, or ought to be, about Two Months.

Therefore 'tis advantageous to hasten, what we can, the Time of Blossoming, and to protract the Time of

---

(b) But now I suspect this to be a Mistake, it being more likely, that the white Colour of the Rind is owing to the Absence of the Sun and free Air, than to the Chyle, as the Skin of those Parts of our own Bodies that are concealed from them, is whiter than of those which are exposed to them, though no Chyle-vessel comes near our Skin.

(c) *Ut enim Mulieres habent ad Partum Dies certos, sic Arbores ac Fruges.* Varro, *Lib.* 1. *Cap.* 44.

Mense Maio florent; sic Frumenta, & Ordeum, & quæ sunt Seminis singularis, Octo diebus florebunt, & deinde per Dies 40. *grandescunt Flore deposito usque ad Maturitatis Eventum.* Palladius, *Pag.* 114, 115.

Quindecim Diebus esse in Vaginis, Quindecim florere, Quindecim exarescere, cum sit maturum Frumentum. Varro, *Lib.* 1. *Cap.* 32.

But the different Heat that there is in different Climates, may alter both the Time that Plants continue in Blossom, and the Time betwixt the Blossoming and the Ripening.

Ripening:

Ripening: And 'tis obferv'd, that the earlieft fown Wheat generally efcapes the Blight the beft, becaufe it comes firft into Bloffom.

Feeding down the Wheat with Sheep prevents the Blight, by doing what the Blight wou'd do, if the Wheat fell down, · *i. e.* caufes the Ears to be light *(a)*.

And we find, that thofe who practife this Method of feeding their Wheat with Sheep in the Spring, to prevent the lodging of it, have moft commonly their Straw weak, and Ears light.

Thefe, inftead of making the Stalks ftrong enough to fupport heavy Ears, make the Ears light enough to be fupported by weak Stalks. They know that heavy Ears make the greateft Crop; and yet they ftill hope to have it from light ones.

They *caufe* the *Blight* by the very means they make ufe of to *cure* it.

This feeding of Wheat much retards the Time of its bloffoming; and that it may bloffom early, is one chief End of fowing it early, to prevent the Blight. But when it is fed, what the Plants fend up next is but a Sort of fecond or latter Crop, which has longer to ftand than the firft would have required, and is always weaker than the firft Crop would have been; and the longer time it has to continue on the Ground, the more Nourifhment is required to maintain it; and yet, as has been fhewn, the longer it has been fown, the more the Earth has loft of its Nonrifhment; and

_(a)_ Heavy Ears never fall. If they did, that would not make them light. Wheat falls fometimes whilft 'tis in Grafs, and before it comes into Ear; fo far are the Ears from caufing it to fall. This was proved by my whole Crop the laft Harveft, and particularly by the *Meafured Acre*, the Ears of which, tho' prodigious large and heavy, were none of them lodg'd, when thofe of fown Wheat on the other Side of the Hedge were fallen down flat, and lodg'd on the Ground.

confe-

confequently, the Crop will be yet weaker, and in more Danger of the ftarving Blight (*b*).

The moft effectual Remedy againft the Blight is that which removes all its Cafes (except fuch extraordinary ones as Lightning); as,

First, *Want of Nouriſhment.*

The Horfe-hoe will, in wide Intervals, give Wheat, throughout all the Stages of its Life, as much Nouriſhment as the difcreet Hoer pleafes.

Secondly, *Want of Air.*

Air, being a Fluid, moves moft freely in a right or ftrait Line ; for there the feweft of its Parts meet with any Refiftance ; as a ftrait River runs fwifter than a crooked one, from an equal Declivity ; becaufe more of the Water ftrikes againft the Banks at

(*b*) I am fure, that whenever Sheep break into my drill'd Wheat in the Spring, it leffens my Crop half, juft as far as they eat the Rows. There are feveral Reafons why Sheep are more injurious to drilled Wheat than fown : I would not therefore be underftood to decry the Practice of feeding fown Wheat, when the Thicknefs and Irregularity of its Plants make it neceffary : I have only endeavoured to ſhew, that that Practice is founded upon a falfe Theory. For, if Wheat fell down by reafon of the Luxuriance of it; a Plant of it would be more likely to fall when fingle, and at a great Diftance from every other Plant, than when near to other Plants, becaufe fuch a fingle Plant is *(cæteris paribus)* always the moft luxuriant ; and I have not feen fuch a one fall (except Birds pull down the Ears), but have obferved the contrary, though its Ears are the largeft.

The Subject I write on is Drilling and Hoeing, and of whatfoever elfe I think relates to the Practice or Theory thereof ; which obliges me to advife againft Drilling too thick upon any Sort of Land ; but more efpecially upon very rich Land : For though I have no fuch Land, yet I apprehend, that a too great Number of Plants may overftock the Rows, and caufe them to be liable to fome of the Inconveniences of fown Wheat ; and in fuch a Cafe, perhaps, Sheep may be rather ufeful than prejudicial to the drilled Wheat ; but of this I have had no Experience : And if it ſhould be too thick, it will be owing to the Fault of the Manager or Driller ; but, I fuppofe, it might be a better Remedy to cut out the fuperfluous Plants by the Hand-hoe, in the manner that fuperfluous Turneps are hoed out.

L 3

the

the Turnings, and is there fomewhat retarded : and the reft moving no fafter than in the ftrait River, the whole Stream of the crooked muft be flower in its Courfe, than that of the ftrait River.

The Air cannot pafs thro' fown Corn in a direct Line, becaufe it muft ftrike againft, and go round every Plant, they ftanding all in the Way of its Courfe, which muft ftop its Current near the Earth.

And the Air amongft fown Corn is like Water amongft Reeds or Ofiers in the Side of a River; it is fo ftopp'd in its Courfe, that it almoft becomes an Eddy; and fince Air is about Eight hundred Times lighter than Water, we may fuppofe its Current thro' the Corn is more eafily retarded, efpecially near the Earth, where the Corn has occafion for the greateft Quantity of Air to pafs : For, tho' the upper Part of the Wheat be not able to ftop a flow Current of Air, yet it does fo much raife even a fwift one, as to throw it off from the Ground, and hinder it from reaching the lower Parts of the Stalks, where the Air muft therefore remain, in a manner, ftagnant; and the thicker the Wheat is, where it ftands promifcu-oufly, the lefs Change of Air can it have, tho' the greater the Number of the Stalks is, the more frefh Air they muft require.

But the confufed Manner in which the Plants of fown Wheat ftand, is fuch, that they muft all oppofe the free Entrance of Air amongft them, from what-ever Point of the Compafs it comes.

Now it is quite otherwife with Wheat drill'd regu-larly with wide Intervals; for therein the Current of Air may pafs freely (like Water in a ftrait River, where there is no Refiftance), and communicate its Nitre to the lower as well as upper Leaves, and carry off the Recrements they emit, not fuffering the Plants to be weaken'd, as an Animal is, when his Lungs are forc'd to take back their own Expirations, if debarr'd from a fufficient Supply of frefh untainted Air. And

this

this Benefit of frefh Air is plentifully, and pretty
equally, diftributed to every Row in a Field of ho'd
Wheat.

Thirdly, *Want of the Sun's Rays.*

Sown Wheat-plants, by their irregular Pofition,
may be faid to ftand in one another's Light, for want
of which they are apt to fall.

'Tis true the whole Field of Plants receive the fame
Quantity of Sun-beams amongft them, whether they
ftand confufedly, or in Order: But there is a vaft
Difference in the Diftribution of them ; for none or
the very leaft Share of Beams is obtain'd by thofe
Parts which need the greateft Share, in the confufed
Plants. And when the crural Parts, that fhould fupport the whole Body of every Plant, are depriv'd of
their due Share of what is fo neceffary to ftrengthen
them, the Plants (like Animals in the fame Cafe) are
unable to ftand.

But in drill'd Wheat, where the Plants ftand in a
regular Order, the Sun-beams are more duly diftributed to all Parts of the Plants in the Ranks; for
which Way foever the Rows are directed, if they be
ftrait, the Rays muft, fome time of the Day, fall on
the Intervals, and be reflected by the Ground, whence
the lower Parts of the Wheat-ftalks muft receive the
greater Share of Heat, being neareft to the Point of
Incidence, having no Weeds to fhadow them.

As to that Caufe of the Blight, *viz.* the Wheat's
dying before the full Time of its Pregnancy be ac-
complifh'd ; the Hoe removes all the Objections
againft planting early, and then it will bloffom the
earlier : And it has vifibly kept Wheat green a whole
Week longer, than unho'd Wheat adjoining to it,
planted the fame Day.

The Antients were perfect Mafters of the Vine-
Hufbandry, which feems to have fo engrofs'd their ru-
ral Studies, that it did not allow them fo much Re-
flection, as to apply the Ufe of thofe Methods to the

L 4   Increafe

Increafe of Bread, which they had difcover'd to be moft beneficial for the Increafe of Wine.   One Method was, to hoe the Vines after they had bloffom'd, in order to fill the Fruit, as in *Columella*, Lib. iv. Cap. 28. *Convenit tum crebris Foffionibus implere: nam fit uberior Pulverationibus.*   And if what *Palladius* fays, *Tit.* ix. be true of the Sarritions and Sarculations in the Month of *January*, and that if Beans do twice undergo that fcratching Operation, they will produce much Fruit, and fo large as to fill the Bufhel almoft as full when fhal'd as unfhal'd.

Faba, fi bis farculetur, proficiet, & multum Fructum & maximum afferet, ut ad Menfuram Modii complendi fresa propemodum ficut integra refpondeat.

This is to be done when Beans are Four Fingers high, and Corn when it has Four or Five Leaves to a Plant; even then the Harrowing-work, tho' it tore up fome of the Plants, yet it was obferv'd to do Good againft the Blight.

. *Si ficcas Segetes farculaveris, aliquid contra Rubiginem praeftitifti, maxime fi Ordeum ficcum farrietur.*

When the Antients obferv'd this, 'tis a Wonder they did not plant their Corn fo as to be capable of receiving this Benefit in Perfection.   They might have imagin'd, that what was effectual againft the Blight, when the Corn was in Grafs, muft, in all Probability, be much more effectual when in Ear.

But the moft general Blight that happens to Wheat in cold Climates, is caufed by Infects, which (fome think) are brought in the Air by an Eaft Wind accompanied with Moifture, a little before the Grain is filling with that milky Juice, which afterwards hardens into Flour.   Thefe Infects depofit their Eggs within the outer Skin (or Rind) of the Stalks; and when the young ones are hatched, they feed on the *Parenchyma,* and eat off many of the Veffels which fhould make and convey this Juice; and then the Grain will be more or lefs thin, in Proportion to the

Number

Number of Veſſels eaten, and as the Inſects happen
to come earlier or later; for ſometimes they come ſo
late, that the Grain is ſufficiently fill'd with the ſaid
milky Juice before the Veſſels are eaten; and then,
tho' the Straw appear thro' a Microſcope to have its
Veſſels very much eaten and torn, and to be full of
black Spots (which Spots are nothing elſe but the
Excrements of thoſe young Inſects), yet the Grain is
plump, and not blighted, there being an Obſervation,
That the early ſown Wheat generally eſcapes this
Blight.   And it has been ſeen, where one Part of a
Field is ſown earlier than the other Part, without any
other Difference than the Time of ſowing, that the
Grain of the lateſt ſown has been much blighted, and
the Grain of the earlier has eſcaped the Blight, tho'
the Straw of both were equally eaten by the Inſects.
Hence it may be inferr'd, that the Milk in the one
had receiv'd all the Nouriſhment neceſſary to its due
Conſiſtence, before the Veſſels were deſtroy'd; but,
in the other, the Veſſels, which ſhould have continued the Supply of Nouriſhment for thickening the
Milk, being ſpoil'd before they have finiſh'd that
Office, it remains too thin; and then the Grain, when
it hardeneth, ſhrinks up, and is blighted; yet the
Grain of one and the other are equally plump until
they become hard: The Difference therefore is only
in the Thickneſs of the Milk, that in the blighted
being more watery than the other.

The chief Argument to prove, that theſe Inſects are
brought by an Eaſt Wind, is, that the Wheat on the
Eaſt Sides of Hedges are much blighted, when that
on the Weſt Sides is not hurt: And as to the Objection, that they are bred in the Earth, and crawl thence
up the Stalks of the Wheat, becauſe ſome Land is
much more ſubject to produce blighted Wheat than
other Land is; perhaps this Difference may be chiefly
owing to the different Situation of thoſe Lands, as
they are oppoſed to the *Eaſt*, or to the *Weſt*.

Another

Another Cause why some Wheat is more blighted than other Wheat on the same Land, is, the different Condition in which the Insects find it; for the Rind of that which is very strong and flourishing (*c*) is soft and tender; into this they can easily penetrate to lay their Eggs; but the Wheat that is poor and yellow, has an hard tough Skin (or Rind), into which the Insects are not able to bore for the Intromission of their Eggs, and therefore can do it no Mischief. It would be in vain to advise to prevent the Blight, by striving to make the Wheat poor; for tho' Poverty may preserve Wheat from this Blight, as well as it does People from the Gout, yet that is a Remedy which few take willingly against either of these Diseases: But this, I think, might be possible to remedy it, if we could, from the strongest Wheat, take away so much Nourishment as to turn its Colour (*d*) a little yellowish just before the Insects come (*e*) which I suppose to be in *June*, after the Ear is out, or at least fully formed.

Yet this can only be done in wide Intervals; for, unless the fine Earth can be thrust to some considerable Distance from the Roots after they are cut off, they will soon shoot out again, and reach it, becoming more vigorous thereby.

In dry Summers this Misfortune seldom happens, much Heat, and very little Moisture, being most agreeable to the Constitution of Wheat; for then its Rind

---

(*c*) Some Sort of Land is more subject to this Blight than others; in such, Lammas Wheat must by no means be drill'd late, and too thin, lest it should not tiller till late in the Spring; and then, for want of a sufficient Quantity of Stalks to dispense with all the Nourishment rais'd by the Hoe, may become too vigorous and luxuriant, and be the more liable to the Injury of the Blight of Insects.

(*d*) But this is a very difficult Matter.

(*e*) Whither those Insects go, or where they reside, from the Time of their eating their Way out of the Straw, until they return the next Year, I cannot learn.

is more firm and hard, as it is, on the contrary, made more foft and fpongy by too much Moifture.

The moft eafy and fure Remedy, that I have yet found againft the Injury of thefe Infects, is, to plant a Sort of Wheat that is leaft liable to be hurt by them; *viz.* The *White-cone* (or bearded) *Wheat*, which has its Stalk or Straw like a Rufh, not hollow, but full of Pith (except near the lower Part, and there 'tis very thick and ftrong): 'Tis probable it has Sap-Veffels that lie deeper, fo as the young Infects cannot totally deftroy them, as they do in other Wheat: For when the Straw has the black Spots, which fhew that the Infects have been there bred, yet the Grain is plump, when the Grey-cone and Lammas Wheat mixt with it are blighted. This Difference might have been from the different times of ripening, this being ripe about a Week earlier than the Grey-cone, and later than the Lammas: But its being planted together both early and late, and at all Times of the Wheat-feed Time, and this White-cone always efcaping with its Grain unhurt, is an Argument, that 'tis naturally fortify'd againft the Injury of thefe Infects, which in wet Summers are fo pernicious to other Sorts of Wheat; and I can impute it to no other Caufe than the different Deepnefs of the Veffels, the Straw of other Wheat being very much thinner, and hollow from Top to Bottom; this having a fmall Hollow at Bottom, and there the Thicknefs betwixt the outer Skin and the Cavity is more than double to that in other Sorts of Wheat; fo that I imagine, the Infects reach only the outermoft Veffels, and enough of the inner Veffels are left untouch'd to fupply the Grain.

This Wheat makes very good Bread, if the Miller does not grind it too fmall, or the Baker make his Dough too hard, it requiring to be made fofter than that of other Flour.

A Bufhel of this White-cone Wheat will make more Bread than a Bufhel of Lammas, and of the
fame

fame Goodnefs ; but it gives a little yellow Caft to the Bread.

Another Sort of lodging Blight there is, which fome call *Moar-Loore*, and moftly happens on light Land · This is when the Earth, finking away from the Roots, leaves the Bottom of the Stalk higher than the fubfided Ground ; and then the Plant, having only thefe naked Roots to fupport it (for which they are too weak), falls down to the Earth.

To remedy this, turn a fhallow Furrow againft the Rows, when they are ftrong enough to bear it, and when the Mould is very fine and dry ; then the Motion of the Stalks by the Wind will caufe fuch Earth to run through the Rows, and fettle about the Roots, and cover them (*f*).

I have never feen any drill'd Wheat fo much fpoil'd by falling, as fown Wheat fometimes is. The drill'd never falls fo clofe to the Ground, but that the Air enters into Hollows that are under it, and the Wind keeps the Ears in Motion. Notwithftanding all the Precaution that can be ufed, in fome unfeafonable Years Wheat will be blighted : I have known fuch a general Blight, when fome of my Lammas Wheat, planted late on blighting Land, was blighted, amongft the reft of my Neighbours, by the Infects, but the Grain of the fown Wheat was vaftly more injured

---

(*f*) Some Land is very fubject to the Misfortune of expofing the Roots, and therefore is lefs proper for Wheat ; for when the Roots are left bare to the Air, they will be fhrivelled, and unable to fupport the Plants : And on fuch Land the Wheat plants have all fallen down, though in Number and Bignefs not fufficient to have produced the Fourth Part of a tolerable Crop, if they had ftood. I am inclined to believe, that a thorough Tillage might be a Remedy to fuch a loofe hollow Soil; for 'tis certain to a Demonftration, that it would render it more *denfe*, and increafe its fpecific Gravity : But to enrich it sufficiently without Manure, the Tillage muft pulverize it much more minutely, and expofe it longer, than is required for the ftrongeft Land : The Fold alfo will be very helpful on fuch hollow Land.

than

than that of the drill'd: The former was fo *light*, that the greateft Part was blown away in winnowing, and the Remainder fo *bad*, that it was not fit to make Bread: The drill'd made as good Bread, and had as much Flour in it, as the fown Wheat had, that was not blighted; for the Grains of the drill'd were much larger than thofe of the fown; being form'd to have been twice as big as the Grains of Wheat gene-rally are, had they not been blighted.

C H A P. XII.

Of S t. F o i n.

ST. F o i n, from the Country we brought it from, is call'd *French Grafs*: And for its long Conti-ance, fome having lafted Forty Years, 'tis call'd *Everlafting Grafs*, tho' it be not ftrictly a *Gramen*.

'Tis call'd in *French, Sain Foin*, i. e. *Sanum Fæ-num*, from its Quality of Wholfomenefs, beyond the other artificial Graffes, green and dry. 'Tis alfo call'd *Sanctum Fænum*, Holy Hay.

'Tis a Plant fo generally known to every Body, that there is no need to give any formal Defcription of that Part of it which appears above-ground, It has many red Flowers, fometimes leaving Ears Five or Six Inches long: I have meafured the Stalks, and found them above Five Feet long, tho' they are com-monly but about Two Feet.

The Reafon why *St. Foin* will, in poor Ground, make a Forty times greater Increafe than the natural Turf, is the prodigious Length (*a*) of its perpendi-cular

---

(*a*) There is a vulgar Opinion, that *St. Foin* will not fucceed on any Land, where there is not an under *Stratum* of Stone or Chalk,

cular Tap-root: It is faid to defcend Twenty or
Thirty Feet. I have been inform'd, by a Perfon of
undoubted Credit, that he has broken off one of thefe
Roots in a Pit, and meafured the Part broken off,
and found it fourteen Feet.

This Tap-root has alfo a Multitude of very long
horizontal Roots at the upper Part thereof, which fill
all the upper *Stratum*, or Staple of the Ground; and
of thoufands of *St. Foin* Roots I have feen taken up,
I never found one that was without horizontal Roots
near the Surface, after one Summer's Growth; and
do much wonder how Mr. *Kerkham* fhould be fo mif-
taken, as to think they have none fuch.

Alfo thefe Tap-roots have the horizontal ones all
the Way down; but as they defcend, they are ftill
fhorter and fhorter, as the uppermoft are always the
longeft.

Any dry Ground may be made to produce this
noble Plant, be it never fo poor; but the richeft Soil
will yield the moft of it, and the beft.

Chalk, to ftop the Roots from running deep; elfe, they fay, the
Plants fpend themfelves in the Roots only, and cannot thrive in
thofe Parts of them which are above the Ground. I am almoft
afhamed to give an Anfwer to this.

'Tis certain that every Plant is nourifhed from its Roots (as an
Animal is by its Guts); and the more and larger Roots it has, the
more Nourifhment it receives, and profpers in proportion to it.
St. Foin always fucceeds where its Roots run deep; and when it
does not fucceed, it never lives to have long Roots; neither can there
ever be found a Plant of it, that lives fo long as to root deep in
a Soil that is improper for it: Therefore 'tis amazing to hear fuch
Reafoning from Men.

An under *Stratum* of very ftrong Clay, or other Earth, which
holds Water, may make a Soil improper for it; becaufe the
Water kills the Root, and never fuffers it to grow to Perfection,
or to attain to its natural Bulk. The beft *St. Foin* that ever I faw,
had nothing in the Soil to obftruct the Roots, and it has been
found to have Roots of a prodigious Depth. If there be Springs
near (or within feveral Feet of) the Surface of the Soil, *St. Foin*
will die therein in Winter, even after it has been vigorous in the
firft Summer; and alfo after it hath produced a great Crop in the
fecond Summer.

If

If you venture to plant it with the Drill, according to the Method wherein I have always had the beſt Succeſs ; let the Land be well prepared before you plant it. The Seed, if not well ordered, will very little of it grow ; therefore 'tis convenient to try it in the manner mention'd in the Chapter of *Hoeing*; where are alſo Directions to find the proper Quantity and Depth to plant it at : I have obſerv'd, that the Heads of theſe Seeds are ſo large, and their Necks ſo weak *(b)*, that if they lie much more than half an Inch *(c)* deep, they are not able to riſe through the incumbent Mould ; or if they are not cover'd, they will be malted *(d)*. A Buſhel to an Acre is full twenty Seeds to each ſquare Foot, in all I try'd ; but there is odds in the Largeneſs of it, which makes ſome Difference in the Number.

The worſt Seaſons to plant it are the Beginning of Winter, and in the Drought of Summer. The beſt Seaſon is early in the Spring.

'Tis the ſtronger when planted alone, and when no other Crop is ſown with it *(f)*.

If

(b) The Kernel or Seed, being much ſwollen in the Ground, I call the Head : This, when it reaches above the Ground, opens in the Middle, and is formed into the Two firſt Leaves ; the Huſk always remaining at the ſame Depth at which it is cover'd : The String that paſſes from the Huſk to the Head, is the Neck ; which, when by its too great Length 'tis unable to ſupport the Head till it reaches to the Air, riſes up, and doubles above it; and when it does ſo, the Head, being turn'd with its Top downwards, never can riſe any higher, but there rots in the Ground.

(c) In very light Land the Seed will come up from a greater Depth ; but the moſt ſecure Way is, not to ſuffer it to be cover'd deep in any Land.

(d) We ſay it is malted, when it lies above-ground, and ſends out its Root, which is killed by the Air. And whether we plant *bad* Seed that does not grow, or *good* Seed buried or malted, the Conſequence will be much the ſame, and the Ground may be equally underſtock'd with Plants.

(f) The worſt Crop that can be ſown amongſt *St. Foin*, is Clover or Rye-Graſs ; Barley or Oats continue but a little while

If Barley, Oats, or other Corn fown with St. Foin, do lodge, it will kill *(g)* the young St. Foin that is under it: But then fo great a Crop of Corn will certainly anfwer the very little Expence of drilling the St. Foin again, either the next Year, or as foon as the Corn is off the Ground.

St. Foin drill'd betwixt Rows of Barley or Oats, always is ftronger than when drill'd amongft Corn that is fown at random; and therefore is in lefs Danger of being kill'd by the Lodging of the Corn; neither is the Corn in Rows fo liable to fall as the other.

The Quantity of Seed to be drill'd on an Acre will depend, in great Meafure, upon the Goodnefs of it; for in fome bad Seed, not more than One in Ten will grow; and in good Seed, not One in Twenty will mifs; which is beft known by ftripping off the Hufks of a certain Number of Seeds, and planting the Kernels in Earth, in the manner directed for

to rob it; but the other artificial Graffes rob it for a Year or Two, until the artificial Pafture is near loft; and then the St. Foin never arrives to half the Perfection as it will do when no other Grafs is fown amongft it.

The Injury thefe Hay-crops do to the St. Foin is beft feen where fome Parts of the fame Field have them, and the other Parts are without them.

(g) When Barley, among which the St. Foin is planted in a dry Summer, is great, there are few Farmers that know till the next Spring, whether the St. Foin fucceeds or not; becaufe the young Plants are not then vifible; unlefs it be to thofe who are accuftomed to obferve them in all the Degrees of their Growth. I have feen a Field of Ten Acres of fuch, wherein, after the Barley was carried off, nothing appeared like St. Foin; but when by the Print of the Chanels I fearched diligently, I found the fmall St. Foin Plants thick enough in the Rows; they had no Leaves, they being cut off by the Scythe; no Part of them that was left had any Green Colour; but from the Plants there came out many Sprigs like Hog's Briftles, or like the Beard of Barley: This whole Piece of St. Foin fuceeeded fo well, that the Third Year its Crop was worth Three Pounds *per* Acre, the Land being good.

finding

finding the proper Depth to plant at, which, in this
Cafe, let be half an Inch : This being done, the
Quality of the Seed will be known.   But until frequent Trials have furnifh'd Experience enough to
the Planter to know the Difference, let him obferve,
that the following are good Signs ; *viz.* The Hufk
of a bright Colour, the Kernel plump, of a light-
grey or blue Colour, or fometimes of a fhining black ;
yet the Seed may be good, tho' the Hufk is of a dark
Colour, if that is caufed by its receiving Rain in the
Field, and not by heating in a Heap, or in the Mow ;
and if you cut the Kernel off in the Middle, crofs-
ways, and find the Infide of a Greenifh frefh Colour, it's furely good ; but if of a yellowifh Colour,
and friable about the Navel, and thin, or pitted, thefe
are Marks of bad Seed.

The Quantity, or rather Number of Seeds convenient to drill, ought to be computed by the Number of Plants (*b*) we propofe to have for making
the beft Crop, allowing for Cafualties (*c*).

In

(b) Not that we need to be fo exact as to the Number of
Plants, whether they be Two, Three, or Four hundred upon a
fquare Perch.   Neither is it poffible to know beforehand the precife Number of Plants that may live ; for fometimes the Grub
kills many, by eating off the firft Two Leaves.

(c) Many even of the beft of Seeds, both fown and drill'd,
are liable to Cafualties, but not equally ; for about Twenty-eight
Years ago, my Servants (being prime Seedfmen) had a Fancy in
my Abfence to try an Experiment of the Difference betwixt fowing and drilling of St. Foin ; and in the Middle of a large Field
of my beft Land they fow'd a fquare Piece of Three Acres, at
the Rate of One Bufhel to an Acre, not doubting but, by their
fkill in fowing even, it would fucceed as well as if drill'd ;
but it fucceeded fo much againft their Expectation, that the
Land all round it, which was drill'd at the fame Time, with
the fame Proportion of the fame Seed, brought extraordinary
good Crops of St. Foin ; but the fow'd Part was fo very thin,
that tho' it lay ftill with the reft for Eight Years, it never was a
Crop, there not being above Three or Four upon a fquare Perch,
taking the Three Acres all together: Not that it can be fuppofed,

M

that

In drilling St. Foin not to be ho'd, and before the Ploughs of my Drill were so perfect in making narrow Chanels as they are now (for, when the Chanels were open, they had Six times the Breadth, wherein Part of the Seed was wasted), then my Quantity was One Bushel to an Acre, sometimes Six Gallons.

But a single Acre (in the middle of a large Field of St. Foin) being drill'd late in *October*, the frosty Winter kill'd at least Nineteen of Twenty Parts (*d*) of that Bushel.   At first it made such a poor Appearance, that 'twas by mere Accident, or it had been plow'd up for a Fallow; but, missing of that, a few Plants were perceiv'd in the Summer, which by their Singleness grew so vigorous, and so very large, that the Second Year of Mowing it (*e*) produc'd a Crop double to the rest of the same Field, which was drill'd in the Spring, with the same Proportion of Seed, and none of it kill'd: tho' all this Field was a much better Crop than some that was sown in the common Manner, with Seven Bushels to an Acre. I have generally observ'd the thin (*f*) to make the best Crop, after the First or Second Year.

I have

that the sown would always meet with so many Casualties as this did; for then Eight Bushels sown to an Acre might have been too thin, and much thinner than all the rest of the Field was, tho' drill'd with only One Bushel to an Acre: And 'tis often seen, that when an Acre is sown with seven Bushels of Seed, the St. Foin is as much too thick, as that sown with One Bushel was too thin.

I do not know, that of the many hundred Acres of St. Foin, that have been drill'd for me, ever one Acre was too thin, except when planted with Wheat: The young Plants were kill'd by the Frost.

(*d*) But I believe, there might remain alive Three or Four Plants to each square Yard, standing single, and at pretty equal Distances.

(*e*) But *Note*, This Acre was dunged, and in better Order than the rest.

(*f*) But, notwithstanding I commend the Planting of St. Foin thin, that most of the Roots may be single; yet I have Fields that

I have also often obferv'd in Lands of St. Foin, lying difperfed in a common Field (but where there was not Common for Sheep), and where the Ends of other Lands kept in Tillage, pointed againft the Pieces of St. Foin, and the Horfes and Ploughs turning out upon the St. Foin (g) did plow and fcratch out a Multitude of its Plants ; fo that it was thought to be fpoil'd, and Law-fuits were intended for Recompence of the Damage; that afterwards this fcratch'd Part, fuppofed to be fpoil'd, became twice as good as the reft of the fame Pieces, where the Ploughs did not come to tear up any Plants.

The Reafon why the fingle St. Foin Plants make the greateft Crops, is, that the Quantity of the Crop is always in Proportion to the Quantity of Nourifhment it receives from the Earth ; and thofe Plants which run deepeft will receive moft ; and fuch as are fingle will run deeper than thofe which are not fingle.

Alfo the fingle do fend out all round them horizontal Roots, proportionably ftronger and larger, whereby they are better able to penetrate, and extract more Nourifhment from the Staple, or upper *Stratum,* than the other can do, if there be a competent Number ; which is, when ho'd, fewer than any-

that were drill'd with but Four Gallons of Seed to an Acre ; and yet the Rows being Seven Inches afunder, the Roots are fo thick in them, that the Ground is cover'd with the St. Foin Plants, which feem to be as thick (in Appearance) as moft fown St. Foin, whereon Seven or Eight Bufhels are fown on an Acre. And I have other Fields that were drill'd with about Two Gallons of Seed to an Acre (which is Five Seeds to each fquare Foot), the Rows Sixteen Inches afunder, that produce better Crops, tho' the Ground be poorer. The drill'd St. Foin, being regular, is more fingle, tho' as thick as the fown; and for that Reafon always makes a better Crop, and lafts longer than the fown that is of the fame Thicknefs, but irregular.

(g) This Plowing and Scratching was a fort of Hoeing, which helped the St. Foin by a fmall Degree of Pulveration, as well as by making the Plants thinner.

M 2   body

body imagines.   'Tis common to fee a fingle St.
Foin have a bigger Tap-root than Twenty thick ones:
Their Length is in Proportion to their Bignefs:
Therefore that fingle Plant may well be fuppofed to
have Twenty times more Depth of Earth to fupply it,
than all thofe Twenty fmall Roots can reach to.   And
tho' thefe under *Strata* are not fo rich as the upper;
yet, never having been drain'd by any Vegetable,
they do afford a very confiderable Quantity of Nourifhment to thofe Roots which firft enter them.

The fmall thick Plants are fo far from equalling
the Product of the fingle, by their Excefs of Number, that the more they are, the fmaller, fhorter, and
weaker they become; lefs Nourifhment they have,
and the lefs Crop they produce; and are foon ftarv'd,
decay, and die, unlefs reliev'd by the Expence of frequent Manure, or that the Soil be very rich.

Single Plants exceed the other by a Multitude of
Degrees, more than a Giant does a Dwarf, in Strength,
as well as Stature; and therefore when natural Grafs
happens to come, are fo much the better able to fhift
amongft it.

The fingle Plants feem alfo to exceed the other in
their Longevity; for 'tis obferv'd, that all St. Foin
that has continu'd great for a good Number of Years
without Manure, has been fo fingle, that the Owners
have determined to plow it up at the Beginning, for
the Thinnefs of it.

How long this may laft by Culture, I can't tell;
but undoubtedly much longer than without it; and
I can fay, that I never knew a Plant of St. Foin die
a natural Death; the moft common End of it is
Starving.   And when an hundred thick Plants have
not the Nourifhment which One fingle Plant has, 'tis
no Wonder that thefe (in a Croud (*b*) thus befieg'd
with Hunger) fhould be ftarv'd before it.

_____

(*b*) Sown Plants, when too thick, are crouded on every Side;
but thofe that are drill'd, have always Room enough on Two
Sides of them; unlefs the Rows are too near together.

Another Advantage the fingle have, in refpect of Moifture : Thefe reach to a Depth where that is never wanting, even when the upper *Stratum* or Staple is parch'd up, as appears by the Experiment of the Mints, that if any Root of a Plant has Moifture, that Root will communicate a Share to all the reft. Hence it is, that, in the drieft Summer, thefe fingle Plants make a great Crop, when the other yield next to nothing. I remember I once faw a Farmer coming out of a Ground with a Load of St. Foin Hay, which he affured me was all he could find worth cutting, out of Forty Acres of this thick fort, in full Perfection, Three Years after fowing : He valued his Load at Three Pounds; but withal faid it came off fo much Ground, that the Expence of Mowing, Raking, &c. was more than the Value ; when, in the very fame dry Summer, there was Three Tun of St. Foin to an Acre in a Field (*i*), where it was drill'd fingle and regularly.

And I have often obferv'd, that where the Plants are thin, the Second Crop of them fprings again immediately after cutting; when Plants that ftand thick in the fame Ground, fpring not till Rain comes ; and I have feen the thin grown high enough to cut the Second time, before the other began to fpring.

The beft way to find what Number of thefe Plants it is proper to have on a Perch of Ground, is to confider what Quantity of Hay one large Plant will produce (for, if cultivated, they will be all fuch).

Without Culture thefe Plants never attain to a Fourth Part of the Bulk they do with it : Therefore very few have feen any one Plant at its full Bignefs. One Plant, well cultivated, has in the fame Ground

---

(*i*) This was on rich deep Land in *Oxfordfhire* ; and the other St. Foin, which was fo poor, was on thin Slate Land near *Caufham* in *Wiltfhire* in the *Bath Road*. It is now about Forty Years fince.

made

made a greater Produce, than One thoufand fmall ones uncultivated.

But the Hay of a large fingle cultivated Plant will weigh more than half a Pound; and 112 Plants upon a fquare Perch, weighing but a Quarter of a Pound apiece one with another, amount to Two Tun to an Acre.

If St. Foin be planted on fome forts of Land early in the Spring, and ho'd, it may bring a Crop the fame Summer; for I once planted a few Seeds of it on fandy Ground in my Garden, at the End of *February*, which produced large Plants above Two Feet high, that went into Bloffom the following *June*; tho' there was a fevere Froft in *March*, which kill'd abundance of Wheat, yet did not hurt thefe Plants: This fhews that St. Foin is a quick Grower, unlefs it be planted on poor cold Ground, or for Want of Culture.

And tho' the poor Land, and ill Management generally allotted to it, caufe it to yield but One mowing Crop a Year; yet it has yielded Two great ones on rich fandy Land, even when fown in the common ordinary matter.

Thin St. Foin cannot be expected to cover all the Ground at firft, any more than an Orchard of Apple-trees will, when firft planted at Thirty Feet Diftance from each other every Way; yet this is reckon'd a proper Diftance to make a good and lafting Orchard. But if thefe fhould be planted at Three Feet Diftance, as they ftand in the Nurfery, it would not be more unreafonoble than the common Method of fowing St. Foin is; and there would be much the fame Confequence in both, from covering all the Ground at firft Planting; except that the St. Foin, being abundantly longer rooted downwards than Apple-trees are, has the greater Difadvantage, when by its Thicknefs 'tis

prevented

prevented from growing to its full Bulk, and Length of Roots (*k*).

The Difference is only this: People are accustom'd to see Apple-trees planted at their due Distance: but few have seen St. Foin planted and cultivated at the Distance most proper to St. Foin; or ever consider'd about it, so much as to make the necessary Trials.

I have constantly found, that, upon doubling any Number of narrow Rows, having equal Number of Plants in each Row, the Crops have been very much diminish'd; and, upon leaving out every other Row, that is, lessening the Number of Rows to half, the Crops are increased; and where Two Rows are wide asunder at one End of a Piece, and near at the other End, the Plants are gradually less and less, as the Rows approach nearer together.

We ought never to expect a full Crop of St. Foin the First Year (*l*), if we intend to have good Crops afterwards, and that it shall continue to produce such, for the same Reasons that must be given for planting an Orchard at other Distances than a Nursery.

The common Error proceeds from mistaking the Cause of a great or small Crop.

Where the Spaces betwixt Rows are wide (if there be not too many Plants in them) we always see the St. Foin grow large, and make the greatest Crop; but when 'tis young, or after cutting, we see room

---

(*k*) Horizontal-rooted Plants suffer no greater Injury by their Pasture's being over-stock'd than Cattle do; because their Pasture lying near the Surface of the Ground, they have it all amongst them: But St. Foin, and other long Tap-rooted Plants suffer yet more, because great Part of their over-stock'd Pasture is lost by them all, when they hinder one another from reaching down to it, by shortening one another's Roots, which they do when they all become Dwarfs by reason of their Over-thickness.

(*l*) But when it has been planted on rich sandy Land, and proper, it has produced very great Crops the first Year; but then the Summer wherein it grew amongst the Barley, must not be reckoned as the first Year.

M 4   (as

(as we fanfy) for more of fuch Plants, to make a yet
larger Crop; not confide ng that 'tis the Widenefs
of thofe Spaces, and lefs Number of Plants, that
caufe the Crop to be fo large, there being more Pafture for thofe Plants.

Where thefe Spaces are narrower, and the Rows
of equal Thicknefs, we fee the Plants lefs when
grown, and that they make a lefs Crop; and yet
there feems to be room for more Rows, which we
fanfy might make the Crop larger, not confidering
that 'tis the Narrownefs of thofe Spaces that caufes
the Plants and Crop to be lefs, for want of fufficient
Pafture.

Thus, fondly increafing the Number of our Rows
and Plants, we bring our Crop (unlefs the Soil be
rich) to nothing, by too much over-ftocking their
Pafture; and, if that Pafture be over-ftock'd, the
Crop will be diminifh'd more than in proportion to
that Over-charge; for perhaps 'tis not impoffible to
prove (if we would be curious), that Plants, by
wanting a Fourth Part of their due *Quantum* of Nourifhment, will be diminifh'd to half *(m)* of the Bulk
they would have attained to, had they been fupply'd
with the other Fourth Part.

I have obferv'd ho'd St. Foin to grow more, and
increafe its Bulk more, in Two Weeks, than unho'd
St. Foin in the fame Ground (and without any other
Difference) hath done in Six Weeks; and the quicker
it grows, by being better fed, the fweeter and richer
Food it will make for Cattle, whether it be fpent green
or dry *(n)*.

(m) When Plants have not their due Nourifhment, they fuffer
the more by Cold and Drought; fo that want of Nourifhment
diminifhing their Gr wth One-fourth, Cold, or Drought, or
both. may diminifh it another fourth.

(n) Cattle are the beft Judges of the Goodnefs of Grafs, and
they always choofe to feed on St Foin that is moft vigorous,
and refufe that which is poor and yellow. And the richeft
fweeteft Grafs will always make the beft Hay; for the drying of
it does not change the Quality of the Grafs.

At

At whatever Diftance the Rows be fet, if they have too many Plants in them, the Crop will be very much injured; and the greater the Excefs is beyond the juft Number, the more void Space there will be amongft them; becaufe the fmaller the Plants are, the lefs Ground they cover.

I have had the Experience of drilling at all Diftances, from Thirty-three Inches to Seven Inches, betwixt the Rows; and recommend the following Diftance, for the different Methods of drilling; whether the *St. Foin* be defign'd for hoeing, or not. As,

Firft, For *Horfe-hoeing*, I think it is beft to drill double Rows with Eight-inch Partitions, and Thirty-inch Intervals; which need only be ho'd alternately, leaving every other Interval for making the Hay thereon.

Indeed I have never yet had a whole Field of ho'd *St. Foin*; but have enough to fhew, that Horfe-hoeing makes it ftrong upon very poor Land, and caufes it to produce two Crops a Year upon indifferent Land.

It is not neceffary to hoe this every Year; but we may intermit the Hoeing for three or four Years together, or more, if the Land be good.

Whilft the Plants are fmall the firft Year, Care muft be taken not to cover them with the Plough: Afterwards there will be no great Danger, efpecially in Winter, the Earth not being fuffered to lie on them too long.

Secondly, For *Hand-hoeing*, drill the Rows Sixteen Inches afunder, and fingle out the Plants, fo as to make them Eight Inches apart at leaft in the Rows, contriving rather to leave the Mafter-plants, than to be exact in the Diftance: This muft be done whilft they are very young, or in Summer; elfe they will come again that are cut off by the Hoe.

Laftly, when *St. Foin* is drill'd without any Intention of hoeing, the beft Way (I think) is to plant fingle Rows, at Eight Inches Diftance, with no greater Quantity of Seed, than when the Rows are at Sixteen Inches Diftance; becaufe, by this Method, the

fame

fame Number of Plants in the Rows, that are but Eight Inches apart, will be much more fingle, than thofe in the Rows at Sixteen Inches apart are, without being fet out by the Hoe.

Which of thefe Methods foever is practis'd, the Land fhould be made as clean from all Grafs, and as well pulveriz'd, as poffible, before Drilling.

The Tines of the Drill-harrow muft exactly follow the Shares, which leaving the Chanels open, the Tines cover the Seed, fome at Bottom, and fome on each Side; fo that it is cover'd very fhallow, tho' it lies deep within the Ground, where there is more Moifture, than nearer to the upper level Surface: This caufes the Seed to come up in dry Weather; and yet it is not in Danger of being buried by a too great Weight of Mould incumbent on it.

But take heed that no other Harrow come on it after 'tis drill'd; for that might bury it. I never care to roll it at all, unlefs on account of the Barley; and then only in very dry Weather, with a light Roller, lengthways of the Rows, immediately after 'tis drill'd; or elfe ftay Three Weeks afterwards before it be roll'd, for fear of breaking off the Heads of the young *St. Foin.*

Be fure to fuffer no Cattle to come on the young *St. Foin* the firft Winter (*a*), after the Corn is cut

that

(*a*) The firft Winter is the Time to lay on Manure, after the Crop of Corn is off; fuch as *Peat-Afhes*, or the like; becaufe, there being no natural Grafs to partake of it, and the Plants being lefs, lefs will fupply them; and becaufe, when made ftrong in their Youth, they will come to greater Perfection: But I never ufed any Manure on my *St. Foin*, becaufe mine generally had no Occafion for Manure before it was old; and *Soot* is feldom to be had of fufficient Quantity in the Country; and little *Coal* is burnt hereabouts, except by the *Smiths*, whofe *Afhes* are not good. The Price and Carriage of *Peat-Afh* will be Ten Shillings for an Acre, which would yet be well beftowed in a Place where Hay is vendible; but, by reafon of the great Quantity of watered Meadows, and Plenty of St. Foin, Clover, and Hay, raifed of late Years by Farmers for their own Ufe,

that grows amongft it; their very Feet would injure it, by treading the Ground hard, as well as their Mouths by cropping it; Nor let any Sheep come at it, even in the following Summer and Winter.

One Acre of well-drill'd *St. Foin*, confidering the different Goodnefs of the Crops, and the Duration of it, is generally worth Two Acres of fown *St. Foin* on the fame Land, tho' the Expence of drilling be Twenty Times lefs than the Expence of fowing it.

One of the Caufes why *St. Foin*, that is properly drill'd, lafteth longer (*b*) without Manure than the fown, is, That the former neither over nor under-ftocks the Pafture; and the latter commonly, if not always, doth one or the other, if not both; *viz.* Plants too thick in fome Places, and too thin in others; either 'tis not fingle, but in Bunches; or if it be fingle, 'tis too thin; it being next to impoffible to have the Plants come true and regular, or nearly fo, by fowing at *random*. Plants too thick foon exhauft the Pafture they reach, which never is more than a fmall Part of that below the Staple: When the Plants are too thin, the *St. Foin* cannot be faid to laft at all, becaufe it never is a Crop.

They who *fow* Eight or Ten Bufhels of good Seed on an Acre, in a good Seafon, among their Corn, with Intent that by its Thicknefs it fhould kill other Grafs, reduce their *St. Foin* almoft to that poor Con-dition I have feen it in, where it grows naturally

Ufe, here are now few or no Buyers of Hay, efpecially thefe open Winters; fo that laying out Money in that Manner would be in Effect to buy what I cannot fell. I think it better to let a little more Land lie ftill in St. Foin, than to be at the Expence of Manure; but yet fhall not neglect to ufe it, when I fhall find it likely to be profitable to me.

(*b*) I have now a great many fingle *St. Foin* Plants in my Fields, that are near Thirty Years of Age, and yet feem as young and vigorous as ever; and yet it is common for thick *St. Foin* to wear out in Nine or Ten Years, and in poor Land much fooner, if not often manured by *Soot*, *Peat-Afh*, or *Coal-Afh*.

wild

wild without fowing or Tillage, upon the *Calabrian* Hills near *Croto :* It makes there fuch a defpicable Appearance, that one would wonder how any body fhould have taken it in their Head to propagate fo unpromifing a Plant ; and yet there has fcarce been an Exotic brought to *England* in this or the laft Age, capable of making a greater or more general Improvement, were it duly cultivated.

Some think the *Cytifus* would exceed it ; but I am afraid the Labour of fhearing thofe Shrubs by the Hands of *Englifh* Servants, would coft too much of its Profit.

Luferne, requiring more Culture, and being much more difficult to be fitted with a proper Soil, never can be fo general as *St, Foin.*

But now let us confider the beft Methods of ordering *St. Foin* for Hay and Seed. The Profit of *St. Foin* Fields, arifing from either of thefe Ways, is a great Advantage to their Owner, above that of natural Meadows ; for, if Meadow-hay cannot have good Weather to be cut in its Seafon, it can ferve for little other Ufe than as Dung, and yet the Expence of mowing it, and carrying it off muft not be omitted. But if there be not Weather to cut *St. Foin* before blofToming, we may expect it till in Flower, or may ftay till the BlofToms are off ; and if it ftill rain on, may ftand for Seed, and turn to as good Account as any of the former : So that it has Four Chances to One of the Meadow.

The elevated, but not mountainous, Situation of the dry Land whereon *St. Foin* is moftly planted, renders it fo commodious for making of Hay, that it efcapes there the Injury of Weather, when Hay in low Meadows is utterly fpoil'd.

On the high Ground the Wind will dry more in an Hour, than on the Meadows in a whole Day. The Sun too has a more benign Influence above, and fends off the Dew about Two Hours earlier in the Morning,

Morning, and holds it up as much longer in the E-vening. By thefe Advantages the *St. Foin* has the more Time to dry, and is made with half the Expence of Meadow-hay.

But before the Manner of making it be defcrib'd, the proper Time of cutting it ought to be determin'd; and upon that depend the Degrees of its Excellence (befides upon the Weather, which is not in our Power); for tho' all Sorts of this Hay, if well made, be good, yet there is a vaft Difference and Variety in them.

The feveral Sorts may be principally diftinguifh'd by the following Terms; *viz.* Firft, The *Virgin.* Secondly, The *Bloffom'd.* Thirdly, The *Full-grown.* And, Fourthly, The *Threfh'd Hay.*

The Firft of thefe is beft of all, beyond Compari-fon; and (except *Luferne*) has not in the World its Equal. This muft be cut before the Bloffoms appear: For when it ftands till full-blown, the moft fpirituous, volatile, and nourifhing Parts of its Juices are fpent on the next Generation; and this being done all at once, the Sap is much depauperated, and the *St. Foin* can never recover that Richnefs it had in its Virgin State. And tho', when in Bloffom, it be *literally* in the *Flower* of its Age, 'tis really in the *Declenfion* of it. If it be faid, that what is not in the Stalk is gone into the Flower, 'tis a Miftake; becaufe much the greateft Part of its Quinteffence perfpires thence into the Atmofphere.

And moreover, That all Vegetables are, in fome Degree, weaken'd by the Action of continuing their Kind, may be inferr'd from thofe Plants which will live feveral Years, if not fuffer'd to bloffom; but, whenever they bloffom, it caufes their Death, tho' in the firft Year of their Life. For in Plants (as Dr. *Willis* obferves in Animals) Nature is more folicitous to continue the Species, than for the Benefit of the Individual.

4

Part

Part of a drill'd *St. Foin* Ground was cut the Beginning of *May*, before bloſſoming (c); and from the Time of cutting, until it was ſet up in Ricks, being about Ten Days, the Sun never ſhone upon it (d); but the Weather was miſty: At laſt it was forc'd to be carried together for fear of Rain, ſo green, that out of the largeſt Stalks one might wring milky Juice; yet by making the Hay up in ſeveral little Ricks, and drawing up a great Chaff Baſket in the Middle of each, its Firing was prevented; but it look'd of a dark Colour by heating; and was the very beſt (e) Hay that ever I had.

The other Part of the Ground was afterwards cut in the Prime of its Flower, and made into Hay by the Heat of the Sun, without Rain or Miſt: This came out of the Ricks at Winter with a much finer Colour, and as fine a Smell as the Virgin Hay; but did not come near it in fatting of Sheep, or keeping

(c) By cutting before bloſſoming, is not meant before any one Bloſſom appears; for here and there a Bud will begin to open with a red Colour long before the reſt: Therefore, when we perceive only a very few Bloſſoms beginning to open (perhaps but One of a Thouſand), we regard them as none.

(d) This alſo was an Advantage to this Hay; for Apothecaries find, that Herbs dried in the Shade retain much more of their Virtue than thoſe dried in the Sun; but Farmers not having any ſuch Conveniency of drying their Hay in the Shade with Safety, muſt always chooſe to dry it by the Sun; becauſe in cloudy Weather there is Danger of Rain; and therefore ſuch excellent Hay muſt be had by Chance; for to be well made in the Shade, it muſt be in Danger of being ſpoiled or damaged by Rain.

(e) This Hay, ſo cut before bloſſoming, has kept a Team of working Stone-horſes, round the Year, fat without Corn; and when tried with Beans and Oats mixed with Chaff, they refuſed it for this Hay. The ſame fatted ſome Sheep in the Winter, in a Pen, with only it and Water; they thrived faſter than other Sheep at the ſame time fed with Peaſe and Oats. The Hay was weighed to them, and the clear Profit amounted to Four Pounds *per* Tun. They made no Waſte. Tho' the Stalks were of an extraordinary Bigneſs, they would break off ſhort, being very brittle. This grew on rich Ground in *Oxfordſhire*.

Horſes

Horses fat at hard Work without any Corn, as the Virgin Hay did.

This superfine Hay cannot well be had of poor uncultivated (*f*) *St. Foin*: because that may not be much above an Handful high, when 'tis in Condition to be so cut; and would then make a very light Crop, and would be a great while ere it sprang up again: But the rich will have Two or Three Tun to an Acre, and spring again immediately for a second Crop; so that little or no Quantity would be lost by so great an Improvement of it's Quality. For ho'd *St. Foin* upon a poor chalky Hill, cut at the same time with that uncultivated on a rich Valley, does in dry Weather grow again without Delay, when the Valley attends a Month or more for a Rain, to excite its vegetative Motion.

This Hay the Owner (if he be wise) will not sell at any common Price; but endeavour to have some of it every Year, if possible, for his own Use.

The Second Sort of *St. Foin* Hay is that cut in the Flower; and tho' much inferior to the *Virgin* Hay, it far exceeds any other Kind, as yet commonly propagated in *England*; and if it be a full Crop, by good Culture, may amount to above three Tun to an Acre. This is that *St. Foin* which is most commonly made; and the larger it is, the more nourishing for Horses. I have known Farmers, after full Experience, go Three Miles to fetch the largest stalky *St. Foin*, when they could have bought the small fine leafy Sort of it at home, for the same Price by the Tun.

The next and last Sort of *St. Foin* that is cut only for Hay, is, the *full-grown*, the Blossoms being gone, or going off: This also is good Hay, tho' it fall short, by many Degrees, of the other Two Sorts: It makes a greater Crop than either of them, because it grows to its full Bulk, and shrinks little in drying.

(*f*) I reckon Manure of *Peat-Ashes*, *Soot*, or the like, to be a Culture.

This

This gives the Owner a Third Chance of having Weather to make good Hay, and spins out the Hay-Season 'till about *Midsummer*; and then in about a Fortnight, or Three Weeks, after the Hay is finish'd, the Seed is ripe.   But, first, of the manner of making *St. Foin* Hay.

In a Day or Two after *St. Foin* is mow'd, it will, in good Weather, be dry on the upper Side: Then turn the Swarths, not singly, but Two and Two together; for by thus turning them in Pairs, there is a double Space of Ground betwixt Pair and Pair, which needs but once raking; whereas, if the Swarths were turn'd singly, that is, all the same Way, suppose to the *East* or *West*, then all the Ground will require to be twice raked; at least, more of it, than the other Way.

As soon as both Sides of the Swarths are dry from Rain and Dew, make them up into little Cocks the same Day they are turn'd, if conveniently you can; for when 'tis in Cock, a less Part of it will be expos'd to the Injuries of the Night, than when in Swarth.

Dew, being of a nitrous penetrating Nature, enters the Pores of those Plants it reaches, and during the Night possesses the Room from whence some Part of the Juices is dry'd out: Thus it intimately mixes with the remaining Sap; and, when the Dew is again exhal'd, it carries up most of the vegetable Spirits along with it, which might have been there fix'd, had they not been taken away in that subtile Vehicle.

If *St. Foin* be spread very thin upon the Ground, and so remain for a Week in hot Weather, the Sun and Dew will exhaust all its Juices, and leave it no more Virtue than is in Straw.

Therefore tis best to keep as much of our Hay as we can from being expos'd to the Dews, whilst 'tis in making; and we have a better Opportunity of doing it in this, than in natural Hay; because the bigger the Cocks are, the less Superficies (in proportion

tion to the Quantity they contain) will be exposed to the Dew, and *St. Foin* may be safely made in much larger Cocks than natural Hay of equal Dryness can, which, sinking down closer, excludes the Air so necessary for keeping it sweet, that if the Weather prevents its being frequently mov'd and open'd, it will ferment, look yellow, and be spoil'd. Against this Misfortune there is no Remedy, but to keep it in the lesser Cocks, until thoroughly dry. *St. Foin* Cocks (twice as big as Cocks of natural Hay), by the less Flexibility of the Stalk admitting the Air, will remain longer without fermenting.

This being able to endure more Days unmov'd, is also an Advantage upon another Account besides the Weather; for tho' in other Countries, People are not prohibited using the necessary Labour on *all Days* for preserving their Hay, even where the certainer Weather makes it less necessary than here, yet 'tis otherwise in *England*; where many a Thousand Load of natural Hay is spoil'd by that Prohibition for want of being open'd; and often, by the Loss of one Day's Work, the Farmer loses his Charges, and Year's Rent; which shews, that to make Hay while the Sun shines, is an exotic Proverb against *English* Laws; whereunto *St. Foin* being, in regard of Sundays and Holidays, more conformable, ought to be the Hay as proper to *England* as those Laws are.

But to return to our Hay-makers: When the first Cocks have stood one Night, if nothing hinder, let them double, treble, or quadruple the Cocks, according as all Circumstances require, in this manner; *viz.* Spread Two, Three, or more, together, in a fresh Place; and after an Hour or Two turn them, and make that Number up into one Cock; but when the Weather is doubtful, let not the Cocks be thrown or spread, but inlarge them, by shaking several of them into one; and thus hollowing them to let in the Air, continue increasing their Bulk, and diminishing their

N Number

Number daily, until they be fufficiently dry to be carried to the Rick.

This I have found the moft fecure Way : Tho' it be fomething longer in making, there is much lefs Danger than when a great Quantity of Hay is fpread at once; for then a fudden Shower will do more Harm to one Acre of that, than to Twenty Acres in Cock.

And the very beft Hay I ever knew in *England*, was of *St. Foin* made without ever fpreading, or the Sun's fhining on it. This Way, tho' it be longer ere finifh'd, is done with lefs Labour than the other.

Not only a little Rain, but even a Mift, will turn *Clover Hay* black; but *St. Foin* will not with any Weather turn black, until it be almoft rotten, its Leaves being thinner than thofe of *Clover*.

If *St. Foin* be laid up pretty green, it will take no Damage, provided it be fet in fmall round Ricks, with a large Bafket drawn up in the Middle of each, to leave a Vent-hole there, thro' which the fuperfluous Moifture of the Hay tranfpires.

As foon as its Heating is over, thefe Ricks ought to be thatch'd; and all *St. Foin* Ricks, that are made when the Hay is full dry'd in the Cocks, ought to be thatch'd immediately after the making them.

That which is laid up moft dry'd, will come out of the Rick of a green Colour, that which has much heated in the Rick, will have a brown Colour.

The Seed is a Fourth Chance the Owner has to make Profit of his *St. Foin*: But this, if the *Hoeing-Hufbandry* were general, would not be vendible in great Quantities for planting; becaufe an ordinary Crop of an Acre will produce Seed enough to drill an Hundred Acres, which would not want replanting in a long Time.

The other Ufe then of this Seed is for Provender; and it has been affirm'd by fome, who have made Trials of it, that Three Bufhels of good *St. Foin*

Seed

Seed given to Horfes, will nourifh them as much as Four Bufhels of Oats. When well order'd, it is fo *fweet*, that moft Sorts of Cattle are greedy of it. I never knew fo much of it given to Hogs, as to make them become fat Bacon ; but I have known Hogs made very good Pork with it, for an Experiment ; and being valued at the Beginning of their feeding, and the Pork by the Score when the Hogs were kill'd, which, computed with the Quantity of Seed they eat, did not amount to near the Value of the fame Seed fold for fowing ; that being Three Shillings *per* Bufhel, and the Profit made by giving it to the Hogs was but Two Shillings a Bufhel.

The Goodnefs of the Seed, and of the Hay out of which it is threfh'd, depends very much upon the manner of ordering them.

This threfh'd Hay, when not damaged by wet Weather, has been found more nourifhing to Horfes than coarfe Water-meadow Hay ; and, when 'tis cut fmall by an Engine, is good Food for Cattle, and much better than Chaff of Corn.

It requires fome Experience in it, to know the moft proper Degree of Ripenefs, at which the feeded *St. Foin* ought to be cut ; for the Seed is never all ripe together ; fome Ears bloffom before others ; every Ear begins bloffoming at the lower Part of it, and fo continues gradually to do upward for many Days ; and before the Flower is gone off the Top, the Bottom of the Ear has almoft fill'd the Seeds that grow there ; fo that if we fhould defer cutting until the top Seeds are quite ripe, the lower, which are the beft, would fhed, and be loft.

The beft time to cut is, when the greateft Part of the Seed is well fill'd, the firft-blown ripe, and the laft blown beginning to be full.

The natural Colour of the Kernel, which is the real Seed, is grey or bluifh when ripe ; and the Hufk, which contains the Seed is, when ripe, of a brownifh

Colour,

Colour. Both Hufk and Seed continue perfectly green for fome time after full-grown ; and if you open the Hufk, the Seed will appear exactly like a green Pea when gather'd to boil, and will, like that, eafily be fplit into Two Parts. Yet St. Foin Seed in this green Plight will ripen after Cutting, have as fine a Colour, and be as good in all Refpects, as that which was ripe before Cutting : Some, for want of obferving this, have fuffer'd their Seed to ftand fo long, till it was all ripe, and loft in Cutting.

St. Foin Seed fhould not be cut in the Heat of the Day, whilft the Sun fhines out : for then much, even of the unripe Seed, will fhed in Mowing : Therefore, in very hot Weather, the Mower fhould begin to work very early in the Morning, or rather in the Night ; and when they perceive the Seed to fhatter, leave off, and reft till towards the Evening.

After Cutting we muft obferve the fame Rule as in mowing it; *viz.* not to make this Hay whilft the Sun fhines.

Sometimes it may, if the Seed be pretty ripe, be cock'd immediately after the Scythe; or if the Swarths muft be turn'd, let it be done whilft they are moift; not Two together, as in the other Hay aforemention'd. If the Swarths be turn'd with the Rake's Handle, 'tis beft to raife up the Ear-fides firft, and let the Stub-fide reft on the Ground in turning; but if it be done by the Rake's Teeth, then let them take hold on the Stub-fide, the Ears bearing on the Earth in turning over. But 'tis commonly Rain that occafions the Swarths to want Turning *(a)*.

If it be cock'd at all *(b)*, the fooner 'tis made into Cocks, the better; becaufe, if the Swarths be dry,

---

(a) If the Swarths be not very great, we never turn them at all, becaufe the Sun or Wind will quickly dry them.

(b) Sometimes when we defign to threfh in the Field, we make no Cocks at all, and but only juft feparate the Swarths in the

dry, much of the Seed will be loſt in ſeparating them, the Ears being entangled together.   When moiſt, the Seed ſticks faſts to the Ear ; but, when dry, will drop out with the leaſt Touch or Shaking.

There are Two ways of threſhing it, the one in the Field, the other in the Barn: The firſt cannot be done but in very fine Weather, and whilſt the Sun ſhines in the Heat of the Day : The beſt Manner of this is, to have a large Sheet pegg'd down to the Ground, for Two Men with their Flails to threſh on : Two Perſons carry a ſmall Sheet by its Corners, and lay it down cloſe to a large Cock, and, with Two Sticks thruſt under the Bottom of it, gently turn it over, or lift it up upon the Sheet, and carry and throw it on the great Sheet to the Threſhers ; but when the Cocks are ſmall, they carry ſeveral at once, thrown upon the little Sheet carefully with Forks ; thoſe which are near, they carry to the Threſhers with the Forks only.   As faſt as it is threſh'd, one Perſon ſtands to take away the Hay, and lay it into an Heap: And ſometimes a Boy ſtands upon it, to make it into a ſmall Rick of about a Load.   As often as the great Sheet is full, they riddle it thro' a large Sieve to ſeparate the Seed and Chaff from the broken Stalks, and put it into Sacks to be carried into the Barn to be winnow'd.

Two Threſhers will employ Two of theſe little Sheets, and Four Perſons in bringing to them ; and when the Cocks are threſh'd, which ſtand at a conſiderable Diſtance all round them, they remove the Threſhing-ſheet to another Place.   There belong to a Set for one Threſhing-ſheet Seven or Eight Perſons ; but the Number of Sheets ſhould be according to the

the Dew of the Morning dividing them into Parts of about Two Feet in each Part.   By this means the St. Foin is ſooner dry'd, than when it lies thicker, as it muſt do, if made into Cocks.

Quan-

Quantity to be thus threſh'd: The ſooner theſe threſh'd Cocks are remov'd, and made into bigger Ricks, the better; and unleſs they be thatch'd, the Rain will run a great Way into them, and ſpoil the Hay; but they may be thatch'd with the Hay itſelf, if there be not Straw convenient for it.

But the chiefeſt Care yet remains; and that is, to cure the Seed: If that be negleſted, it will be of little or no Value *(a)*; and the better it has eſcap'd the Wet in the Field, the ſooner its own Spirits will ſpoil it in the Barn or Granary. I have known it lie a Fortnight in Swarth, till the wet Weather has turn'd the Husks quite black: This was threſh'd in the Field, and immediately put into large Veſſels, holding about Twenty Buſhels each. It had by being often wet, and often dry, been ſo exhauſted of its fiery Spirits, that it remain'd cool in the Veſſels, without ever fermenting in the leaſt, till the next Spring; and then it grew as well as ever any did that was planted.

But of Seed threſh'd in the Field, without ever being wetted, if it be immediately winnow'd, and a ſingle Buſhel laid in an Heap, or put into a Sack,

---

(a) But there is yet another Care to be taken of St. Foin Seed, beſides the curing it; and that is, to keep it from Rats and Mice after 'tis cured; or elſe, if their Number be large, they will in a Winter eat up all the Seed of a conſiderable Quantity, leaving only empty Huſks, which to the Eye appear the ſame as when the Seeds are in them. A Man cannot without Difficulty take a Seed out of its Huſk; but the Vermin are ſo dextrous at it, that they will eat the Seed almoſt as faſt out of the Huſks, as if they were pulled out for them. I ſaw a Rat killed as he was running from an Heap of it, that had Seven peeled Seeds in his Mouth not ſwallowed; which is a Sign, that he was not long in taking them out. They take them out ſo cleverly, that the Hole in the Huſk ſhuts itſelf up when the Seed is out of it. But, if you feel the Huſk between your Finger and Thumb, you will find it empty. Alſo a Sackful of them is very light; yet there have been ſome ſo ignorant and incurious as to ſow ſuch empty Huſks for ſeveral Years ſucceſſively; and none coming up, they concluded their Land to be improper for St. Foin.

it

it will in few Days ferment to fuch a Degree, that the greateſt Part of it will loſe its vegetative Quality : The larger the Heap, the worſe: During the Fermentation it will be very hot, and ſmell ſour.

Many, to prevent this, ſpread it upon a Malt-Floor, turning it often; or, when the Quantity is ſmall, upon a Barn-floor; but ſtill I find, that this Way a great deal of it is ſpoil'd; for it will heat, tho' it be ſpread but an handful thick, and they never ſpread it thinner: Beſides, they may miſs ſome Hours of the right times of turning it; for it muſt be done very often; it ſhould be ſtirr'd in the Night as well as the Day, until the Heating be over; and yet, do what they can, it never will keep its Colour. ſo bright as that which is well houſed, well dry'd, and threſh'd in the Winter: For in the Barn the Stalks keep it hollow; there are few Ears or Seeds that touch one another; and the Spirits have room to fly off by Degrees, the Air entering to reeeive them.

The only Way I have found to imitate and equal this, is to winnow it from the Sheet; then lay a Layer of Wheat-ſtraw (or if that be wanting, of very dry-threſh'd Hay); then ſpread thereon a thin Layer of Seed, and thus *Stratum ſuper Stratum*, Six or Seven Feet high, and as much in Breath; then begin another Stack; let there be Straw enough, and do not tread on the Stacks; by this means the Seed mixing with the Straw, will be kept cool, and come out in the Spring with as green a Colour as when it was put in, and not one Seed of a Thouſand will fail to grow when planted. A little Barn-room will contain a great Quantity in this Manner.

I have had above One hundred Quarters of clean Seed thus manag'd in one Bay of a ſmall Barn. We do not ſtay to winnow it clean before we lay it up in the Straw; but only paſs it through a large Sieve, and with the Van blow out the Chaff, and winnow. it clean in the Spring.

N 4   This

This Field-threshing requires extraordinary fine Sun-shiny Weather, which some Summers do not afford at the Season, for threshing a great Quantity of it; for 'tis but a small Part of the Day in which the Seed can be thresh'd clean out. They who have a small Quantity of it, do carry it into a Barn early in the Morning, or even in the Night; whilst the Dew is on it; for then the Seed sticks fast to the Ear: As it dries, they thresh it out; and if they cure it well, have thus sometimes good Seed, but generally the Hay is spoil'd.

There is one Method of saving all the Seed good, and the Hay too, by carrying it unthresh'd to the Barn or Rick, in a particular Manner, tho' it be a great Quantity, more than can presently be thresh'd; but must be laid up in Mows or Ricks, as Corn is. Then if it be carry'd in, in the Dews or Damp, the Hay is sure to be spoil'd, if not both Hay and Seed: When 'tis taken up dry, the Seed comes out with a Touch, and the greatest Part is lost in pitching up the Cocks, binding and jolting in carrying home.

To avoid this Dilemma, a Person who happen'd to have a great Crop of Seed on One hundred and Fifty Acres together (and being by Weather delay'd 'till Wheat-harvest came on, so that most Labourers went to Reaping) was forc'd to a Contrivance of getting it in as follows; *viz* Three Waggons had each a Board with an Hole in, fix'd cross the Middle of each Waggon, by Iron Pins, to the Top of the Rades or Sides: There was a Crane which a Man could lift, and set into the Hole in the Board, and, having an Iron Gudgeon at the Bottom, which went into a Socket in the Bottom of the Waggon, would turn quite round: The Post of the Crane was Ten Feet Four Inches long, its Arm Four Feet Eight Inches long, brac'd; having a treble Pulley at the End of it, and another to answer it with an Hook.

About

About Forty Sheets were provided, capable of holding each One hundred and Fifty, or Two hundred Pounds Weight of it; these had Knots or Buttons at the Corners and Middles, made by sewing up a little Hay in these Knots, as big as Apples, into Part of the Sheet; for if any Buckle, or other thing, be sew'd to a Sheet plain, it will tear the Sheet. Half these Buttons have Strings ty'd to them; these Sheets are spread among the Cocks, fill'd by Two, and ty'd up by Two other Persons: There is also a light Fir Ladder, wide at Bottom, the Top of it fasten'd by a Piece of Cord to the brace of the Crane: they hitch the Hook of the lower Pulley to a fill'd Sheet, and by a little Horse at the End of the Pulley-rope, draw it up sliding on the Ladder; 'tis up in a Moment: Then the Man who is below, hitches the Crook of the Pulley to the lower Round of the Ladder, and the Loader above pulls up the Ladder from the Ground, till the Waggon comes to another Sheet. The Waggons are lengthen'd by Cart-Ladders before and behind, for the more easy placing of the Sheets. When about Twelve or Fifteen of them are loaded, they have a Rope fix'd to the Fore-part of each Waggon, which they bring over the Top of all the loaded Sheets, and wrest it at the Tail, to hold on the Sheets fast from falling off with Jolting. Then the Loader pulls out the Crane, and puts it into the next Waggon in the same Manner. One Waggon is loading whilst another is emptying in the Barn, by treble Pulleys likewise; because 'tis inconvenient to take it out of the Sheets by Prongs; but the Pulleys will easily draw off Two or Three Sheets together. One Waggon is always going to the Field, or coming home. This Contrivance makes more Expedition than one would imagine: Three Loads have been loaded, and sent off, in the same Time this way, that one Load of Hay has been loading, binding, and raking off the Out-

sides

fides of it, in the next Ground, in the common
Way.

I will not relate the manner of making a Rick of
this Seed in its Hay, of monstrous Dimensions, by a
sort of Mast-pole Forty-four Feet high, with a Ten
Feet Crane at the Top, which made the same Expedition; because I think, that where such a Quantity
is, *Dutch* Barns with moving Roofs are better. Such
a Rick is troublesome to thatch, and the Wind has
more Power to blow the Thatch off so high in the
Air, than if it were lower. Neither would I advise
any one to reserve much more St. Foin for Threshing, than his Barn will contain; because tho' sometimes it brings the greatest Profit by Threshing, yet
some Years 'tis apt to be blighted.

I have been told by my Neighbour, that he had a
Crop of Five Quarters of St. Foin Seed on an Acre;
but the most Profit that ever I took notice of, was
on half an Acre, which was drill'd very thin, and
had no Crop of Corn with it; by which Advantage
it produc'd a good Crop of Seed the next Year after
it was planted, and the Third Year this Half-Acre
produc'd (as was try'd by a Wager) within a Trifle of
Two Quarters of Seed, which was sold for Two
Pounds and Ten Shillings: The thresh'd Hay of it
was sold in the Place for One Pound, and Two Quarters of Chaff sold for Twelve Shillings; in all Four
Pounds and Two Shillings. There was also a very
good Aftermath, which was worth the Charges of
Cutting and Threshing: So that the clear Profit of
the One Year of this Half Acre of Ground amounted to Four Pounds Two Shillings: And it was remarkable, that at the same Time the rest of the same
Field, being in all Ten Acres, had a Crop of Barley
sown on Three Plowings, which (the Summer being
dry) was offered to be sold at One Pound *per*
Acre.

I believe

I believe the greateſt Part of the St. Foin that is ſown, is ſpoil'd by being indiſcreetly fed by Sheep *(b)*; which Damage is occaſion'd merely by ſuffering them to continue feeding it too long at a Time, eſpecially in the Spring; for then the Sap moves quick, and muſt be depurated by the Leaves; and as the Sun's nearer Approach accelerates the Motion or Ferment of the Juices, more *Pabulum* is receiv'd by the Roots; but for want of Leaves to diſcharge the Recrements, and enliven the Sap with nitro-aereous Particles (the Sheep devouring the Buds continually as faſt as they appear), the St. Foin's vital Flame (if I may ſo call it) is extinguiſh'd; the Circulation ceaſing, the Sap ſtagnates, and then it ends in Corruption *(c)*.   But let the Sheep eat it never ſo low, in a ſhort time, without continuing thereon, or cropping the next Buds which ſucceed thoſe they have eaten, the Plants will recover and grow again as vigorouſly as ever, and if with a Spade, in the Winter you cut off the St. Foin Heads an Handful deep, and take them away, together with their upper Earth, the Wound in the remaining Root will heal, and ſend out more Heads as good as thoſe cut off, if thoſe ſecond Heads be preſerv'd from Cattle, until they attain to a Bigneſs competent to bear Leaves ſuffi-

---

(b) I never ſuffer Sheep to come upon St. Foin, except betwixt Mowing-time and *All-Saints.*   And there is ſo much Danger of ſpoiling St. Foin by the Fraud of Shepherds, that I knew a Gentleman that bound his Tenant never to ſuffer any Sheep to come thereon; and by this means his St. Foin continued in Perfection much longer than is uſual, where St. Foin is ſuffer'd to be fed by Sheep.

(c) Natural Graſs is not kill'd by conſtant feeding, becauſe no ſort of Cattle can bite it ſo low as to deprive it of all its Leaves; and 'tis, like Eels, more tenacious of Life than the reſt of its Genius, and will ſend out Leaves from the very Roots when reverſed, as is too often ſeen where turffy Land is plow'd up in large Furrows.

cient

cient for the Use of the reviving Plants: Nay, I have seen Plants of St. Foin cut off in the Winter a Foot deep, and the Earth of that Depth taken away; and the remaining Root recover'd, and grew to an extraordinary Bigness: But this was preserv'd from Cattle at first.

I esteem St. Foin to be much more profitable than Clover, because St. Foin is never known to do any perceivable Damage to the Corn amongst which 'tis planted; but Clover often spoils a Crop of Barley (a); and I have known, that the Crop of Barley has been valued to have suffer'd Four Pounds *per* Acre Damage by a Crop of broad Clover's growing in it in a wet Summer: In a dry Summer both Sorts of Clover are apt to miss growing; and if it does grow, and the next Summer (wherein it ought to be a Crop) prove very dry, it fails on most sorts of Land, tho' it was vigorous enough to spoil the Barley the Year it was sown; at best, 'tis of but very short Duration, and therefore is not to be depended on by the Farmer, for maintaining his Cattle, which the broad Clover will also kill, sometimes by causing them to swell, unless great Care be taken to prevent it. The broad Clover is esteem'd a foul Feed for Horses. The Hop Clover is gone out of the Ground sooner than the broad Clover; I never knew it cut more than once: Indeed Cattle are never swollen by feeding on it; but then it affords but very little Feeding for them, except the Land whereon it grows be very rich.

St. Foin is observ'd to enrich whatever Ground 'tis planted on, tho' a Crop be taken off it yearly.

(a) But this Damage may be prevented by drilling the Clover after the Barley is an Handful high or more; for then the Barley will keep it under, and not suffer it to grow to any considerable Bigness till after Harvest; nor will this Drill, being drawn by Hand, do any Damage to the Barley.

Poor

Poor Slate Land (*a*), when it has borne fown St. Foin for Six or Seven Years, being plow'd up, and well till'd, produces Three Crops of Corn; and then they fow it with St. Foin again.

Rich arable Land was planted with it, and mow'd annually with very great Crops ('twas drill'd in Nine-inch Rows, with Six Gallons of Seed to an Acre; One Crop of it was fold at Four Pounds*per* Acre): This, after about Seven Years, and in full Perfection, was plow'd up by a Tenant, and continued for many Years after fo rich, that, inftead of dunging or fallowing it for Wheat, they were forc'd to fow that upon Barley-ftubble, and to feed the Wheat with Sheep in the Spring, to prevent its being too luxuant.

But 'tis to be noted, that the Land muft be well till'd at the breaking up of old St. Foin, or elfe the Firft Crops of Corn may be expected to fail: For I knew a Tenant, who, the laft Year of his Term, plow'd up a Field of St. Foin, that would have yielded him Three Pounds *per* Acre; but, thinking to make more Profit of it by Corn, he fow'd it with White Oats upon once Plowing; and it proving a dry Summer, he loft his Plowing and Seed; for he had no Crop of Oats, and was forc'd to leave the Land as a Fallow to his Succeffor.

Many more Inftances there are of this Failure of the Crop of Corn after St. Foin has been broken up, and not well till'd.

(*a*) The Poverty of this fort of Land, lying upon Slate or Stone, generally proceeds from the Thinnefs of it; and, if it were thicker, it would be good Land: Much of this Earth, being difperfed among the Crannies or Interftices of the Slate and Stone to a great Depth, is reach'd by the Tap-roots of the St. Foin, but cannot be reach'd by the Roots of Corn; and therefore, when conftantly kept in Tillage, is of fmall Value: Upon which Account fuch Land is greatly improveable by St. Foin, even when fown in the common manner.

When

When St. Foin is grown old, and worn out, as 'tis said to be when the artificial Pasture is gone, and the natural Pasture is become insufficient for the Number of Plants that are on it, to be maintained; and is so poor, that it produces no profitable Crop, so that the Ground is thought proper to be plow'd up, and sown with Corn, in order to be replanted (*a*); the most effectual Way to bring it into Tilth speedily, is, to plow it up in the Winter, with a Four-coulterd Plough, and make it fit for Turneps by the following Season; and if the Turneps be well ho'd, and especially if spent by Sheep on the Ground, 'twill be in excellent Order to be sown with Barley the following Spring; and then it may be drill'd with St. Foin amongst the Barley.

To return to the Benefit Land receives by having been planted some Years with St. Foin : All the Experienc'd know, that Land is enriched by it; but they do not agree upon the Reason why.

They agree as to the Ὅτι, but not the Διότι.

Some are of Opinion, 'tis because the St. Foin takes a different Sort of Nourishment to that of

(*a*) Or if you perceive, that there is a competent Number of Plants alive, and tolerably single; be they never so poor, you may recover them to a flourishing Condition in the following manner, without replanting : Pulverize the whole Field in Intervals of about Three Feet each, leaving betwixt every Two of them Four Feet Breadth of Ground unplow'd. When the Turf of these Intervals, being cut by the Four coulter'd Plough, is perfectly rotten, one Furrow made by any sort of Plough will hoe one of these Intervals, by changing the whole Surface of it. The poorer the Land is, the more Hoeings will be required ; and the oftener 'tis ho'd, with proper Intermissions the first Year, the stronger the St. Foin will become, and the more Years it will continue good, without a Repetition of Hoeing.

The Expence of this cannot be great ; because the Plough, in hoeing an Acre in this manner Nine Times, travels no farther than it must to plow an Acre once in the common Manner.

I need not tell the Owner, that the Earth of these Intervals must be made level, before the St. Foin can be mowed.

Corn :

Corn: But that I think is difprov'd in the Chapter of *Change of Species*, where 'tis fhewn, that all Plants in the fame Soil muft take the fame Food.

Mr. *Kirkham* thinks St. Foin has no collateral or horizontal Roots in the upper Part of the Ground where the Plough tills for Corn; and therefore has no Nourifhment from that Part of the Soil which feeds the Corn. This would be a very good Account for it, were it not utterly contrary to Matter of Fact, as every one may fee.

But fo far it is right, that large *(a)* St. Foin draws the greateft Part of its Nourifhment from below the Reach of the Plough; and what Part it does receive from the Staple is overbalanc'd by the Second Crop, or After-leafe, being fpent by Cattle on the Ground; different from Corn, which is very near wholly maintain'd by the plow'd Part of the Earth, and is all carry'd off.

For tho' the under *Stratum* of Earth be much poorer than the upper; yet that, never having been drain'd by any fort of Vegetables, muft afford confiderable Nourifhment to the Firft that comes there.

And befides, in fuch Land whofe Poverty proceeds from the Rain's carrying its Riches too quickly down through the upper *Stratum*, the under *Stratum* muft be the richer *(b)* for receiving what the upper *Stratum* lets pafs unarrefted.

(a) For large St. Foin, being fingle, has large Roots, and very long, which probably defcend Twenty Feet deep: Now, if we allow Four or Five Inches the Depth of the Staple, to afford a Supply equal to Two Feet below it, taking the lower Nineteen Feet Seven Inches together, upon this Computation, the Part below the Staple gives the St. Foin about Nine Parts in Ten of its Suftenance.

(b) In light poor Land the Water carrying fome impregnated Earth along with it down lower than it does in ftrong Land, that is more tenacious of fuch impregnated Particles, the under *Strata* of ftrong Land are likely to be poorer than thofe of light Land.

'Tis

'Tis well known, that many Eſtates have been much improv'd by St. Foin; therefore there is no occaſion to mention Particulars.   Only I will take Notice, that the Firſt in *England* was one of about One hundred and Forty Pounds *per Annum*, ſown with St. Foin, and ſold for Fourteen Thouſand Pounds; and as I hear, continues, by the ſame Improvement, ſtill of the ſame Value.   This is, I ſuppoſe, the ſame that Mr. *Kirkham* mentions in *Oxfordſhire*.

Another Farm of Ten Pounds *per Annum* Rent, which, whilſt in Arable (*a*), was like to have undone the Tenant; but being all planted with St. Foin by the Owner, was lett at One hundred and Ten Pounds *per Annum*, and prov'd a good Bargain.

If it ſhould be aſk'd, Why St. Foin is an Improvement ſo much greater in *England*, than in other Countries? it might be anſwer'd by ſhewing the Reaſon why *Engliſh* Arable is of ſo much leſs Value than Foreign (*b*) where the Land is of equal Goodneſs, and the Corn produc'd of equal Price.

CHAP. XIII.

Of LUSERNE.

*L*A *Luſerne* is that famous *Herba Medica* ſo much extoll'd by the Antients.

The high Eſteem they had of its Uſe appears by the extraordinary Pains they beſtow'd on its Culture.

(*a*) Theſe Eſtates conſiſted of thin Slate Land; which before it was planted with St. Foin, was valued at two Shillings *per* Acre, and ſome Part of it at One Shilling *per* Acre (as I have been inform'd); and yet Oxen are well fatted by the St. Foin it produces.

(*b*) 'Tis doubtleſs from the extraordinary Price of *Engliſh* Labour above that of other Countries, occaſioned by *Engliſh* Statutes being in this Reſpect different from all other Laws in the World.

Its

Its Leaves refemble thofe of Trefoil: It bears a blue Bloffom very like to double Violets, leaving a Pod like a Screw, which contains the Seeds about the Bignefs of broad Clover, tho'-longer, and more of the Kidney-fhape.

The Stalks grow more perpendicular than any of the other artificial Graffes that I know, flender, full of Knots and Leaves: 'Tis of very near an equal Bignefs from Bottom to Top: When cut, if vigorous, the Stalks will fpring out again from the Stubs, immediately below where the Scythe parted them; which makes them the fooner ready for another Mowing; an Advantage which no other Grafs has.

It has a Tap-root that penetrates deeper into the Bowels of the Earth, than any other Vegetable fhe produces.

Tho' one Luferne-root be much more taper than another towards the upper Part of it, 'tis fometimes feen, that a fingle ho'd Plant of it has many of thefe perpendicular Roots, fome of them fpringing out from the very Branches of its Crown.

Its Roots are abundantly longer than the Roots of St. Foin: I have One that meafures very near Two Inches Diameter: Thofe which are higher than the Ground have a Bark like a Tree. Upon this account, and by its Stalks fpringing again juft below the Place where cut off, and by the woody Hardnefs of its Stalks, when they ftand too long without cutting, it feems that Luferne is of a Nature nearly approaching to that of a Shrub.

Luferne is the only Hay in the World that can pretend to excel or equal St. Foin. I have known Inftances of the pinguefying Virtue of this *Medica Hay*, that come up to the higheft Encomiums given it by the *Romans*; which being to the Vulgar incredible, I forbear to relate, but leave to be confirm'd by the Experience of others, when it becomes frequent in *England*.

O   . Luferne

Luserne in Grafs is much fweeter than St. Foin, or any other artificial or natural Grafs. This, when ho'd, may be given to Cattle cut green, for Six Months; but then Care muft be taken to (a) prevent their Swelling by its Lufcioufnefs, and not to give them too much at once, until they be accuftom'd to it.

The Quantities of Luferne Seed annually imported, and fown without Succefs, not difcouraging People from continuing its Importation, fhews there is more need of a fuccefsful Way of Planting, than recommending it in *England*.

I fhall take Notice of fome of the Reafons why I conclude there is no Hope of making any Improvement by planting it in *England*, in any manner practis'd by the Antients or Moderns.

I wonder how any one fhould attempt to plant it here, who has feen in *Columella*, and other Authors, the Defcription of the manner the old *Romans* planted it in. They chofe out the very beft Land, that was both *pinguis* and *putris*; they dung'd and till'd it to the greateft Perfection, and laid it out in Beds, as we do for Onions or Afparagus; they fow'd it

(a) The Swelling of Cattle by eating too much green Luferne, Clover, or Turnep-leaves, happens only to fuch as chew the Cud, becaufe they fwallow more in lefs Time than other Cattle do; and a large Quantity of fuch lufcious Greens being fwallow'd by a Beaft, fermenting to a great Degree, heats and rarifies the internal Air, which by its Spring becoming too ftrong for that Column of the Atmofphere that enters at the Trachea, it preffes the Lungs againft the Thorax fo clofely, that the Weight of the external Column is not of Force to open their Veficles, and then the Circulation of the Blood is ftopt, and the Beaft is ftrangled.

· Moft Farmers know how to prevent the Swelling, fo that now-a-days it feldom happens; but when it does, there is an effectual way of curing it, if taken in Time: They cut a Hole into the Maw near the Back in a proper manner, whereat the rarified Air rufhes out, and the Lungs again perform their Action of Refpiration.

very

very thick, for that miserable Reason of enabling it
by its Thickness the better to kill the Grass.   The
Beds being harrow'd very fine before Sowing, which
was in the End of *April*; the Seed required to be
speedily cover'd, left the Sun's Heat should spoil it.
But with what Instrument must it be cover'd? For,
after Sowing, the Place must not be touch'd with
Iron.   *At medica obruitur non aratro, sed ligneis
rasteltis*. ' *Medica*-seed is cover'd,   not with the
' Plough, but with little (or rather light) wooden
' Harrows.' Two Days Work (of a Team) were spent
on this Harrowing of one Acre.   Some time after it
came up, they scratch'd it again and again with the
same wooden Instruments: This was call'd Sarrition:
Then by Runcation they weeded it over and over, *Ne
alterius generis herba invalidam medicam perimat*. ' Left
' other Grass should kill it whilst it was weak.' The
First Crop they let stand till some of the Seed shat-
ter'd, to fill the Ground yet fuller of Plants: After
that they might cut it as young as they pleas'd; but
must be sure to water it often after cutting.   Then
after a few Days, when it began to spring, they repeated their Runcation : and so continuing to weed out
all manner of Grass for the First Two or Three Years,
it used to bring Four or Six Crops a Year, and last
Ten Years.

English Gardeners make Forty Pounds of an Acre
of Asparagus, or Cabbage-plants, with half the Labour and Expence that was bestow'd on an Acre of
Roman Medica.

We know not the Price Hay and Grass were at in
Italy, while the *Roman Empire* was in its Glory, and
Rome, then the Metropolis of the World, drew the
Riches of all Parts thither; its Price must be then
very high.

And the *Romans* had not only Servants, but plenty of Slaves, for whom they had scarce sufficient
Employment: This might lessen the Expence of this

tedious

tedious Method of Planting, and ordering the *Medica*. But when the *Romans* were brought down to the Level of other Nations, and in Danger of being Slaves, inftead of having them ; and the Lands of *Italy* came to be cultivated by *Italian* Hands only; they found fomething elfe more neceffary to employ them in, than the Sarritions, Runcations, and Rigations of the *Medica*. Their Labour being beftow'd in getting Bread for themfelves, they fubftituted other artificial Graffes of more eafy Culture, in the room of *Medica*, for the Food of their Cattle. They were fo bigotted to all the Superftitions of their Anceftors, that they were content to lofe the Ufe of that moft beneficial Plant, rather than attempt to cultivate it by a new, tho' more rational Method, when they were become unable any longer to continue it by the old.

Thus, as I take it, Superftition has chafed *Medica* from the *Roman* Territories, and fo little of it is planted there, that beyond the *Alps* I could not find one whole Acre of it.

Luferne makes a great Improvement in the South of *France* : There, when their low fandy Land is well prepar'd, and very clean, they fow it alone, in *March*, and at *Michaelmas*, as we do Clover: Their fowing it at thofe Seafons is of a double Advantage : Firft, it faves the Labour of watering it, which would be impracticable for fo many thoufand Acres, as there are planted. Secondly, Thofe Seafons being much moifter than that wherein the *Romans* fow'd it, the Grub has Opportunity of eating more of it at its firft coming up; and often the Froft kills fome of it. By thefe Advantages the Ground is lefs over-ftock'd.

The Summers there are much drier than in *Italy*, fo that the Sun fcorches up the natural Grafs, and fuffers it not to come to a Turf till after fome Years; and therefore has lefs need of Weeding.

But,

But as that natural Grafs increafes, the Crops of Luferne are proportionably diminifh'd: And tho' Luferne is faid to laft Ten or Twelve Years; yet it is in Perfection only for a very few Years. Whilft it is at beft on their richeft Land, and in a kind Summer, they have at Seven Crops Ten Tuns to an Acre, as I have computed them from the Relation of fome of the Inhabitants of *Pezenas*. This was extraordinary: for I obferv'd, that moft of their common Crops made a very thin Swarth.

When the Ground begins to be turffy and hard, many of the Luferne-plants die, and the reft fend up very few Stalks: The People know this is the Deftruction of it, and therefore I have feen fome of them, in that Cafe, half-plow it, thinking thereby to deftroy the Turf: This does for a time much ftrengthen the Luferne-plants; but it fo much ftrengthens the Grafs alfo, that the Turf grows the ftronger; and then there is no Remedy but to plow it up, make the Ground clean, and replant it.

In more Northern Climates, where it rains oftener, the Ground fooner becomes hard; and in the Land otherwife moft proper for Luferne, the Grafs grows infinitely fafter, and will be as ftrong a Turf in Two Years, as in the hot Countries in Ten. Upon this Account, about *Paris*, even near the Walls, they plow up Luferne, and fow St. Foin in its room, becaufe that endures Grafs and hard Ground better, tho' it brings but One Crop a Year, or Two at moft.

And in many Places in *Franche Comtè* and *Switzerland*, I have feen Luferne in the Corners of Vineyards, not above Two or Three Perches together, which they will at any Expence have to cure their Horfes when fick; fince they cannot obtain, by their Culture, Quantities fufficient to maintain them as their ordinary Food, there being too much Rain, and too little

of

of the Sun's violent Heat, to prevent the speedy Increase of Grass amongst it.

How then can we expect Success in sowing it in
England, where Rains are yet more frequent, and the
Sun is weaker ? 'Tis not One Year in Ten, that the
natural Grass is here scorch'd up.   In our rich Land
the Grass comes to a Turf very soon, and poor Land
will not by the common Sowing bring Luserne to any
Perfection, tho' no Grass should annoy it.

I have here seen Part of a Meadow Breast-plow'd,
and, when the Turf was dead, dug up and planted as
a Garden: After it had been drill'd with Carrots, ho'd,
and made, in all Appearance, perfectly clean, it was
sown with Luserne, which came up and flourish'd
very well the First Year, and indifferently the Second;
but, after that, the Grass came, and the Luserne grew
faint; and in Three or Four Years time there was no
more left, but just to shew by here-and-there a single
poor Stalk, that there had been Luserne sown, except one Plant of it, which was cleansed of Grass the
Third Year; and this recover'd, and sent up Abundance of Stalks for Two Years after it; and then the
Grass returning, that Plant dwindled again.

I have often try'd it in the richest Part of my
Garden, and constantly find, that, however vigorously
it grows at the first, yet it soon declines, when the
Grass appears amongst it, which is always the sooner,
by how much the Soil (in *England*) is richer, unless
the Spade or Hoe prevent it.

Here have been also many Fields of a poorer white-
ish Soil sown with it, which are not very subject to
be over-run with Grass, as the rich Land is; and
tho' these were so well till'd as scarce any Grass appear'd, during the many Years the Luserne liv'd
therein, yet it never grew to any Perfection here
neither; nor was there any one Crop worth much
more than the Cutting, it was always so poor, thin,
and short.   And, by what Intelligence I can get, all
Ex-

Experience proves, that every Soil in this Island is too rich, too poor, or too cold, for the Luserne Improvement by the common Husbandry.

I believe every one will be confirmed in this, who shall upon full Inquiry find, that, amongst the great Quantities which have been sown in this Kingdom in that manner, never any of it was known to continue good and flourishing Three Years; and that, on the contrary, never any one Plant of it in any warm Soil, cultivated by the Hoeing manner, was known to fail here, or in any other Country, as long as the Hoeing (or Digging about it, which is equivalent) was continued to it with proper Repetitions.

A Multitude of such hoed Plants have I known, and are now to be seen in both poor and rich Lands: Therefore it seems possible, that Thousands of *English* Acres may be capable, by the Hoeing Culture, to produce Crops of Luserne every Year for an Age. For as the greater Moisture, and less intense Heat of this Climate, are, upon the Accounts mentioned, injurious to Luserne, yet this is only to such as is sown and cultivated in the common Manner, because our Climate, upon the very same Accounts, is very advantageous to hoed Luserne.

In hot Countries, when the Summer is drier than ordinary, the Sun so scorches it, that they have fewer and much poorer Crops, than in moister Summers; *viz.* only Four or Five, instead of Six or Seven; but, in the driest Summer I ever knew in *England*, hoed Luserne yielded the most Crops.

Our Summer Days are longer, have more of the Sun's Warmth, and less of his fiery Heat; he cherishes, but never burns Luserne, or any other hoed long Tap-rooted Plant in *England*.

The well hoed Earth, being open, receives and retains the Dews; the benign solar Influence is sufficient to put them in Motion, but not to exhale them

O 4.   from

from thence. The Hoe prevents the Turf, which
would otherwise by its Blades or Roots intercept, and
return back the Dews into the Atmosphere, with the
Assistance of a moderate Heat. So that this Husbandry
secures Luserne from the Injury of a wet Summer,
and also causes the Rain-water to sink down more
speedily, and disperse its Riches all the Way of its
Passage; otherwise the Water would be more apt to
stand on the Surface, chill the Earth, and keep off
the Sun and Air from drying it: For, when the Surface is dry and open, Luserne will bear a very great
Degree of Heat, or grow with a mean one. I have
seen this hoed Luserne, in a sheltry Place of my
Garden, so much grown in a mild Winter, as to be
measured Fourteen Inches and an half high at *Christ-
mas*; and a very large single Plant of it, which had
not been hoed for Two Years before, was laid bare
by digging out the Earth all around it a Foot deep,
to observe the Manner of its Tap-root; and then the
Earth was thrown in again, and the Hole filled up.
This was on the Twenty-seventh of *September*. Upon
this mellowing of the Soil about it, it sent out more
Stalks in *October*, than it had done in the whole ' um-
mer before; they grew very vigorously, until a great
Snow fell in *December*, which also preserved the Ver-
dure of them, till that was melted away, and a black
Frost came after it, and killed those Stalks. It is
probable this Plant sent out immediately new fibrous
horizontal Roots, which did grow apace to extract the
Nourishment from this new-made Pasture, in pro-
portion to the quick Growth of the Stalks, which in
Summer have been measured, and found to grow in
Height Three Inches and an half in a Night and a
Day; this being almost One Inch in Six Hours.

And it has been my Observation, that this Plant,
in hot and cold Countries, thrives both with a much
greater, or less Degree of Heat and Moisture, when
it is hoed; for if it has Plenty of Nourishment, which

Hoeing

Hoeing always gives it, a very little Heat above, and the Moisture alone (which is never wanting to the deep Tap-root) suffice, and that Plenty of Food enables it the better to endure the Extremes of either Heat or Cold.

We need not much apprehend the Danger of *English* Winters; for Luserne will endure those which are more rigorous. In the Principality of *Neufchâtel* the Winters are so severe, as to kill all the Rosemary left abroad; yet Luserne survives them there: This proves it more hardy than Rosemary, which is planted for Hedges in *England*; and here is scarce twice in an Age a Frost able to kill it.

I have one single Luserne-plant in a poor Arable Field, that has stood the Test of Two-and-twenty Winters, besides the Feeding of Sheep at all Seasons, and yet remains as strong as ever. What Quantity of Hay this Plant yearly produces, cannot be known, because at those times that Cattle are kept from it, the Hares constantly crop it, being sweeter than any other Grass.

But this happens to be fortunately situate, where 'tis not altogether destitute of the Benefit of Hoeing. 'Tis in an Angle, where, every time the Field is till'd, the Plough goes over it in turning from the Furrows of one Land and one Head-land; but it is after the Plough is lifted out of the Ground, and turned up on one side, so that the Share only breaks the Turf very small all around it, without plowing up the Plant: Yet it has escaped it so narrowly, that the Fin of the Plough-share has split it into Four Parts; Three of which remain, and grow never the worse, but the Fourth is torn off, and the Wound healed up.

By the extreme hard Winter that happened about the Year 1708, or 1709, some of the Luserne in *Languedoc* was killed: Yet this was no Argument of its Tenderness, but rather the contrary; because then all the Olive-trees and Walnut-trees were there killed,

tho'

tho' the greateft Part of the Luferne efcaped unhurt: And I did not hear one Walnut-tree was killed that Winter in *England*. Perhaps thofe in *France*, having being accuftomed to much hotter Summers, were unable to endure the Rigour of the fame Winter, that could do no Harm to the fame Species in *England*, where our Winters do not feem to exceed fome of theirs in Cold, fo much as their Summers do ours in Heat. And fince the Extremes are not fo far afunder here, the fame Degree of Cold may to our Plants feem tepid, which to thofe in *Languedoc* muft feem rigorous, differing a more remote Degree from the oppofite Extremity of Heat in Summer.

And, befides the Difference of Heat and Cold in different Climates, there is another more neceffary to be obferved ; and that is, the Difference of the Hardinefs in different Individuals of the fame Species : The fame Froft that kills a faint languifhing Plant of Luferne, will be defpifed by a robuft one, which, being well fed by the Hoe, becomes a Giant cloath'd and fenced with a thick Bark, that renders it impregnable againft all Weather; its Rind is to it a Coat of Mail or Buff, impenetrable by Froft: But the unhoed is generally fmall and weak; its thin tender Bark expofes it almoft naked to the Froft; it being, for want of a fufficient Pafture, ftarv'd and half-dead already, 'tis the more eafily killed by the Cold.

I formerly lived fome Years in *Languedoc*, where are many Hundred Acres of Luferne ; and I never could find a very large Plant amongft it, unlefs in fuch Pieces as had been plowed up, tilled, and fown with Corn : Here indeed thofe Plants that remained (as always fome would do) grew to an extraordinary Bulk ; and One of thofe fingle tilled Plants did feem to produce a greater Quantity of Stalks, than Twenty of fuch as had not been plowed up ; and as there were no large Plants amongft the unplowed, fo there were no fmall amongft the plowed ones. The fame thing has

has been obferved in all other Places where Luferne
has been plowed (*a*).

And in *Wiltfhire* feveral Grounds of it ftood fome
Years without ever coming to a Subftance to be of
any Value, tho' the Land was whitifh, and fcarce any
Grafs appeared amongft the Luferne ; and therefore
its Poornefs was thought to proceed from the Soil's
being improper ; but when it had been broken up,
and fown feveral Years with Corn, and afterwards
lain down with St. Foin, all the Luferne-plants which
remained (and they were many) grew large and ftrong,
fhooting up a Yard in Height foon after the St. Foin
was cut ; and if there had been a competent Number
of them undeftroyed by the Plough, they would have
yielded Crops of an extraordinary Value, where before Plowing it grew but few Inches above the
Ground.

It feems that in this fort of Land the Earth grows
ftale, ere the Luferne arrives at a Tenth Part of its
Stature : But this is moft remarkable, that Tillage
transforms thofe Luferne-plants from Dwarfs to Gi-
ants ; and then they are able to contend with, if not
conquer, fo ftrong Plants as St. Foin is, tho' before
Plowing they were unable to refift the Depredations
of a few hairy Spires of Grafs.

Since Tillage can thus recover Luferne, after it has
long languifhed in the loweft Ebb of Life, and reftore
it to Health, Youth, and Vigour, and augment its
Stature even after it has paffed the Age of its full
Growth ; to what Bulk would it arrive, regularly
planted, and hoed from its Infancy to Maturity without any Check to ftint it !

We can never know how poor a Soil will bear this
Plant, unlefs it be tried by the Hoeing Culture.

For 'tis wondrous how fo great a Man as Dr.
Woodward fhould imagine, that Difference of Soil

- ` (*a*) This Plowing is a Hoeing to the Luferne.

fhould

fhould be the Reafon why Apples in *Herefordfhire*,
and Cherries in *Kent*, fucceed better than in other
Places, when in truth they are feen to profper as well
almoft all over *England*, where planted, cultivated,
and preferved.

I believe Plants are more altered as to their Growth,
by being cultivated or not, than by Change of Climates differing in very many Degrees of Latitude.
I fay, in their Growth, not always in their Fruit; for
tho' a Peach-tree, well cultivated in a Standard, will
grow here vigoroufly, and be very beautiful; yet
its Fruit will be of little Value, unlefs it be planted
againft a good Wall: So Luferne, unlefs cultivated
upon a well expofed Gravel, will yield little Seed in
England.

The Soil to plant it on is either an hot Gravel, a
very rich dry Sand, or fome other rich warm Land,
that has not an under *Stratum* of Clay, nor is too
near the Springs of Water; for, if the Earth below
be of a cold Nature, which I take to be occafioned
by its holding of Water, the Luferne will not long
profper therein, of whatever Sort the upper *Stratum*
of Earth may be: This may be guefled at by the Vegetables a Soil naturally produces, as Fern, and the
like; which, Mr. *Evelyn* obferves, do indicate a Soil
fubject to Extremities of Heat and Cold; and con-
demns fuch a Soil as accurfed.   I agree to that Sen-
tence, as far as relates to Cold; but am not fatisfied of
its abounding with Heat; and I am fure I know fome
Land very fubject to Fern, which is very far from
being barren, when well cultivated, and well fuited
with Vegetables; but, from among thefe, Luferne
muft be excluded.

Luferne in hot Countries grows beft near Rivers,
where its Roots reach the Water, which helps to mi-
tigate the exceflive Heat of the Climate; but here the
Heats are fo moderate, that if Luferne-roots are in
Water (for 'tis that that makes Earth cold) it dimi-

nifhes

nifhes too much the juft Proportion of Heat, which Luferne requires.

The natural Poornefs of an hot Gravel may be compenfated by Dung, more Heat, and the Benefit of the Hoe.

The natural Richnefs of the other forts of Land being increafed by hoeing and cleanfing it from Grafs, Luferne will thrive therein with the lefs Heat; for what the Soil wants of one of thefe Two Qualities, muft be made up with the other; and it has grown high in hoed rich Ground at *Chriftmas,* when that in Land of an hotter Nature, but poorer, has not been able to peep out, for want of more Nourifhment: So, if rich Land be clayey, very wet and cold, tho' very rich, it requires much Heat, for as high a Growth of Luferne at *Midfummer.*

The beft Seafon of planting it in *England* is in *April,* after the Danger of Froft is over; for a fmall Froft will deftroy the whole Crop, when the Plants firft appear; and too much Wet, with cold Weather, will rot the Seeds in the Ground; fo that about the Middle of *April* may be generally efteemed as the beft Seafon for fowing this Seed.

The hoed Plants of Luferne having larger Roots, and yielding more Crops than thofe of St. Foin, Reafon feems to require, that the Number of the former be lefs.

But, on the other hand, if we confider, that as the Luferne-roots exceed the St. Foin in Bignefs, fo they alfo do in Length, by as great a Proportion; being generally lefs taper, and as they go deeper, they have more Earth to nourifh them; they alfo require a better Soil, and more frequent Aids from the Hoe; and, by their extraordinary quick Growth, receive a fpeedier Relief from it, than the Roots of St. Foin do.

Thus, if by reaching deeper in a better Soil, and being more hoed, Luferne receives, from a fquare

Perch

Perch of Ground, Nourifhment in a proportion double to that whereby its Roots exceed thofe of St. Foin in Bignefs, then I do not fee why we fhould not leave the Number of Luferne-plants double to the Number of thofe we leave in St. Foin.

But if the Excefs of Nourifhment were no more than the Excefs of Bignefs of Roots, I think an equal Number of Plants fhould be left in Luferne, and in St. Foin: Yet fince the hot or cold Conftitution of a Plant, and alfo the Quantity it can produce, ought to be confidered, as well as its Bulk, in relation to the Nourifhment it requires, more Trials are necef- fary for determining the exact Number of Luferne- plants proper to be placed on a fquare Perch, than have been hitherto made.

Perhaps it will be thought heterodox to maintain by any Arguments, that to err in falling fomewhat fhort of the juft Number, is not of worfe Confe- quence, than exceeding it.

Where they ftand at Four or Five Inches afunder in the Rows, 'tis obferved, that tho' the Intervals be- twixt the Rows be wide, yet the Plants are much the . larger, and produce more that ftand in the outfide Rows (the Ground without being clean) ; and efpe- cially thofe at each End of the outfide Rows, that is, the Corner-plants, are largeft of all. I need not fay, that had all the other Plants as much Room and Tillage as the Corner ones have, they would be as large, and produce each as much Hay ; for thofe which ftand perfectly fingle in Places by themfelves, are feen to be larger, and produce more, than thofe Corner ones ; and of the larger and longer Roots our Stock does confift, the more Nourifh- ment they are capable of taking, as has been fhewn. Where fome Plants of the Luferne have been planted Two Feet afunder, in poor dry Land, which was kept clean from Weeds, and frequently digged, each Plant has fent forth upward of Three Hundred Stalks,

and

and thefe have been Six or Seven Inches high by the Middle of *March*.

And it muft be likewife obferv'd, that the Crop will be produc'd in Proportion to the Nourifhment it receives; for if the moft gigantic Luferne plant, which, when pamper'd by the Hoe, has made a Produce more like a Tree than an Herb, remains a few Years without that or fome equivalent Culture, it will by little and little ceafe to produce more than a few poor fickly Stalks, juft to fhew its Species; and then, if this Culture be repeated, will recover its priftine Strength, and yield as great a Crop as ever; but, if that be longer omitted, will die: The Vaftnefs of its Root avails nothing, unlefs it has Food in proportion to it.

Hence it appears, that the moft fatal Difeafe incident to Luferne is ftarving, and that rarely fuffers any of its Plants to arrive at the full Period of their Growth or Age; it prevents their Fertility even in the Prime of their Youth, and kills them before they have liv'd out Half, or perhaps the Tenth Part, of their Days. How long its Life might otherwife be, nobody knows, unlefs a Plant could be found to die when well fed; for when it is, 'tis fo tenacious of Life, that, I am told, beheading will not difpatch it (*a*).

'Tis therefore neceffary, that our Rows be plac'd at fuch a Diftance, as that their Intervals may be wide enough for the Hoe-plough to raife an artificial Pafture, fufficient to fuftain the Number of Plants in them.

Whoever fhall make Trials of this Hufbandry (for that is all I propofe to others), I would advife them to begin with Rows that have Intervals of Thirty-three Inches; for, if they begin with much

(*a*) But I have cut off the Heads of fome myfelf to try, and could not find that any one would fprout again, tho' *St. Foin* will; perhaps I tried at the wrong Seafon.

narrower

narrower Diftances, they may be by that means dif-appointed of Succefs : But tho' they fhould after-wards find a Way to hoe them at fomewhat nearer Diftances ; yet the Lofs of a few Perches of Ground would not be much; neither can they be wholly loft, fince the Roots of thefe Plants may be prov'd to ex-tend much farther horizontally, than from Row to Row at that Diftance.   And the wider the Intervals are, the more Earth will be till'd in a Perch of Ground; becaufe Six Rows, which will be therein at Thirty-three Inches Diftance, will admit the Hoe-plough to till more Earth, than Nine Rows at Twenty-two Inches Diftance from each other · And, befides, 'tis not proper, that every time of hoeing, the Plough fhould come very near to the Plants, unlefs when Grafs comes amongft them; and then they may, in Thirty-three Inch Spaces, be perfectly cleanfed in this manner : *viz.* Plow a good Furrow from each Side of every Row ; and then with Harrows, or other Inftru-ments proper for that Purpofe, going crofs them, you will pull out both Earth and Grafs from betwixt the Plants ; then, after a convenient Time, plow thefe Furrows back again to the Rows; this will in a man-ner tranfplant the upper Part of the Roots, and bury the Grafs, tho' it be not dead, by lying open to be dry'd by the Sun : Then harrow the Ground to break it more, and to level it, and go once over it with a very light Roller, to the End that the Hay may be raked up the cleaner.

I am aware of the common Prejudice, which is, that People, when they have never feen a Plantation of thefe Plants in Perfection, are apt to form to themfelves the Idea of fuch fmall ones as they have been ufed to fee; and thence imagine it impoffible that this (tho' a double) Number fhould be fufficient to make a Crop.   But they might, with equal Rea-fon, imagine the fame of Apple-trees at a Year's Growth, which are lefs than thefe at the fame Age;

and

and ſo plant a Thouſand Trees in the Room proper
for one.   The Antients direct the Planting of Seventeen *Cytiſus* Plants in a Perch of Ground; and I do
not believe, that ever thoſe Seventeen could yield a
Crop equal to Two hundred Twenty-four Luſerne-
plants; for as many Ounces of Hay as each of theſe
yields, ſo many Ton of Hay will one Crop of an
Acre produce: Thus by weighing the Product of one
Plant (ſuppoſing them all equal) the Quantity of the
Crop may be determin'd, and prov'd greater than
Fancy from their Number repreſents.

	s.	d.
April 14. One ſingle unho'd Plant of Luſerne had Thirty-one Stalks, which, by Silver-Money, weigh'd green —	23	0
24. The ſame dried to Hay, weigh'd	6	6
14. The Stalks of one ſingle ho'd Luſerne-plant green, weigh'd —	56	0
24. The ſame dry'd —— —	14	6
14. Eighteen Inches in Length of a Row, being five indifferent Plants, weigh'd green one Pound and an half *Avoirdupois*		
24. Dry'd to Hay, it weigh'd —	28	6
25. One Foot of an ho'd Row, being One hundred and Sixty-Stalks of two Luſerne Plants of Six or Seven Years old, weigh'd Two Pound green —		
But the ſame dry'd, to the 9th of *May*, weigh'd no more than —— —	31	6

Which laſt is about Three Tons to an Acre.

This I am certain of, that the leaſt competent
Number of Plants will bring the greateſt Number of
Crops: ſince I ſee the Stalks of a ſingle ho'd Plant
grow higher in Fifteen Days, than one amongſt near
Neighbours does in Thirty Days.

The greateſt Difference between the Culture of this
and St. Foin is, that Luſerne Rows ſhould be more
grown, before the Plants be made ſingle in them by
the Hand-hoe, leſt the Fly ſhould deſtroy ſome

after-

afterwards, and then they might become too thin. For Luferne is fometimes eaten by the Fly, as Turneps are, tho' St. Foin be never liable to that Misfortune, if fown in a proper Seafon. Luferne muft alfo be more frequently ho'd (*a*), in fome Proportion to the more frequent Crops it produces.

I fhall not go about to compute the Difference of Expence beftow'd in the *Roman* Culture and in this; yet it will appear theirs was incomparably more chargeable, and that the Excefs of Charge was occafioned by their Error in the Theory of Hufbandry.

They fow'd it fo thick, that the Plants muft needs be very fmall; and when Ten of them were no bigger than one good fingle ho'd Plant would have been, in the fame Space of the Earth's Surface, they could have but a Ninth Part of the Earth's Depth, which the one would have had. The Defect of Depth muft be therefore made up, in fome Meafure, by the extraordinary Richnefs of the Surface. Upon this Account few Lands were capable of bearing *Medica*. Their fowing it fo late made the firft Waterings neceffary; and the Shortnefs of the Roots required the repeated Rigations, after the Crops were cut: For

(*a*) The Hoe-plough is the Inftrument to bring it to Perfection: but then I doubt it muft lie ftill fome Years, left the plow'd Earth injure the Hay that is made upon it; and when it is come to a Turf, and the Luferne wants renewing, the Four coulter'd Plough is the only Inftrument that can prepare the Turf to be kill'd, and cure the Luferne; which Plough muft be ufed in the following Manner: Turn its Furrows toward one Row, and from the next; that is, plow round one Row, and that will finifh Two Intervals, and fo on; and the next Plowing muft be towards thofe Rows, from whence they were turn'd the firft time; take care the firft Furrows do not lie long enough on the Rows to kill the Plants, which will be much longer in Winter than in Summer. But you may leave every Third or Fourth Interval unhoed for making the Hay on, which will be yet more beneficial, if the Swarths in mowing fhould fall thereon. This unhoed Interval may be plowed when there is Occafion, and another left in its ftead.

Columella

Columella faith in *Lib*. ii. *Cap*. 11. *Cum fecueris autem, fæpius eam rigato*.   But had it been cultivated by the hoeing Method, the Tap-roots would have defcended as deep as a Well, and, from the Springs below, have fent up Water to the Plants, befides what the Hoe would have caufed the horizontal Roots to receive from Dews at the Surface above.   At how much a cheaper Rate Water is fupply'd by thefe Means, than by carrying it perhaps a great Way, and then fprinkling it by Hand over the Beds, which were made Ten feet wide between Path and Path for that Purpofe, let any one judge; as alfo what a laborious Tafk it was to pick out the Grafs with Fingers from amongft it, in the hard dry Ground in the Summer, after mowing the Crop, as *Columella* directs in his foremention'd Chapter, which the Horfe-hoe would have done with Eafe, at a Twentieth Part of that Expence.   However, fince they faw the *Medica* was as impatient of Grafs as the Vineyards were, 'tis a Wonder they did not give it the fame Culture with the *Bidens*, which would have been much better and cheaper, than to cleanfe the *Medica* with Fingers. Indeed Fingers were made before the *Bidens*; but fure the Effect of its Ufe in raifing Juices to the Vine, had infpired the *Romans* with more judicious Speculations, than to give that for a Reafon why they ho'd the *Medica* with their Fingers, rather than with the *Bidens*.

Oh! But this was made with Iron, and *Medica* had, in thofe Times, an Antipathy to Iron; and after it was fown, the Place muft not be touch'd by that Metal; therefore the Seed muft not be cover'd with a Plough, nor with Iron Harrows.   But if they had made Trials enough, to know that half an Inch was a proper Depth to cover this Seed at, thefe *Virtuofi* would have been convinc'd, that it had no lefs Antipathy to thefe Inftruments, of what *Matter* foever they were made, if they bury'd it Five or Six

Inches deep, which the Plough muſt do, and the
Weight of Iron Harrows in ſuch fine Ground not
much leſs. Had the Plough been all of Wood, the
Furrow would have lain never the lighter upon the
Seed ; and if the wooden Harrows had been loaded
with a Weight capable of preſſing it down as deep,
it would have been no more able to riſe, than if it
had been buried with Iron Harrows : This *Columella*
ſeems to be ſenſible of, when he ſays, *Raſtellis ligneis*; *viz*. That it was not ſufficient for them to be
made of Wood, unleſs they were diminutive ; for
then they were light ones. 'Tis probable the Plough
ſuffer'd none to come up, and the heavy Harrows
very few, tho' perhaps Plants enough, had they cal-
culated what Number were ſufficient: But unleſs the
Ground were cover'd with them at firſt, it ſeems
they had not Patience to wait till the Plants grew
large enough, to fill it with a bare competent Number, and thought it not worth while to weed and water,
what they fanſied to be an inſufficicient Number.
'Twas expected that the Thickneſs of the Plants
ſhould help to kill the Graſs: Yet upon due Obſervation 'tis found, that when their exceſſive Numbers
have brought a Famine amongſt them, they are forc'd
to prey upon one another ; and tho' the ſtronger ſur-
vive, yet even thoſe are ſo weaken'd by Hunger,
that they become the leſs able to contend with Graſs,
whoſe good Fortune it was, that Superſtition would
not permit the *Romans* to interpoſe, by attacking it
with Iron Weapons.

I hope theſe Hints may be improv'd for the Abo-
lition of old Errors, and for the Diſcovery of new
Truths; to the end that Luſerne may be planted in
a more reaſonable Method than has been commonly
practis'd: And when the Theory is true, 'tis impoſſible the Practice ſhould be falſe, if rightly apply'd ; but if it fail of Succeſs, the Event will be a

Proof

Proof either of a Mifapplication, or that the Theory is falfe.

Luferne fhould be order'd for Hay in the fame Manner as is directed for St. Foin in the foregoing Chapter : But it muft be obferv'd, that Luferne is more worfted by being fuffer'd to furvive its Virginity before cutting ; and therefore the richeft and moft nourifhing Hay is cut whilft the Stalks are fingle, without any collateral Branches fhooting out of them ;. and when they are fo, neither Bloffoms nor even their Buds appear.   But of that fown in the old Fafhion, the laft Crops, for want of a new Supply of Nourifh-ment, grow fo flowly, that ere it is high enough to be cut, the Bloffoms are blown out, and the Stalks, tho' very fmall, are become *woody*, *hard*, and *dry*, and make the Hay nothing near fo nourifhing as that of the firft Crops.

But in that which is ho'd, the laft Crops of it will, by virtue of the greater Quantity of Nourifhment it receives, grow fafter, and be of an Height fit to cut before bloffoming, and thence being as young and vigorous, make as good Hay as the firft Crops ; fo that Hoeing does not only procure more and larger Crops, but alfo better Hay.

This is moft certain, that unlefs we can keep our Luferne pretty clean from natural Grafs, we cannot expect it to fucceed, let the Soil be never fo proper.

C H A P.

C H A P. XIV.

Of Change of SPECIES.

I. *That Plants of the moſt different Nature feed on the ſame Sort of Food.*

II. *That there is no Plant but what muſt rob any other Plant within its Reach.*

III. *That a Soil which is proper to one Sort of Vegetable once, is, in Reſpect of the Sort of Food it gives, proper to it always.*

IF any one of theſe *Three Propoſitions* be true, as I hope to prove all of them are, then it will follow, that there is no need to change the Species of *Vegetables* from one Year to another, in reſpect to the different Food the ſame Soil is, tho' falſely, ſuppoſed to yield *(a)*.

The common Opinion is contrary to all theſe (as it muſt be, if contrary to any one of them): And ſince an Error in this fundamental Principle of *Vegetation* is of very ill Conſequence; and ſince Dr. *Woodward*, who has been ſerviceable in other reſpects *(b)* to this Art, has unhappily fallen in with the Vulgar in this Point; his Arguments for this Error require to be anſwer'd in the firſt Place.

(a) For if all Plants rob one another, it muſt be becauſe they all feed on the ſame Sort of Food; and, admitting they do, there can be no Neceſſity of changing the Species of them, from one Soil to another; but the ſame Quantity of the ſame Food, with the ſame Heat and Moiſture which maintains any Species one Year, muſt do it any other Year.

(b) By proving, in his Experiments, that Earth is the *Pabulum* of Plants.

The

The Doctor says (c) ' It is not possible to imagine
' how one uniform, homogeneous Matter, having its
' Principles, or original Parts, all of the same Sub-
' stance, Constitution, Magnitude, Figure, and Gra-
' vity, should ever constitute Bodies so egregiously
' *unlike*, in all those Respects, as Vegetables of dif-
' ferent Kinds are ; nay, even as the different Parts
' of the *same* Vegetable.

  ' That there should be that vast Difference in
' them, in their several Constitutions, Makes, Pro-
' perties, and Effects, and yet all arise from the very
' same Sort of Matter, would be very strange.'

Answer. 'Tis very probable, that the terrestrial
Particles which constitute *Vegetables*, tho' inconceiv-
ably minute, may be of great Variety of Figure, and
other Differences ; else they could not be capable of
the several Ferments, &c. they must undergo in the
Vessels of Plants.   Their Smalness can be no Objection to their Variety, since even the Particles of Light
are of various Kinds.

But as the Doctor asserts, ' That each Part of the
' same *Vegetable* requires a peculiar specific Matter
' for its Formation and Nourishment ; and that there
' are very many and different Ingredients to go to the
' Composition of the same individual Plants ;'

From hence must be inferred, that the same Plant
takes in very many and different Ingredients (and it
is proved, that no Plant refuses any Ingredient (d)
that is capable of entering its Roots.   Tho' the terrestrial Particles which nourish *Vegetables*, be not
perfectly homogeneous ; yet most of the various

(c) In *Philos. Transf.* No. 253.
(d) Dr. *Grew*, in his Anatomy of Plants, by microscopical
Inspection, found, that the outer Superficies of Roots was of a
spongy Substance; and 'tis well known, that no such Body can
refuse to imbibe whatever Liquor comes in Contact with it, but
will by its springy Porosity absorb any sort of Moisture.

Taftes and Flavours of Plants are made in and by
the Veffels (e).

Doctor *Woodward* fays, ' That Water will pafs
' Pores and Interftices, that neither Air, nor any
' other Fluid, will: This enables it to enter the fineft
' Tubes and Veffels of Plants, and to introduce the
' terreftrial Matter, conveying it to all Parts of them ;
' whilft each, by means of Organs 'tis endow'd with
' for the Purpofe, intercepts, and affumes into itfelf,
' fuch Particles as are fuitable to its own Nature (f);
' letting the reft pafs on *through the common Ducts.*'

Here then he fays plainly, That each Plant receives the terreftrial Matter in grofs, both fuitable and

(e) We are convinced, that 'tis the Veffels of Plants that make
the different Flavours ; becaufe there is none of thefe Flavours in
the Earth of which they are made, until that has enter'd and been
alter'd by the vegetable Veffels.

(f) If the Doctor's Plants were fo nice in leaving vegetable
Matter *behind, quiet and undifturb'd,* 'tis a Wonder they would
take up the mineral Matter, as, he fays, they did, that kill'd
themfelves with Nitre.

Thefe Plants might, with much lefs Difficulty, have diftinguifh'd
the mineral Matter from the vegetable Matter, than they could
diftinguifh the different Particles of vegetable Matter from one
another, and muft have been very unwife to chufe out the Nitre
(their Poifon) from the Water and Earth, and to leave the vegetable Particles behind ; none of which could be fo improper to
them as the Nitre.

It may perhaps be objected, that fuch like pernicious Matter
kills a Plant by only deftroying its Roots, and by clofing the
Pores; which prevents the Nourifhment from entering to maintain
its Life; and that fuch Matter doth not itfelf enter to act as
Poifon upon the Sap, or upon the Veffels of the Body, or Leaves :
But it plainly appears that it doth enter, and act as Poifon ; for
when fome of the Roots of a Mint, growing in Water, are put
into falt Water, it kills the whole Plant, although the reft of the
Roots remaining in the frefh Water were fufficient to maintain it,
if the other Roots had been cut off at the Time they were removed into the Salt Water ; and alfo all the Leaves, when dead,
will be full of Salt.

Or if the Juice of wild Garlick-feed be made ufe of inftead of
the falt Water, it will have the fame Effect ; and every one of the
Mint-leaves will have a ftrong Tafte of Garlick in it.

unfuit-

unfuitable to its Nature, retains the fuitable Particles
for its Augment, and the unfuitable lets pafs through
it.   And in another Place he fays they are exhal'd
into the Atmofphere.

And this will appear to be the true Cafe of Plants;
and directly contradicts what he advances, in faying,
' That each Sort of Grain takes forth that peculiar
' Matter that is proper for its own Nourifhment.
' Firft, the Wheat draws off thofe Particles that fuit
' the Body of that Plant, *the reft lying all quiet and*
' *undifturb'd the while*.   And when the Earth has
' yielded up all them, thofe that are proper for Bar-
' ley, a different Grain, remain ftill behind, till the
' fucceffive Crops of that Corn fetch them forth too;
' and fo the Oats and Peafe in their turn, till, in fine,
' all is carried off.'

In the former Paragraph he fays, each Plant *lets
pafs through it* the reft of the Particles that are not
fuitable to its own Nature.   In the latter Paragraph
he fays, That each *leaves* the unfuitable *all behind* for
another Sort; and fo on.

Both cannot be true.

If the latter were true, Change of Sorts would be
as neceffary as it is commonly thought.   But if the
former be true, as I hope to prove it is, then there
can be no Ufe of changing of Sorts in Refpect of
different Nourifhment.

If in this Series of Crops each Sort were fo juft
as to take only fuch Particles, as are peculiarly proper to it, letting all the reft alone to the other Sorts
to which they belonged, as the Doctor imagines;
then it would be equal to them all, which of the
Sorts were fown firft or laft: But let the Wheat be
fown after the Barley, Peafe, and Oats, inftead of
being fown before them, and then it would evi-
dently appear, by that ftarv'd Crop of Wheat,
either that fome or all of thofe other Grains had
violated this natural Probity, or elfe that Nature
has

has given to *Vegetables* no fuch Law of *Meum* and *Tuum* (g).

If thefe Things were, as the Doctor affirms, why do Farmers lofe a Year's Rent, and be at the Charge of fallowing and manuring their Land, after fo few Crops; fince there are many more Sorts of Grain as different from thefe and one another, as thofe are which they ufually fow?

They ftill find, that the firft Crops are beft; and the longer they continue fowing, the worft the laft Crops will prove, be they of never fo different a Species; unlefs the Land were not in fo good Tilth for the firft Crop as for the fubfequent; or unlefs the laft fown be of a more robuft Species.

This Matter might be eafily clear'd, could we perfectly know the Nature of thofe fuppofed *unfuitable* (h) *Particles*; but, in Truth, there is no more to be

---

(g) A Charlock could not rob a Turnep, and ftarve it, more than feveral Turneps can do, unlefs the Charlock did take from it the fame Particles which would nourifh a Turnep: and unlefs the Charlock did devour a greater Quantity of that Nourifhment than feveral Turneps could take.

Flax, Oats, and Poppy, could not burn or wafte the Soil, and make it lefs able to produce fucceeding Crops of different Species, unlefs they did exhauft the fame Particles which would have nourifh'd Plants of different Species: For let the Quantity of Particles thefe Burners take be never fo great, the following Crops would not mifs them, or fuffer any Damage by the Want or Lofs of them, were they not the fame Particles which would have nourifhed thofe Crops, if the Burners had left them *behind, quiet and undifturbed.* Neither could Weeds be of any Prejudice to Corn, if they did draw off thofe Particles only that fuit the Bodies of Weeds, *the reft lying all quiet and undifturbed the while.* But conftant Experience fhews, that all Sorts of Weeds, more or lefs, diminifh the Crop of Corn.

(h) But we muft not conclude, that thefe Particles, which pafs through a Plant (being a vaftly greater Quantity than thofe that abide in it for its Augment), are all unfuitable, becaufe no one of them happens to hit upon a fit *Nidus:* For fince the Life of Animals depends upon that of Plants, 'tis not unreafonable to imagine, that Nature may have provided a confiderable Over-plus

be known of fuch of them, than that they are carried
away by the Atmofphere to a Diftance, according to
the Velocity of the Air; perhaps feveral Miles off,
at leaft, never like to return to the Spot of Ground
from whence the Plants have raifed them.

But fuppofe thefe caft-off Particles were, when
taken in, unfit for the Nourifhment of any manner
of Vegetables: Then the Doctor muft fanfy the Wheat
to be of a very fcrupulous Confcience, to feed on
thefe Particles, which were neither fit for its own
Nourifhment, nor of any other Plant ; and at the
fame time to forbear to take the Food of Barley, Peafe,
and Oats, letting that *lie ftill and undifturb'd the while,*
as he fays it does, tho' he gives no manner of Reafon
for it.

'Tis needlefs to bring ftronger Arguments, than the
Doctor's Experiments afford, againft his own vulgar
Opinion, of Plants diftinguifhing the particular Sort
of terreftrial Matter, that, he fays, is proper to each
Sort of *Vegetable,* in thefe Words ; *viz.* ' Each Sort
' takes forth that peculiar Matter that is proper for its
' own Nourifhment, the *reft lying all quiet and undifturb'd*
' *the while.*

He fays, that great Part of the terreftrial Matter,
mixed with the Water, paffes up into the Plant along
with it; which it could not do, if only the peculiar
Matter, proper to each Plant, did pafs up into it:
And after he has fhewed how apt the vegetable Matter is to attend Water in all its Motions, and to follow it into each of its Receffes; being by no Filtrations or Percolations wholly feparable from it ; 'tis
ftrange he fhould think that each Plant leaves the
greateft Part of it behind, feparated from the Water
which the Plant imbibes.

plus for maintaining the Life of individual Plants, when fhe has
provided fuch an innumerable Overplus for continuing every
Species of Animals.

There

There are, doubtlefs, more than a Million of Sorts of Plants, all of which would have taken up the Water, and had each as much Right to its Share, or proper Matter in it, as the Doctor's Plants had ; and then there would be but a very fmall (or a Millionth) Part of it proper to each of his Plants : And thefe leaving all the reft behind, both of the Water wherewith the Glaffes at firft were filled, when the Plants were put into them ; and alfo of all the additional Water daily fupply'd into them afterwards; I fay, fo much more terreftrial Matter brought into thefe Glaffes, in Proportion to the added Water, and fo very fmall a Part as could be proper to each of his Plants being carried off; there muft have remain'd in thefe Glaffes a much greater Quantity of terreftrial Matter at the End of the Experiment, than remained in the Glaffes *F* or *G*, which had no Plants in them, nor any Water added to, or diminifhed from them ; but the quite contrary appear'd. ' And the Water in
' the Glaffes *F* and *G*, at the End of the Experiment,
' exhibited a larger Quantity of terreftrial Matter,
' than any of thofe that had Plants in them did. The
' Sediment at the Bottom of the Glaffes was greater,
' and the *Nubeculæ* diffufed thro' the Body of the
' Water thicker.'   Had the *Cataputia* infum'd, with the Two thoufand Five hundred and One Grains of Water, no more than its proper Share of the vegetable Matter, it could not have attained thence an In-creafe of Three Grains and a Quarter, nor even the Thoufandth Part of One Grain.   But he found ' this
' terreftrial Matter, contained in all Water, to be of
' Two Kinds : The one properly, a vegetable Matter,
' but confifting of very different Particles ; fome of
' which are proper for the Nourifhment of fome
' kind of Plants, others for different Sorts,' &c.

This, indeed, would have been a moft wonderful Difcovery, and might have given us a great Light, if he had told us in what Language and Character
                                                        thefe

thefe proper Differences were ftamp'd or written upon the vegetable Particles; which Particles themfelves, he fays, were fcarce vifible. Certainly it muft be a great Art (much beyond that of Dr. *Wallis*) to decypher the Language of Plants, from invifible Characters.

But that this Dream may deceive none, except fuch who are very fond of old Errors, there is an *Experimentum Crucis* which may convince them; *viz.* At the proper Seafon, tap a Birch-tree in the Body or Boughs, and you may have thence a large Quantity of clear Liquor, very little altered from Water; and you may fee, that every other Species of Plants, that will grow in Water, will receive this; live and grow in it, as well as in common Water. You may make a like Experiment by tapping other Trees, or by Water diftilled from Vegetables; and you will find no Species of Plants, into which this Water will not enter, and pafs through it, and nourifh it too; unlefs it be fuch a Species as requires more Heat than Water admits; or unlefs the peculiar Veffels of that it has firft paffed through, have fo altered the vegetable Particles contained in that Water, as that it acts as Poifon upon fome other particular Species.

The Doctor concludes, ' That Water is only the ' Agent that conveys the vegetable Matter to the ' Bodies of Plants, that introduces and diftributes ' it to their feveral Parts for their Nourifhment: ' That Matter is fluggifh and inactive, and would ' lie eternally confin'd to its Beds of Earth, without ' ever advancing up into Plants, did not Water, or ' fome like Inftrument, fetch it forth, and carry it ' unto them.'

That Water is very capable of the Office of a Carrier to Plants, I think the Doctor has made moft evident; but as to the Office of fuch an Agent as his Hypothefis beftows upon it, it feems impoffible to be executed by Water. For it cannot be imagined,

that

that Water, being itſelf but mere homogenial Matter, void of all Degrees of Life, ſhould diſtinguiſh each Particle of vegetable Matter, proper and peculiar to every different Species of Plants, which are innumerable; and when 'tis to act for the Wheat, to find out all the Particles proper to that ſort of Grain, to rouſe only thoſe particular Sluggards from their Beds of Earth, letting all the reſt lie quiet and undiſturbed the while. This Agent frees the Wheat-Particles from their Confinement, and conveys, introduces, and diſtributes them, and only them, into the ſeveral Parts of the Wheat.

Since 'tis unreaſonable to believe, that Water can have ſuch extraordinary Skill in Botany, or in Micrography, as to be qualified for a ſufficient Agent in ſuch an abſtruſe Matter, I conceive Water to be only an Inſtrument or Vehicle, which takes up indifferently any Particles it meets with (and is able to carry), and advances them (or the *Pabulum* they yield) up into the Firſt Plant, whoſe Root it comes in Contact with; and that every Plant it meets with does accept thereof, without diſtinguiſhing any different Sorts or Properties in them, until they be ſo far introduc'd and advanc'd up into the vegetable Veſſels, that it would be in vain to diſtinguiſh them; for whether the terreſtrial Matter, Plants imbibe with the Water, will kill or nouriſh them, appears by its Effects; but which cannot be foreknown or prevented without the Help of Faculties, which Plants are not endow'd with.

Mr. *Bradley* ſeems to have carried this Error farther than any Author ever did before; but he ſupports it by Affirmations only, or by ſuch Arguments (I cannot ſay Reaſons; for no Reaſon can be againſt any Truth) as go near to confute the very Opinion he pretends to advance by them.

He aſcribes to Vegetables the Senſe of Taſte, by which he thinks they take ſuch Nouriſhment as is
moſt

moft agreeable to their refpective Natures, refufing the reft; and will rather ftarve, than eat what is difagreeable to their Palate.

In the Preface to his *Vol.* I. *Page* 10. of his *Hufbandry* and *Gardening*, he fays, ' They feed as dif' ferently as Horfes do from Dogs, or Dogs from ' Fifh.'

But what does he mean by this Inftance, *Vol.* I. *p.* 39. *viz.* ' That Thyme, and other Aromatics, being planted ' near an Apricot-tree, would deftroy that Tree?' Does it not help to confirm, that every Plant does not draw exactly the fame Share of Nourifhment?

I believe there is no need for him to give more Inftances to difprove his Affertion than this one. His Conclufion, taken by itfelf, is fo far right; *viz.* ' That ' if the Nourifhment the Earth afforded to the Thyme ' and Apricot-tree, had been divided into Two ' Shares, both could not have had them.'

But this his Inftance proves, That thofe Aromatics robb'd the Apricot-tree of fo much of its Share as to ftarve it; and that they, tho' of fo very different a Nature, did draw from the Earth the fame Nourifhment which the Apricot-tree fhould have taken for its Support, had not the Aromatics been too hard for it, in drawing it off for their own Maintenance:

Unlefs he believes, that all the Juices of the Aromatics were as Poifon to the Apricot; and that, according to my Experiment of the Mint, fome of their Roots might difcharge fome kind of Moifture in dry Weather, given them by others, that had it for their Ufe; and that the Apricot-roots, mingling with them, might imbibe enough of that Liquor, altered fufficiently by their Veffels, to poifon and kill the Tree.

But then, where was the Tree's diftinguifhing Palate? Why did it not refufe this Juice, which was fo difagreeable as to kill it? And as to his Notion of

Vege-

Vegetables having Palates, let us fee how it agrees with what he affirms.

' That 'tis the Veffels of Plants that make, by
' their Filtrations, Percolations, *&c.* all the different
' Taftes and Flavours of the Matter, which is the
' Aliment of Plants ; and that, before it be by them
' fo filtred, *&c.* it is only a Fund of infipid Subftance,
' capable of being altered by fuch Veffels, into any
' Form, Colour, or Flavour.'

And *Vol.* I. *p.* 38. ' The different Strainers, or
' Veffels of the feveral Plants, growing upon that
' Spot of Earth, thus impregnated with Salts, alter
' thofe Salts or Juices, according to the feveral Fi-
' gures or Dimenfions of their Strainers ; fo that one
' Plant varies, in Tafte and Smell, from others, tho'
' all draw their Nourifhment from the fame Stock
' lodged in the Earth.' See Mr. *Bradley*'s *Palates of*
Plants, and the infipid Subftance he allots them to diftinguifh the Tafte of, how they agree.

They muft, it feems, within their own Bodies, give the Flavour to this infipid Subftance, before their Palates can be of any Ufe ; and, even then, 'tis im-poffible to be of any Ufe, but in the manner of the the Dog returning to his Vomit.

They would have as much Occafion for the Senfe of Smelling, as of Tafte ; but, after all, of what Ufe could either of the Two be to Plants, without local Motion of their Roots ? which they are fo deftitute of, that no Mouth of a Root can ever remove itfelf from the very Point where it was firft formed, becaufe a Root has all its longitudinal Increafe at the very End ; for, fhould the Spaces betwixt the Branchings increafe in Length, thofe Branches would be broken off, and left behind, or elfe drawn out of their Ca-vities ; which muft deftroy the Plant. All the Branches, except the foremuft, would be found with their Ex-tremities pointing towards the Stem ; the contrary of
which

which Pofture they are feen to have: And if they
moved backwards, that would have much the fame
Effect on all the collateral Branchings to deftroy them.
Smell and Tafte then could be of no manner of Ufe
to Vegetables, if they had them; they would have
no Remedy or Poffibility to mend themfelves from
the fame Mouths, removing to fearch out other Food,
in cafe they had Power to diflike or refufe what was
offered them.

Therefore the crude Earth, being their Food, fimple and free from any Alterations by Veffels, remaining infipid, cannot give, neither can Plants receive,
require, or make ufe of, any Variety from it, as Animals do from their Diet. It would be loft upon them,
and Nature would have acted in vain, to give Smell
and Tafte to Vegetables, and nothing but infipid
Earth for an Object of them: or to give them a
charming Variety of Relifh and Savour in their Food,
without giving them Senfes neceffary to perceive or
enjoy them; which would be like Light and Colours
to the Blind, Sound and Mufic to the Deaf, or like
giving Eyes and Ears to Animals, without Light or
Sound to affect them.

The Mouths of Plants, fituate in the convex Superficies of Roots, are analogous to the Lacteals, or
Mouths, in the concave Superficies of the Inteftines
of Animals.

Thefe fpongy Superficies of animal Guts, and
vegetable Roots, have no more Tafte or Power of
refufing whatever comes in Contact with them, the
one than the other.

The free open Air would be equally injurious to
both; and if expofed to it, it would dry and clofe up
the fine Orifices in Guts and Roots: Therefore Nature has guarded both from it.

Nature has alfo provided for the Prefervation of
both Vegetables and Animals (I do not fay equally)

Q   in

in refpect of their Food ; which might poifon them, or might not be fit to nourifh them.

The Security of Plants (the beft that can be) is their Food itfelf, Earth ; which, having been altered by no Veffels, is always fafe and nourifhing to them ; For a Plant is never known to be poifoned by its own natural Soil, nor ftarved, if it were enough of it, with the requifite Quantities of Heat and Moifture.

Roots, being therefore the Guts of Plants, have no need to be guarded by Senfes ; and all the Parts and Paffages, which ferve to diftinguifh and prepare the Food of Animals, before it reach the Guts, are omitted in Plants, and not at all neceffary to them.

But as the Food of moft Animals is Earth, very varioufly changed and modified by vegetable or animal Veffels, or by both, and fome of it is made wholfome, fome poifonous ; fo that if this doubtful Food fhould be committed to the Inteftines, without Examination, as the pure unaltered Earth is to Roots, there would, in all Probability, be very few Animals living in the World, except there be any that feed on Earth at firft Hand only, as Plants do.

Therefore, left this Food, fo much more refined than that of Plants, fhould, by that very means, become a fatal Curfe, inftead of a Bleffing to Animals, Nature has endowed them with Smell and Tafte, as Sentinels, without whofe Scrutiny thefe various uncertain Ingredients are not admitted to come where they can enter the Lacteals, and to diftinguifh, at a fufficient Diftance, what is wholfome and friendly, from what is hurtful ; for when 'tis once paffed out of the Stomach into the Guts, 'tis too late to have Benefit from Emetics ; its Venom muft then be imbibed by the Lacteal Mouths, and mix with the Blood, as that muft mix with the Sap, which comes in Contact with the Lacteals in the Superficies of Roots, Nature having left this unguarded.

Yet

Yet Plants feem to be better fecured by the Salubrity and Simplicity of their Food, than Animals are by their Senfes: To compenfate that Inequality of Danger; Animals have Pleafure from their Senfes, except fome miferable Animals (and fuch there are) that have more Pain than Pleafure from them. But I fuppofe, more Animals than Plants are poifon'd; and that a poifonous Animal is lefs fatal to a Plant, than a poifonous Plant is to an Animal.

It being fufficiently proved, that every fort of Vegetables, growing in the fame Soil, takes, and is nourifhed, by the fame Sort of Food; it follows from hence, that the beneficial Change of Sorts of Seeds or Plants, we fee in the common Hufbandry, is not from the Quality of the Sorts of Food, but from other Caufes; fuch as,

    I. *Quantity of the Food.*
    II. *Conftitution of the Plants.*
    III. *Quantity of the Tillage.*

In Dr. *Woodward*'s Cafe, upon his Hypothefis, the Three Proportions of Seeds, *viz.* Barley, Oats, and Peafe, might be fown all together in the fame Acre of Ground, the fame Year, and make Three as good Crops as if fown fingly in Three fucceffive Years, and his Two Crops of Wheat in one Year likewife. But every Farmer can tell, that thefe Three Proportions of Seed would not yield half the Crop together, as one would do fingle; and would fcarce produce more than to fhew what Grains were fown, and which of the Sorts were the ftrongeft, and the moft able Robber.

Though this Failure would, in Truth, be from no other Caufe than want of the fufficient Quantity of Food, which thofe Three Crops required; yet, perhaps, the Doctor might think, that all Three Crops might fucceed together very well, taking each its proper Nourifhment, were it not for want of Room, Air, and Sun.

I have

I have been credibly inform'd, that on One Perch of Ground there has grown a Bushel of Corn, which is Twenty Quarters to an Acre. Mr. *Houghton* relates Twenty-six, and even Thirty Quarters, of Wheat on One Acre. There have certainly grown Twelve Quarters of Barley to an Acre, throughout a whole Field : Therefore, unlefs a Crop exceed the leaft of thefe, or indeed the greateft of them (if the Relation be true), a Crop cannot fail for want of Room ; for one Acre (be it of what Nature it will, as to the Soil of it) muft have as much room for a Crop to grow on, as any other Acre.

Then there was room for all Dr. *Woodward*'s Three Crops together, to produce as much as Three common Crops do. Yet all thefe together will fcarce yield one Quarter of Corn, tho' there is room, at leaft, for Twelve.

The fame *Air* and *Sun* that had Room to do their Office to Mr. *Houghton*'s Acre, why fh'ould they not have Room to do the fame to Doctor *Woodward*'s Acre, when the Three Crops growing on it at once, through pretty good ones, might require lefs Room than Mr. *Houghton*'s Crop did ?

I perceive that thofe Authors, who explain *Vegetation*, by faying the Earth imbibes certain Qualities from the Air, and by fpecific Qualities, and the like, do alfo lay a great Strefs upon the *perpendicular* Growth of *Vegetables* ; feeming to fanfy there is little elfe neceffary to a good Crop, but Room.

Mr. *Bradley*, in his Arguments concerning the Value of an Hill, does implicitly fay as much.

But if they would but confider the Diameters of the Stems, with the Meafure of the Surface of an Acre, they would be convinced, that many, even of Mr. *Houghton*'s Crops, might ftand in a perpendicular Pofture upon an Acre, and Room be left.

One true Caufe of a Crop's failing, is want of a Quantity of Food to maintain the Quantity of Vegetables, which the Food fhould nourifh.

When the Quantity of Food which is sufficient for another Species (that requires less), but not for that which last grew, to grow again the next Year, then that other is beneficial to be planted after it.

The Second true Cause is from the Constitution of Plants; some require more Food than others, and some are of a stronger Make, and better able to penetrate the Earth, and forage for themselves.

Therefore Oats may succeed a Crop of Wheat on strong Land, with once plowing, when Barley will not; because Barley is not so well able to penetrate as Oats, or Beans, or Pease, are.

So a Pear-tree may succeed a Plum-tree, when another Plum-tree cannot; because a Pear is a much stronger Tree, and grows to a much greater Bulk; so inclined to be a Giant, that 'tis hard to make it a Dwarf; and will penetrate and force its Way thro' the untill'd Earth, where the other cannot; being of a weaker and less robust Constitution, not so well able to shift for itself.

The Pear could penetrate Pores, that the other could not. Mr. *Evelyn* says, in his Discourse of Forest-trees, ' That a Pear will strike Root thro' the ' roughest and most impenetrable Rocks and Clifts ' of Stone itself.' He says likewise, in his *Pomona*, ' That Pears will thrive where neither Apple or other ' Fruit could in Appearance be expected.'

I can scarce think, that a large Plant takes in larger Particles than a small one, for its Nourishment: If it did, I can't believe, that the Thyme could have starv'd the Apricot-tree; it must have left the larger Particles of Food for that Tree, which probably would have sufficed to keep it alive: I rather think, that great and small Plants are sustain'd by the same minute Particles; for, as the fine Particles of Oats will nourish an Ox, so they will nourish a Tom-tit, or a Mite.

Some

Some Plants are of an hotter Conftitution, and have a quicker Digeftion, like Cormorants or Pigeons, devouring more greedily, and a greater Quantity of Food, than thofe of a colder Temperature, of equal Bulk, whofe Sap, having a more languid Motion, in proportion to the lefs Degree of Heat in it, fends off fewer Recrements; and therefore a lefs Supply of Food is required in their room. This may make fome Difference in the one's fucceeding the other; becaufe the hot-conftitution'd leaves not enough for its own Species to fucceed again, but leaves enough for a Species of a colder Conftitution to fucceed it.

But the Third and chiefeft Caufe of the Benefit of changing Sorts is Quantity of Tillage, in proportion to which the Food will be produced.

The true Caufe why Wheat is not (efpecially on any ftrong Soil) to be fown immediately after Wheat, is, That the firft Wheat ftanding almoft a Year on the Ground, by which it muft grow harder; and Wheat Seed-time being foon after Harveft in *England*, there is not Space of Time to till the Land fo much as a fecond Crop of Wheat requires.

Tho' fometimes in poorer Land, that is lighter, Wheat has fucceeded Wheat with tolerable Succefs; when I have feen, on very rich ftrong Land, the firft Crop loft by being much too big, and one following it immediately, quite loft by the Poornefs of it, and not worth cutting.

This was enough to fatisfy, that the Tillage which was fo much eafier perform'd in lefs Time, fufficed for the light Land, but not for the ftrong : and, if the ftrong Land could have been brought into as good Tilth as the light (like as in the new Hufbandry it may), it would have produced a much better fecond Crop than the light Land did.

From all that has been faid, thefe may be laid down as Maxims; *viz.* That the fame Quantity of
Tillage

Tillage will produce the fame Quantity of Food in the fame Land (*a*) ; and that the fame Quantity of Food will maintain the fame Quantity of Vegetables.

'Tis feen, that the fame Sort of Weeds, which once come naturally in a Soil, if fuffer'd to grow, will always profper in proportion to the Tillage and Manure beftow'd upon it, without any Change. And fo are all manner of Plants, that have been yet try'd by the new Hufbandry, feen to do.

A Vineyard, if not tilled, will foon decay, even in rich Ground, as may be feen in thofe in *France*, lying intermingled as our Lands do in common Fields. Thofe Lands of Vines, which by reafon of fome Law-fuit depending about the Property of them, or otherwife, lie a Year or two untilled, produce no Grapes, fend out no Shoots hardly : the Leaves look yellow, and feem dead, in Comparifon of thofe on each Side of them; which, being tilled, are full of Fruit, fend out an hundred times more Wood, and their Leaves are large and flourifhing ; and continue to do the fame annually for Ages, if the Plough or Hoe do not neglect them.

No Change of Sorts is needful in them, if the fame annual Quantity of Tillage (which appears to provide the fame annual Quantity of Food) be continued to the Vines.

But what in the Vineyards proves this Thefis moft fully is, That where they conftantly till the low Vines

(*a*) And *cæteris paribus* ; for when the Land has been more exhaufted, more Tillage (or Dung) or Reft will be required to produce the fame Quantity of Food, than when the Land hath been lefs exhaufted. By Tillage is here meant, not only the Number of Plowings, but the Degree of Divifion or Pulveration of the Soil ; or, if perchance the Soil is extraordinary much exhaufted by many Crops, without proper Tillage between them, the greater Degree of Pulveration, by Plowing or Dung (which is only a *Succedaneum* of Tillage), and alfo a longer Time of Expofure, may be neceffary to counterpoife that extraordinary Exhauftion.

with

with the Plough, which is almoſt the ſame with the Hoe-plough, the Stems are planted about Four Feet aſunder, chequerwiſe; ſo that they plow them Four ways.   When any of theſe Plants happen to die, new ones are immediately planted in their room, and exactly in the Points or Angles where the other have rotted; elſe, if planted out of thoſe Angles, they would ſtand in the Way of the Plough : Theſe young Vines, I ſay, ſo planted in the very Graves, as it were, of their Predeceſſors, grow, thrive, and proſper well, the Soil being thus conſtantly tilled : And if a Plum-tree, or any other Plant, had ſuch Tillage, it might as well ſucceed one of its own Species, as thoſe Vines do.

'Tis obſerved, that White-thorns will not proſper, ſet in the Gaps of a White thorn Hedge : But I have ſeen the Banks of ſuch Gaps dug and thrown down one Summer, and made up again, and White-thorns there replanted the following Winter, with good Succeſs.

But note, That the annual plowing the Vines is more beneficial than the one Summer Tillage of the Banks, the Vines having it repeated to them yearly.

I have, by Experience and Obſervation, found it to be a Rule, That long Tap-rooted Plants, as Clover and St. Foin, will not ſucceed immediately after thoſe of their own or any other Species of long Tap-roots, ſo well as after horizontal-rooted Plants; but, on the contrary, horizontal will ſucceed thoſe Tap-roots as well or better than they will ſucceed horizontal.

I confeſs, this Obſervation did, for a great while, cheat me into the common Belief, That different Species of Plants feed on different Food; till I was delivered from that Error, by taking Notice, that thoſe Tap-roots would thrive exceedingly well after Turneps, which have alſo pretty long Tap-roots, though Turneps never thrive well immediately after
Clover,

Clover *(a)*, or St. Foin: I found the true Cause of this Exception to that Rule to be chiefly the different Tillage *(b)*.

Land must be well tilled for Turneps, which also are commonly hoed; they stand scarce ever above Three-quarters of a Year, and are then fed on the Ground; and then the succeeding Crop of Corn has, by that means, the Benefit of twice as much Tillage from the Hoe, as otherwise would be given to it; and the Broad Clover, or St. Foin, sown with the Corn (if the Corn be not so big as to kill it), will enjoy, in its Turn, a Proportion of the extraordinary Tillage, and of the Dung of Cattle, which feed the Turneps, and thrive accordingly: But Broad Clover and St. Foin, being perennial Plants, stand on the Ground so long, that it lies several Years untilled; so that Turneps, sown immediately after these, do fail, for want of their due Tillage, for which there is not sufficient time, by plowing often enough; because, by the common Ploughs, it requires Two or Three Years to make it fine enough for Turneps, or for a Repetition of Clover, or St. Foin, in strong or swerdy Land.

Another Reason why any Crop succeeds well after Turneps (and besides their being spent on the Ground where they grow) is their cold Constitution, by which they are maintained with less Food than another Plant of the same Bulk.

The *Parenchyma*, or fleshy Part of a Turnep, consisting of a watry Substance, which cools the Vessels, whereby the Sap's Motion is very flow, in proportion to the very low Degree of Heat it has, and

(a) But when Clover has been fed by Cattle, the Ground being good, and well tilled, Turneps may thrive immediately after Clover: Therefore this is an Exception to the general Rule.

(b) Very mellow rich Land is so full of vegetable Food, that 'tis an Exception to most Rules; and therefore I speak not of that.

fends off its Recrements in the fame Proportion likewife; and therefore requires the lefs of the terrene
Nourifhment to fupply thofe Recrements.

This is feen, when a Bufhel of Turneps, mixed
with a Quantity of Wheaten Flour, is made into
Bread, and well baked: This Bufhel of Turneps
gives but few Ounces Increafe in Weight, more than
the fame Quantity of Wheaten Flour made into
Bread, and baked without any Turneps.   This fhews
there is in a Turnep very little Earth (which is the
moft permanent Subftance of a Plant); the Oven
difcharges in Vapour near all but the largeft Veffels:
Its earthly Subftance being fo fmall, is a Proof 'tis
maintained by a fmall Quantity of Earth: and, upon
that Account alfo, of lefs Damage to the next Crop
than another Plant would be, which required more of
the folid Nourifhment to conftitute its firmer Body,
as a Charlock does; for when a Charlock comes up,
contiguous to, and at the fame time with a Turnep,
it does fo rob the Turnep, that it attains not to be of
the Weight of Five Ounces; when a fingle Turnep,
having no more Scope of Ground, and, in all refpects
(but the Vicinity of the Charlock), equal, weighs
Five Pounds, yet that Charlock does not weigh One
Pound.

And where Three Turneps coming up, and growing thus contiguous, will weigh Four Pounds; a
Charlock joined with Two or Three Turneps, all
together, will be lefs than one Pound, upon no lefs
Space of Ground.

This Obfervation cannot be made, except where
Turneps are drilled in Rows; and there 'tis eafy to
demonftrate, that a Charlock, during the time of its
fhort Life, draws much more Earth than a Turnep of
equal Bulk, from an equal Quantity of Ground (*c*).

The

(*c*) 'Tis certain that Turneps, when they ftand for Seed, fuck
and impoverifh the Ground exceedingly: For though they are of

a

The true Caufe why Clover and St. Foin do not fucceed fo well after their own refpective Species, or that of each other, as Corn, &c. can, is, that they take great Part of their Nourifhment from below the Plough's Reach, fo as that under Earth cannot be tilled deep enough, but the upper Part may be tilled deep enough for the horizontal Roots of Corn, &c. towards which, the Rotting of the Clover and St. Foin Roots, when cut off by the Plough, do not a little contribute *(d)*; And there's no doubt but that, if

the

a cold Conftitution, and confequently confume lefs Food than Plants of an hotter Conftitution, and of the fame Bulk; yet thefe Seed-turneps being of fo vaft a Bulk, as fometimes Eighty Quarters of their Roots grow on an Acre, and their Stalks have been meafured Seven Feet high, and their Roots having continued at near their full Bignefs for about Ten Months together, and then carried off, they drain the Land more than a Crop of other Vegetables of a lefs Bulk, and an hotter Conftitution, and which live a lefs time; or than Wheat, which, though it lives as long, is very fmall, except in the Four laft Months.

(d) That the Rotting of vegetable Roots in the Ground doth ferment therein, and improve it for horizontal-rooted Plants, I am convinced by an Accident; *viz.* My Man had plowed off the Earth clofe to the Rows in a Field of extraordinary large Turneps defigned for Seed. This Earth was neglected to be thrown back to the Rows, until a fevere Froft in the Winter came, and killed the Turneps; upon which, in the Spring, the Field was fown with Barley upon the Level, with only *once* plowing, and that crofs-ways of the Rows The Turneps had ftood fo wide afunder, that the Spot whereon each had rotted, appeared like the Spot whereon an Horfe had urined in till'd Ground, and was of a deeper Colour, and much higher, than the Barley that grew round thofe Spots; and yet none of it was poor. As the Roots of Clover, and St. Foin, are very much lefs; yet the greater Number rotting in plowed Ground muft be of great Ufe to a following Crop of Corn.

I will here relate Two Examples of this in St. Foin: The one is, That a Field of Twenty-five Acres drilled with St. Foin, except Three Acres in the Middle of it, which was, at the fame time, fown with Hop-Clover; after Eight Years the whole Field was plowed up by a Tenant, and fown with Corn: The St. Foin had been mowed yearly, as the Hop-Clover was not mowed at

all,

the under Earth could be as well tilled for the Tap-roots, as the upper Earth is for the horizontal, the Tap-roots would succeed one another as well as the horizontal would succeed them, or those of their own Species, or as the Tap-roots do the horizontal.

all, but fed by Horses teddered (or staked) thereon the First and Second Years; and after that had nothing on it but poor natural Grass.

The whole Field was managed alike, when plowed up; but the Three Acres produced visibly worse Crops of Corn than the rest all round it, which had produced St. Foin.

The other Example or Instance was, Where an Acre, Part of a Field, was, by a Fancy, drilled with St. Foin in single Rows, about Thirty-three Inches asunder, but was never hoed: After Seven Years it was plowed up with the rest of the Field crofs the Rows, and sown with Oats upon the Back Three Months after plowing. These Rows were as visible in the Oats, as if the St. Foin had been still remaining there: The Oats in the Rows where the St. Foin had been, looked of a deep green flourishing Colour, at first coming up, and until they were about half a Foot high, and the Spaces between them looked yellowish; but afterwards the Difference of their Colour disappeared, all the Crop being very good. Upon this I imputed it to the Rotting of the Roots, which by their Singleness were very large; and when the different Colours disappeared, I suppose the Roots of all the Oats had reached to the Benefit of the rotted Roots, which might also be then spread farther into the Spaces; and I doubt not but that the Rotting of Broad Clover-roots has the same Effect as of St. Foin, for manuring of Land, especially when the Roots are large.

Some have objected against this Opinion, and say the Effect was rather to be imputed to the Rows of St. Foin shadowing the Earth under them, or else from their keeping the Earth under them free from Couch-grass, of which the Intervals were full: But I think it more probable, that the Couch-grass, having very long horizontal Roots, might draw Nourishment from the Earth under the Rows, and from the Intervals equally.

And as to the Shadow of the Rows, tho', for the First and Second Years, the St. Foin Plants were very large; yet, being afterwards, for Five or Six Years, until plowed up, constantly fed by Cattle, and being more sweet, was eaten very low, whilst the Couch-grass remained intire in the Intervals, and shadowed them more than the Earth of the Rows was shadowed by the St. Foin: Besides, the rotten Turneps, which were freed from both these Objections, had the same Effect on the Barley, as the St. Foin had on the Oats.

The

The under Earth, in fome time, is replenifhed by what the Rains leave, when they fink through it; and then Tap-rooted Plants may be there nourifhed again, tho' the upper Earth be drained by the Corn; fo that no Change is fo beneficial, as that betwixt Tap-rooted Plants, and thofe which have only horizontal ones. The former are provided for by Rains, though not fo fpeedily as the latter are by Tillage and Hoeing.

Paftures require no Change of Herbs; becaufe they have annually the fame Supply of Food from the Dunging of Cattle that feed on them, and from the Benefit of the Atmofphere.

Meadows hold out without Change of Species of Grafs, tho' a Crop be carried off every Year; the Richnefs of that Soil, with the Help of the Atmofphere, Dung of Cattle in feeding the After-Crop, or elfe Flooding, from the overflowing of fome River, fome, or all of which, fupply the Place of the Plough to a Meadow.

Woods alfo hold out beyond Memory or Tradition, without changing Sorts of Trees; and this by the Leaves, and perhaps old Wood, rotting on the Soil annually, which operate as a Manure; becaufe, as has been faid, Earth which has once paffed any Veffels, is fo changed, that, for a long time after, it does not retain its Homogeneity (e) fo much as to mix with pure Earth, without fermenting; and by the Defcent of the Atmofphere, the Trees fhadowing the Soil, to prevent the Re-afcent of what that brings down; all this, refembling Tillage, continually divides the Soil, and renews the Food equal to the Confumption of it made by the Wood.

And the laft Argument I fhall attempt to bring for Confirmation of all I have advanced, is that

(e) Not that the Particles of Earth are ftrictly homogeneous, but that they are much lefs heterogeneous, before they are altered by Veffels, than afterwards.

which

which proves both the Truth and Ufe of the reft; *viz.* That when any Sort of Vegetable, by the due Degrees of Heat and Moifture it requires, is agreeable to a Soil, it may, by the new Horfe-hoeing Hufbandry, be continued without ever changing the Species.

C H A P. XV.

Of Change of INDIVIDUALS.

SEEDS, in their natural Climate, do not degenerate, unlefs Culture has improved them; and then, upon Omiffion of that Culture, they return to their firft natural State.

As the Benefit of changing of Species of Seeds is from Difference of Tillage, fo the Benefit of changing Individuals of the fame Species appears to be from thofe Caufes which are, generally, themfelves, the Effects of different Climates, fuch as Heat and Moifture, which may alfo vary very much in the fame Latitude and Neighbourhood; as the fame Mountain in the Country of the *Mogul* (related by Mr. *Evelyn*, from Monfieur *Bernier*), on the South Side produces *Indian* Plants, and on the North Side *European* Plants, from different Expofures; and fome Land, retaining Water longer, is colder; fome, fuffering it to pafs down quicker, and by the Nature and Figure of its Parts, caufes fuch a Refraction and Reflexion of the Sun's Rays, which give a great Warmth, as in Sand, and gravelly Grounds, that are well fituate, and have an under Stratum of fome Sort of hollow Matter, next under the Staple (*a*),

(*a*) This hollow Matter lets the Water pafs down the fooner from the Surface, whereby the Staple of the Ground becomes the drier, and confequently warmer.

or

or upper Stratum, wherein the Plough is exer-
cifed.

This beneficial Change of Individuals feems rather
to be from the forementioned Caufes, than from
Change of Food ; and thefe Caufes fhew their Efficacy, chiefly in the Generation or Fœtation of
thofe Seeds ; as Flax-feed brought from *Holland*,
and fown here, will bring as fine Flax as there ; but
the very next Generation of it coarfer, and fo dege-
nerating gradually, after Two or Three Defcents,
becomes no better than the common ordinary Sort ;
yet its Food is the fame, when the Flax is fine, as
when 'tis coarfe.

And fo it is, when Individuals of Wheat are
changed: So Silk-worms, hatched and bred in *France*,
of Eggs or Seed brought from *Italy*, will make as
fine Silk as the *Italian* ; but the Eggs of thefe laid
in *France* and their Iffue, will make no better Silk
than the *French*; though their Food be from Leaves
of the fame Mulberry-trees, when they make fine Silk
and coarfe : Therefore 'tis from the Climate, where
the Eggs are impregnated, not where they have their
Incubation or Food, when hatched, and fed to their
Lives End, that this Difference happens.

Common Barley, fown once in the burning Sand
at *Patney* in *Wiltfhire*, will, for many Years after, if
fown on indifferent warm Ground, be ripe Two or
Three Weeks fooner than any other *(b)*, which has
never

(b) Barley is far from being improved by becoming rath-ripe;
for it lofes more good Qualities than it gets by being fown at *Patney*: 'Tis fo tender, that if it be fown early, the Froft is apt to
kill it ; or if it be fown late in *May*, on the fame Day, and in
the fame Soil, with the fame Sort of Barley that is not rath-ripe,
it will be much thinner bodied than the late-ripe ; and befides,
if it happens to have any Check by Cold or Drought, it never
recovers it as the other doth, at what time foever it is fown. It
is now, I am informed, gone out of Fafhion, and very few Farmers have fown it of late Years. I know a little Parifh, that.

I

never been impregnate at *Patney:* But if fown a Degree farther North, on cold clayey Land, will, in
Two or Three Years, lofe this Quality, and become
as late ripe as any other.

Indeed *Patney* is far from improving the Species of
Barley, except we think it improved by becoming
more weak and tender, and fhorter-lived; which laft-
mentioned Quality fits it for fuch Countries, where
the Summers are too fhort for other Barley to ripen.

The Grains or Seeds of Vegetables are their Eggs;
and the individual Plants, immediately proceeding
from them, have not only the Virtues they received
in Embryo (or rather *in plantulis*), but the Difeafes
alfo; for when fmutty Wheat is fown, unlefs the
Year prove very favourable, the Crop will be fmutty;
which is an evident Token of *mala ftamina.*

The fmutty Grains will not grow; for they turn
to a black Powder: But when fome of thefe are in a
Crop, then, to be fure, many of the reft are infected;
and the Difeafe will fhew itfelf in the next Generation,
or Defcent of it, if the Year wherein 'tis planted
prove a wet one.

Weeds, and their Seed, in the Fields where they
grow naturally, for Time immemorial, come to as
great Perfection as ever, without Change of Soil.

Thefe Weeds, with Acorns, and other Mafts,
Crabs, Sloes, Hips, and Haws, are thought to have
been, originally, the only natural Product of our
Climate: Therefore other Plants being Exotics, many
of them, as to their Iudividuals, require Culture and
Change of Soil, without which they are liable more
or lefs to degenerate.

But to fay, that the Soil can caufe Wheat to degenerate into Rye, or convert Rye into Wheat, is what

I believe, formerly loft about Two hundred Pounds *per Ann.* by
fowing rath-ripe Barley: But long and dear Experience hath now
convinced them of their Error, and obliged them totally to dif-
ufe it.

                                                    reflects

reflects upon the Credit of *Laurembergius:* 'Tis as
eafy to believe, that an Horfe, by feeding in a certain
Pafture, will degenerate into a Bull, and in other
Pafture revert to an Horfe again; thefe are fcarce of
more different Species than Wheat and Rye are: If
the different Soil of *Wittemberg* and *Thuringia* change
one Species, they may the other.

C H A P. XVI.

Of RIDGES.

THE Method of plowing Land up into Ridges
is a particular Sort of Tillage; the chief Ufe
of which is, the Alteration it makes in the Degrees
of Heat and Moifture, being two of the grand Re-
quifites of Vegetation; for very different Degrees of
thefe are neceffary to different Species of Vegetables.

Thofe Vegetables commonly fown in our Fields,
require a middle Degree of both, not being able to
live on the Sides of perpendicular Walls in hot Countries, nor under Water in cold ones, neither are they
amphibious, but muft have a Surface of Earth not
cover'd, nor much foak'd with Water, which de-
prives them of their neceffary Degree of Heat, and
caufes them to languifh. The Symptoms of their
Difeafe are a pale or yellow Colour in their Leaves,
and a Ceffation of Growth, and Death enfues as fure
as from a Dropfy.

The only Remedy to prevent this Difeafe in Plants
is, to lay fuch wet Land up into Ridges, that the Water may run off into the Furrows, and be convey'd
by Ditches or Drains into fome River.

The more a Soil is fill'd with Water, the lefs Heat
it will have.

The Two Sorts of Land moſt liable to be over-glutted with Water, are Hills, whereof the *Upper Stratum* (or Staple) is Mould lying upon a *Second Stratum* of Clay; ·

And generally all ſtrong deep Land.

Hills are made wet and ſpewy by the Rain-water, which falls thereon, and ſoaks into them as into other Land; but being ſtopp'd by the Clay lying next the Surface or Staple, cannot enter the Clay; and for want of Entrance, ſpreads itſelf upon it; and as Water naturally tends downwards, it is by the incumbent Mould partly ſtopp'd in its Deſcent from the upper towards the lower Side of an Hill; and being follow'd and preſs'd on by more Water from above, is forced to riſe up into the Mould lying upon it, which it fills as a Ciſtern does a Fountain (or *Jet d'Eau*). The Land of ſuch an Hill is not the leſs wet or ſpewy for being laid up in Ridges, if they be made from the higher to the lower Part of the Field; for the Force of the Water's Weight continued will raiſe it ſo, as to cauſe it to iſſue out at the very Tops of thoſe Ridges; the Earth becomes a ſort of Pap or Batter, and being like a Quagmire, in going over it, the Feet of Men and Cattle ſink in till they come to the Clay.

There are two Methods of draining ſuch a 'wet Hill: The one is to dig many Trenches, croſs the Hill horizontally (*a*), and either fill them up with Stones looſe or archwiſe, through which the Water, when it ſoaks into the Trenches, may run off at one or both Ends of them into ſome Ditch, which is lower,

---

(*a*) For if they are made with the Deſcent, and not acroſs it, then they will be parallel to the Rills of Water, that run upon the Surface of the Clay under the Staple (or upper *Stratum* of Mould), and would be no more effectual for draining the Hill, than the digging of one River parallel to another, without joining it in any Part, would be effectual for draining the other River of its Water.

and

and carries it away; then they cover the Trenches with Mould, and plow over them as in dry level Ground.

This Method has been found effectual for a time, but not of long Continuance; for the Trenches are apt to be ftopp'd up, and then the Springs break out again as before: Befides, this is a very chargeable Work, and in many Places the Expence of it may almoft equal the Purchafe of the Land.

Therefore 'tis a better Method to plow the Ridges crofs the Hill almoft horizontally, that their parting Furrows, lying open, may each ferve as a Drain to the Ridge next below it; for when the Plough has made the Bottom of thefe horizontal Furrows a few Inches deeper than the Surface of the Clay, the Water will run to their Ends very fecurely, without rifing into the Mould, provided no Part of the Furrows be lower than their Ends.

Thefe parting Furrows, and their Ridges, muft be made more or lefs oblique, according to the Form and Declivity of the Hill; but the more horizontal they are, the fooner the Rain-water will run off the Lands; for in that Cafe it will run to the Furrows, and reach them at right Angles, which it will not do when the Ridges (or Lands) are oblique; and therefore the Water's Courfe crofs the Lands will be longer (*a*). Every one of thefe horizontal Trenches receives

(*a*) The natural Courfe of Water being downwards, it would always run by the neareft Way to the Bottom of the Hill, if nothing ftopt it; but the Water runs from an Hill in Two Manners; *viz.* Upon the Surface of the Staple, and upon the Surface of the Clay that is under the Staple; that which runs under keeps its ftrait Courfe from the Top to the Bottom of an Hill, under a Ridge that is made exactly with the Defcent of the Hill, except that Part of the Water that rifes up into the Mould, and a very little that foaks into the Furrows, for when the Furrows are not made exactly with the Defcent, the more oblique they are to the Defcent, the longer will be the Water's Courfe under the Ridges; and the fhorter, as they are nearer being at Right Angles to the

receives all the Water from the Rills, or little Gutters, wherein the Water runs betwixt the Mould and the Clay; thefe are all cut off by the Trenches, which receive the Water at their upper Sides, and carry it away, as the Trunks of Lead plac'd under the Eaves of a Houfe do carry away the Rain-water.

If there were no other Manner of plowing Ridges on the Sides of Hills than what is commonly prac-tifed on the Plains, this Method of leaving open Fur-rows (or Drains on Declivities) would be impracti-cable; becaufe the Plough could not turn up the Furrows againft the Hill, and againft the Ridge alfo, from the lower Side of it: But the eafy Remedy againft that Inconvenience is, to plow fuch Ridges in Pairs, without throwing any Earth into the Trenches, and then the Ridges will be plain a-top, and the Rain-water will run fpeedily downward to the next Trench, and thence to the Head-land, and fo out of the Field. Thefe Trenches will be made, as well as kept always open, by this plowing in Pairs; and is abundantly more eafy than the Way of plowing Ridges fingly. This plowing in Pairs prevents alfo another Inconveniency, which would otherwife happen to thefe horizontal Ridges; and that is, they being higheft in the Middle, the Rain-water could not run freely from the upper Half of a Ridge towards the next Furrow below it, but would be apt to fink in there, and foak thro' the Ridge; but when Ridges lie in Pairs, the Water will run off from a whole Ridge, as well as off the lower Half of a Ridge that is plow'd fingly, and higheft in the Middle.

Defcent. 'Tis alfo the fame with the Water that falls upon the Surface of the Ridges; for the more horizontal they are, the fhorter its Courfe will be from them to the Furrows, which carry it off; and the lefs of the Water will fink into the Ridges, the lefs oblique and the nearer to Right Angles to the Defcent they are made.

Note,

Note, That every time of plowing, the Pairs muft
be changed, fo that the Furrow, which had Two
Ridges turned towards it one time, muft have Two
turned from it the next time: This Method keeps the
Surfaces of all the Ridges (or Lands) pretty near
even *(a)*.

Farmers are at more Trouble and Pains to drown
fuch Land (it being common to break their Horfes
Wind in plowing up Hill) than they would be at, if
they laid their Ridges in the abovefaid Manner,
which would effeftually make them dry. Many
hundred Acres of good Ground are fpoiled; and
many a good Horfe, in plowing againft the Hill, and
againft all Reafon, Demonftration, and Experience
too; which might be learned even from the *Irifh*,
who drain their Bogs, and make them fruitful, whilft
fome *Englifh* beftow much Labour to drown and make
barren many of their Hills, which would more eafily be made dry and fertile.

I have obferved, that thofe Places of fuch an Hill,
that, when plowed with the Defcent, were the wetteft,
and never produced any thing that was fown on
them, became the very richeft, when made dry by
plowing crofs the Defcent. This fhews that Water
does not impoverifh Land, but the contrary; tho',
whilft it ftands thereon, it prevents the Heat which
is neceffary to the Produftion of moft Sorts of Vegetables: And where it runs fwiftly, it carries much
Earth away with it; where it runs flowly, it depofits
and leaves much behind it.

Though in all Places, where this Way of making
the Ridges crofs the Defcent of Hills is practifed,
the Land becomes dry; yet very few Farmers will

(a) *Note*, This cannot be done on an Hill, whofe Declivity is
fo great, that the Plough is not able to turn a Furrow againft it.
But in this Cafe, perhaps, it may be fufficient to plow the Ridges
obliquely enough for the Furrow to be turned bo:h Ways.

R 3   alter

alter their old Method *(a)* ; no, not even to try the Experiment ; but ftill complain their Gronnd is fo wet and fpewy, that it brings them little or no Profit; and if the Year prove moift, they are great Lofers by fowing it *(b)*.

(a) But fome of late are convinced, by obferving that an Hill of mine has been made dry by this means for Fourteen Years paft, which before was always more wet and fpewy than any Field in the Neighbourhood ; and from the time of inclofing it out of an Heath (or Common), and the converting it to arable, which was about Seventy Years ago, it had been reputed as little better than barren, on account of its Wetnefs ; and that it has been the moft profitable Field of my Farm ever fince it has been under this new Management. I have alfo another Field, that lies about a Mile and an half from me : It doth not belong to the Farm where I live, but was thrown upon my Hands, no Tenant caring to rent it, becaufe great Part of it was full of Springs, and barren : This alfo, having been kept in Lands plowed crofs the Defcent (which is but a fmall Declivity), is become dry : And now the moft prejudiced Farmers agree, that keeping the Lands or Ridges of wet Ground always crofs the Defcent doth cure its Spewinefs. Hereupon fome have attempted to put this Method in Practice on their wet Land ; and, after it has been well tilled up Hill and down, have plowed it the laft time for fowing of Wheat in flat Lands crofs the Defcent ; but by Mifmanagement their Furrows are higher at each End than the Middle, fo that none of the Water can run off either downwards or fideways, or any other Way.

Had the Furrows carried off the Water at both or either of their Ends, it might have been effectual, notwithftanding the broad Lands, becaufe their Ground hath a much lefs Declivity, and is much lefs fpewy, than my Hill was : They will doubtlefs find their Miftake, and amend it, having a Precedent before their Eyes ; but if they had none within their own Infpection, I queftion whether this Mifmanagement might not difcourage them from profecuting their Project any further.

(b) Remember, in making Ridges of all Sorts, and of whatfoever Figure the Piece is, that no Ridge ought to have any more Furrows at one End, than at the other End ; for if there be, the Plough muft be turned in the Middle of the Piece, which will caufe the Land to be trodden by the Horfes ; but if each End have an equal Number of Furrows, the Horfes in turning will tread only upon the Head lands, which may be plowed afterwards ; or if defign'd to be Horfe-ho'd, the Head-lands fhould be narrow, and not plowed at all.

The

The Benefit of laying up ftrong deep Land into Ridges is very great; tho' there be no Springs in it, as are in the Hills aforementioned.

This Land, when it lies flat, and is plowed fometimes one Way, fometimes the other, by crofs-plowing, retains the Rain-water a long time foaking into it; by that Misfortune, the Plough is kept out Two or Three Weeks longer than if the fame were in round Ridges; nay, fometimes its Flatnefs keeps it from drying till the Seafon of plowing, and even of fowing too, be loft.

The Reafons commonly given againft fuch Ridges are thefe following.

I. *They prevent the fanfied Benefit of crofs-plowing.*

II. *Farmers think they lofe Part of their Ground, by leaving more Furrows betwixt Ridges, than when they lay their Land flat, where the Lands are made much larger than round Ridges can conveniently be; and becaufe alfo the Furrows betwixt Ridges muft be broader, and lie open; but the other they fill up by the Harrows.*

The firft of thefe I have already anfwered elfewhere, by fhewing, that Crofs-plowing is oftener injurious than beneficial.

The Second I fhall fufficiently confute, if I can make appear, that no Ground is loft, but much may be gained, by Ridges.

What I mean by gaining of Ground, is the increafing of the Earth's Surface: For if a flat Piece be plow'd up into Ridges, and if in each Sixteen Feet Breadth there be an empty Furrow of Two Feet; and yet, by the Height and Roundnefs of the Ridges, they have Eighteen Feet of Surface capable of producing Corn, equally to Eighteen Feet whilft the Piece was flat; there will be one Eighth Part of profitable Ground or Surface gain'd, more than it had

R 4 when

when level; and this, I believe, Experience will prove, if the thing were well examined into.

But againſt this Increaſe of profitable Ground, there is an Objection, which I muſt not call a frivolous one, in reſpect to the Authors who bring it; yet, I hope, the Deſire of finding the Truth will juſtify me to examine it; and the Arguments brought to ſuſtain it.

This Opinion of theirs is founded upon their Notion (which I think very erroneous) of the perpendicular Growth of Vegetables; and is, by Mr. *Bradley*, ſet in its beſt Light, in his *Vol.* I. *Pag.* 8. *uſque ad Pag.* 13. and in his Cuts, repreſenting Three Hills; but his Arguments ſeem to be ſuch as all Arguments are, which pretend to prove a thing to be what it is not; *viz.* Sophiſtical ones.

The Hypotheſis he endeavours to prove, is in *Pag.* 8. thus: ' An Hill may contain Four equal Sides,
' which meet in a Point at the Top; but the Contents
' of theſe Four Sides can produce no more, either of
' Grain or Trees, than the plain Ground, upon which
' the Hill ſtands, or has at its Baſe: and yet, by the
' Meaſure of the Sides, we find twice the Number of
' Acres, Roods, and Poles, which meaſure in the
' Baſe, or Ground-plat; and therefore *Page* 9. Hills
' are worth no more than half their Superficial Meaſure; *i. e.* Two Acres upon the Side of the Hill to
' pay as much as one upon the Plain, provided the
' Soil of both is equally rich.'

To prove it, he gives an Example in *Fig.* III. of Buildings upon an Hill; ſhewing, that the Two Sides of the Hill will only bear the ſame Number of Houſes, that may ſtand in the Line at the Baſe.

This is foreign to the Queſtion, of how much Grain, or how many Trees, the Hill will produce. For Vegetables, being fed by the Earth, require much more of its Surface to nouriſh them, than is neceſſary for them to ſtand on; but Buildings require no more

of

of the Surface but Room to ftand on: Therefore no fuch Argument, taken from Buildings, can be applied to Vegetables.

This Argument of Mr. *Bradley*'s gives no more Satisfaction to the Queftion about producing of Vegetables, than a Grazier would do, being afked, how many Oxen a certain Pafture-ground would maintain, if he fhould anfwer, by fatisfying you with the Number of Churches which might ftand thereon.

The like Anfwer, in effect, may be given to the Argument in *Fig.* IV. of the Pales; only he has forgot to fhew, that to mound over the Hill would require double the Rails, or double the Hedge-wood (except Stakes) as to mound the Bafe; if it did not, the Hill would be yet of the more Value, becaufe thereon more Surface might be fenced in at lefs Expence.

In his *Fig.* II. he gives no good Reafon why the Hill fhould not bear twice the Number of Trees as the Bafe can do; for there is as much Room for Two hundred Trees on the Hill, as for One hundred on the Bafe, becaufe he allows the Surface to be double to that of the Bafe. He ought to meafure the Diftances of the Trees on the Hill, by a Line parallel to the Surface they grow on, as well as he does the Diftances of thofe below.

And fuppofe the Row at the Bafe, together with the Surface they grow on, were rais'd up, fo that it fhould become parallel to half the Row on the Hill, would not the Trees in the Bafe Row be twice as near to one another as the Trees in the Hill Row are? And fuppofe a Line had been ty'd from the Tops of all the lower Trees, before the Row was fo rais'd up at one End, and then, after the Situation of the Row was fo alter'd, if by this Line the Trees fhould be pull'd from being perpendicular to the Surface they grow on, and made to ftand oblique to that, and perpendicular to the Horizon, as the upper Trees are; would the Diftances of the Trees from one another be

alter'd

alter'd by this Change of Posture ? No, for their Bottoms would be at the same Distances, because not removed ; and their Tops, because the same Line holds them, at the same Distances in both Postures.

Mr. *Bradley*'s Lines, drawn from the Trees below, which are one Perch asunder, make the Two Rows of Trees falsly seem to be at equal Distances, because these Lines are parallel to each other : But this is a Deceit; for, in Truth, the Distances of the Trees are not measured by the Distances of those Lines, but by the extreme Points at the Ends of the Lines (*a*) ; and those Two Points above, where the Lines cut the Row obliquely, and at unequal Angles are twice as far asunder as the endmost or extreme Points below are, where the Lines cut the Row at right Angles. Hence may be inferr'd, that there is Room for twice as many Trees to grow on the Hill as on the Base, and twice as much Grain for the same Reason ; because there is twice the Surface for the Roots to spread in.   And since Mr. *Bradley* allows the Hill to contain Two Perches to One of the Base, and the Soil of both to be of equal Goodness ; and yet affirms, that the Two can produce no more of Grain or Trees than the one Perch can ; I cannot see, why it should not be as reasonable to say, that Two Quarters of Oats will maintain an Horse no longer, nor better, than One Quarter of Oats, of equal Goodness, will do.

In *Page* 13. he concludes thus : ' That Hills, in ' their Measure, contain only as much profitable ' Land as the Plain or Plat of Ground they stand ' upon; and as a Proof of that, all Vegetables or ' Plants have an erect Method of Growth.'

This Proof of Mr. *Bradley*'s is founded upon an Argument which has no Consequence, unless it were

(a) These upper Trees are measured by the unequal Length of the Lines, not by their parallel Distance, as the lower Trees are ; therefore his Measure is a Quibble.

first

firſt proved, that the Surface of Earth could produce and maintain as many Vegetables or Plants as could ſtand thereon in an erect Poſture; which Suppoſition is as impoſſible, as that half an Acre ſhould produce and maintain and Hecatomb, without Mr. *Bradley's* teaching Oxen to live upon Air for their Food, as he thinks *Van Helmont's* Tree did.

All expert Huſbandmen muſt needs be convinced, that the greateſt Crop of Vegetables that ever grew, might ſtand in an erect Poſture, upon a twentieth (and I may ſay the Hundredth) Part of the Surface that produced it; therefore there muſt be Nineteen Parts for the Roots to ſpread, unoccupied by the Trunks Stems, or Stalks.

And tho' it be true, than an Hill will ſupport no more of theſe, than its Baſe, when placed in an erect Poſture, cloſe together, as in a Sheaf; yet this cloſe Poſition is only proper for them when they are dead, and require no more Nouriſhment than Houſes and Pales do; and conſequently require no Room but to ſtand on. Therefore this Argument of Mr. *Bradley's* muſt not be admitted in vegetative Growth, where there is always required Nineteen times more Room in the Surface, for the Uſe of the Roots, than what the Stems, Trunks, or Stalks, do poſſeſs upon it: And the more Room there is for the Roots, the greater Number of Plants may be produced.

Neither can I admit, that all Vegetables or Plants have an erect Method of Growth; becauſe the contrary is ſeen in Chamomile, and divers other Vegetables, which have an horizontal Method of Growth.

But what is more material to this Purpoſe, to be obſerved, is, that all Vegetables have horizontal Roots, and Roots parallel to the Earth's Surface or Superficies; and unleſs thoſe Roots have a ſufficient Superficies of Earth to range in, for Nouriſhment of a Plant, the Stem and Branches cannot proſper,

what-

whatever be their Method of Growth above the Earth; and if there be not a due Quantity of Food for the Roots within the Earth, a very little Space may contain the external Parts of Vegetables upon it.

From what has been faid, I think we may conclude, that Mr. *Bradley*'s Hill may produce more Vegetables than the Bafe whereon it ftands; and therefore it is of more Value than half its fuperficial Meafure; *i. e.* Two Acres on the Hill are worth more than one Acre on the Plain, the Soil being equally rich, as he allows it to be, in his Cafe.

Now, indeed, whether Mr. *Bradley* might not poffibly be deceived in his Opinion of the equal Richnefs of his Hill, and his Plain, I will not difpute: I will only fay this, that 'tis generally otherwife. But where a Plain is plow'd up into moderate Ridges, their Height being in proportion to the Depth of the Staple, below which the Plough muft take nothing into the Ridges, the Soil is equally rich, whether it be plowed plain, or ridged up. And as the Surface is in the Ridges increafed, there is nothing in all Mr. *Bradley*'s Arguments, that fhews, why that increafed Surface fhould not produce more Vegetables than the fame Earth could do whilft it was level.

There are other Reafons why it fhould produce more when ridged *(a)*, befides the Increafe of Surface; as,

I. *'Tis then more free from the Injuries of too much Water.*

(a) To the Three we may add a Fourth Reafon, *viz.* the raifing the Thicknefs of the Staple in the Ridges, keeping the Surface drier in wet Weather, and moifter at the Bottom of the Staple in dry Weather. And I have feen Barley that was drilled on my raifed little Ridges flourifh in a dry Summer on the Brow of my chalky Hill, and on my loweft Land in wet Weather, when the Barley hand-fown contiguous to it on each Side thofe Ridges, fown on the Level the fame Day that the Ridges were drilled, have looked yellow and fickly; and yet it is not wet Land.

II.

II. *'Tis better protected against cold Winds; because the Ridges are a Shelter to one another.*

III. *If the Surface be much exhausted, by too frequent Sowing, the Ridges may be made just where the Furrows were, and then the Surface will be intirely changed.*

The following general Rules ought to be obferved about Ridges; *viz.*

That, as to their Height, regard muft be had to the Nature of the Soil, in its difficult Admiffion of Water; for the greater that is, the greater Declivities the Ridges fhould have; and then, if the Soil be not deep, they fhould generally be made the narrower.

There is one thing which Mr. *Bradley* takes no notice of; *viz.* That no more of the Rain, or other Benefits of the Atmofphere, which defcend perpendicularly, can fall on an Hill, or on a Ridge, than what would fall on the Bafe, or Ground-plot. But 'tis probable, that more of the fine Vapour, which fwims in the Current of the Air horizontally, does ftrike and break againft thofe Eminences, and fo make an Equivalent *(b)*, except that it runs off more quickly.

Notwithftanding all I have here faid, in behalf of Ridges, I muft confefs, that, for my Hoeing-Hufbandry, I fhould prefer Land that is naturally dry enough, without a Neceffity of being laid up in any larger or higher Ridges than what may contain Six Feet in Breadth *(c)*, that Size being the largeft that is proper for the regular Operation of the Horfehoe.

CHAP.

(b) But though Ridges do alter or increafe the Surface, the Quantity of Soil or Earth remaining the fame as on the Level, and of no greater Depth than can be tilled, it may produce equal Crops of Corn with the Level, and no more; except from the Advantage the Ridges may give it in lying drier.

(c) Since the Printing of my Effay, I find, upon Trial, that thefe narrow Ridges are as effectual as any for carrying the Water off from my clayey Hill; and that they be made much lefs horizontal

CHAP. XVII.

Of Differences *between the* Old *and the* New Hu∫bandry.

IN order to make a Compari∫on between the Hoe-ing-Hu∫bandry, and the old Way, there are Four Things, whereof the Differences ought to be very well con∫idered.

    I. *The Expence* ⎫
    II. *The Goodne∫s* ⎬   of a Crop.
    III. *The Certainty* ⎭
    IV. *The Condition in which the Land is left after a Crop.*

The Profit or Lo∫s ari∫ing from Land, is not to be computed, only from the Value of the Crop it produces; but from its Value, after all Expences of Seed, Tillage, *&c.* are deducted.

Thus, when an Acre brings a Crop worth *Four Pounds,* and the Expences thereof amount to *Five Pounds,* the Owner's Lo∫s is *One Pound*; and when an Acre brings a Crop which yields *Thirty Shillings,* and the Expence amounts to no more than *Ten Shillings,* the Owner receives *One Pound*, clear Profit, from this Acre's very ∫mall Crop, as the other lo∫es *One Pound* by his greater Crop.

horizontal than broad Ridges, whereby their Furrows are the more ea∫ily turned upwards again∫t the Declivity.

I have not tried any narrower Ridge than that of Six Feet upon this Hill: But I have had full Experience of Five-feet and of Four-feet Ridges upon other Land; and find that all Sizes of the∫e narrow Ridges are very advantageous, even where the Crop is to be ∫own upon the Level; for fewer Furrows are nece∫∫ary for the Tilling of an Acre, when 'tis kept in ∫uch Ridges, than in broad Lands; and after wet Weather the Ridges will be fit to be plowed much ∫ooner than level Ground.

The

The ufual Expences of an Acre of Wheat, fown in the old Hufbandry, *in the Country where I live, is, in in fome Places, for Two Bufhels and an half of Seed; in other Places Four Bufhels and an half; the leaft of thefe Quantities at* Three Shillings per *Bufhel, being the prefent Price, is* Seven Shillings *and* Six-pence. *For Three Plowings, Harrowing, and Sowing,* Sixteen Shillings; *but if plow'd Four times, which is better,* One Pound. *For Thirty Load of Dung, to a Statute Acre, is* Two Pounds Five Shillings. *For Carriage of the Dung, according to the Diftance, from* Two Shillings *to* Six-pence *the Load,* One Shilling *being the Price moft common, is* One Pound Ten Shillings. *The Price for Weeding is very uncertain; it has fometimes coft* Twelve Shillings, *fometimes* Two Shillings *per Acre.*

	l.	s.	d.
In Seed and Tillage, nothing can be abated of	01	03	06
For the Weeding, one Year with another, is more than	00	02	00
For the Rent of the Year's Fallow	00	10	00
For the Dung; 'tis in fome Places a little cheaper, neither do they always lay on quite fo much; therefore abating 15s. in that Article, we may well fet Dung and Carriage at	02	10	00
Reaping commonly 5s. fometimes lefs	00	04	06
Total	04	10	00

Folding of Land with Sheep is reckoned abundantly cheaper than Cart-dung; but this is to be queftioned, becaufe much Land muft lie ftill for keeping a Flock (unlefs there be Downs); and for their whole Year's keeping, with both Grafs and Hay, there are but Three Months of the Twelve wherein the Fold is of any confiderable Value; this makes the Price of their Manure

5   qua-

quadruple to what it would be, if equally good all the Year, like Cart-dung: And folding Sheep yield little Profit, besides their Dung; because the Wool of a Flock, except it be a large one, will scarce pay the Shepherd and the Shearers. But there is another thing yet, which more inhances the Price of Sheep-Dung; and that is, the dunging the Land with their Bodies, when they all die of the Rot, which happens too frequently in many Places; and then the whole Crop of Corn must go to purchase another Flock, which may have the same Fate the ensuing Year, if the Summer prove wet; and so may the Farmer be served for several more successive Years, unless he should break, and another take his Place, or that dry Summers come in time to prevent it. To avoid this Misfortune, he would be glad to purchase Cart-dung at the highest Price, for supplying the Place of his Fold; but 'tis only near Cities, and great Towns, that a sufficient Quantity can be procured.

But, supposing the Price of Dunging to be only Two Pounds Ten Shillings, and the general Expence of an Acre of Wheat, when sown, at Three Shillings per Bushel, to be Four Pounds Ten Shillings, with the Year's Rent of the Fallow;

The Expences of planting an Acre of Wheat in the Hoeing-Husbandry, is Three Pecks of (a) of Seed, at *Three Shillings per* Bushel, is *Two Shillings* and *Three-pence.* The whole Tillage, if done by Horses, would be *Eight Shillings*; because our Two Plowings, and Six Hoeings (b), are equal to Two Plowings;

(a) Sometimes half a Bushel is the most just Quantity of Seed, to drill on an Acre.

(b) But we sometimes plow our Six-feet Ridges before Drilling, at Five or Six Furrows, which is a Furrow or Two more than I have reckoned: But we do not always hoe Six times afterwards. But it is better for successive Wheat-crops to bestow the Labour of as many Hoeings as amount to three plain Plowings in a Year, it being a greater Damage to omit one necessary Hoeing, than is the Expence of several Hoeings.

the

the common Price whereof is *Four Shillings* each; but this we diminish half, when done by Oxen kept on St. Foin, in this manner ; *viz.* Land worth *Thirty Shillings* Rent, drill'd with St. Foin, will well maintain an Ox a Year *(a)*, and sometimes Hay will be left to pay for the Making: We cannot therefore allow more than *One Shilling* a Week for his Work, because his Keeping comes but to *Seven-pence* a Week round the Year.

In plain Plowing, Six Feet contains Eight Furrows; but we plow a Six-feet Ridge at Four Furrows, because in this there are Two Furrows cover'd in the Middle of it, and one on each Side of it lies open. Now what we call one Hoeing, is only Two Furrows of this Ridge, which is equal to a Fourth Part of one plain Plowing; so that the Hoeing of Four Acres requires an equal Number of Furrows with one Acre that is plow'd plain, and equal Time to do it in (except that the Land, that is kept in Hoeing, works much easier than that which is not).

All the Tillage we ever bestow upon a Crop of Wheat that follows a ho'd Crop, is equal to Eight Hoeings *(b)*; Two of which may require Four Oxen each, One of them Three Oxen, and the other Five Hoeings Two Oxen each. However, allow Three Oxen to each single Hoeing, taking them all one with another, which is Three Oxen more than it comes to in the Whole.

(a) Or an Ox may be well kept Nine Months, with an Acre of indifferent Horse-ho'd Turneps ; and if we value them only at the Expence and Rent of the Land, this will be a yet cheaper Way of maintaining Oxen. Upon more Experience it is found, that St. Foin Hay alone, or with a small Quantity of Turneps, is best for working Oxen in the Winter ; but a Plenty of Turneps with the same Hay is better for fatting Oxen that do not work.

(b) But the Number of Oxen required will be according to their Bigness and Strength, and to the Depth and Strength of the Soil, which also will be the easier Draught for the Oxen, the oftener the Intervals are hoed.

S   Begin

Begin at Five in the Morning, and in about Six Hours you may hoe Three Acres, being equal in Furrows to Three Rood; *i. e.* Three Quarters of an Acre. Then turn the Oxen to Grafs, and after refting, eating, and drinking, Two Hours and an half, with another Set of Oxen begin Hoeing again ; and by or before half an Hour after Seven at Night, another like Quantity may be ho'd. Thefe are the Hours the Statute has appointed all Labourers to work, during the Summer Half-year.

To hoe thefe Six Acres a Day, each Set of Oxen draw the Plough only Eight Miles and a Quarter, which they may very well do in Five Hours ; and then the Holder and Driver will be at their Work of Plowing Ten Hours, and will have Four Hours and an half to reft, *&c.*

The Expence then of hoeing Six Acres in a Day, in this manner, may be accounted, at *One Shilling* the Man that holds the Plough, *Six-pence* the Boy that drives the Plough, *One Shilling* for the Six Oxen, and *Six-pence* for keeping the Tackle in Repair. The whole Sum for hoeing thefe Six Acres is *Three Shillings*, being *Six-pence per* Acre (*a*).

They who follow the old Hufbandry cannot keep Oxen fo cheap, becaufe they can do nothing without the Fold, and Store-fheep will fpoil the St. Foin. They may almoft as well keep Foxes and Geefe together, as Store-fheep and good St. Foin. Befides, the fowed St. Foin coft Ten times as much the Planting as drill'd St. Foin does, and muft be frequently manured, or elfe it will foon decay ; efpecially upon all forts of chalky Land, whereon 'tis moft commonly fown.   The

---

(*a*) But where there is not the Convenience of keeping Oxen, the Price of Hoeing with Horfes is One Shilling each time.

When a Roller is ufed, which is lefs than a Hoeing, becaufe one Perfon to lead is enough, and that may be a Boy; and once in an Interval may fuffice ; then 'tis lefs Labour than half a Hoeing ; and for this we may well abate One Hoeing of the Eight.

The Expence of drilling cannot be much ; for as we can hoe Six Acres a Day, at Two Furrows on each Six-feet Ridge, so we may drill Twenty-four Acres a Day, with a Drill that plants Two of those Ridges at once ; and this we may reckon a *Peny Half-peny* an Acre.   But because we find it less Trouble to drill single Ridges, we will set the Drilling, at most, *Six-pence per* Acre.

As every successive Crop (if well managed) is more free from Weeds than the preceding Crop ; I will set it all together at *Six-pence (a)* an Acre for Weeding (*b*).

For a Boy or a Woman to follow the Hoe-plough, to uncover the young Wheat, when any Clods of Earth happen to fall on it, for which Trouble there is seldom necessary above once (*c*) to a Crop, *Two-pence* an Acre.   *One Peny* is too much for Brine and Lime for an Acre.

Reaping this Wheat is not worth above half as much as the Reaping of a sown Crop of equal Value ; because the drill'd standing upon about a Sixth Part of the Ground, a Reaper may cut almost as much of the Row at one Stroke, at he could at Six, if the same stood dispersed all over the Ground, as the sowed does ; and because he who reaps sowed Wheat,

(*a*) This is when the Land has been well cleansed of Weeds in the preceding Crop, or Fallow, or both.

(*b*) This may be enough, if the Land be well cleansed the Year before, and considering that several Years in such there is no Occasion for Weeding at all : And as this Calculation is comparative with the old Way, we should examine the Price of weeding the sown Corn, which by the best Information I can get, was in the Year 1735. about 4 *s. per* Acre for Weeding of Barley ; and of Wheat, round about where I live, about 6 *s.* and in *Wiltshire*, 15 *s. per* Acre for their Wheat, amongst which much Damage is done by the Weeder's Feet, and yet some Weeds are left.

(*c*) But this Expence being so small, 'tis better that a Person should follow at every Hoeing, where we suspect, that any Damage may happen from any Earth's falling on, or pressing too hard against some of the Plants.

S 2   must

muft reap the Weeds along with the Wheat; but the drilled has no Weeds; and befides, there go a greater Quantity of Straw, and more Sheaves, to a Bufhel of the fowed, than of the drilled (*a*).   And fince fome Hundred Acres of drilled Wheat have been reaped at *Two Shillings* and *Six-pence per* Acre, I will count that to be the Price.

The whole Expence *of an Acre of drilled Wheat.*

	l.	*s.*	*d.*
For Seed — — — — —	00	02	03
For Tillage — — — —	00	04	00
For Drilling — — — —	00	00	06
For Weeding — — — —	00	00	06
For Uncovering — — —	00	00	02
For Brine and Lime — —	00	00	01
For Reaping — — — —	00	02	06
Total	00	10	00
The Expence of an Acre of fowed Wheat is — —	04	00	00
To which muft be added, for the Year's Rent of the Fallow	00	10	00
Total	04	10	00

If I have reckoned the Expence of the drilled at the loweft Price, to bring it to an even Sum; I have alfo abated in the other more than the whole Expence of the drilled amounts unto.

And thus the Expence of a drilled Crop of Wheat is but the Ninth Part of the Expence of a Crop fown in the common Manner.

'Tis alfo fome Advantage, that lefs Stock is required where no Store-fheep are ufed.

(*a*) One Sheaf of the latter will yield more Wheat than Two of the former of equal Diameter.

II.

II. *Of the different Goodness of a Crop.*

The Goodness of a Crop consists in the Quality of it, as well as the Quantity; and Wheat being the most useful Grain, a Crop of this is better than a Crop of any other Corn, and the ho'd Wheat has larger Ears (and a fuller Body) than sow'd Wheat. We can have more of it, because the same Land will produce it every Year, and even Land, which, by the Old Husbandry, would not be made to bear Wheat at all: So that, in many Places, the New Husbandry can raise Ten Acres of Wheat for One that the Old can do : because where Land is poor, they sow but a Tenth Part of it with Wheat.

We do not pretend, that we have always greater Crops, or so great as some sown Crops are, especially if those mention'd by Mr. *Houghton* be not mistaken.

The greatest Produce I ever had from a single Yard in Length of a double Row, was Eighteen Ounces: The Partition of this being Six Inches, and the Interval Thirty Inches, was, by Computation, Ten Quarters (or Eighty Bushels) to an Acre.

I had also Twenty Ounces to a like Yard of a Third successive Crop of Wheat; but this being a treble Row, and the Partitions and Interval being wider, and supposed to be in all Six Feet, was computed to Six Quarters to an Acre. And if these Rows had been better order'd than they were, and the Earth richer, and more pulveriz'd, more Stalks would have tillered out, and more Ears would have attained their full Size, and have equall'd the best, which must have made a much greater Crop than either of these were.

But to compare the different Profit, we may proceed thus : The Rent and Expence of a drill'd Acre being One Pound, and of a sow'd Acre Five Pounds; One Quarter of Corn, produced by the drill'd, bears an equal Proportion in Profit to the One Pound, as Five Quarters, produced by the other, do to the Five

Pounds.   As fuppofe it be of Wheat, at Two Shillings and Six-pence a Bufhel, there is neither Gain
nor Lofs in the one nor the other Acre, though the
former yield but One Quarter, and the other Five;
but if the drill'd Acre yield Two Quarters, and the
fow'd Acre Four Quarters at the fame Price, the
drill'd brings the Farmer One Pound clear Profit, and
the fown, by its Four Quarters, brings the other One
Pound Lofs.   Likewife fuppofe the drilling Farmer
to have his Five Pounds laid out on Five Acres of
Wheat, and the other to have his Five Pounds laid
out on One dung'd Acre; then let the Wheat they
produce be at what Price it will, if the Five Acres
have an equal Crop to the one Acre, the Gain or
Lofs muft be equal: But when Wheat is cheap, as
we fay it is when fold at Two and Six-pence a Bufhel,
then if the Farmer, who follows the old Method, has
Five Quarters on his Acre, he muft fell it all to pay
his Rent and Expence; but the other having Five
Quarters on each of his Five Acres, the Crop of One
of them will pay the Rent and Expence of all his
Five Acres (*a*), and he may keep the remaining
Twenty Quarters, till he can fell them at Five Shillings a Bufhel, which amounts to Forty Pounds,
wherewith he may be able to buy Four of his Five
Acres at Twenty Years Purchafe, out of One Year's
Crop, whilft the Farmer who purfues the old Method,
muft be content to have only his Labour for his
Travel; or if he pretends to keep his Wheat till he
fells it at Five Shillings a Bufhel, he commonly runs
in Debt to his Neighbours, and in Arrear of his Rent;
and if the Markets do not rife in time, or if his Crops

(*a*) Or fuppofe a drill'd Acre to produce no more than One
Third of the fow'd Acre's Crop, whofe Expence is Five times as
much as of the drill'd, 'tis much more profitable, becaufe a Third
of Five Pounds is One Pound Thirteen and Four-pence; and a
Fifth of the Rent and Expence being only One Pound, fuch
drill'd Acre pays the Owner Thirteen and Four-pence more Profit,
than the other which brings a Crop treble to the drill'd.

fail

fail in the Interim, his Landlord seizes on his Stock, and then he knows not how it may be sold ; Actions are brought against him ; the Bailiffs and Attorneys pull him to Pieces ; and then he is undone (*a*).

III. *The Certainty of a Crop.*

The Certainty of a Crop is much to be regarded; it being better to be secure of a moderate Crop, than to have but a mere Hazard of a great one.   The Farmer who adheres to the old Method is often deceiv'd in his Expectation, when his Crop at coming into Ear is very big, as well as when 'tis in Danger of being too little.   Our hoeing Farmer is much less liable to the Hazard of either of those Extremes ; for when his Wheat is big, 'tis not apt to lodge or fall down, which Accident is usually the utter Ruin of the other ; he is free from the Causes which make the contrary Crop too little.

A very effectual Means to prevent the failing of a Crop of Wheat, is to plow the pulveriz'd Earth for Seed early, and when 'tis dry.   The early Season also is more likely to be dry than the latter Season is.

1. *The Advocate for the old Method is commonly late in his sowing ; because he can't fallow his Ground early, for fear of killing the Couch, and other Grass that maintains his folding Sheep, which*
2. *are so necessary to his Husbandry : And when 'tis sow'd late, it must not be sow'd dry, for then the*
3. *Winter might kill the young Wheat.   Neither can he at that time plow dry, and sow wet, because he commonly sows under Furrow ; that is, sows the Seed first, and plows it in as fast as 'tis sown.   If he*
4. *sows early (as he may if he will) in light Land, he must not sow dry, for fear the Poppies and other Weeds should grow, and devour his Crop ; and if his*
5. *Land be strong, let it be sown early, wet or dry (tho'*

(*a*) Tho' only Five Acres and one Acre be put, yet we may imagine them Two hundred and Fifty, and Fifty to enrich the one, or break the other Farmer.

wet is worſt), 'tis apt to grow ſo ſtale and hard by Spring, that his Crop is in Danger of ſtarving, unleſs the Land be very rich, or much dung'd : and then the Winter and Spring proving kind, it may not be in leſs Danger of being ſo big as to fall down, and be ſpoil'd.

6. Another thing is, that though he had no other Impediment againſt plowing dry, and ſowing wet, 'tis ſeldom that he has time to do it in ; for he muſt plow all his Ground, which is Eight Furrows in Six Feet ;

7. and, whilſt it is wet, muſt lie ſtill with his Plough. When he ſows under Furrow, he fears to plow deep, leſt he bury too much of his Seed ; and if he

8. plows ſhallow, his Crop loſes the Benefit of deep plowing, which is very great. When he ſows upon

9. Furrow (that is after 'tis plow'd) he muſt harrow the Ground level to cover the Seed ; and that expoſes the Wheat the more to the cold Winds, and ſuffers the Snow to be blown off it, and the Water to lie longer on it ; all which are great Injuries to it.

Our Hoeing Huſbandry is different in all of the fore-mentioned Particulars.

1. We can plow the Two Furrows whereon the next Crop is to ſtand, immediately after the preſent Crop is off.

2. We have no Uſe of the Fold ; becauſe our Ground has annually a Crop growing on it, and it muſt lie ſtill a Year, if we would fold it, and that Crop would be loſt ; and all the Good the Fold could do to the Land, would be only to help to pulverize it for one ſingle Crop ; its Benefit not laſting to the Second Year. And ſo we ſhould be certain of loſing one Crop for the very uncertain Hopes of procuring one the enſuing Year by the Fold ; when 'tis manifeſt by the adjoining Crops, that we can have a much better Crop every Year, without a Fold, or any other Manure.

3. We can plow dry, and drill wet, without any manner of Inconvenience.

4. He

4. He fears the Weeds will grow, and destroy his Crop : We hope they will grow, to the end we may destroy them *(a)*.

5. We do not fear to plant our Wheat early (so that we plow dry), because we can help the Hardness or Staleness of the Land by Hoeing.

6. The Two Furrows of every Ridge whereon the Rows are to be drilled, we plow dry ; and if the Weather prove wet before these are all finished, we can plow the other Two Furrows up to them, until it be dry enough to return to our plowing the first Two Furrows ; and after finishing them, let the Weather be wet or dry, we can plow the last Two Furrows. We can plow our Two Furrows in the Fourth Part of the Time they can plow their Eight, which they must plow dry all of them, in every Six Feet ; for they cannot plow part dry, and the rest when 'tis wet, as we can.

7. We never plant our Seed under Furrow, but place it just at the Depth which we judge most proper ; and that is pretty shallow, about Two Inches deep ; and then there is no Danger of burying it.

8. We not only plow a deep Furrow, but also plow to the Depth of Two Furrows ; that is, we trench-plow where the Land will allow it *(b)*; and we have the greatest Convenience imaginable for doing this, because there are Two of our Four Furrows

(a) For, before they grow, they cannot be killed ; but if they are all killed as soon as they appear, there will be no Danger of their exhausting the Land, or re-stocking it with their Seed ; and 'tis our Fault if we drill more than we can keep clean from Weeds by the Horse-hoe, Hand-hoe, and Hands ; the First for the Intervals, the Second for the Partitions, and the Third for the Rows : By the Two former, as soon after they appear as they can ; but by the last, when they are grown high enough to be conveniently taken hold of.

(b) Very little of my Land will admit the Plough to go the Depth of Two common Furrows without reaching the Chalk ; But deep Land may be easily thus Trench-plowed with great Advantage; and even when there is only the Depth of a single Furrow, that may sometimes be advantageously plowed at twice.

always

always lying open ; and Two plowed Furrows (that is, one plowed under another) arc as much more advantageous for the nourifhing a Crop, as Two Bufhels of Oats are better than one for nourifhing an Horfe : Or if the Staple of the Land be too thin or fhallow, we can help it by raifing the Ridges prepared for the Rows the higher above the Level.

9. We alfo raife an high Ridge in the Middle of each Interval above the Wheat before Winter, to pro-tect it from the cold Winds, and to prevent the Snow from being driven away by them.　And the Furrows or Trenches, from whence the Earth of thefe Ridges is taken, ferve to drain off the Water from the Wheat, fo that, being drier, it muft be warmer than the harrowed Wheat, which has neither Furrows to keep it dry, nor Ridges to fhelter it *(a)*, as every Row of ours has on both Sides of it.

IV. *The Condition in which the Land is left after a Crop.*

The different Condition the Land is left in after a Crop *(b)*, by the one and the other Hufbandry, is

not

(a) This is a Miftake ; for the Ridges in the Middle of the Intervals do not always, nor often in thin fhallow Land lie high enough to make a Shelter to the Rows, they being higher : But when Wheat is drilled on the Level, 'tis fheltered by the Ridges raifed in the Intervals : But we never weed or hand-hoe Wheat before the Spring.

(b) If indifferent Land be well pulverized by the Plough for one whole Year, it will produce a good Crop : But then, if, in-ftead of being fown, it be kept pulverized on for another Year without being exhaufted by any Vegetables, it will acquire from the Atmofphere an extraordinary great Degree of Fertility more than it had before fuch Second Year's Pulveration and Unex-l.auftion.　This being granted, which no Man of Experience can deny, what Reafon can there be why fuch a Number of Plants, competent for a profitable Crop, may not be maintained on it the Second Year, that may keep the Degree of their Exhauftion in *Æquilibrio* with that Degree of Fertility, which the fame Land had acquired at the End of the Firft Year of its Pulveration, the fame Degree of Pulveration being continued to it by Hoeing in the Second Year ? Or why may it not produce annual Crops al-ways, if the fame *Equilibrium* be continually kept? Two unan-fwerable

not lefs confiderable than the different Profit of the Crop.

A Piece of Eleven Acres of a poor, thin, chalky Hill was fown with Barley in the common Manner, after a hoed Crop of Wheat; and produced full Five Quarters and an half to each Acre (reckoning the Tythe); which was much more than any Land in all the Neighbourhood yielded the fame Year; tho' fome of it be fo rich, as that One Acre is worth Three Acres of this Land: And no Man living can remember, that ever this produced above half fuch a Crop before, even when the beft of the common Management has been beftowed upon it.

A Field, that is a fort of an Heath-ground, ufed to bring fuch poor Crops of Corn, that heretofore the Parfon carried away a whole Crop of Oats from it, believing it had been only his Tythe. The beft Management that ever they did or could beftow upon it, was to let it reft Two or Three Years, and then fallow and dung it, and fow it with Wheat, next to that with Barley and Clover, and then let it reft again; but I cannot hear of any good Crop that it ever produced by this or any other of their Methods; 'twas ftill reckoned fo poor, that nobody cared to rent it. They faid Dung and Labour were thrown away upon it, then immediately after Two fown Crops of black Oats had been taken off it, the laft of which was fcarce worth the mowing, it was put into the

fwerable Reafons may be given why this *Equilibrium* cannot be kept in the random Sowing, as it may in the Hoeing Method; *viz.* Firft, In the former, the Land is by the Number of fown Plants and Weeds much more (we may fuppofe at leaft Five times more) exhaufted: And, Secondly, No Pulveration is continued to the Soil, whilft the Crop is on it; which is that Part of the Year wherein is the moft proper (if not the only proper) Seafon for pulverizing. Therefore, allowing, that, in the random way, a Soil cannot, for want of Quantity of vegetable Food, continue to produce annual Crops without Manure, or perhaps with it; yet that is no Reafon why it may not produce them in the Hoeing Culture duly performed.

Hoeing

Hoeing Management; and when Three hoed Crops *(a)* had been taken from it, it was fown with Barley, and brought a very good Crop, much better than ever it was known to yield before; and then a good Crop of hoed Wheat fucceeded the Barley, and then it was again fown with Barley, upon the Wheat-ftubble; and that alfo was better than the Barley it ufed to produce.

Now all the Farmers of the Neighbourhood affirm, that it is impoffible but that this muft be very rich Ground, becaufe they have feen it produce Six Crops in Six Years, without Dung or Fallow, and never one of them fail. But, alas! this different Reputation they give to the Land, does not at all belong to it, but to the different Sorts of Hufbandry; for the Nature of it cannot be altered but by that, the Crops being all carried off it, and nothing added to fupply the Subftance thofe Crops take from it, except (what Mr. *Evelyn* calls) the celeftial Influences; and that thefe are received by the Earth, in proportion to the Degrees of its Pulveration.

A Field was drilled with Barley after an hoed Crop; and another adjoining to it on the fame Side of the fame poor Hill, and exactly the fame Sort of Land, was drilled with Barley alfo, Part of it after the fown Crop, the fame Day with the other; there was only this Difference in the Soil, that the former of thefe had no manner of Compoft on it for many Years before, and the latter was dunged the Year before: Yet its Crop was not near fo good as that which followed the hoed Crop *(b)*; tho' the latter had twice the Plowing that the former had before drilling, and the fame Hoeings afterwards; *viz.* Each was hoed Three times.

A Field of about Seventeen Acres was Summer-fallowed, and drilled with Wheat; and with the Hoeing brought a very good Crop (except Part of it,

(*a*) Thefe Three hoed Crops were of Turneps and Potatoes.
(*b*) This was a Wheat Crop, and often well hoed.

which

which being eaten by trefpaffing Sheep in the Winter, was fomewhat blighted) ; the *Michaelmas* after that was taken off, the fame Field was drilled again with Wheat, upon the Stubble of the former, and hoed: This Second Crop was a good one, fcarce any in the Neighbourhood better.   A Piece of Wheat adjoining to it, on the very fame Sort of Land (except that this latter was always reckoned better, being thicker in Mould above the Chalk), fown at the fame time on dunged Fallows, and the Ground always dunged once in Three Years; yet this Crop failed fo much, as to be judged, by fome Farmers, not to exceed the Tythe of the other: That the hoed Field has re-ceived no Dung or Manure for many Years paft, is becaufe it lies out of the Reach for carrying of Cart-Dung, and no Fold being kept on my Farm : But I cannot fay, I think there was quite fo much Odds betwixt this Second undunged hoed Crop and the fown ; yet this is certain, that the former is a good, and the latter a very bad Crop.

I could give many more Inftances of the fame Kind, where hoed Crops and fown Crops have fucceeded better after hoed Crops than after fown Crops, and never yet have feen the contrary ; and therefore am convinced, that the Hoeing *(a)* (if it be duly per-formed) enriches the Soil more than Dung and Fal-lows, and leaves the Land in a much better Condition for a fucceeding Crop.   The Reafon I take to be very

(a) This is more efpecially meant of Fallows in the common Hufbandry, and a moderate Quantity of common Dung, or the Fold : And there may be fuch a poor Sand, or other barrenifh Soil, fo fubject to Conftipation in the Winter, as to require Dung when planted with Wheat, there being no general Rule without Exceptions; and 'tis impoffible for me to know the Number of thefe Exceptions.   Well it is for the Hoer, whofe Land is of fuch a kind, that he can keep it in Heart without Dung by Hoeing : for when he has no Fold, he plows his Ground with Oxen, and plants it moftly with Wheat, the Straw whereof being for other Ufes, he can make but very little Dung.

obvious:

obvious: The artificial Pasture of Plants is made and increased by Pulveration only; and nothing else there is in our Power to enrich our Ground, but to pulverize it *(a)*, and keep it from being exhausted by Vegetables.

(a) These Two are all we have in our Power; for pulverizing includes an Exposure to the Atmosphere; without which, I think, it cannot be reduced to Particles minute enough, or have their Superficies so impregnated as to become a fertile Pasture for Plants. The Experiment related by Mr. *Evelyn* of artificial Pulveration, seems to prove such an Exposure necessary; as also the frequent turning (or incessantly agitating) that fine Dust for a Year, before the barren exhausted Earth was made rich and prolific: For, besides the Benefit of Pulveration and Impregnation, Land is more enriched in proportion to the Time of Exposure, during which it is free from Exhaustion, and continually receiving from the Atmosphere: Therefore frequent Turning and Exposure are both contained in the Words *pulverize, and not exhaust*; and to comply with the latter, we should endeavour, that our Land may be never exhausted by any other Plants than by those we would propagate, and by no more of them neither, than what are necessary for producing a reasonable Crop; which, upon full Trial, will be found a very small Number in comparison to those that are commonly sown; and then, if the Supply from the Atmosphere by Help of the Pulveration exceeds the Exhaustion, the Land will become richer, tho' constant Crops are produced of the same Species; as in the Vineyards; and the Soil of these is so much improved by a bare competent Exhaustion, and the usual Pulveration, that after producing good annual Crops without Dung, until Age has killed the Vines, they leave the Soil better than they found it; and better than contiguous Land of the same Sort kept in arable Field-culture.

By Pulveration are meant all the Benefits of it that accrue to the Pasture of Plants; and by Exhaustion, all the Injuries that can be done to that Pasture, except Burning. And as the Benefits of Pulveration visibly continue for several Years, so do the Injuries of Exhaustion; which appear by the Ends of some of my Rows that have been cleansed of Weeds in their Partitions by the Hand-hoe, and the other Ends of the same Rows not cleansed; the Difference is visible in the Colour of the Wheat in the Third and Fourth following Crops, equally managed; and this is no more to be wondered at, than that Two unequal Sums, being equally increased or diminished, should remain unequal, until an Addition to the lesser, or a Subtraction from the greater, be made; which, in case of the Soil, must be either by a greater Pulveration, or a lesser Exhaustion. 'Tis by this that both Ends

of

getables *(a)*.   Superinductions of Earth are an Addition of more Ground, or changing it, and are more properly purchafing than cultivating.

Their

of thefe Rows in time become equal : For tho' Ten Plants that produce an Ounce of Wheat, infume more *Pabulum* than one Plant that produces the fame Quantity (the Reafon for which is given in the Note on *p.* 121.) ; yet a Plant that produces Six or Seven Drams, infumes lefs than one that produces an Ounce ; for a Plant which produces Six Drams of Wheat cannot be a poor one, and therefore infumes no more *Pabulum* than in proportion to its Augment and Product.   Thus the Soil of thofe Ends, which, by being doubly exhaufted by Weeds and Wheat plants, was made poorer, gradually recovers an Equality with the other Ends, by being for feveral Years lefs exhaufted than the other Ends are by larger Plants, whilft the Number of Plants, and the Pulveration of each, are equal.

To the Reafons already given there is another to be added, why Horfe hoed Wheat exhaufts the Soil lefs than fown Crops, where the Product of Wheat produced by each is equal: Which Reafon is, that the former has much lefs Straw than the latter ; as appears by the different Quantities of Grain that a Sheaf of each of equal Diameter yields ; one of the former yielding generally double to one of the latter ; for a Sheaf of the fown has not only more fmall Under-ears, but alfo its beft Ears bear a lefs Proportion to their Straw than the other ; for a Straw of fown Wheat Six Feet high, I have found to have an Ear but of half the Size of an Ear of drilled Wheat on a Stalk Five Feet high, having meafured both of them ftanding in the Field, and rubbed out the Grain of them.   This Difference I impute to the different Supply of Nourifhment at the time when the Ears are forming. Thus the fown Crop exhaufts a Soil much more by its greater Quantity of Straw.

And this is one Reafon why annual Crops of fown Wheat cannot fucceed as Crops of Horfe hoed Wheat do.   There muft be Dung and Fallow to repair the Exhauftion of the fown ; neither of which are neceffary for Crops of the Horfe-hoed.

(a) It may be afked, How 'tis poffible that Eight Hoeings, which are but equal, in Labour, to Two plain Plowings, fhould fo much exceed Three plain Plowings, as to procure as good or a better Crop without Manure, than the common Three Plowings can do with Manure, and enrich the Land alfo.

The Anfwer is, That each Hoeing of the Five or Six being done to the Wheat-plants, though it does not clean plow the whole Interval underneath, yet it changeth the whole external Superficies (or Surface) thereof, whereby it becomes impregnate

by

Their One Year's Tillage, which is but Two Plowings before Seed-time, commonly makes but little Duſt ; and that which it does make, has but a ſhort time to lie expoſed for Impregnation ; and after the Wheat is ſown, the Land lies unmoved for near Twelve Months, all the while gradually loſing its Paſture, by ſubſiding, and by being continually exhauſted in feeding a treble Stock of Wheat-plants, and a Stock of Weeds, which are ſometimes a greater Stock. This puts the Advocates for the old Method upon a Neceſſity of uſing of Dung, which is, at beſt, but a Succedaneum *of the Hoe ; for it depends chiefly on the Weather, and other Accidents, whether it may prove ſufficient by Fermentation to pulverize in the Spring, or no : And it is a Queſtion whether it will equal Two additional (a) Hoeings, or but one ; tho', as I have computed it, one Dunging coſts the Price of One hundred Hoeings.*

When they have done all they can, the Paſture they raiſe is generally too little for the Stock that is to be maintained upon it, and much the greateſt Part of the Wheat-plants are ſtarved ; for from Twenty Gallons of Seed they ſow on an Acre, they receive commonly no more than Twenty Buſhels (b) of Wheat in their Crop, which is but an Increaſe of Eight Grains for one : Now, conſidering how many Grains there are in one good Ear, and how many Ears

by the nitrous Air, as much as if it were all clean plowed at the time of every Hoeing, and the Weeds are as much ſtifled, or ſuffocated.

(a) Additional, becauſe there muſt firſt be ſeveral Hoeings to make our treble Row equal to an undunged Six-feet Ridge of ſown Wheat.

(b) And they have oftener leſs than Sixteen Buſhels ; and in the Harveſt 1735, a ſubſtantial experienced Farmer had no more than Four Buſhels of Wheat to an Acre throughout a Field of Forty Acres, being robbed by Poppies ; and I have known a Crop that has amounted to do more than Two Buſhels to an Acre, and ſome Crops leſs, tho' dunged and fallowed ; ſo that, taking the common ſown Crops of Wheat one with another, they are thought not to amount to Sixteen Buſhels to an Acre, *communibus annis.*

on

on one Plant, we find, that there is not One Plant in
in Ten that lives till Harvest, even when there has
not been Frost in the Winter sufficient to kill any of
them; or if we count the Number of Plants that come
up on a certain Measure of Ground, and count them
again in the Spring, and likewise at Harvest, we shall
be satisfied, that most or all of the Plants that are
missing, could die by no other Accident than want of
Nourishment.

They are obliged to sow this great Quantity of Seed,
to the end that the Wheat, by the great Number of
Plants, may be the better able to contend with the
Weeds; and yet, too often, at Harvest, we see a
great Crop of Weeds, and very little Wheat among
them. Therefore this Pasture, being insufficient to
maintain the present Crop, without starving the greatest Part of its Plants, is likely to be less able to maintain a subsequent Crop, than that Pasture which is not
so much exhausted.

When their Crop of Wheat is much less than ours,
their Vacancies, if computed all together, may be
greater than those of our Partitions and Intervals;
theirs, by being irregular, serve chiefly for the Pro-
tection of Weeds; for they cannot be plow'd out,
without destroying the Corn, any more than Cannons
firing at a Breach, whereon both Sides are contending,
can kill Enemies, and not Friends.

Their Plants stand on the Ground in a confused
manner, like a Rabble; ours like a disciplin'd Army:
We make the most of our Ground; for we can, if
we please, cleanse the Partitions with a Hand-hoe (*b*);
and for the rest, if the Soil be deep enough to be
drill'd on the Level (*c*), in treble Rows, the Par-

(*b*) Of all annual Weeds.
(*c*) This is only put as a Supposition; for I have for these
several Years left off drilling on the Level, and do advise against
it; because altho' Mould should not be wanting for the Partitions
in deep rich Land, yet it is much more difficult to hoe on the
Level than on Ridges.

titions

titions at Six Inches (*d*), the Intervals Five Feet; Five Parts in Six of the whole Field may be pulveriz'd every Year, and at proper times all round the Year.

The Partions being one Sixth-part for the Crop to ftand on, and to be nourifhed in the Winter, one other Sixth-part being well pulveriz'd, may be fufficient to nourifh it from thence till Harveft (*e*); the Remainder, being Two-thirds of the Whole, may be kept unexhaufted, the One-third for one Year, and the other Third of it Two Years; all kept open for the Reception of the Benefits defcending from above, during fo long a time; whilft the fowed Land is fhut againft them every Summer, except the little time in which it is fallow'd, once in Three Years, and a little, perhaps, whilft they plow it for Barley in the Winter, which is a Seafon feldom proper for pulverizing the Ground.

Their Land muft have been exhaufted as well by thofe fupernumerary Plants of Wheat, while they lived, as by thofe that remain for the Crop, and by the Weeds. Our Land muft be much lefs exhaufted, when it has never above one Third-part of the Wheat-plants to nourifh that they have, and generally no Weeds; fo that our ho'd Land having much more vegetable Pafture made, and continually renewed, to fo much a lefs Stock of Plants (*f*), muft needs be

(*d*) But when it is drilled upon Ridges, the Proportion is lefs, by how much the Partitions, being thicker in Mould, contain more than a Sixth-part of the whole Six Feet of Earth, and the Proportion of unexhaufted Earth will be alter'd likewife; and I only mention thefe Diftances to avoid Fractions.

(*e*) This may be done, tho' the Roots of a competent Number of Plants run through the Whole, in the manner herein before explained.

(*f*) Therefore, whenever a Soil receives more Supplies of fine Earth from the Atmofphere, than is exhaufted by all the Plants that grow in the Soil, it becomes richer; but if the contrary, then it becomes poorer.

left,

left, by every Crop, in a much better Condition than
theirs is left. in by any one of their fown Crops,
altho' our Crops of Corn at Harveft be better than
theirs (g).

They object againft us, faying, That fometimes
the Hoeing makes Wheat too ftrong and grofs,
whereby it becomes the more liable to the Blacks (or
Blight of Infects): But this is the Fault of the Hoer;
for he may choofe whether he will make it too ftrong,
becaufe he may apply his Hoeings at proper times
only, and apportion the Nourifhment to the Number
and Bulk of his Plants.   However, by this Objection
they allow, that the Hoe can give Nourifhment
enough, and therefore they cannot maintain, that there
is a Neceffity of Dung (h) in the Hoeing-Hufbandry;
and

(g) On an undung'd low Six feet Ridge, we have Three Rows,
Eight Inches afunder, all which being equal, during the Winter,
but each of the Two outfide Rows at Harveft producing Ten
times as much Wheat as the middle Row doth, all Three together
produce a Quantity equal to One-and-twenty of this middle
Row. Now, fuppofing the Roots of this Row not to reach through
the outfide Rows, fo as to receive any Benefit from the ho'd Intervals, then this Row might only be equal to one of Nine Rows,
which fhould have been drilled Eight Inches afunder on this
Ridge, and then our Three would only be equal to Twenty-one
of fuch Nine Rows.   But fince it can be demonftrated, that the
Roots of our middle Row do pafs through both the outfide Rows
far into the ho'd Intervals, we may well fuppofe it to be at leaft
double to what it would have been, if it had no Benefit from the
Hoeing, and then our Three will be equal to Forty-two of fuch
Nine unho'd Rows.   Thus our Crop is Thirty-three in Forty-
two (or almoft Four Parts in Five) increafed by the Hoeing; for
though many Fields of Wheat have been drilled all over in Rows
Eight Inches afunder, it never has been judged, in Twenty Years
Experience, that a Crop fo planted, though not ho'd, was, by its
Evennefs and Regularity, lefs, *cæteris paribus*, than a Crop fown
a random.

(h) As for the Quantity of vegetable Matter of Dung, when
reduced to Earth by Putrefaction, it is very inconfiderable, and,
of many forts of Manure, next to nothing.

The almoft only Ufe of all Manure is the fame as of Tillage:
viz. the Pulveration it makes by Fermentation, as Tillage doth

and that, if our Crops of Wheat fhould happen to
fuffer, by being too ftrong, our Lofs will be lefs
than theirs, when that is too ftrong, fince it will coft
them Nine times our Expence to make it fo.

A Second Objection is, That as Hoeing makes
poor Land become rich enough to bear good Crops
of Wheat for feveral Years fucceffively, the fame muft
needs make very good Land become too rich for
Wheat.   I anfwer, That if poffibly it fhould fo happen, there are Two Remedies to be ufed in fuch a
Cafe; the one is to plant it with Beans, or fome
other Vegetables, which cannot be over-nourifhed,
as Turneps, Carrots, Cabbages, and fuch-like, which
are excellent Food for fatting of Cattle; or elfe they
may make ufe of the other infallible Remedy, when
that rich Land, by producing Crops every Year in
the Hoeing-Hufbandry, is grown too vigorous and
refty, they may foon take down its Mettle, by fowing it a few Years in their old Hufbandry, which will
fill it again with a new Stock of Weeds, that will
fuck it out of Heart, and exhauft more of its Vigour,
than the Dung (*i*), that helps to produce them, can
reftore.

There is a Third Objection, and that is, That the
Benefit of fome Ground is loft where the Hoe-plough
turns at each End of the Lands: But this cannot be
much, if any, Damage; becaufe about Four Square

---

by Attriti n or Contufion; and with thefe Differences, that Dung,
which is the moft common Manure, is apt to increafe Weeds, a
Tillage (of which Hoeing is chief) deftroys them, and Manure is
fcanty in moft Places, but Tillage may be had every-where. Another Difference is, the vaft Difproportion of the Price of Manure
and that of Tillage.

Note, As we have no way to enrich the Soil, but by Pulveration of Manure, or of Inftruments, or of both; fo Nature has
ordain'd, that the Soil fhall be exhaufted by nothing, but by the
Roots of Plants.

(*i*) Dung made of the Straw of fown Corn generally abounds
with the Seed of Weeds.

Perch

Perch to a Statute Acre is fufficient for this Purpofe;
and that, at the Rate of *Ten Shillings* Rent, comes
to but *Three-pence*, tho' this varies, according as the
Piece is longer or fhorter; and fuppofing the moft
to be Eight Perch, that is but *Six-pence per* Acre;
and that is not loft neither; for whether it be of
natural or artificial Grafs, the Hoe-plough, in turning on it, will fcratch it, and leave fome Earth on
it, which will enrich it fo much, that it may be worth
its Rent for Baiting of Horfes or Oxen upon it. And
befides, thefe Ends are commonly near Quick-hedges
or Trees, which do fo exhauft it, that when no Cattle
come there to manure it, 'tis not worth the Labour
of plowing it.

C H A P. XVIII.

Of P L O U G H S.

BY what means Ploughs and Tillage itfelf came
at firft to be invented is uncertain; therefore
we are at Liberty to guefs: And it feems moft probable, that it was, like moft other Inventions, found
out by Accident, and that the firft Tillers or Plowers
of the Ground were Hogs: Men in thofe Days,
having fufficient Leifure for Speculation, obferv'd,
that when any fort of Seed happen'd to fall on a
Spot of Ground well routed up by the Swine (which
Inftinct had inftructed to dig in Search of their Food),
it grew and profpered much better than in the whole
unbroken Turf. This Obfervation muft naturally in-
duce rational Creatures to the Contrivance of fome
Inftrument, which might imitate, if not excel Brutes
in this Operation of breaking and dividing the Surface of the Earth, in order to increafe and better its
Product.

T 3   That

That fome fuch Accident gave Men the Firft Hints of *original Agriculture*, may be inferr'd from the very little (or no) Probability of its being invented originally upon Arguments which might convince the Underftanding (by juft Conclufions from Ideas of the Earth and Vegetation) of any reafonable Grounds to hope, that the Effect of increafing the Earth's Produce fhould follow the Caufe of Tillage; or, in other Words, why it fhould produce more when tilled than when untilled.   Therefore it is very unlikely, that Men fhould begin to take Pains to till the Land without any Sort of Reafon why they did it.   And no fuch Reafon could they have before the Invention, as they had afterwards: For when they accidentally faw that Effect follow that Caufe, then they were well convinced it did fo.   But tho' this Argument, *viz.* Tillage increafes the Product of the Earth, becaufe it does, has been fufficient to continue the Practice of Tillage ever fince; yet it is impoffible for the Inventors to have had this Argument before the Invention, in cafe it had been invented by Men, and not fortuitoufly difcover'd.

Had there ever been extant any other or better Arguments, whereon this Practice, fo ufeful to Mankind, was founded ; fure, fome of all the great and learned Authors, who have written on this Subject, would have mention'd them. Philofophers, Orators, and Poets, have treated of it in the fame Theory by which it was firft difcover'd, and by no other ; *viz.* Land produces more when tilled ; and fome feem to fay, the more it is tilled, the more it produces.   It does, becaufe it does; not a Word of the Pafture of Plants, or any thing like it.   So that all the antient *Scriptores de re ruftica* have done, was only to keep that Theory in the fame Degree of Perfection in which the firft Difcoverers received it.

The briftled Animals broke up the Ground, becaufe they ufed to find their Food there by digging ;

Men

Men till it, becaufe they find Tillage procures them better Food than Acorns.

The Reafons are the fame for one and the other.

Thefe Writers, afham'd to acknowlege fo noble a Difcovery to be owing to fo mean a Foundation, make no mention of the true Teachers, but attribute the Invention to *Ceres*, a Goddefs of their own makeing; fhe, as they pretend, firft taught the Art of Tillage. With this Fable they were fo well pleafed, that they never attempted to improve that Art, left they fhould derogate from the Divinity of *Ceres*, in fuppofing her Invention imperfect.

With what Inftrument Men firft tilled the Ground we don't know exactly; but there may be Reafons to believe it was with the Spade, and probably a wooden one, and very rough.

For whilft People liv'd on Acorns, there was no need of the Smith; fuch Food required no Knives for eating it, nor was it worth while to make Swords to fight for it; and without Iron the Spade could not be well hewn, or fhap'd; but if it had been fuch as it is at prefent, there never was any thing comparable to it, for the true Ufe of Tillage. Yet the Spade could not make that Expedition, which was neceffary when Tillage became general in the Fields; and therefore in time the Spade came wholly to be appropriate to the moft perfect Sort of Tillage in the Garden. Then the Plough fupply'd the Place of the Spade in the Field; and tho' it could not (fuch as it was) till the Land near fo well, yet it could till ten times more of it, and with lefs human Labour.

Why they did not improve the Plough, fo that it might alfo till as well as the Spade, feems owing to their Primitive Theory, which gave no Mathematical Reafon to fhew wherein the true Method of Tillage did confift; *viz.* in dividing the Earth into many Parts, to increafe its internal Superficies, which is the Pafture of Plants.

The

The Difference betwixt the Operation of the Spade, and that of the common Plough, is only this; that the former commonly divides the Soil into fmaller Pieces, and goes deeper.

How eafy and natural it is to contrive a Plough that may equal the Spade, if not exceed it, in going deeper, and cutting the Soil into fmaller Pieces, than the Spade commonly does, I leave to the Judgment of thofe who have feen the Four-coulter'd Plough.

The Plough defcrib'd by *Virgil* had no Coulter; neither do I remember to have feen any Coulter in *Italy*, or the South of *France*; and, as I have been informed, the Ploughs in *Greece*, and all the *Eaft*, are of much the fame Fafhion: Neither is it practicable to ufe a Coulter in fuch a Plough; becaufe the Share does not cut the Bottom of the Furrow horizontally, but obliquely; in going one way, it turns off the Furrow to the right Hand; but in coming back, it turns it to the Left (*a*). Therefore, if it had a Coulter, it muft have been on the wrong Side every other Furrow: And befides, as the Handle (for it has but one) always holds the Plough towards one Side, with the Bottom of the Share towards the unplow'd Land, it would caufe the Coulter to go much too low when it went on the Furrow-fide, and it would not touch the Ground, when it went on the Land-fide.

'Tis a great Miftake in thofe who fay *Virgil*'s Plough had Two Earth-boards; for it had none at all; but the Share itfelf always going obliquely, ferved inftead of an Earth-board; and the Two Ears, which were the Corners of a Piece of Wood lying under

(*a*) *Note,* This *Eaftern* Plough always goes forward, and returns back in the fame Furrow, making only one Land of a whole Field: Though it turns its one Furrow towards the Right, and the other towards the Left of the Holder; yet every Furrow is turned towards the fame Point of the Compafs, as when we plow with a Turn-wrift Plough.

the Share, did the Office of Ground-wrefts : This Fafhion continues to this Day in thofe Countries, and in *Languedoc.*

This fort of Plough performs tolerably when Ground is fine, and makes a fhift to break up light Land; and I could never find any other Land there; I am fure none comparable to ours for Strength: And it would be next to impoffible, to break up fuch as we in *England* call ftrong Land with it.

I do not find, that the Arable Lands about *Rome* are ever fuffered to lie ftill long enough to come to a Turf; but I have obferved in the low rich Lands in the *Calabria*'s, fubject to the Invafions of the *Turks,* that there is Turf, and that thefe Ploughs go over the Land Two or Three times before the Turf of it is all broken, tho' the Soil be a very mellow Sort of Garden-mould. Having no Coulters to cut it, they break and tear Turf into little Pieces. This was done in the Month of *November*; and had I not feen Men and Oxen at the Work, or had there been Oaks in the Place, I fhould rather have thought that Tillage performed by a Race of the firft Teachers of it, in muzzling Acorns, than by Ploughs. Howe-ver, the Mould being naturally very mellow, when the Turf is broken with fhallow Plowing, they can plow deeper afterwards.

The *Englifh* Ploughs are very different from the *Eaftern,* as in general the Soil is.

Thefe, when well made, cut off the Furrow at the Bottom horizontally; and therefore, it being as thick on the Land-fide as on the Furrow-fide, the Plough cannot break it off from the whole Land, at fuch a Thicknefs (being Six times greater than the *Eaftern* Ploughs have to break off), and muft of Ne-ceffity have a Coulter to cut it off: By this means the Furrow is turned perfectly whole, and no Part of the Turf of it broken ; and if it lie long without new turning, the Grafs from the Edges will fpread,

and

and form a new Turf (or Swerd) on the other Side,
which was the Bottom of the Furrow before turning,
but is now become the Surface of the Earth, and
may foon become greener with Grafs than before
Plowing; and often the very Roots fend up new
Heads to help to ftock the reverfed Furrow, the former Heads being converted into Roots, fo that it is
doubly cloathed and braced on both Sides, or, as
it were, kay'd together, firm and folid, almoft as a
Plank; it may be drawn from one Side of a Field
to the other without breaking, and might poffibly
be made ufe of, inftead of *Virgil*'s *Crates Viminea*,
for harrowing or fmoothing of fine-tilled Ground;
but not without much Time, Labour, and Difficulty,
can it be made fuch itfelf.

If you plow whole ftrong turfy Furrows crofs-ways,
as *Virgil* directs, and as it is too commonly practifed,
the Coulter cannot eafily cut them, becaufe, being
loofe underneath, they do not make a fufficient Refiftance or Preffure againft its Edge, but move before
it, and fo are apt to be drawn and driven up into
Heaps, with their Surfaces lying all manner of Ways,
and fituate in all manner of Poftures: So the Turf,
which is not turned, continuing in the open Air,
grows on, and with its vigorous Roots holds the
Earth faft together, and will not fuffer the neceffary
Divifion to be made, which would be, if the Turf
were rotten, and which is the End of all Tillage,
viz. to increafe the Pafture of Plants.

Next, fome have vaft heavy Drags, with great long
Iron Tines in them; and tho' thefe huge broken
Pieces of Furrows, being loofer than before, require
keener Edges to cut them; yet thefe Drag-tines have
no Edge at all, but are as blunt as the Furrows they
fhould cut. Thefe Drags draw them fometimes into
larger Heaps, leaving the under *Stratum* bare betwixt
them, only fhaking off fome of their Mould in tum-
bling them about, and fcratching their Surfaces,
                                        without

without reducing them to a moderate Finenefs, until this ill-broken Land has, for above a Year, and fometimes longer, entertained Ploughs, Cattle, and Men, with a frequent laborious Exercife, for which they are obliged to the one Coulter.

If the Soil be fhallow, it may be broken up with a narrow Furrow, which will the fooner be brought in Tilth; but if it be a deep Soil, the Furrows muft be proportionably large, or elfe a Part of the good Mould muft be left under unmoved, and fo loft; for a narrow Furrow cannot be plowed deep, becaufe the Plough will continually flip out from the hard Land toward the Right-hand, unlefs the rifing Furrow be of fufficient Weight to prefs the Plough towards the Left, and keep it in its Work: The deeper you plow, the greater Weight is required to prefs it; fo that the deeper your Land is, the worfe (or into the larger Furrows) muft it be broken up with one Coulter, infomuch that, if the Land be ftrong (as moft deep Ground in *England* is), it is a Work of fome Years to conquer it, after it has been refted. And often it happens, that the exceffive Charge of this Tillage reduces the Profit of rich Land below that of poor.

This gives an Opportunity to deceitful Servants, of impofing upon their ignorant Mafters. They plow fuch deep Land with a fmall fhallow Furrow, to the end the Turf and Furrows may be broken, and made fine the fooner; pretending they will plow it deeper the next time (which is called Stirring), which thefe Rogues know very well cannot be done, and intend no more than that the Plough coming the eafier after the Horfes, their Coats may fhine the better; and tho' there be no Crop at Harveft, they muft have Four Meals a Day all the Year, and extravagant Wages at *Michaelmas*, or at any time of the Year, when they think fit to mifbehave themfelves.

This

This fort of Land muft not be ftirred, *i. e.* plowed the Second time in wet Weather; for that will caufe the Grafs and Weeds to multiply, befides the treading the Ground into hard Dabs, &c. And, in dry Weather, the Plough will never enter any deeper than it went the firft time; the Refiftance below being fo much more than the Preffure above, the Plough will rife up continually; or, if it goes deep enough for the Weight of Earth to keep it down, another Inconvenience will follow, which is that mentioned by *Columella*, Page 47. *Quod omnis humus, quamvis lætiſſima, tamen inferiorem partem jejuniorem habet, eamque attrahunt excitatæ majores glebæ; quo evenit, ut infœcundior materia miſta pinguiori ſegetem minus uberem reddat.* The vulgar *Engliſh* Phrafe is, It fpaults up from below the Staple. Hence the treacherous Plowman is fecure of an eafy Summer's Work, if he can perfuade his Mafter to fuffer him to fallow the Ground with a fhallow Furrow.

Another way to conquer a ftrong Turf is, to plow it firft with a Breaft-plough, very thin; and, when the Swerd is rotten, then plow it at the proper Depth: But this Method is (befides the extraordinary Charge of it) liable to other great Misfortunes. If the Turf be pared up in Winter, or early in the Spring, it is a Chance but the Rains caufe it to grow ftronger than before, inftead of its Rotting.

And if it be pared later, tho' dry Weather do follow, and continue long enough to kill the Turf, yet this lofes time; the Seafon of plowing is retarded; for all the Staple ftill remains untilled; and, before that can be well done, the Year is too far fpent for fowing it with Wheat, which is the moft proper Grain for fuch ftrong Land (*a*); and few will have Patience to wait, and plow on till another Wheat-feed

(*a*) Befides, moft ftrong Land has Stones in it, which will not admit the Ufe of the Breaft-plough.

time.

time. The dry Weather alſo, which in Summer kills the Swerd, renders the Plowing obnoxious to moſt or all the Evils afore-mentioned.

A Farmer inquires concerning the Four-coulter Plough, as in the following DIALOGUE.

Farm. What *muſt we do then? Muſt we have re-courſe to the Spade for 'breaking up our rich, ſtrong, ſwerdy Land?*

Reſp. If you can procure Men to dig it faithfully in Pieces, not above Two Inches and an half thick, at the Price of about Eight Shillings *per* Acre, it would do very well, and anſwer all the Ends of Till-age; but, tho' you bargain with them to dig it at that Size for Three Pounds *per* Acre, you will find, upon Examination, moſt of the Pieces or Spits, which are dug out of your Sight, to be of twice that Thickneſs. And no great Quantities can be this way managed, altho' the Price of Corn ſhould anſwer ſuch an extravagant Expence.

Farm. Since it is ſo difficult to bring our ſtrong Land *into Tilth, after it has reſted, that it cannot be ſpeedily done by a Plough without a Coulter, or by one with a Coulter, in wet Weather or dry, nor with a Breaſt-plough, without a certain Expence, and an uncertain Succeſs, the Spade is too chargeable a Tillage for the Field : It ſeems to me, upon the Whole, that we are Loſers by this* inaratæ gratia terræ, *unleſs we could con-trive ſome other Method of reducing it ſooner, and with leſs Charge, into Tilth ; for I obſerve, that, when we ſow it upon the Back, the Corn and Graſs (or Couch), coming both together, exhauſt the Ground ſo much, that by that time we can (which is about Three Years) re-duce the great Lumps to a tolerable Fineneſs, it grows full of Graſs and Weeds (which we call Foul), and loſes that Fertility we expected it ſhould acquire by Reſt, be-coming,*

4

coming, in our Terms, both out of Tilth, and out of Heart.

Resp. If you know all this to be true, and that without a Coulter you cannot break it up at all; and that with one Coulter you cannot any way cut the Furrow fmall enough, or lefs than Ten Inches broad; why do not you cut it with Four Coulters, which will reduce the fame Furrow into Four equal Parts, of Two Inches and an half each in Breadth, and of the Depth of the Staple, tho' that fhould be Two Spit, or Sixteen Inches deep?

Farm. *How can that be done?*

Resp. Every jot as eafily as with one Coulter: For, before the Furrow is raifed by the Share, it lies faft, and makes a fufficient Refiftance equally againft the Edges of all the Coulters; tho', after it be raifed and loofe, it yields and recedes every way, except downwards; fo that it cannot be cut by any Edge, but fuch as attacks it perpendicularly from above, as that of the Spade does.

Farm. *This feems to me reafonable; and, having very lately heard talk of this Plough, I would gladly know more of it.*

Resp. The Furrow, being cut into Four Parts, has not only Four times the Superficies on the Eight Sides which it would have had on Two Sides; but it is alfo more divided crofs-ways; *viz.* The Ground-wreft preffes and breaks the lower (or Right-hand) Quarter; the other Three Quarters, in rifing and coming over the Earth-board, muft make a crooked Line about a Fourth longer than the ftrait one they made before moved; therefore their Thinnefs not being able to hold them together, they are broken into many more Pieces, for want of Tenacity to extend to a longer Line, contrary to a whole Furrow, whofe great Breadth enables it to ftretch and extend from a fhorter to a longer Line, without breaking; and, as

it

it is turned off, the Parts are drawn together again by the Spring of the Turf or Swerd *(a)*, and so remain whole after Plowing. Thus the Four-coultered Plow can divide the Soil into above Twenty times more Parts than the common Plough ; and sometimes, when the Earth is of a right Temper betwixt wet and dry, the Earth-board, in turning the Furrows off, will break them into Dust, having more Superficies than is made by Four common Plowings; and it is impossible there should be any large Pieces amongst it.

Now, what a prodigious Advantage must the Influences of the Atmosphere have upon these small Parts, for making a further Division of them! Frost, Water, Drought, and nitrous Air, easily penetrate to their very Centers, which cannot in the largest of them be more than one Inch and a Quarter distant from their Superficies. This Advantage, with a few subsequent common Plowings, performed in proper Seasons, resolves the Earth almost all to a Powder. The Swerd, some being immersed or buried and mixed among so great a Proportion of Mould, is soon rotten and lost ; some of the Swerd lying loose a-top, the Earth presently drops out of it ; and then the Roots are dried up, and die. Thus is the whole Staple of the Ground brought into perfect Tilth in

(a) A swerdy Furrow cut off by only one Coulter, being whole, is apt to stand up on its Edge, or lie hollow ; and then, being open to the Air, it does not rot; but when it is cut by several Coulters, it has not Strength to support itself, it falls down, lies close to the Earth under it, and, excluding the free Air from the Turf, it soon becomes rotten. And for killing the Turf of swerdy Land is the chief Use of the Four-coultered Plough : For doing of which there is this Advantage, that as in a whole Furrow there are often Strings of Couch-grass, Three or Four Feet long; but, when cut by this Plough, there is scarce a String left of one Foot long: And these Strings being apt to send out Roots from every Knot or Joint, the shorter they are cut, the more they will be exposed to the Air and Sun, which will kill them the sooner.

a very

a very fhort time beyond what the Spade ever does in fuch fwerdy Land.

Farm. What fort of Weather is beft for ufing this Plough ?

Refp. Any Weather, except the Ground be fo dry and hard that the Plough cannot enter it; but it is very proper to be done, when the Earth is fo wet, that by no means it ought to be plowed with any other Plough; for it never can be too moift for this, unlefs the Cattle which draw it be mired; becaufe, tho' all the Cattle fhould not go in the Furrow, yet their Treadings are cut fo fmall by the Coulters, that the Earth is not kept from diffolving, as when turned off whole in common Tillage. 'Tis obferved, that the Incifions made by the Coulters on fwerdy Land, will not heal, or fo clofe up, but that they will open again by the next Plowing, though it be a great while after. A Farmer who ufes this Plough, may till in all Weathers and all Seafons of the Year, either in fallowing with this, which is beft in wet, or in ftirring with the common ones, which muft be done in dry Weather; and when the Ground is broken up with this, it may be ftirred in the drieft Weather that can be, without the Danger of tearing (or fpaulting) up of the under *Stratum* along with the Staple, becaufe this is all broken before, and then no more can rife with it ; as it does to the Ruin of the Soil, when in common Tillage they go deeper the Second time than the Firft : Alfo, if there be a Neceffity of ftirring fome fort of Land when it is wet, it ought either to be done with this Plough, or elfe with a common one drawn by a fingle Row of Cattle treading all in the Furrow; for tho' fome Land be very fine, yet, when plowed by a double Row of Cattle in wet Weather, it will be made into large Pieces by the Treading, and perhaps not diffolve again in a long time : Therefore it is better to be prevented.

Farm.

Farm. I perceive this Plough lays the Foundation for all good Husbandry; and there can be no other way to bring Land into perfect Tilth in so short a Time, or with so little Expence. And I am convinc'd, that no Farmer ought to be without it, who desires to be free from the Danger of his Land being ever out of Tilth: But I have heard it objected, that it is harder to draw than the common Ploughs; and that its Beam being longer, upon account of the Four Coulters, it lies farther behind, and comes harder after the Horses.

Resp. I must confess, there is something in that Objection; for this Plough, being something longer, may be a little the harder Draught; and also its Weight and Strength must bear a Proportion to the Length of it. But this small Increase of the Draught would have been a much stronger (if not a fatal) Objection, had that Custom been general, of Horses drawing by their Tails, as 'tis said to have been formerly in some Places; for then, perhaps, a sufficient Strength of Horses could not be applied to the Plough. But in Countries where Traces are in Use, every Horse of the Team may draw the Plough equally, and then there will be no other Inconvenience, besides the adding one Horse, or keeping a stronger Team: And he cannot be wise, who would lose the Profit of his Land, for the Odds of sometimes adding a Horse to his Plough. And I am very certain, that this Plough requires a much less Strength of Cattle to draw it in moist Weather, which is the most proper to use it in, than to draw a common Plough in the same Ground, and at the same Depth, in dry Weather; and can seldom be used safely in any other. And the Vulgar, who have always a wrong Cause ready at hand to apply to every thing, impute that Draught to the Fashion of the Plough, which ought to be imputed to its going deeper; and this great Depth at which 'tis capable of plowing, *viz.* Two

U   Spit

Spit deep, is one extraordinary Benefit of it, tho' it may, on Occasion, go as shallow as any.

The Draught is not so much increased by adding Three Coulters, as may be imagined; for when the Ground is moist, the Incisions are easily made by the Edges; and when they are cut small, the Furrows rise much more easily upon the Share and Earth-Board, than if whole.

Farm. If this Plough be so beneficial, having so many Advantages, and only the Two Inconveniencies, one of requiring a little more Strength to draw it, and the other its being unfit for dry hard Ground, I wonder why it is not become more common?

Resp. It has been used with very great Success for these several Years last past, but never like to be common, unless it be described in a more geometrical Manner, than any Plough has hitherto been; for the Plough-wrights find it difficult enough to make a common Plough with one Coulter to perform as it ought, for want of the necessary Rules of their Art. It is upon this Account that the Two-coulter'd Ploughs are used in few Places, though they have been found of excellent Use, and have been formerly common: But, alas! when the Makers, who by their diligent Study and much Practice had attained the Perfection of their Art, died for want of learning to write their Rules mathematically, and shew how the mechanical Powers were applicable to them, the Art was in a Manner lost, at the Death of those Artists; and then the unskilful Plough-wrights, destitute of the true Rules, were not able to make a Two-coulter'd Plough to perform well, and then it was left off. Very lately 'tis revived, since the Three and Four-coulter'd ones have been used; from whence some have made a Shift to take the Rules of placing Two Coulters into a Plough, and they begin to be common again; and, no doubt, will cease again as soon as the Rules are forgot.

'Tis

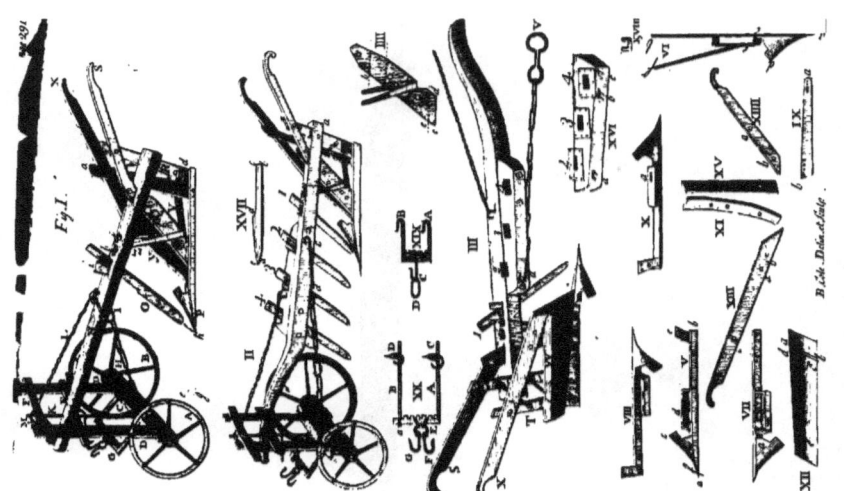

'Tis ftrange that no Author fhould have written fully of the Fabric of Ploughs! Men of the greateft Learning have fpent their Time in contriving Inftruments to meafure the immenfe Diftance of the Stars, and in finding out the Dimenfions, and even Weight, of the Planets: They think it more eligible to ftudy the Art of plowing the Sea with Ships, than of tilling the Land with Ploughs; they beftow the utmoft of their Skill, learnedly, to pervert the natural Ufe of all the Elements for Deftruction of their own Species, by the bloody Art of War. Some wafte their whole Lives in ftudying how to arm Death with new Engines of Horror, and inventing an infinite Variety of Slaughter; but think it beneath Men of Learning (who only are capable of doing it) to employ their learned Labours in the Invention of new (or even improving the old) Inftruments for increafing of Bread.

The eafieft Method of perpetuating the Ufe of the many coulter'd Ploughs, and other newly-invented Inftruments of Hufbandry, is by Models, *i. e.* the Things themfelves in little; and thefe may be all portable even in a Man's Pocket: Every Part muft be fully defcribed, with the true Dimenfions, and the mathematical Reafons, on which their Contrivance is founded. Directions alfo for ufing them muft be given at the fame time that their Manner of making is defcribed. In fome, the very Horfes which draw muft be reprefented, to fhew the manner of fixing the Horfes, and the Traces: Cautions againft all the Errors that may happen by the want of Experience in the Makers or Ufers, muft be given.

When this is done, and the Rules put into a Method, the new Hoeing-Hufbandry, in all its Branches, will be much more eafy and certain than the old; becaufe there are no mathematical Rules extant in any Method; and a Man may practife the old random Hufbandry all his Life, without attaining fo much Certainty in Agriculture as may be learned in a few Hours from fuch a Treatife. U 2 The

The Rules, indeed, require much Labour, Study, and Experience, to compofe them; but when finifh'd, will be moft eafy to practife: Like the Rules for meafuring Timber; their Ufe is, at firft Sight, eafy to every Carpenter, and to moft Artificers who work in Wood; but no illiterate Perfon is able to compofe thofe Rules, or to meafure Timber without them.

C H A P.   XIX.

The Defcription of a Four-coulter'd Plough.

TO defcribe all Parts of a Plough geometrically, would require more Time and Learning than I am Mafter of: Therefore leaving that to be done by fomebody elfe, who is better qualified for it, I fhall at prefent attempt little more than what relates to the Three added Coulters.

In *Plate* 1. *Fig.* 1. is the Portrait of a common Two-wheel'd Plough ufed in *Berkfhire, Hampfhire, Oxfordfhire,* and *Wiltfhire,* and in moft other Countries of *South-Britain*; and is generally efteemed the beft Plough for all Sorts of Land, except fuch miry Clays that ftick to the Wheels, and clog them up, fo as they cannot turn round.

But they have, in fome Places, a Contrivance to prevent this Inconvenience; which is done by winding Thumb-ropes of Straw about the Iron Circles of the Wheels, and about the Spokes. The Wheels preffing againft the Ground, the Thumb-ropes are diftended on each Side: which Motion throws off the Dirt, and prevents its fticking to the Wheels, which it would otherwife do.

'Tis commonly divided into Two Parts; *viz.* the Plough-head, and the Plough-tail.

The Plough-head contains the Two Wheels A, B, and their Axis or Spindle of Iron paffing thro' the

Box

Box C, turning round both therein, and in the Wheels; the Two Crow-ſtaves D, D, faſtened into the Box perpendicularly, and having in each Two Rows of Holes, whereby to raiſe or ſink the Beam, by pinning up or down the Pillow E, to increaſe or diminiſh the Depth of the Furrow; the Gallows F, thro' which the Crow-ſtaves paſs at top, by Mortiſes, into which they are pinned; G the Wilds with its Links and Crooks of Iron, whereby the whole Plough is drawn; H the Two-chain, which faſtens the Plough-tail to the Plough-head, by the Collar I at one End, and by the other End paſſing thro' a Hole in the Middle of the Box, is pinned in by the Stake K; L the Bridle-chain, one End whereof is faſtened to the Beam by a Pin, and the other End to the Top of the Stake, which Stake is held up to the left Crow-ſtaff, by the With M, paſſing round it above, and under the End of the Gallows below; or inſtead of this With, by a Piece of Cord, and ſometimes by the End of the Bridle-chain, when that is long enough.

The Plough-tail conſiſts of the Beam N: the Coulter O; the Share P; and the Sheat Q; the Hinder-ſheat R, paſſing thro' the Beam near its End; S the ſhort Handle, faſtened to the Top of the Hinder-ſheat by a Pin, and to the Top of the Sheat by another Pin; T the Drock which belongs to the right Side of the Plough-tail, and whereto the Ground-wriſt V is faſten'd; as is the Earth-board, whoſe Fore-part W is ſeen before the Sheat; and alſo the long Handle X, whoſe Fore-part Y appears before the Sheat, and is faſten'd to the Drock by a Pin at *a*, the other End of which Pin goes into the Beam. Z is the double Retch, which holds up the Sheat, and paſſes through the Beam to be faſten'd by its Screws and Nuts at *b* and *c*.

But without intrenching much farther upon the common Plough-wright's Art, whoſe Trade is his Living, I'll haſten to ſhew the neceſſary Difference

U 3   there

there is betwixt the common Plough, and the Four-coulter Plough, beginning with *Fig.* 2. where it is reprefented as ftanding upon a level Surface.

Fig. 2. And, Firft, The Beam differs in Length, being Ten Feet Four Inches long, as the other Plough-beam is but Eight Feet; it differs in Shape, as the other is ftrait from one End to the other, but this is ftrait only from *a* to *b*, and thence turns up of a fudden, in the manner that is fhewn in the Cut; fo that a Line let down perpendicular, from the Corner at *a*, to the even Surface whereon the Plough ftands, would be Eleven Inches and an half, which is its Height in that Place; and, if another Line were let down, from the turning of the Beam at *b*, to the fame Surface, it would be One Foot Eight Inches and an half, which is the Height that the Beam ftands from the Ground, at that Part; and a Third Line let down to the Surface, from the Bottom of the Beam, at that Part which bears upon the Pillow, will fhew the Beam to be Two Feet Ten Inches high above the Surface in that Part.

From the End *a*, to the Back-part of the firft Coulter, is Three Feet Two Inches; from thence, to the Back of the next Coulter, is Thirteen Inches; thence to the Third, Thirteen Inches; and from thence to the Fourth, the fame. From *a* to *b* is Seven Feet.

This Crookednefs of the Beam is to avoid the too great Length of the foremoft Coulters, which would be neceffary if the Beam was ftrait; and then, un-lefs they were vaftly thick and heavy, they would be apt to bend, and the Point of the Fourth would be at fo great a Diftance from its Coulter-hole, that it would have the greater Power to loofen the Wedges, whereby the Coulter would rife up out of its Work, as it never doth when the Beam is made in this bending Manner. This Beam is made either of Afh, which is the lighteft, or of Oak, which is the moft
durable.

durable.   Its Depth and Breadth may vary, according to the heavier or lighter Soil it is to till; but this before us is in Depth Five Inches at the firſt Coulter-hole, and in Breadth Four Inches.

Fig. 4. Is the Sheat Q in *Fig.* 1. (broad Seven Inches) with the Iron Retch on it, the left Leg of which Retch muſt ſtand foremoſt, to the end that the Edge of its Fore-part, that is flat, may ſit cloſe to the Wood of the Sheat: This Retch holds the Sheat faſt up to the Beam by its Nuts and Screws; as alſo doth a Pin driven into the Hole *a*, which Hole being a ſmall Part of it within the Beam, the Pin being driven into the Hole, draws up the Sheat very tight to the Beam.   The principal thing to be taken notice of here, is the Angle *b c d*, which ſhews the Elevation of the Sheat; the Line *c d* is ſuppoſed to be equal with the Bottom of the Share (or rather with the plain Surface whereon it ſtands); when this Angle at *c* is larger than of Forty-five Degrees, a common Plough never goes well: In my Four-coulter Plough I chooſe to have it of Forty-two or Forty-three at the moſt.

Fig. 5.   Is the Share; *a* is the End of the Point; *b* is the Tail of the Share, long from *a* to *b* Three Feet Nine Inches; *c* the Fin; *d* the Socket, into which the Bottom of the Sheat enters; *e* a thin Plate of Iron riveted to the Tail of the Share : By this Plate, the Tail of the Share is held to the hinder Sheat, as at *d* in *Fig.* 1. by a ſmall Iron Pin with a Screw at its End, and a Nut ſcrew'd on it on the inner or right Side of that Sheat.   From *a* to *f* is the Point, long about Three Inches and an half, flat underneath, and round at Top: It ſhould be of hard Steel underneath.   From *f* to *c* is the Edge of the Fin, which ſhould be well ſteeled; the Length of it is uncertain, but it ſhould never make a leſs Angle at *f* than it appears to make in this *Fig.*   The Socket is a Mortiſe of about a Foot long, at the upper Part,

Two

Two Inches deep: The Fore-end of this Mortife muft not be perpendicular, but oblique, conformable to the Fore-part of the Sheat which enters it; the upper Edge of which Fore-part muft always bear againft the Sheat at *e* in *Fig.* 4. but if this End of the Socket fhould not be quite fo oblique as the Sheat, it may be help'd, by taking off a little of the Wood at the Point *c*.

Fig. 6. Shews the Share, with its right Side upwards, in the fame Pofture as when it plows; whofe Side *a b* fhould be perfectly ftrait, but its under Side at *c*, which is its Neck, fhould be a little hollow from the Ground, but never more than half an Inch in any Plough, and a Quarter of an Inch in a Four-coulter Plough; fo that the Share, when it is firft made, ftanding upon its Bottom, bears upon the level Surface only in Three Places; *viz.* at the very Point *a*, at the Tail *b*, and at the Corner of the Fin *d*.

Fig. 7. Is the Share, turn'd Bottom upwards; and fhews the Concavity of the Fin at *a*; which muft be greateft in a ftony rubbly Soil.

Fig. 8. Shews the Share, the right Side upwards, but leaning towards the Left.

In placing of the Share rightly upon the Sheat, confifts the well going of a Plough, and is the moft difficult Part of a Plough-wright's Trade, and is very difficult to be fhewn. Suppofing the Axis of the ftrait Beam, and the left Side of the Share, to be both horizontal, they muft never be parallel to each other; for if they were, the Tail of the Share, bearing againft the Side of the Trench, as much as the Point, would caufe the Point to incline to the right Hand, and go out of the Ground into the Furrow. If the Point of the Share fhould be fet, fo that its Side fhould make an Angle on the right Side of the Axis of the Beam, this Inconvenience would be much greater; and if its Point fhould incline much to the

5

Left,

Left, and make too large an Angle on that Side
with the Axis of the Beam, the Plough would run
quite to the left Hand; and if the Holder, to prevent its running out of the Ground, turns the upper
Part of his Plough towards the left Hand, the Fin
of the Share will rife up, and cut the Furrow diagonally *(a)*, leaving it half unplow'd; befide, the
Plough will rife up at the Tail, and go all upon the
Point of the Share: To avoid thefe Inconveniences,
the ftrait Side of the Share muft make an Angle on
the left Side of the Beam, but fo very acute, that
the Tail of the Share may only prefs lefs againft the
Side of the Trench than the Point does. This Angle is fhewn by the prick'd Lines at the Bottom of
Fig. 1. where the prick'd Line *e f* is fuppofed to be

(a) This is the greateft Misfortune incident to a common Two-
wheeled Plough, and happens generally by the Fault of the
Maker, though fometimes by the Plowman's fetting it fo, that
the Point of the Share turns too much to the Left. I have feen
Land plowed in this manner, where not half of it has been
moved, nor better tilled than by Raftering, not only cut diagonally, but alfo half the Surface hath remained whole, where
when the Earth that was thrown on it was removed, the Weeds
appeared unhurt on the unplowed Surface. In this Cafe, they
for a Remedy fet the Plough to go deeper; and then, if it go
deep enough for the Fin to cut off the Furrow at a juft Depth, the
Point will go below the Staple, which may ruin the Soil, unlefs
it be very deep

When our *English* Ploughs go in this manner, they make much
worfe Work than the *Eaftern* Ploughs, that have no Coulter; for
thefe, contrar. to ours, though they always cut their Furrow diagonally, cut it thin on that Side from which it is turned, as our
bad Ploughs leave it thin on that Side towards which it is turned.
The Earth the *Eafterns* leave by their Diagonal in one Furrow,
is taken off by the next; but ours leaving Part of their Furrow
behind them, on the Side next to the plowed Part of the Field,
come at it no more; but the other can plow cleaner, their Diagonal being contrary to ours, which leaves the Trench deepeft on
the Side next to the unplowed Part of the Field; but unlefs the
Fin of the Four-coulter'd Plough go parallel to the Surface of the
Earth, it will not plough at all; or will leave Two or Three of
its Four Furrows untouched.

the

the Axis of the Beam let down to the Surface, and
the prick'd Line *g f* parallel to the left Side of the
Share; but this Angle will vary as thofe Two prick'd
Lines are produc'd forwards to the Fore-end of a
long and a fhort Beam, keeping the fame Subtenfe:
For Plough-wrights always take this Subtenfe at the
Fore-end of a Beam, whether it be a long Beam or
fhort one; and it is the Subtenfe *e g*, that determines
the Inclination the Point of the Share muft have toward the left Hand.   Plough-wrights differ much in
this Matter; but, by what I can learn by thofe that
make the Ploughs I fee perform the beft, this Subtenfe at the Fore-end of an Eight-feet Beam fhould
never be more than one Inch and an half; and by full
Experience I find, that whether the Beam be long or
fhort, the Subtenfe muft be the fame; for when my
Plough-wrights take this Subtenfe at Eight Feet from
the Tail, when they make my Four-coulter Plough,
whofe Beam is Ten Feet Four Inches long, the Point
of the Share will incline too much to the Left, and
it will not go well until this Fault be mended, by
taking the fame Subtenfe quite at the End of the
Beam; which makes the mentioned Angle more
acute.

Fig. 3. Shews the right-hand Side, and upper Side
of the Four-coulter Plough, of which V the Iron
Ground-wrift is fhewn in *Fig.* 9. long Two Feet Five
Inches, deep at the End *b* Four Inches, and Three-
eighths of an Inch thick, except at the End *a*, where
it is thin enough to bend, fo as to fit clofe to the
Share, as at *e*, in *Fig.* 6.   The Ground-wrift has
Four fmall Holes near its End *a*, into one of which
goes a Nail, to faften it to the Sheat, thro' the long
Hole in the Side of the Socket of the Share, as at
a, in *Fig.* 10. and then it will ftand in the Pofture
fhewn by *e f*, in *Fig.* 6. From the Outfide of the
Ground-wrift at *f*, to the Outfide of the Share at *b*,
is Eleven Inches and an half, which is the Width of
the

the lower Part of the Plough-tail at the Ground; the Ground-wrift has feveral Holes at the upper Side of its broadeft End, as at *b*, in *Fig.* 9. by which it is nailed to the lower Part of the Drock T, as in *Fig.* 3. which Drock with its Perforations is fhewn in *Fig.* 11.

Fig. 12. Is the Earth-board, with its Infide upwards; the Notch *a b* fhews the Rifing of the Wood, which takes hold of the Edge of the Sheat, to hold it the firmer, to which it is faftened by the Holes *c* and *d*; and at the other End it is faftened to the Drock, at the Hole *e*. All which is feen as it ftands mark'd with W, in *Fig.* 3. But this Pin, with which it is faftened to the Drock, is bigger in the Middle than at each End; which prevents the Earth-board from coming near the Drock: By this Pin, the Earth-board is fet at a greater or lefs Diftance from the Drock, as there is Occafion to throw off the Furrow farther from the Plough at fome times than at others: It always ftands confiderably farther out on the right Hand than the Ground-wrift does, which is one Reafon that the Drock is made crooked, bending outwards in that Part.

The long Handle X is *Fig.* 13. long Five Feet Four Inches, broad in the wideft Part Four Inches, pinned to the Sheat thro' the Holes *a b*, and pinned to the Drock through the Hole *c*.

The fhort Handle S is *Fig.* 14. and is long Three Feet Nine Inches, pinned to the hinder Sheat (being *Fig.* 15.) by the Hole *a*, and to the Top of the Fore-fheat above the Beam by the Hole *b*.

The Handles are made fo long, for the more eafy guiding of the Plough; but the lazy Ploughman is apt to cut them off fhorter, clofe up to the Plough, to the end that, bearing his whole Weight thereon, he may in a manner ride inftead of walking; but if he fhould thus ride on long Handles, he would tilt up the Fore-end of the Beam, and raife the Share out of the Ground. The

The chief, and moſt indeſpenſably neceſſary thing
to be obſerved, is, to place the Four Coulters in ſuch
a manner, that the Four imaginary Planes deſcribed
by the Edges of the Four Coulters, as the Plough
moves forwards, be all of them parallel to each other,
or very nearly ſo ; for if any one of them ſhould be
much inclined to, or recede from, either of the other
three, they could not enter the Ground together. In
order to place them thus, the Coulter-holes muſt be
made through the Beam, in the manner as they are
ſhewn in _Fig._ 3. _viz._ the Second Coulter-hole is Two
Inches and an half more on the Right than the Firſt,
the Third, Two and an half more on the right Hand
than the Second, and the Fourth, Two Inches and
an half more on the right Hand than the Third, conformable to the Four Inciſions or Cuts they are to
make in a Ten-inch Furrow: And becauſe no ſingle
Beam is broad enough to hold the Four Coulter-holes
at this Diſtance, we are forced to add the Piece ſhewn
in _Fig._ 16. The Second Hole is made Part in the
Beam, and Part in this Piece; the Third and Fourth
are made wholly in this Piece, in which _a_, _b_, _c_, are
the Ends of the Three Screws, which faſten the Piece
to the right Side of the Beam by their Nuts.

The Diſtance of Two Inches and an half, by
which each of the Three added Coulters ſtand more
to the right Hand than that immediately behind it,
muſt be reckoned from the Middle of one Hole to
the Middle of the other.

The Fore-part of every Hole muſt incline a little
towards the Left ; ſo that the Backs of the Coulters
may not bear againſt the left Side of the Inciſions
made by the Edges.

Each Hole, being a Mortiſe, is one Inch and a
quarter wide, with its Two oppoſite Sides parallel
from Top to Bottom ; each of theſe Mortiſes, or
Holes, are long at Top Three Inches and an half, and
at Bottom Three Inches; the Back-part, or Hinder-
end,

end, of each Coulter-hole is not perpendicular, but oblique, and determines the Obliquity of the Standing of the Coulter, which is wedged tight up to it by the Poll-wedge *i*, *Fig*. 1. as all Coulters are.

.*Fig*. 17. Is a Coulter; *a b* is its Length, being Two Feet Eight Inches, before it is worn; *e d* is its Edge, Sixteen Inches long; *d c* is the Length of its Handle, Sixteen Inches; this is made thus long, at first, to stand above the Plough, that it may be driven down lower, according as the Point wears shorter; this Handle is One Inch and Seven Eighths broad, and Seven Eighths of an Inch thick, equally thro' its whole Length: Its Breadth and Thickness might be described by a rectangled Parallelogram.

In all Ploughs this first Coulter is, or ought to be, placed in the Beam in manner following; *viz*. its Back to bear against the Back of the Coulter-hole, its right Side above to bear against the upper Edge of the Coulter-hole, and its left Side to bear against the lower Edge of the Coulter-hole; so that always Three Wedges at least will be necessary to hold the Coulter; the Poll-wedge before it, as at *i*, in *Fig*. 1. another Wedge on the left Side of it above, and a Third on the right Side underneath: The Coulter-hole must be so made, that the Coulter standing thus across the Hole, its Point may incline so much towards the Left, as to be about Two Inches and an half farther to the Left (*a*) than the Point of the Share, if it were driven down as low as it; but it never ought to be so low in any Plough: As to its bearing forwards, the Point of the Coulter should never be before the Middle of the Point of the Share: What Angle the Coulter would make with the Bottom of the Share, may be seen by the Posture it stands in, in *Fig*. 1. If it should be set much more obliquely, it would have a

(*a*) I find that sometimes it is necessary in some of these Ploughs for the Point of this Coulter to stand yet farther on the Left of the Share's Point.

greater

greater Force to raife up the Poll-wedge, and get loofe.

The Three added Coulters fhould ftand in the fame Pofture with this already defcribed, in regard to the Inclination of their Points towards the Left : And this is a very great Advantage to them; for by this means, when the Fin is rais'd up, by turning the Handles towards the Left, their Points do not rife out of the Ground on the right Hand, as they would do without this defcribed Inclination towards the Left; but in regard to their Pointing forwards, I find it beft, that every one of the Three fhould be a little more perpendicular than that next behind it. So the Coulter 4 ftands the nearest to Perpendicular of any of them. By this means there being more Room betwixt them above than below, they are the more eafily freed from the Turf, whenever the Pieces, being covered with a great Quantity of Couch-grafs, or the like, rife up betwixt them : which tho' this feldom happens, makes a Neceffity for a Man, or a Boy, to go on the Side with a forked Stick, to pufh out the Turf and Grafs, which might otherwife fill the Spaces betwixt the Coulters, and raife up the Plough out of its Work.

'Tis to be obferved, that none of thefe Coulters ought to defcend fo low as the Bottom of the Share, except when you plow very fhallow: 'Tis always fufficient that they cut through the Turf, let the Plough go never fo deep in the Ground.

It is neceffary alfo, that when you plow very fhallow, the Fin of the Share be broad enough to cut off the Fourth Piece or Furrow ; elfe that, lying faft, will be apt to raife up the Ground-wrift, and throw out the Plough : But when you plow deep, the Ground-wrift will break off this Fourth Furrow, altho' the Fin be not broad enough to reach it.

Sometimes the Firft or left Furrow is apt to come through betwixt the Firft Coulter and the Sheat, and

fo

ſo falls on the left-hand Side of the Plough ; This is no Injury; but yet it is prevented, by letting the Second Coulter ſtand a lighter higher than the Third; and then the Second Furrow, holding the Firſt at its Bottom, will carry it over, together with itſelf, on the right Side by the Earth-board ; but yet never ſet this, or any of the Three added Coulters, ſo high that they may not cut through the Turf.   But as for the firſt Coulter, tho' it ſhould cut but an Inch or Two within the Ground, the Share will break off the firſt Furrow in raiſing it up.

Remember, as often as the Point of any Coulter is worn too ſhort, that you drive down the Coulter with a large Hammer, carried for that Purpoſe; and when it is driven low enough, faſten the Wedges again, ſo as to keep the Coulters in their right Poſtures, that their Inciſions may be all of them equidiſtant.

Fig. 18. Is a Nut, with Two of its oppoſite Corners turn'd up, by which it is driven round by a Hammer, and has ſo great a Force, that Three of them, with their Screws properly placed, hold the Piece, *Fig.* 16. as faſt to the Plough-beam, as if they both were made of one Piece of Wood ; but as often as the Wood ſhrinks in dry Weather, the Nuts muſt be ſcrew'd farther on, both here and in all other Places where they are uſed : particularly, thoſe which hold up the Retch ; for if the Sheat ſhould once get looſe, there is no Cure but by a new one.

Betwixt this Nut and the Wood, there ſhould be a thin Iron Bolſter, about the Thickneſs of a Shilling, broader than the Nut, to prevent the Nut from eating into the Wood, eſpecially when it is to be often ſcrew'd, as on the Retch of theſe Ploughs, and moſt of all on the Hoe-plough; but ſometimes we uſe a Piece of Shoe-leather inſtead of an Iron Bolſter.

Note, There muſt be Iron Plates upon all the Coulter-holes both above and below, Three of which

are

are feen on the Piece in *Fig.* 16. There is no need
to fay how they muft be nailed on with many Nails
made for the Purpofe.

Fig. 19. Is the Iron Collar, faftened to the Beam
by Two fhort Crooks A, B, which take hold of Two
fhort Pins driven into the Plough juft behind the Second Coulter-hole, one on one Side, and the other on
the other Side of the Beam. The Crook A is feen
on the left Side of the Beam near *c,* in *Fig.* 2. the
Crook B doing the fame on the other Side of the
Beam, which is feen near *a,* in *Fig.* 3. C is the
Crook (for its Shape called a C) which holds the Tow-
chain to the Collar by the Link D, being Part of the
faid Chain taking hold of its Fore-claw; the other
Claw taking hold of one of the Five Notches of the
Collar: This Collar is partly feen at *d,* in *Fig.* 2.
Both the Claws of the Crook (or C) turn upwards, fo
that they cannot take hold of any thing that may rife
under the Plough: The Ufe of the Notches is to
help the Direction of the Point of the Share, which
has been defcribed by the prick'd Lines under *Fig.* 1.
As the Point of the Share wears, it inclines a little
more towards the Right, and is remedied by moving
the Crook into a Notch nearer to the Left, which
will direct the Point a little more towards the Left:
This is more eafy to be done here than in the common
Plough, whofe Collar moves round the Beam: We
can, by changing the Crook from one Notch to another, incline the Point of the Share towards the
Right or Left at Pleafure. The Length of each
Side of this Collar is a Foot long.

The Tow-chain is beft feen in *Fig.* 3. where the
Link Y is that which paffes thro' the Box, and is pinned in by the Stake, as has been fhewn in *Fig.* 1.
which Stake is commonly nailed to the Box, to prevent its rifing up. When we would draw up the
Plough a little nearer to the Crow-ftaves, we take
hold of the Crook by a Second or Third Link.

Note,

Note, That the fhortening of the Chain does alfo a little incline the Point of the Share towards the Left.

Fig. 20. is the Iron-wilds. The Leg A is of one Piece with that which has the Notch, and that paffes thro' the Leg B by the Loop at *a*; both which Legs pafs thro' the Box, and are pinned in behind it, by the crooked Pins C, D. This Figure is feen with its Crooks on it, both in *Fig.* 1. and *Fig.* 2. *Note,* That the Holes in the Box, thro' which thefe Legs pafs, muft not be made at right Angles with the Box, but muft incline upwards, fo that the Fore-part of the Wilds may be higher than the Hinder-part, or elfe the Upper-part of the Crow-ftaves would lean quite back when the Plough is drawn. If the Beafts that draw immediately next to the Plough be very high, their Traces muft be the longer; elfe they and the Wilds making too fmall an Angle with the Tow-chain at the Box, when they draw hard, the Wheels will rife from the Ground, and be apt to overturn: This Angle I fuppofe fhould not be lefs than of 160 Degrees, and the Angle made by the Tow-chain or Traces that are drawn by the Cattle that go before them, will make an Angle with the Tow-chain at the Box yet much more obtufe. The Ufe of thefe Notches in the Wilds is, to give the Plough a broader or narrower Furrow: If the Links are moved to the Notches on the right Hand, it brings the Wheels towards the left Hand, which gives a greater Furrow; and when the Links are moved towards the left Hand, it gives a lefs Furrow, by bringing the Wheels towards the right Hand.

The Diftance betwixt the Two Legs of the Wilds is Eight Inches and an half; the Length of the Legs is Nineteen Inches. They muft be of convenient Strength. The Links being placed in Notches diftant from one another, prevents one Wheel from advancing before the other; which would happen, if the Links were both in One Notch, or in Two adjoining

Notches,

Notches, except they were middle Notches: Thefe Links are each Six Inches and an half long.

E is the Ring, by which the Two Links, and the Two Crooks F and G, are held together, and on which they all move.

The Height of the Wheels in *Fig.* 2. The left-hand Wheel is Twenty Inches Diameter; the Diameter of the right Wheel is Two Feet Three Inches; the Diftance the Wheels are fet from each other at the Ground, is Two Feet Five Inches and an half; the Crow-ftaves are One Foot Eleven Inches high, from the Box to the Gallows; they both ftand perpendicular to the Box, and the Diftance between the Crowftaves is Ten Inches and an half. The Pillow is pinned up at its Ends by Two fmall Iron Pins, which are chained to it, that if they drop, they may not be loft. Thefe appear in *Fig.* 1. and *Fig.* 2. The Height from the level Surface, up to the Hole in the Box, where the Tow-chain paffes through it, is Thirteen Inches (being Two Inches below the Holes of the Wilds, on the Hinder-fide of the Box); the Height at the other End, where the Crook of the Collar takes hold of the Pin in the Beam at *c*, in *Fig.* 2. is Twenty Inches high above the fame level Surface, and fhews how much the Chain defcends forward, for drawing down the Plough, and by which Defcent may be known what Angle the Chain would make with the Surface, if it were produced forwards in a ftrait Line; which is a thing material for the good going of a Plough; and fo is the Angle the Towchain makes with the Beam: About the Middle of this Tow-chain, there fhould be a Swivel, whereby one End of the Chain may turn without the other.

When this Four coulter Plough is made, I would advife, that it be tried with only the firft Coulter, before the other Three are put in; for if the Plough does not go well with One Coulter, it is not likely it fhould go well with Four; and I never yet have feen

or

Plate II. P.307

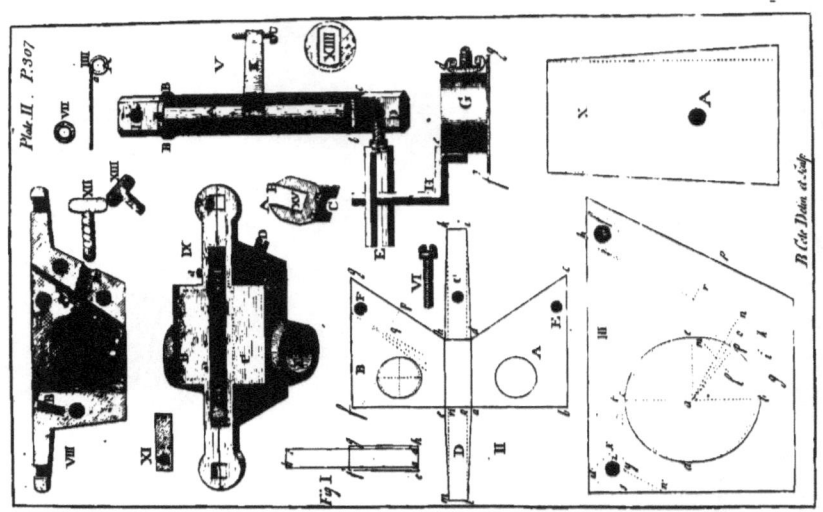

or heard of any that went well with One Coulter, that did not alfo go well with Four, being placed as is here directed.

The Proofs of a Plough's performing well are thefe; *viz.* If it makes a Furrow of an equal Depth on the right Hand and on the left, and turns it off fairly: If, in its going, the Tail of the Shate, and the Bottom of the Drock, bear againft the Bottom of the Furrow, and if it goes eafy in the Hands of the Holder, without preffing one Arm more than the other, then the Plough is certainly a good one.

The Ploughman who is accuftom'd to a Two-wheel'd Plough, never fuffers the Wheels to overturn, in turning out at the Land's End, from one Furrow to another; for which Purpofe, after he has lifted the Plough a little round, he has a Knack of holding up the Crow-ftaves with the End of the Beam, by preff-ing his Hand hard againft the Handle, whilft the Plough lies down on one Side, until the Horfes, the Wheels, and the Plough, come near to a Line in the Beginning of the Furrow; and then he lifts up his Plough, and goes on.

C H A P.   XX.

Of the Drill-Boxes.

THE Drill is the Engine that plants our Corn and other Seeds in Rows: It makes the Chanels, fows the Seed into them, and covers them at the fame time, with great Exactnefs and Expedition.

The principal Parts of the Drill are, the Seed-box, the Hopper, and the Plough, with its Harrow.

Of thefe the Seed-box is the Chief: It meafures (or rather numbers) out the Seed which it receives

from the Hopper: It is for this Purpofe as an artificial Hand, which performs the Tafk of delivering
out the Seed, more equally than can be done by a
natural Hand.

It is defcribed, together with fome of its Appurtenances, in *Plates* 2 and 3.

The MORTISE.

As the Seed-box is the principal Part of a Drill,
fo is the Mortife the principal Part of the Seed-box.

The following Defcriptions fhew how this Mortife
differs from a common Mortife.

Fig. 1. *Plate* 2. fhews both the upper and lower
Edges of a Turnep-Seed-box, and the Manner how
they are pofited one over another. *a b c d* is a rectangled Parallelogram, and fhews the upper Edges (or
Top) of the Mortife. *e f g h*, being a Figure of
the fame Denomination with the former, is the lower
Edges (or Bottom) of the Mortife. The Line *e h* is
the Length of the lower Edge of the Hinder-end of
the Mortife. *a d* is the upper Edge of the Hinder-end
of the Mortife, and pofited juft over the lower Edge of
the fame End. The Space between the Line *a b*,
and the Line *e f*, fhews half the Excefs whereby the
Bottom of the Mortife exceeds the Top in Breadth ;
as the Space on the oppofite Side, betwixt the Line
c d, and the Line *g h*, fhews the other Half of that
Excefs, both which Halves, taken together, fhew
the whole Bevel (or Angle of Inclination) defcribed
in *Fig.* 2. That Part of the Line *a b*, from the
Angle at *b* to the Line *f g*, which interfects it, fhews
the Excefs whereby the Top of the Mortife exceeds
the Bottom in Length.

Fig. 2. Is the Mortife cut down by its Four Corners, and laid open. *a b c d* is a Trapezium, with
Two parallel Sides, and mark'd A, the right Side
of the Mortife ; its oppofite Side *e f g h*, mark'd B,

the

the left Side of the Mortife; the Areas of both being true Planes (*a*).

d i k b Shew the Fore-end of the Mortife, mark'd C. *a l m e* fhew the Hinder-end of the Mortife, mark'd D. *a d b e* fhew the Bottom of the Mortife already defcribed in *Fig.* 1.   If thefe oppofite Sides and Ends were all raifed up, until the Angle at *b* join the Angle at *l,* and that at *m* join *f,* and that at *g* join *k,* and that *i* join *c,* the Top of the Mortife would be formed, and the fame with the Parallelogram *a b c d,* in *Fig.* 1. and then the intire Mortife of the Turnep Seed-box would appear in its true Form, ftanding upon its Bottom.

This differs from a common Mortife, in that it is impoffible to fit it with a Tenon; becaufe it is narrower above, and fhorter below, as in *Fig.* 1.

The Areas, or imaginary Planes, of the Top and Bottom of the Mortife, are parallel to each other, but not equal.

Its Two oppofite Sides are equal, but not parallel, by reafon of their Inclination to each other upwards, which is the Bevel hereafter to be defcribed.

The Two Ends are neither parallel nor equal, becaufe the Hinder-end D is perpendicular to the Top and Bottom, and the Fore-end oblique, and therefore longer.

(*a*) Take care that thefe oppofite Sides be fure to be true Planes, efpecially all that Part of their Areas, that is before the tranfverfe Axes of their Ellipfes herein after defcribed ; for fhould they be otherwife, the Bevel of the Mortife would be fpoiled, and fo would the Ellipfes, and the acute Triangles, on the Sides of the Tongue ; which how neceffary they are to be true, is fhewn in the proper Place.   Workmen are very apt to fail in this when they file by Hand, and make thefe Sides of the Mortife convex inftead of plane.   Therefore this might be done with lefs Difficulty, and more Exactnefs, with a File placed in a Frame, whereby it might move upon a true Level without rifing or finking of either End.

When

When Two oppofite Sides, or Surfaces, are inclined to each other upwards, I call that Inclination a Bevel ; but when they are inclined downwards, I call it a Bevel revers'd.

The Line *a e*, being the Bottom, or Bafe, of the Hinder-end D, by being longer than the Line *l m*, fhews that the Mortife is bevel.

The Two prick'd Lines *m n* and *l o*, with the Line *l m*, and Part of the Line *a e*, make a rectangled Parallelogram, which fhews the exact Depth of the Mortife, and forms on each Side of it a rectangled Triangle, the one *m e n*, and the other *l o a*; which Triangles being fimilar and equal, and their acute Angles at *l* and *m* being each of Four Degrees, make the whole Bevel, or Inclination of the Sides of the Mortife, to be of Eight Degrees, their Hypothenufes being the fame with the Sides of the Mortife.

This End D, being raifed up to its Place, will be at right Angles with the Plane of the Top and of the Bottom of the Mortife ; which, being both rectangled Parallelograms, prove that Bevel, or Angle of Inclination, to be the fame from one End to the other of the Sides, which Sides are the Hypothenufes of thofe Two Triangles: But this could not be proved by the Triangles in the oppofite End C ; becaufe the Bafes being the fame with the other, and having their Legs longer, the vertical Angles at *k* and *i* are more acute. The Legs are longer ; becaufe the End C, when in its Place, is not at right Angles with the Top and Bottom of the Mortife, as the End D is.

The next thing to be defcribed in the Mortife, is the Bore, great Hole, or Perforation ; which is beft fhewn in the Side of a Mortife of a Wheat-drill, being larger, as in *Fig. 3.* wherein *c e b d* is the great Hole, and is a Section of an hollow Cylinder, that paffes through the Mortife, with its Axis parallel to the Edges of the Ends of the Mortife : This

Cylinder,

Cylinder, being cut by the Side of the Mortife ob-liquely, and not parallel to its Bafe, is an Ellipfe.

The prick'd curve Line is a Circle parallel to the Bafe of the Cylinder, and the curve Line *b d c e* is the Ellipfis; and this Curve is more or lefs elliptical (or oval) in proportion to the Angle of Inclination, or Bevel, of the Sides of the Mortife.

Of this Ellipfe the longeft Diameter (or *Axis tranf-verfus*) *b c* is at right Angles with the upper and lower Edges of the Sides of the Mortife.

Its fhorteft Diameter (or *Axis rectus*) *d e*, is the Diameter of the Cylinder, bifecting the *Axis tranf-verfus* at right Angles in the Centre *a*; and is in this Figure one Inch and an half.

This Ellipfe being concentric with the Circle, the Letter *a* is the Centre of both.

The Semi-ellipfis *c e b* is the Part of chief Ufe; and therefore the Edge muft of Neceffity be fmooth, and without Flaws, as muft the Surfaces of the Sides of the Mortife betwixt the Ellipfe and the Fore-end.

The Tongue of the Seed-box (*Plate 3. Fig. 1.*) differs from that in the Sound-board of an Organ (from which I took the Idea of it) in Shape, in Situation, and in the Manner of its being fix'd to the Mortife.

The Tongue, in the Organ, is on its Surface a long Square, or rectangled Parallelogram, a little broader and longer than the Mortife (or Grove) it fhuts againft; but this Tongue on its upper Surface, which is here turned downwards, being a Plane, is a Trapezium, of the fame Shape with the Fore-end of the Mortife juft now defcribed, except that the Tongue has a lefs Bevel.

The Situation of that in the Organ is on the Out-fide of the Mortife, which it fhuts by its Spring behind it, and opens immediately by the Finger of the Organift preffing down the Key to let in the com-preffed Air to its Pipes; but this Tongue is fituate

within the Mortife of the Seed-box, and placed almoft, in a manner, diagonally ; for, had it been placed like the other, the Seed getting betwixt it and the
Edges of the Mortife, would not have given Way to
its Shutting (as the Air does to the other), but have
kept it always open ; which would have render'd it
ufelefs for fowing of Seeds.

The Manner of faftening the Organ-tongue to its
Mortife is by Parchment and Leather glu'd to its
Surface, and alfo to the Sound-board, at its End
which is oppofite to that preffed open by the Key,
and fhut by the Spring; but this our Tongue is held
within the Mortife, and moves on an Axis, which
paffes thro' its upper and narrower End, which Axis
is the Pin A (which muft be exactly parallel to the
Edge of the End of the Mortife), and alfo thro' the
Hole *f* in *Fig. 3.* in *Plate* 2. which is feen in its
Place at A in *Fig. 3. Plate 3.* and likewife through
both Sides of the Mortife near their upper Edges,
and as near the Fore-end of the Mortife as may be,
without the Tongue's rubbing againft the faid Fore-
end,

The Breadth of the Tongue muft be conformed to
the Breadth and Bevel of the Mortife, and when it is
on its Axis, it being raifed tight up as far as the
fhort prick'd Line *l m* in *Fig. 3. Plate* 2. being One-
eighth Part of the great Hole, and being there, you
fee its upper Edges touch both Sides of the Mortife
by their whole Length: Then it is rightly made: and
by this touching both Sides of the Mortife tightly and
clofely, when raifed up to that Degree, it appears,
that the Two upper Edges of the Sides of the Tongue
are inclined to each other in an Angle that is more
acute, by about One-third, than is the Angle of Inclination of the Sides of the Mortife.

Hence, when the Tongue is let down to its Place,
there will be on each Side of it an empty Space, betwixt it and the Mortife, of the Form of a very
acute

acute Triangle, whofe vertical Angle is more or lefs acute, according as the Tongue approaches nearer to, or recedes farther from the Spindle.

This *Fig.* 1. *Plate* 3. is the brafs Tongue with its Back-fide upwards. The Two outer Lines *a b* and *c d* are the Edges of the upper Surface (tho' turned downwards in this Figure), which are inclined to each other, as afore-mentioned; but the Two inner Lines *e f* and *g b* are nearer to each other, whereby this under Surface is narrower than the upper: Both muft be plain Surfaces, but the upper and its Two Edges very free from Flaws, and fmooth, or polifhed.

The Reafon why the under Surface is narrower than the upper, is to preferve the Bevel of the empty Triangle: For though the Bevel of the Sides of the Mortife would be fufficient for this, if both Sides of the Tongue were fure to keep equally diftant from the Spindle; yet as the Tongue never is fo tight on its Axis, but that fometimes one Corner of it may be nearer to the Spindle than the other, in this Cafe, that Side which is neareft to the Spindle would reverfe that Bevel, fo as to make the fmall empty Space that is betwixt the Mortife and the Tongue, wider above than underneath.

C C are the Two little Knobs that prevent the Spring from flipping to either Side, and are at the Diftance from one another of the Breadth of the Spring.

Fig. 2. fhews one Side, and the Thicknefs of the Tongue the other Side, being the fame. *a b* fhews the polifhed Surface (being a true Plane), whereon the Seed runs down to the Spindle. *c d* the Back-fide, which lies turned uppermoft in *Fig.* 1. *b e d* fhews one End of the hollow Cylinder of the Tongue, thro' which its Axis paffes.

The Length of the Tongue muft be fuch, as will reach lower than juft to touch the Bottom of the

great

great Hole as a Tangent: for, if it be not longer than that, it might happen, that when the Mortise is empty of Seed, and the Tongue set up close, a Wheel might, in Turning, or otherwise, go a little backwards, and cause a Notch of the Spindle to take hold of the End of the Tongue, and tear it out of the Mortise: Therefore let the Tongue reach a little below the Spindle, as the pricked Line *g h*, in *Fig.* 3. of *Plate* 2. doth.

As for the Posture in which the Tongue ought to stand in the Mortise, it is shewn by the Three pricked Lines in *Fig.* 3. *Plate* 2. where the pricked Line *g h* makes an Angle of Forty-five Degrees, being the nearest that it can stand to the Spindle; the pricked Line *i h* makes a somewhat greater Angle, and it is a mean (or middle) Distance from the Spindle; and the pricked Line *k h* is supposed to be its greatest Distance, where the Tongue makes its greatest Angle with the Top and Bottom of the Mortise. If the Tongue stood so obliquely as to make an Angle much less than Forty-Five, the Tongue would rise too much against the Bevel of the Mortise, and the Spring would have the greater Difficulty in returning it to its Place, when driven back by the Force of the Notches.

And beside, when the Tongue stood wide from the Spindle, there might be so much Room betwixt it and the Sides of the Mortise, that some Seeds might fall thro' there.

The Steel Spring is D, properly placed upon the Back of the Tongue, in *Fig.* 1. *Plate* 3.

At first, I made the Spring double, *i. e.* with Two Legs, in Imitation of that in the Organ, and fastened into its Tongue, much after the same manner as the Spring of the Organ is into its Tongue or Flap, which prevents the compressed Air from passing out of the Sound-board, except whilst the Key is thrust

down

down by the Finger of the Player; but the Drill-spring requiring to be of a vaftly greater Strength than that, I made it of Steel, of the Breadth of half an Inch, inftead of Brafs Wire: This performed very well, and feveral Drills are yet extant, that have only this Sort of Springs: Yet I found there was great Difficulty to fet the Legs at their due Diftance from each other; for their Seafoning would alter them from what they were, whilft the Steel was foft: They alfo took up too much Room in the upper Part of the Mortife.   Then, to remedy thefe Inconveniencies, I made it fingle, with only one Leg, which by full Experience is found to be much better than the double one; it does not contain a Fourth Part of the Metal, and is moft eafily made, requiring none of that Trouble and Nicety that the double Spring doth.   I fhall therefore give a Defcription of the fingle Spring only.

B, the End of the Screw, which holds the Spring to the Tongue, thro' a Hole near the upper End of the Spring; D, the Middle, againft which the End of the Setting-fcrew bears.

Its Length is almoft the whole Length of the Tongue; the End E reaching very near to the lower End of the Tongue, and the End B is as near the upper End of the Tongue; as it can be placed without touching the Cylinder of the Tongue.

The Breadth is ufually about half an Inch; the Thicknefs muft be in proportion to its other Dimenfions, and according to the Degree of Stiffnefs required.

The longer it is, the thicker it muft be, to have the fame Stiffnefs; but the broader it is, the thinner it muft be of the fame Length; fo that it is hard to determine its Thicknefs.   It is made ftiffer or ftronger by being cut fhorter; it is made weaker, or lefs ftiff, by filing or grinding it either thinner or narrower.

The

The common Thickneſs is about that of a Shilling *(a)*.

The Degrees of Stiffneſs are meaſured in this manner; *viz.* Fix Two Boards together, leaving a Chink betwixt them, in one Place of an Inch long; lay the Spring (when ſeaſoned acroſs this Chink) with its Middle exactly over it; then put a String over the Spring, which may paſs with both Ends thro' the Chink, and tie ſo much Weight to the Ends of the String under the Boards, that will pull down the Middle of the Spring, till it touch the Chink, and is ſtrait with both its Ends; This will ſhew the Degree of Stiffneſs. But note, That the Spring muſt be crooked, and bear only upon its Ends, with the hollow Side upwards.

If ten or a dozen Pounds Weight pull it down to the Board, it is a good Degree of Stiffneſs, for a large Box: We are not confined to be very nice or exact in the Degree of Stiffneſs; for by our Fingers preſſing it, we that are practiſed in it, know well enough, whether a Spring be of a ſufficient Degree of Stiffneſs, without weighing it; but for ſuch who are unacquainted with them, it is beſt not to truſt to Gueſs, but Weights; and to adjuſt the Stiffneſs to that of a Spring, that has been known to perform well.

The Spring muſt bear againſt the Back of the Tongue at each End, and lie hollow in the Middle: But the Degree of Hollowneſs of the Spring is very material; for thereon depends the Diſtance of the Tongue's Motion towards the Spindle by Force of the Spring, and back again quite to the Setting-ſcrew, by the Seed that is preſſed againſt it by Force of the Notches, when they are moved by the Wheels; becauſe the more the Spring is curved, the farther

---

(a) Not quite ſo thick as a milled Shilling, but rather of an old broad ſtamped Shilling, which is a little thinner.

will

will it thruſt the Tongue from its Middle, if its Strength be ſuperior to the Force that reſiſts it, as it ought to be when a Notch is paſſed and before the next: This Motion of the Tongue is called its Play.

In order to meaſure the Diſtance (or Quantity) of this Motion, we muſt conſider, that the Tongue, moving on its Axis above, deſcribes with its lower End the Arch of a Circle, the Chord of which Arch is the Meaſure required.

To meaſure this by the Angle the Tongue makes at its Centre, would be no Rule for making Boxes; becauſe ſome Tongues are longer, ſome ſhorter, in proportion to the different Diameters of the Spindles they move againſt; and yet the Play of the ſhorteſt muſt be as much as that of the longeſt, that is, it muſt deſcribe as great an Arch at the Place of Preſ-ſure (deſcribed in *Fig.* 3. *Plate* 2.); and therefore the ſhorteſt Tongue would make the greateſt Angle.

A ſhort and eaſy Way, then, for a Mechanic to meaſure, is thus: Screw in the Setting-ſcrew until the Tongue come within a quarter of an Inch of touching the Spindle; then take out the Spindle, and from the Centre of the Hole draw a Line on the Side of the Mortiſe, perpendicular to the Tongue, and at the Tongue's Edge make a Mark with the Compaſſes, or a Pen; then force back the Tongue againſt the Setting-ſcrew as far as it will go (that is, until the Spring touch the whole Back of the Tongue); produce the ſaid Line to the ſame Edge of the Tongue, or ſet the End of the Rule thereon, and draw another Line, by the Rule, from the Mark to the Edge of the Tongue, when fartheſt back, and there make the ſecond Mark. The Ruler uſed this Way will ſhew both the Perpendicular, and the Mea-ſure.

But yet a quicker Way is, to ſet the Tongue, by the Setting-ſcrew up to the Edge of the Hole; and, when it is forced back, meaſure from the Tongue

3   to

to the neareft Part of the Hole, which will ever be a perpendicular Line drawn from the Centre of the Hole to the Place of Preffure above-mentioned, and make another Mark there : Now the Diftance between thefe Two Marks is the Meafure (near enough) of the Tongue's Play at the Place of Preffure. Tho' this Line drawn on the Side of the Mortife be not exactly perpendicular to the Surface of the Tongue, but only to its Edge; yet the Difference is next to nothing, and not to be regarded.

If its Meafure be a quarter of an Inch, it is what Experience fhews to be of a good Size for all Corn and Peas; a little lefs is no Harm, but greater is the moft fatal Error, into which moft of the Pretenders to the making of this Machine have fallen; they give the Tongue half an Inch, fometimes Three quarters of an Inch Play. The Mifchief of this Error is yet farther increafed, if the Spring be weak, if the Mortife have too great a Bevel, or if the Angle made by the Tongue at the upper Edge of the Mortife be too acute.

When the Tongue has too great Play, the Seed is apt to be turned out too faft, or elfe too flow, in fpite of the Driller. For when the Tongue is fet at its due Diftance from the Spindle, and is thruft quite back by the Seed preffed againft it by the Turning of the Notches; but the Spring being unable to return the Tongue to its former Place at fuch a Diftance, at the time of paffing the Intervals which are betwixt the Notches; then the Space between the Spindle and the Tongue being too open, the Seed is fent down too faft.

To prevent that, they fet up the Tongue to the Spindle; and then, as often as the Spring happens to overcome the Force of the Seed's Preffure (as fometimes it will), it is fent out too flowly.

The Inequality of the Running of the Seed makes fuch Boxes ufelefs, which the Expence of Two-pence

(for

(for another Spring, or new Seafoning of that) at moft would rectify, if the Maker underftood how to mend his own Work.   If time did permit, more fhould be faid on this Point, becaufe I find it is the *Pons Afini* of a Workman.   Sometimes it may be prevented, when the Spring is too hollow, and gives too much Play.   Screw the Screw, that holds it on the Tongue, down clofer, fo that the lower Part of the Screw's Head prefs againft the Spring, and thereby force its Middle nearer to the Tongue, until you find its Play leffened to its juft Diftance.

The Spring, remaining in this compreffed State, has loft the weakeft, and retains only the ftrongeft, Part of its elaftic Force.   Therefore, if you find it then too ftiff, make it weaker by Filing or Grinding, or elfe put another into its Place, which is honeftly worth no more than Two-pence.

This Holding-fcrew has a pretty broad Head, and is fcrewed in by a Notch, like the Screw-pin of a Gun-lock.

The Hole in the Spring muft be fomewhat bigger than the Holding-fcrew, becaufe the Spring muft have room to move and play thereon.

If the Middle of the Spring were againft the Middle of that Part of the Tongue, that is betwixt its Axis and the Place of Preffure, the Diftance of the Spring's Hollownefs would be juft half the Diftance of the Spring's Play, to wit, the One-eighth Part of an Inch ; but as the Spring does not quite reach up to the Axis, and reaches much below the Place of Preffure, the Hollownefs at the Place where the Setting-fcrew bears againft the Middle of the Spring at D, is confiderably nearer to the Place of Preffure than to the Axis of the Tongue ; this Hollownefs of the Spring at the Setting-fcrew may be fomething more than the One-eighth Part of an Inch, to give the Spring a Quarter of an Inch Play : but it feldom has fo much.

Fig.

Fig. 4. in *Plate* 2. ſhews the Length and Thick-neſs of the Steel Spring of a Turnep Seed-box: This ſerves both for a Tongue and Spring: It is made firſt ſtrait, and then the narroweſt End of it is turned round, till it reach to *a*, and forms the Cylinder A, thro' which its Axis paſſes; but is not welded or joined to the other Part of the Spring at *a*: It is placed in the Box with the Cylinder Part underneath. The Face of this Spring is ſeen upon its Axis, mark'd K. in *Fig.* 5. Its Axis is to paſs thro' the Hole E, and ſcrew into the Hole F, in *Fig.* 2. as is ſeen more plainly at *a* in *Fig.* 9.

As the Top of every Tongue ought to be even with the upper Edges of the Mortiſe, the Thickneſs of the Cylinder of the Braſs Tongue cauſes the Hole in the Sides of the Mortiſe, into which it is held by its Axis, to be far enough from the Edges of the Mortiſe, to be bored and ſcrewed without Danger of breaking the ſaid Edges; but the Spring of the Turnep-drill being ſo very thin, there is ſome Dif-ficulty in making the Hole ſo high, and near the Edges: To prevent which Danger, *Fig.* 7. ſhews the End of a ſmall hollow Cylinder of Iron or Braſs, of the Thickneſs of the Mortiſe; which, being put into the Cylinder A, in *Fig.* 4. raiſes the Spring higher above the Hole; ſo that it may be made as low in a Turnep Mortiſe, as that is which holds the Braſs Tongue in the Wheat-drill. But we do not always uſe this inner Cylinder *(a)*; but muſt then take the more Care in boring the Hole, or elſe it will burſt out at the Edges of the Mortiſe.

Its Shape muſt conform to that of the Braſs Tongue already deſcribed.

(a) For, inſtead of this, we may uſe a Bit of Woolen Cloth of the Breadth of the Mortiſe, glued on to the Bottom of the Hop-per, which, filling the Vacuity above the Steel Tongue, prevents any Seed from running over it, though the Holes are bored as low in the Mortiſe as if the Cylinder *Fig.* 7. were to be uſed.

The

The Degree of its Stiffneſs is known by weighing, as has been directed for the other Spring ; and being laid with its Face downwards over a Chink, with a ſmall Piece of Wood of the Thickneſs of a Barley-corn at Each end, and a String taking hold of its Middle, and deſcending thro' the Chink, the Weight of Five Pounds, tied to the End of the String, will juſt bend the Spring, till it touch the Edges of the Chink ; and this is the Stiffneſs of a Spring that has performed well, for many Years, in drilling of Tur-nep-feed.

The SETTING-SCREW.

Fig. 6. is the Iron Setting-ſcrew, which paſſes thro' the Hole in the Fore-end of the Mortiſe, *Fig.* 2. and paſſes up to the Middle of the Spring by the prick'd Line *p q* in the ſame Figure. The Uſe of this Setting-ſcrew is, to increaſe or diminiſh the Pro-portion of Seed to be turned out by the Notches ; and this it does by forcing up the Spring and Tongue (where there is one) nearer to, or farther from the Spindle, whereby the Seed-paſſage is made wider or narrower, as is ſhewn by the Three prick'd Lines in *Fig.* 2. and *Fig.* 3.

Obſerve, that the prick'd Line *p q*, *Fig.* 2. (being the Mortiſe of the Turnep-box) ſtands higher than the ſame Line doth in *Fig.* 3. which is the Mortiſe of the Wheat-box. The Reaſon of this Difference is, becauſe the Spring in the Wheat-box bears at its lower End againſt the Tongue below the Seed-paſſage, and at its upper End below the Axis of the Tongue, whereby the Middle of that Spring is lower than the Spring of the Turnep-box, which, being both Spring and Tongue, bears againſt its Axis above, and againſt the Seed-paſſage below ; therefore its Middle is higher. This Setting-ſcrew ſhould be placed perpendicular to the Tongue when at its mean or middle Diſtance from the Spindle, which may be ſuppoſed to be the

Y   middle-

middlemoſt of the Three mention'd prick'd Lines. This Setting-ſcrew ought to be ſmooth and round at its End, which bears againſt the Spring ; for, if it ſhould have ſharp Corners or Edges, the Spring might be wounded by them, and in time might break there, being preſs'd by every Notch that turns againſt it ; and, as I have computed it, a Spring undergoes One hundred thouſand of theſe Preſſures in one Day's Work ; and yet, in my whole Practice, I have had only one Spring broken, and that was in drilling a large Sort of Peas with a Wheat-drill, and was oc-caſioned by a jagged End of the Setting-ſcrew, which was not placed perpendicular to the Spring, by which means the rough End of the Screw made Scratches againſt it a Quarter of an Inch long, and ſo deep, that the Spring broke off there : Let not this Setting-ſcrew be any longer than juſt to force the Tongue up to the Spindle ; for, if it ſhould be longer, an ignorant Driller might happen, by the Force of the Screw, to break the Tongue, or its Axis ; but in the Turnep-drill, which has only a Spring inſtead of a Tongue, the Setting-ſcrew may be a Thread or Two longer ; becauſe the Spring will yield a little to it, after it touches the Spindle, and is ſometimes of Uſe in that reſpect, when the Notches are too large. This Screw muſt be of ſuch a Bigneſs, that it may not be in Danger of bending ; for if it ſhould be bent, it could not be ſcrew'd up with any Certainty, becauſe its End, being crooked, would be below its Place at one Half-turn, and above it at the other Half-turn, and ſo the Spring might be ſet farther from the Spindle inſtead of nearer, and nearer in-ſtead of farther, by the Crookedneſs of the Setting-ſcrew. Its Head may be made with a Notch in it, to be ſcrew'd in with a Knife, or elſe with a Head like a T, to be turn'd with the Fingers, which I think is beſt, eſpecially for a Wheat-drill ; becauſe as the Brine and Lime, which ſtick on the Wheat, grow drier,

drier, it will run fafter; and therefore the Setting-
fcrew muft be frequently fcrew'd in to leffen the Seed-
paffage.

The Seed-paffage, or Place of Preffure, is where
the Seed paffes down betwixt the Spindle and the
Tongue; and is in that Part where they are neareft
together; for there the Seed is prefs'd hardeft by the
Force of the Notches, which carry it down : And this
Paffage is higher or lower, as the Tongue ftands
nearer or farther from the Spindle; for as it ftands
wider, it becomes nearer to perpendicular to the Top
of the Mortife; and then the Seed-paffage is higher;
and when it ftands neareft to the Spindle, then the
Seed-paffage is loweft.   This appears in *Fig.* 3. by
the Three prick'd Lines *a n*, *a o*, and *a p*.

The Spindle, with its Notches, is beft fhewn where
it is large, and made of Wood, as that of the Wheat
Seed-box; it is a folid Cylinder that paffes thro', and
fills the great Hole, or hollow Cylinder, of the Seed-
box; it is of various Lengths, according to the
Diftance its Wheels go afunder; it is always in large
Boxes the Axis of Two Wheels, and turns round
with them, as the Axis of the One Wheel of a
Wheelbarrow does with that: Thefe Wheels, by their
Circumferences, meafure out the Ground over which
they carry the Seed-box, and, by the Notches in their
Axis, deliver down the Seed equally, whether they
move fwift or flow; becaufe an equal Number of
Notchfuls of Seed will be deliver'd thro' the Seed-
paffage at each Revolution of the Wheels.

The Notches refemble thofe in the Hinder-Cylinder
of a Cyder-mill, which break the Apples by turning againft the Notches of the Fore-cylinder, as our
Notches turn againft the Tongue; and bruife the Apples which come betwixt them, as our Notches might
fometimes bruife foft Seeds, if the Tongue ftood clofe
to the Notches, without any Spring behind it to give
Way to their Preffure, and return the Tongue again

to its Place, at every Interval betwixt Notch and Notch.

The beſt Way, that I can think of, to ſhew the making of theſe Notches, is by a Section of the Spindle at right Angles, in the Middle of the Notches, as in *Fig.* 4. of *Plate* 3. which is a Circle whoſe Circumference is cut off by Six Notches; which ſhew the different Sort of Notches, that increaſe or diminiſh the Proportion of Seed to be carried thro' the Seed-paſſage by them: The Length of the Notches we never alter; but make them always parallel to the Axis of the Spindle, and of the Length of the Diſtance there is between the lower Ends of the oppoſite *Axes tranſverſi* of the Ellipſes, or great Holes, of the Mortiſe; for if any Part of the Surface of the Spindle ſhould be betwixt the End of a Notch and the Hole, one or more Seeds coming betwixt that Surface and the Tongue, might hold it open, and prevent its preſſing againſt the Notch, to hold the Seed therein from falling without the Turning of the Wheels.

This Proportion of Seed is alter'd by the Number of Notches, and by their Depth or Breadth, or by both. *b c* is the Depth of a Notch, which we call its Side; and is that which takes hold of the Seed, and carries it down thro' the Seed-paſſage. The Manner of cutting this is ſeen by its being a Portion of the *Radius* A *c.* The Bottom of a Notch is made in different Forms (*a*): As, firſt, it may be convex,

as

(*a*) The convex Form is beſt for turning out a great Proportion of Seed; becauſe ſuch a Bottom may be broader than one of any other Form, in a Notch of the ſame Depth and Capacity; and ſuch a Notch, having its Capacity more in Breadth than Depth, will be leſs liable to let fall any Seed without the Turning of the Wheels, than a Notch that is deeper and narrower, except it be very narrow, which it cannot be for throwing out a large Proportion of Seed; for a great Number of Notches cannot have altogether the ſame Capacity as a leſſer Number of the ſame Depth as is fhewn by the curve Line *b d.* We may enlarge the Capacity of this Notch, by taking off the Convexity of its Bottom, as in the Bottom of the Notch fhewn by the Line *e f*; and if we would increafe it more, we make it concave, as *g h.*

But of whatever Sort or Dimenfions one Notch is made, all the reft fhould be the fame exactly; and confequently, the Interftices (or Intervals) between Notch and Notch, of which the Line *f c*, being an Arch of the Circle, is the Breadth, muft be equal *(a)*, and cannot be otherwife, if the Notches are all equal and equidiftant, as they appear in the adjoining *Fig.* 5. which is a Section like the former, and fhews Six Intervals, with their Six Notches, of the Size wherewith we drill St. Foin with high Wheels; but when we would drill very thin, it is better to have but Four or Five Notches inftead of Six.

Fig. 6. fhews a Notch of the Spindle. *a b* is the upper Edge of the Side of the Notch, being always an acute folid Angle. *c d* is the Edge of its Bottom, being always an obtufe Angle. *e f* is the Angle made by the Side and Bottom, and is always fhorter than the aforefaid Two Edges, by reafon of the Obliquity of the Two Ends; this Angle is never obtufe, except when the Bottom of the Notch is concave. Thefe Three Lines muft be parallel to the Axis of the Spindle.

Fig. 7. is one End of the afore-defcribed Notch; the Line *a b* being joined to the Line *f d* of *Fig.* 6.

Depth may. The concave Notch, if it were as broad as the convex may be, would make the Interftice, that is before it, liable to be broken out, and fo Two Notches would become One; but the Convexity of the other fupports the Interftice like an Arch, and for that Reafon may be made to reach almoft quite to the Notch that is before it, without that Danger.

(a) But thefe cannot be equal, unlefs the Notches are all of equal Breadth, and equidiftant from one another; and if they are otherwife, the Seed will not be equalfy delivered to the Ground.

and the Line *a c*, being joined to the Line *b f* in *Fig.* 6. would be the End of that Notch in its proper Posture ; and then the Line *b c*, being an Arch of the cylindrical Spindle, would be the Edge of the upper End of the Notch. *a b c*, being the Area of this End, is a Plane, and, when in its Place, makes an Angle of Forty-five Degrees with the Axis of the Spindle.   The other End is the fame with this in all respects, except that, being opposite to it, it is inclined to it in an Angle of Ninety Degrees, at the bottom Angle of the Notch, at the Line *e f* in *Fig.* 6.

Fig. 8. is a Notch lying with its Ends near it, and is of the fame Dimensions with those appearing in the Seed-box, *Fig.* 3.

The Cover B appears with its upper Surface rightly placed in the Mortise, in *Fig.* 3. of *Plate* 3. where its Breadth is shewn to be the fame with that of the Mortise ; but its Shape, and other Dimensions, are beft feen in *Fig.* 3. of *Plate* 2. where *f t* is its Length, and reaches from the Hinder-end of the Mortise, to within the Tenth of an Inch of the upper End of the *Axis transversus* of the Ellipsis ; its greatest Depth is from *v* to *w*, and is made fo deep, that its Bottom, at *w*, bearing against the End of the Mortise, may prevent its Point, which is at *t*, from finking down to touch the Spindle, which it neither muft do, nor be fo high above it as to fuffer a Seed to pafs between the Spindle and it, tho' the Seed is not apt to pafs that Way, becaufe the Notches throw it forwards from the Cover. *z* is the Hole, thro' which an Iron Screw-pin paffes, and fcrews into the oppofite Sides of the Mortise, to hold it firm in its Place : 'Tis made fo thin betwixt x and *y* both for Lightnefs, and that the Seed may come the more freely to the Notches, without Danger of Arching at that End.   The Ufe of the *Cover* is to prevent any Seed from falling down behind the Spindle.

Fig.

Fig. 10. *Plate* 2. is the Fore-end of a Wheat Mortife, with its Hole A, thro' which the Setting-fcrew is fcrew'd, and paffes up to the Back of the Tongue by the Line *q r* in *Fig.* 3.

Fig. 9. in *Plate* 3. is the hinder End of a Wheat Mortife, which by its prick'd Lines, and the Two right-angled Triangles they make, fhews the Bevel of the Mortife, and alfo its Depth; it alfo fhews the Difference of the Bevel of the Mortife, and that of the Tongue, *Fig.* 1. which is placed againft it: Thefe Figures having been already demonftrated in the Defcription of the Turnep Mortife, and in thefe, I need fay no more of it, but that I think thefe laft-mention'd Figures fufficient Directions for under-ftanding and making the Mortife of a Wheat-drill.

Fig. 3. of *Plate* 3. exhibits to View a Wheat Seed-box, with its Appurtenances, ftanding upon its Bottom; B the Brafs Cover; C the Tongue hanging upon its Axis; *c* the End of the Iron Screw that holds on the Spring, coming thro' the Tongue, and filed fmooth with it; *a, a, a,* are Three Notches of the Spindle, with their bevel Ends; *b, b,* are Two Interftices betwixt the Notches.

Hitherto we have been fpeaking of the Parts contained in the Wheat Seed-box; let us now come to the Parts containing: As, firft, *d e f g* is the upper Surface of the Brafs Seed-box, fhewing the Top of the Mortife, and what it contains; *h h h,* and *h h h,* fhew the Ends of the hollow Cylinder, and its Bafes coming out on each Side, farther than the Box; for if it did not project farther out than the Sides of the Box, the Surface of it would be fo narrow, that it would cut the wooden Spindle by the Friction made between it and the Spindle; but the Surface, being of this Breadth, never wears into the Spindle, but makes it fmooth and fhining; *i i i,* and *i i i,* fhew a Portion of the wooden Spindle (of an Inch and an

Y 4   half

half Diameter) coming out of the hollow Cylinder, on each Side of the Brafs Box.

The Spindle is kept from moving end-ways, by Wreaths, in the fame manner as the Axis of a Wheelbarrow is; which Wreaths fhall be defcribed together with the Hopper. *k* is the Hole by which the Fore-end of the Seed-box is held up to the Bottom of the Hopper, by a Screw and Nut. *l* is the Hole where the Hinder-end of the Box is held up, in the fame manner as the Fore-end is. *m n o p* fhew where the Two Halves of the Seed-box are joined together.

Fig. 10. fhews the Outfide of One Half of the Brafs Seed-box. A A A fhew the Thicknefs of the projecting Bafe of the hollow Cylinder, which is made the thicker, to the end that the Hole may be bored large, and made an Inch and Three Quarters Diameter, when a Spindle that is to go therein is required to be of that Bignefs, by reafon of its extraordinary Length, as it is in the Fore-hopper of the Wheat-drill. B C fhews the Thicknefs of the Ends of the Seed-box, whereby it is held up to the Bottom of the Hopper; if they are not quite a quarter of an Inch thick, they will be ftrong enough; efpecially C, which is the hindermoft, and which is never pull'd down by the Turning of the Spindle, but is rather raifed up by it.

D is the Head of the Counter-fcrew, to be turn'd by the Fingers, to prefs againft the Side of the Setting-fcrew, to keep it from turning of itfelf, when it is worn loofe.

E is the Hole for the Axis of the Tongue. F is the Hole of an Iron Screw-pin, which both holds the Cover to its Place, and alfo the Two Halves of the Box together. G is the Hole for another Screw-pin, which holds the Two Sides of the Box together. H and I are Holes for Two other Screw-pins, which likewife hold the Two Halves of the Box together,

and

and are placed one above, and the other below, the Setting-ſcrew ; for otherwiſe that Screw, and its Counter-ſcrew, might force open the Joining of the Box, and then the Setting-ſcrew might be looſe, and the Bevel of the Box might be altered ; but theſe Screws, being one on each Side of it, prevent this Inconvenience.

Fig. 8. in *Plate* 2. is one Half of a Braſs Turnep Seed-box, lying with its Inſide uppermoſt, which ſhews the left Side of the Mortiſe, and half the Fore-end, and half the Hinder-end, of the Mortiſe, and half of each Screw-pin Hole, by which it is held up to the Bottom of the Hopper. A is half the Hole of the Setting-ſcrew, ſhewing in the Middle of it the End of the Counter-ſcrew. B is half the Hole, by which the Steel Spring-cover is held in with a Screw. All the other Holes are for the ſame Pur-poſes, as have been ſhewn in the Wheat Seed-box.

Fig. 9. is the whole Turnep Seed-box, ſtanding upon its Bottom ; Part of its Steel Spring-tongue appears in its Place, as alſo ſome of the Notches of the Spindle ; but more eſpecially the Cover A, which differs from the Cover of the Wheat Mortiſe, this being a very thin Spring, whoſe lower End juſt reaches to touch (but not to bear upon) the Spindle at the upper End of the tranſverſe *Axes* of the Ellip-ſes ; the Mortiſe being filed away at the End, in order that the upper End of this Spring, and the Screw which holds it, may not lie above the upper Surface of the Box. This Spring is made very weak, to the end that, if by any Chance a ſoft Seed ſhould ſtick in a Notch, and be turned round, this Spring might ſuffer it to paſs by without breaking it. B, C, are the Two Flanks or Sides, made neceſſarily of this Breadth, for bearing againſt the Wood of the Bottom of the Hopper, to prevent the Seed from falling out betwixt the Wood and the Braſs, and that the Hole in the Hopper may be broader than this narrow Mor-

tiſe

tife of the Seed-box. The left Flank B, being next the wide Side of the Hopper, lies all open, except on the outfide of the pricked Lines, where it is covered by the Wood of the End of the Hopper, when it is fcrewed on to its Place ; but the Flanch C, on the right Side, will be all covered by the End of the Box, that will ftand upon it, and will reach to the pricked Line that touches the Edge of the Mortife. D is the End of the Setting-fcrew, appearing in its Place with a Notch, whereby it is to be turned by a Knife ; but I think it better to have an End like a T, to be turned with the Fingers. E is one End of the hollow Cylinder, which projects beyond the Flanch, that there may be more Room for the Crank to turn (without ftriking againft the End of the Hopper, or againft the Flanch) on the Outfide of the Box or Hopper ; and for that, the longer this Cylinder is, the better the Brafs Spindle will turn in it.

Fig. 11. is the Spring-cover, with its Hole, whereby it is fcrewed into its Place, as it is feen marked A, in *Fig.* 9.

Fig. 12. is the Setting-fcrew pointing againft its Hole, its Head being flat, that it may be turned by the Finger and Thumb.

Fig. 13. is the Counter-fcrew, to be turned in the fame manner.

Fig. 5. fhews the Brafs Spindle of the Turnep Seed-box, and the Manner of turning it againft its Steel Tongue, or Spring ; which Manner is different from that of turning the larger Spindles for Boxes of a larger Size, fuch as the Wheat Seed-box.

This Spindle (*a*), being but half an Inch Diameter, is too fmall to be turned by the Two Wheels, as the .

(*a*) I believe, if it were lefs by a Fourth or Third of its Diameter, it might be better, as being more proportionable to the Smalnefs of the Turnep-feed. I have had the Mortife much wider ; but it cannot well be made much narrower, whilft the

Tongue

the larger Spindles are; not only becaufe it would be in Danger of breaking by the Weight of the Hopper, and by the Twifting (or Wrenching) of the Wheels; but alfo becaufe it would foon become loofe, by wearing the hollow Cylinder thro' which it paffes; and it would be apt to open the Brafs Flanches from the Bottom of the Hopper, whereby the Seed might run out, befide feveral other Inconveniencies; all which are prevented by turning the Spindle in the manner fhewn in this Figure; for here the Spindle never preffes againft the hollow Cylinder, with any greater Force than that of its own Weight, which is fo very little, that the Friction made by it is next to nothing.

A the Spindle, exactly fitting the Bore of the hollow Cylinder; which, when it enters the faid Cylinder at its left End, in *Fig.* 9. will be ftopped by the Wreath B B B; which Wreath, being circular, is caft on the Spindle, and is Part of it; the other End of the Spindle will then appear without the right-hand End of the faid hollow Cylinder, at E in *Fig.* 9. and is kept there by the Wreath *Fig.* 14. which is to be put on upon the End of the Spindle, until it come to the Shoulder at *a*, which Shoulder is exactly even with the End of the hollow Cylinder; fo that this Wreath will touch the End of the faid Cylinder by its whole Surface. Then, to fix in this Wreath from coming off, we make ufe of the Slider, *Fig.* 15. whofe Two Claws A, B, being thruft down by the Two Notches of the Spindle, at *b* and *c*, until its other Part

Tongue is of this Fafhion; for this Steel Tongue, if narrower, would either be too ftiff, or elfe apt to break, nor would there be Room in the Mortife for a fufficient Setting-fcrew to follow it. But there is another Fafhion, wherein a narrower Brafs Tongue has a broad Spring behind it; and when it is in this Manner, the Mortife may be a Fourth of the Breadth of this. I have had many of thefe when I made my Boxes in Wood; but cannot defcribe them by thefe Cuts; neither are fuch narrow Mortifes neceffary, unlefs it were for drilling Tobacco feed, Thyme-feed, or fome other Sort of an extraordinary Smalnefs.

C₃

C, which is perpendicular to its Claws, comes down to the Flat of the Spindle, and environs one half of the Hole, covering the Part of the Flat which appears of a darker Colour; and then the upper Part of C, in *Fig.* 15. makes one level Surface with the Flat D of the Spindle; and then the Iron Fork E., being screwed into the Hole F, holds down the Slider faſt, ſo that it cannot riſe up; and then the Spindle, being in its Place, will run round without moving endways, being confined by theſe Wreaths.

The Spindle being thus placed, ſo that it may turn eaſily, we place the Seed-box upon its Flanches with its Bottom upwards; and then ſetting one ſharp Point of a Pair of Compaſſes, or ſome ſuch Inſtrument, upon the Spindle, within the Mortiſe, cloſe to the Edge of the Hole or Ellipſe at the End of the tranſverſe Ax, turn round the Spindle, until the ſaid Point makes a Mark round the Spindle, which will be a Circle; by the ſame means make ſuch another Mark at the oppoſite Ax; then unſcrew the Fork, and take out the Slider, pull off the Wreath, and take out the Spindle, and cut the Notches between the Two ſaid Circles and Marks; the Edges of the Ends of the Notches muſt be Arches of theſe Circles. Theſe Notches ſhould differ from thoſe already deſcribed in the Wheat-drill, in nothing but the Smalneſs of their Dimenſions; their Depth ſhould be about the Thickneſs of a Turnep-ſeed, or ſomething deeper. The Breadth of their Bottoms is uncertain, and muſt be greater or leſs according to their greater or leſs Number; but we commonly have Seven or Eight Notches, and make them about the Breadth in which they appear in this Figure; but whatever their Number be, they muſt be all equal, and ſo muſt all their Interſtices.

G is the End of a wooden Spindle, thro' which paſſes the Iron Crank H. and is faſtened to it by its Screw and Nut, at *d*; Part of which Crank enters the

the Wood at *e*, which prevents its Turning in the Spindle.

This Crank, by its other End, paffing thro' the Two Legs of the Fork E, and equally diftant from the Top and Bottom of it, turns the Spindle by the Motion of the Wheel which is fixed on the other End of the wooden Spindle. If this Crank were to turn the Spindle by a fingle Pin, inftead of this Fork, the Seed could never be delivered out equally to the Ground; for as foon as the Pin began to defcend, and decline from being perpendicular to the Horizon, it would, by its own Weight falling down, turn the Spindle half round in a Moment, and there remain with its other End downwards perpendicular to the Horizon under the Spindle, until the Crank reached it there, and fo no Seed would be turned out by one Semicircle of the Wheel, and a double Proportion would be turned out to the Land that was meafured by the other Semicircle; but the hinder Leg of the Fork, bearing againft the hinder Part of the Crank, prevents this Inconvenience.

The Line *f g* is Part of the Surface of a Board, thro' which the wooden Spindle paffes, and by which it is held in its Place; as fhall be fhewn hereafter.

The Axis of this wooden Spindle ought to fall into a Line with the Axis of this Brafs Spindle; but, unlefs Care be taken to prevent it, the wooden Spindle will fo much wear the Hole thro' which it paffes, and be worn by it, as to have Room in the Hole to deviate from this Exactnefs, and may defcend fo low, that the Crank may come out of the Ends of the Fork; and for this Reafon it is, that the Fork is made fo long as it is; but when this wooden Spindle does, by the Contrivances hereafter fhewn, keep its Axis in a Line with the Axis of the Brafs Spindle, or very nearly fo, then the Legs of the Fork need be no longer than half an Inch; and in that Cafe, the Joint of the Crank, which is perpendicular to the

Spindle,

Spindle, muſt be ſhorter, or elſe deſcend deeper into the Wood, ſo that its End, which turns the Fork, may be in the Middle betwixt its Bottom and the End of its Legs.

The Uſe of the other End of the Spindle is this: When we have a mind that it ſhould be turned by the left Wheel inſtead of the right, we ſcrew in the Fork into the Hole I, and place a ſhort Screw in the room of the Fork, to hold down the Slider.

Note, It is not abſolutely neceſſary, that the hollow Cylinder, which appears on the Sides of the Seed-box, ſhould both, or either of them, project farther than the Flanches; but I think it better that it ſhould do ſo, at leaſt, on that Side which is next to the Fork.

This Cylinder ſhould be bored as true, and as even, as the Barrel of a Fuſil is bored: and the Edges and Surfaces of its Ends muſt be ſmooth, and without Jaggs, to the end that the Wreaths may turn glibly againſt them.

The Figure or Shape of all Sorts of Seeds diſpoſes them, more or leſs, to form an Arch, when they are preſſed from above, and confined on all Sides.

The moſt effectual Way to prevent this is, to take care, whenever many Seeds are to deſcend together by their own Gravity thro' a narrow Paſſage, that ſuch Paſſage be never narrower downwards than upwards; but, on the contrary, that it be wider downwards, on ſome or one of its Sides; in which Caſe, if the Surfaces of all the Sides of this Paſſage be ſmooth, it is impoſſible, that Seeds ſhould of themſelves form an Arch therein.

On this Maxim depends the infallible Performance of a Drill, and from hence are derived the Uſes of the Bevel of the Mortiſe: What I mean by the Word Bevel, in general, has been already defined.

The Bevel of the Mortiſe of the Seed-box is that Inclination of its Sides, whereby it is wider downwards,

wards, and narrower upwards; by which means the Seed is prevented from arching in the Mortife before it defcends to the Notches of the Spindle.   And this is the Firft Ufe of our Bevel; for this Arching might happen in the Mortife, if the Planes of its Sides were parallel to each other; and would be unavoidable, if their Inclination were downwards, as it is upwards; but thefe Planes opening downwards, the lower the Seed defcends, the more Room it has to expand; fo that the very Weight, which would otherwife caufe it to arch and ftop, does by means of this Bevel force it to defcend to the Notches, and then it is fafe from all manner of Danger of ftopping.   The Ends of the Mortife are at fuch a great Diftance from each other, and the Cover fo very thin, as to lie almoft even with the upper Part of the Spindle, that the Seed can never form an Arch that way; or, if it did, the continual Motion of the Tongue would immediately break it down at the Fore-end of the Mortife.

The Second Ufe of this Bevel is, that it gives room for the Tongue to be in the fame manner bevel, tho' in a lefs Degree: By this means, the Seed cannot by any Impediment be ftopped in its oblique Defcent to the Notches, from the Fore-end, and all that other Length of the Mortife, along and upon the Surface of the Tongue.

But if the Mortife had not this Bevel, the Tongue could not have it; for then either the upper Surface of the Tongue muft have no Bevel at all, which would deftroy the Two empty Triangles which ought to be on its Sides; or elfe it muft have a Bevel the contrary Way (*i. e.* a Bevel reverfed), and be narrower downwards than upwards, which would caufe the Seed to arch thereon, and hinder its free Defcent to the Notches.

A Third great Ufe of this Bevel is, that, befides the Bevel of the Tongue aforementioned, it gives place for Two empty Triangles, one on each Side the Tongue,

Tongue, which have each its vertical Angle extremely acute at the Axis of the Tongue, and have their Bases at the Bottom of the Mortife, and of the Tongue: These Triangles are also Bevels, which confist of the Difference, or Complement, of the Bevel of the Tongue, and that of the Mortife, the latter being about One-third greater than the former; *i. e.* One-third of the whole Bevel of the Mortife is divided between these Two Triangles, to each a Sixth Part; so that if the Angle of Inclination of the Sides of the Mortife were Nine Degrees, then the vertical Angle of each of these empty Triangles would be of One Degree and Thirty Minutes, and Six Degrees, would be left for the Bevel of the Tongue. And these triangular Spaces help to secure the free Motion of the Tongue, and free Defcent of the Seed down its Surface; because they permit no Impediment to lodge in them, they being, by means of the Bevel of the Mortife, wider downwards, both obliquely and perpendicularly, fo that no Duft, nor whatever elfe happens to get in betwixt the Tongue and the Side of the Mortife, can reft there; for it will be immediately removed thence by the Motion of the Tongue, and its own Gravity, and either thrown perpendicularly down, or elfe obliquely to the Notches, and the firft Notch that takes it will carry it out at the Seed-paffage.

The Fourth Ufe of the Bevel is, that thereby the Sections of the hollow Cylinder (before defcribed) do form Ellipfes inftead of Circles; which they muft have been, if cut parallel to the Bafes of that Cylinder; and the Sections muft have been thus parallel, had the Mortife been without any Bevel.

Now the Two Semi-ellipfes, which are on the Fore-fides of their longeft Axes or Diameters, and next to the Tongue, are oppofite to, and do ftill uniformly depart from each other, even from the upper End of their faid longeft Axis, until they

arrive

arrive at the lower End of the fame Axis, which is below the Seed-paffage, as its upper End is very near the Cover.

This Opening of thefe oppofite Semi-ellipfes makes it impoffible for any thing, of itfelf, to get into the remaining Parts of this hollow Cylinder, betwixt them and the folid Cylinder, call'd the Spindle, which turns continually therein, when the Wheels are going: For you will fee, that if you make a Mark on the Spindle, clofe to the Side of the Mortife, at the upper End of the longeft Ax of the Ellipfe; and then turn the Spindle until this Mark come againft the lower End of the fame Ax; and there make another Mark on the Spindle, clofe to the Side of the Mortife; and draw a Line from one Mark to the other, parallel to the Ax of the Spindle, which will be the Meafure of that Part of the Bevel of the Diameter of the Hole; every Point in this Line will, by an intire Revolution of the Spindle, generate a Circle, which will cut the Ellipfe in Two Places, once on the Forefide of its longeft Axis, and once on the Back-fide or hinder Half of it; and that all thefe Points, in this Surface of the Spindle, defcribed by thefe Circles, will enter the Hole, by the faid hinder Semi-ellipfe, as the Spindle there turns upwards (as it always does); and they will all again come out on the fore Semi-ellipfe, as they defcend towards the lower End of the faid Ax of the Ellipfe.

As thefe Points thus come out of the Hole, or (if I may ufe the Expreffion) as they emerge, they oppofe every thing that would enter the Hole, they ftill moving from the Hole, and pufh away from it whatever they meet; nay, if any thing were in the Hole, thefe Points (whereof this Surface confifts) would bring it out by this Semi-ellipfe, which is always prefs'd by the Seed when the Drill is at Work; but as thefe Points immerge by the other Semi-ellipfis which is behind the Spindle, they can carry with

them

them into the Hole nothing but Air, becaufe the Cover never fuffers any thing elfe to come there from
above; and the Seed falls out of the Notches by its
own Gravity, juft before it reaches the lower End of
the tranfverfe Ax, being the Place where the oppofite
Ellipfes are fartheft afunder; and none of it is ever
carried fo far back as the hinder Semi-ellipfes; and
therefore nothing can be carried into the Hole from
below.

Thus that Part of the Surface of the Spindle will
keep the Hole empty and clear, before ever any
Notches are cut; but when the Notches are made on
the Spindle, they have yet a much greater Force to
drive and expel whatever would enter the Hole, their
Shape being fuch as nothing can enter againft their
bevel Ends; but what is at their Ends will be thrown
prefently into the Mortife; infomuch that when a
Spindle has been too little for the Hole by a Quarter
of an Inch, that is, a fixth Part of the Diameter of
the Hole, it will perform very well in drilling large
Species of Seeds; and when the Mortife is run empty,
nothing at all is found in the Hole, it being thus
kept void and clean by the Notches.

Note, That what is here, and elfewhere, faid of
the Ellipfe of the one Side of the Mortife, muft be
underftood the fame of its oppofite Ellipfe, on the
oppofite Side of the Mortife.

All thefe Advantages accruing from this Bevel of
the Mortife, I believe that, without it, all Attempts
of making a Machine to perform the Work, which this
does, would have been vain.

There is alfo within the Mortife unavoidably another Bevel, which is as the Reverfe of the former,
and notwithftanding is as ufeful; and this Bevel is,
the Inclination which Part of the curvilineal Surface of
the Spindle, beginning a little above the fore End of
the fhorteft Diameter of the Ellipfes, and defcending
down to the Seed-paffage, has to the lower Part of
the

the Surface of the Tongue oppofite againft it. Thefe Two Surfaces meeting one another below, when the Tongue is fet up clofe to the Spindle, form a mix'd Angle, which ftops up the Seed-paffage, except when a Notch comes againft it.

When the Tongue is fet from the Spindle, to the Diftance of feveral Diameters of one of the Seeds that are to be drill'd, this revers'd Bevel caufes the Seed to arch at the Seed-paffage, and ftop there, till the Notches force it thro', which would, without this Arching, fall out by its own Gravity, without the Turning of the Wheels.

The Seed arches here the more firmly, the more it is prefs'd upon by the incumbent Seed from above it; and the former Bevel (which I call the Bevel of the Mortife) permits the incumbent Weight to prefs the harder on the Seed that is near the Seed-paffage; and this might be reckon'd a fifth Ufe of the former Bevel : For as it prevents the Seed from arching in any other Part of the Mortife, fo it does, by the fame means, caufe it to arch the more ftrongly at the Seed-paffage, which is fometimes (*viz.* when the Tongue muft be fet wide) as neceffary, as it is for it to efcape arching before it comes thither. And the more ftrongly this Arch preffes againft the Tongue, the more the Tongue by its Spring preffes againft it ; and this Preffure being reciprocal and equal, the Seed cannot fall out fpontaneoufly; for when the Paffage is thus wide, if you throw into the Mortife a few Seeds, fuppofe Five or Six at a time only, they will all pafs through immediately, without any Motion of the Wheels; but if you throw in a large Quantity together, there will only a few of the lowermoft fall through, unlefs the Wheels do turn and throw them down by the Force of the Notches.

Indeed we do not care to fet the Tongue fo very wide from the Spindle, unlefs it be when we are obliged to plant a very much larger Proportion of Seed

than

than the Notches are defign'd for, and when we have no Opportunity of changing the Wheels for such as are lower, nor of changing the Spindle for another that has greater or more Notches in it.

Four-and-twenty Gallons of large Peas are as proper a Proportion to drill on an Acre, as Six Gallons of Wheat are.

There are divers Ways to vary (*i. e.* increase or diminish) the Proportion of Seed; as, Firft, by the Setting-screw, with which we can, without any Inconveniency, set the Tongue so far from the Spindle, as to permit one Round of the Notches to turn out Four times the Quantity, as it will do when the Tongue is set close up to the Spindle; and thus we can vary the Proportion by innumerable intermediate Degrees.

Next, if we would increase the Proportion yet farther, we can inlarge the Notches; but we cannot add to their Number, unlefs there be room to double it, by making a new Notch between every Two; but we cannot diminish the Proportion of Seed by the fame Notches, becaufe they cannot be made lefler or fewer.

If we would make any other Alteration in the Proportion of Seed by the Notches, it muft be done by making another Set of them; which we may do, becaufe the wooden Spindle may have Three Rows of Notches in it, of which we may ufe either, by moveing the Wreaths and Wheels towards one End or the other of the wooden Spindle; as fhall be fhewn in the Defcriptions of the Hoppers.

But as for the Brafs Spindle of the Turnep-drill, we can have but one Set of Notches in it *(a)*: And there-

---

(a) But by putting on a Wreath (that is a little broader than the Mortife) upon the Spindle (made longer for that Purpofe) we can, by changing this Wreath from one End of the Spindle to the other, have Two fets of Notches of different Sizes, and of different

therefore, tho' we can increafe the Proportion of Seed by enlarging the Notches, or perhaps by doubling their

different Numbers in it : Or if we would have Three Sets, we need only make Ufe of Two fuch Wreaths, and let the Spindle be long enough to receive them.   So we may ufe which Set we pleafe.

Tho' feveral Sets of Notches may be ufeful to thofe who drill many Sorts of fine Seeds different in Magnitude in a very great Degree; yet I never found more than one Set of Notches neceffary in this Spindle.

Nor have I ufed any more than one Set of Notches in one Mortife of any Sort; but in a wide Mortife, there may be made a double Set of Notches, confifting of Two Rows, all of equal Bignefs, and half of the Length, and double the Number of a fingle Row, one End of each Notch reaching to the Middle of the Mortife, and pointing againft the End of an Interftice, that is between Two of its oppofite Notches.

If ever there fhall be Occafion for this Sort of Notches, it muft be when a great Proportion of Seed is to be drill'd by a fmall Spindle, and low Wheels : The Smalnefs of the Spindle may not, by a fingle Set, admit of a fufficient Number of Notches (of a proper Bignefs) in its Circumference; not that a double Set, by its double Number, will throw down a greater Quantity of Seed than a fingle Set of the fame Width and Depth, but a lefs Quantity : But it may be feared, that a very fmall Number of Notches might not fpread the Seed fo much as to caufe it to lie even in the Chanels, one Notchful falling all to the Ground, before any of the next Notchful reaches it, which would make Chafms or Gaps in the Row of Corn or Legumes: This, fuch a double Number of Notches will certainly prevent.

It would feem, that the higher the Wheels, the more need there fhould be for this double Set of Notches : But it appears to be otherwife ; for the greater Diftance the Seed has to fall, the more it fpreads, and ftrikes oftener againft the Funnel and Trunk; and by that means a Notch from high Wheels will, with the fame Quantity of Seed, fupply a greater Length of the Chanel (or Furrow) than a Notch will from low Wheels.

In all my Practice I never had any Occafion for fuch a double Set of Notches, either with high or low Wheels, or even when I drilled into open Chanels, without Funnels or Trunks to my Drill-plough ; and yet my Rows of St. Foin, and of Corn, were always free from Gaps, being equally fupply'd with Seed from one End to the other.

If ever there is Occafion for more than a fingle Set, it muft be for Beans, for which alfo I think a large Spindle is better than a

double

their Number; yet we cannot leſſen the Proportion of Seed by the Notches, unleſs we have a new Set of them, and that will occaſion a Neceſſity of having another Spindle; but, as to the Setting-ſcrew of the Turnep-drill, it will increaſe the Proportion of Seed with the ſame Notches, much more than the Setting-ſcrew of the Wheat-drill will do.

The other Way of varying the Proportion of Seed in the ſame Boxes, is by the Diameter of the Wheels, when we can alter them; for Wheels, of what Diameter ſoever they are, muſt turn round all the Notches at one Revolution; ſo that Wheels of Twenty Inches Diameter will deliver out a third Part more Seed than Wheels of Thirty Inches Diameter, into the ſame Length of the Chanels; but we ſeldom have any Occaſion to alter the Wheels, unleſs it be on account of planting a Species of Seed of a different Magnitude, as the largeſt Sort of Peas, and ſmall-grain'd Wheat, or St. Foin Seed are.

Theſe are all the Ways we have to alter the Proportion of Seed, we drill with the ſame Seed-boxes;

double Set of Notches in a ſmall one one. The largeſt Spindle I have known made, is of Two Inches and an half Diameter, and that only for Horſe-Beans.

The beſt Sort of Notches for a double Set are thoſe which have convex Bottoms; becauſe ſuch are leſs liable to drop their Seeds without the turning of the Wheels, than any other Sort: And a double Set muſt be in greater Danger of this, as the Tongue is always hindered from preſſing ſo cloſely againſt any Notch, being held open by the Seeds on the oppoſite Interſtice; which is contrary to a ſingle Set, where no Seed can lodge at either End of a Notch, to hold open the Tongue, or hinder its preſſing againſt it.

Note, When I made my Boxes of Wood, I had double Boxes, with a Partition between ſuch a double Set of Notches; but never made ſuch in Braſs, not knowing whether that Partition, by its Thinneſs of hard Metal, might not cut the Spindle: Yet I never found any Occaſion for a double Row of Notches. I made thoſe double Boxes only for drilling Two Sorts of Seeds at once into the ſame Chanel.

theſe

thefe Two Sizes, already defcribed, being fufficient
for all Sorts of Corn and Seeds which we commonly
fow, from Marrow-peas to Turnep-feed; but, for
drilling of Beans, the Boxes muft be larger, and are,
commonly made of Wood, the Spindle Two Inches
Diameter, or more, and the Boxes Two Inches wide :
Where note, That this Increafing of the Width of
the Mortife, from an Inch and an half, to Two Inches,
increafes the Quantity of Seed to almoft double; becaufe this Half Inch is all added to the Middle of the
Notches, where they are deeper than their Ends; the
Bevel of which takes up a confiderable Part of the
Length of the Notches.   For Beans, they alfo contrive to have their Wheels as low as conveniently they
can. Thefe Wooden Drills are now become common
in many Places.

The Wooden and Brafs Seed-boxes differ not in
any of the moft effential Parts of them ; only the
Wooden Box muft be thicker, as the Wood is not fo
ftrong as Brafs ; the Spring is made ftrait inftead of
crooked ; and, being let into the Back of the Wooden
Tongue, bears againft it at each End; and the Chanel,
into which it is placed, being made hollow in the
Middle, the Spring has its Play there, and muft be
ftiffer and have a little more Play in the Bean-drill,
than in any leffer Seed-box.

I, at firft, made all my Seed-boxes of dry Box-
tree Wood, which performed very well, and are ftill
ufed: But, a few Years ago, a Gentleman advifed me
to make them in Brafs ; the doing of which has put
me to a great deal of Trouble and Expence, for want
of underftanding the Founder's Art: Yet this I do not
repent, becaufe they are, in fome refpect, better than
thofe made in Wood; efpecially to thofe who do not
well underftand their Fabric; for, to fuch, the Swelling and Shrinking of the Wood was inconvenient
in fmall Boxes : And I now am told, that they are
caft in *London* of the beft Brafs, at the Price of One

Z 4   Shilling

Shilling *per* Pound, and fo fmooth as to require very little filing. And thefe Brafs Boxes being alfo more lafting than Wood, and not much more expenfive, when Workmen know how to make them, I think it not worth while to give any particular Directions for making them in Wood.

As to the Spindles of the Turnep-boxes, I have often made them with a mix'd Metal, of half Pewter, and half Spelter, which perform very well, and are eafily made; becaufe this Metal will melt, almoft as foon as Lead, in a Fire-fhovel, to be caft in a Mould; but Brafs will not melt without a Crucible.

The firft Idea that I form'd of this Machine, was thus: I imagin'd the Mortife, or Groove, brought from the Sound-board of an Organ, together with the Tongue and Spring, all of them much alter'd; the Mortife having an Hole therein, and put on upon one of the Iron Gudgeons of the Wheelbarrow; which Gudgeon being enlarg'd to an Inch and an half Diameter, having on it the Notches of the Cylinder of a Cyder-mill, on that Part of it which fhould be within the Mortife, and this Mortife made in the Ear of the Wheelbarrow (thro' which the Gudgeon ufually paffes), made broad enough for the Purpofe; this I hoped, for any thing I faw to the contrary, might perform this Work of Drilling; and herein I was not deceived.

As for placing a Box over this Mortife to carry a fufficient Quantity of Seed, it was a thing fo obvious, that it occafion'd very little Thought; and an Inftrument for making the Chanels, not much more; neither for applying Two Wheels, one at each End of the Axis, inftead of the fingle Wheel in the Middle of the Axis of the Wheelbarrow.

At firft my Plough made open Chanels, and was very rude, being compofed of Four rough Pieces of Planks, of little Value, held together by Three Shoots, or Pieces of Wood, which held them at a Foot Diftance

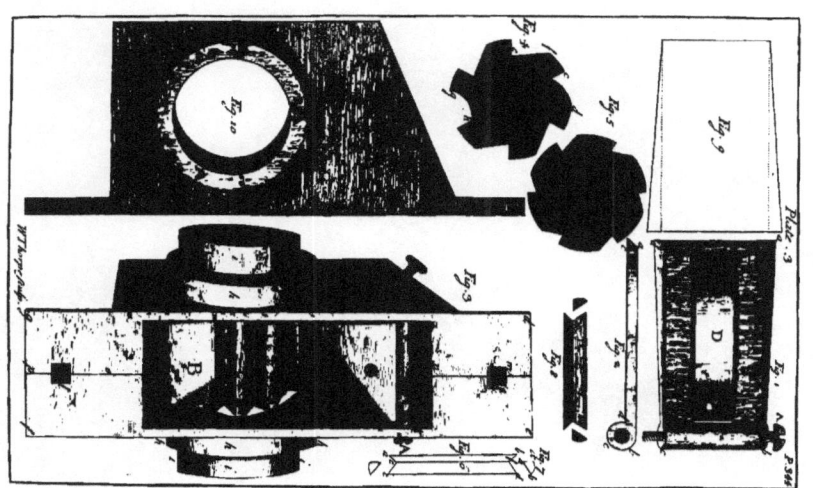

Plate 3

Fig. 2

Fig. 3

Fig. 4

Fig. 5

Fig. 6

Fig. 7

Fig. 8

Fig. 9

Fig. 10

Fig. 1

P. 344

ftance one from the other : Thefe Pieces, being cut
fharp at Bottom, made the Chanels tolerably well in
fine Ground. But I foon contrived a Plough with
Four Iron Shares, to make Chanels in any Ground :
This drew a Hopper after it, having Four Seed-boxes
at its Bottom, carried on a Spindle by Two low
Wheels, which had Liberty to rife and fink by the
Clods that they pafs'd over : The Seed-boxes delivered
their Seed immediately into the open Chanels.

This Plough and Hopper were drawn by an Horfe,
and the Seed, lying open in the Chanels, was covered
fometimes by a very light Harrow, and fometimes by
an Hurdle ftuck with Bufhes underneath it.

I foon improv'd this Plough to perform better,
and to make Six Chanels at once, and fometimes a
great many more.

This Plough and Hopper, with their Improvements and Alterations, are fhewn in *Plates* 4. and 5.

C H A P. XXI,

Of the *Wheat-Drill.*

*F*IG. 1. in *Plate* 4. is the Drill-plough, which makes
the Chanels for a treble Row of Wheat, at
Seven-inch Partitions, and covers the Seed by the
Harrow which moves on its Beams. A, is the Plank,
Three Feet and an half long, Eight Inches and an
half broad, one Inch and a quarter thick ; its upper
and under Surfaces are true Planes. B, B, the Two
Beams, each Two Feet Four Inches long, Two Inches
Three quarters broad, and Two Inches and a quarter
deep, ftanding under the Plank at right Angles with
it, and held up to it by the Four Screws and Nuts
$a, a, a, a,$ the one being at the fame Diftance from
the

the right, as the other is from the left End of the Plank.

This Plough makes its Chanels by Three Sheats, and their Shares and Trunks; the First or Foremost of which Sheats stands under the Middle of the Plank, with Part of it appearing at *b*; and is fully describ'd in *Fig.* 2, where A is the Tenon, of a convenient Size, Two Inches broad between Shoulder and Shoulder, Three quarters of an Inch thick: It is driven into the Plank thro' a Mortise, and pinn'd up by its Hole: It stands thus obliquely, and pointing forwards, that it may stand the more out of the Way of the Funnel. The Shoulder at *a* is a quarter of an Inch. The hinder Shoulder, from the Tenon to the Angle at *b*, is Three quarters of an Inch. The Depth of the Back of the Sheat, and Thickness of the Share, when it is on, from *b* to *c*, is Nine Inches and a quarter; and the Angle at *c* must be a right Angle, contrary to the Opinion of some, who fansy it ought to be acute, supposing that when this Angle is right, whilst the Seed is descending by the Back of the Sheat, the Plough, as it moves forwards, would get before the Seed, and so it might fall to the Ground behind the Trunk; but this Mistake is for want of considering the vast Disproportion between the Celerity of the Seed's descending near the Earth, and the slow Progress of the Plough; the Seed descending at the Rate of Sixteen Feet in a Second of Time, and the Plough proceeding but about Three Miles an Hour, does not advance the Thickness of a Seed, whilst it is falling to the Ground by the whole Depth of the Sheat.

The Thickness of the Sheat is an Inch, at its upper Part. The rest of it is to be no thicker than the Breadth of the Share.

Fig. 3. is the Share, lying Bottom upwards. *a* is its Point. *b* the Socket, Three Inches long, Seven Sixteenths of an Inch broad. *c* is the Hole, by which it is fastened up to the Sheat. *d* is another Hole, which is never made use of, except when the Share,

being

being faften'd up by the other Hole, inclines to either Side; then we draw it right by a Nail driven into this Hole. *e, e,* are Two very fmall Notches, into which the Sides of the Trunk are jointed, to protect them from being torn out by the Earth or Stones that might rub againft them. *f* is the Tail of the Share, which, when it is in its Place, will make the right Angle before defcribed in *Fig.* 2. and from which Tail, to the Forepart of the Socket, is the Length of the Bottom of the Sheat, *viz.* Six Inches and an half. The Breadth of the Share Three quarters of an Inch.

Fig. 4. fhews one Side of the Share. The prick'd Line *a e* fhews the Bevel of the Fore-end of the Socket, the upper Edge of which muft bear upon the Fore-part of the Sheat below *f* in *Fig.* 2. and the other Part of the Share will bear againft the Bottom of the Sheat, from *d* to *c,* and will be faftened up by a flat Nail, paffing thro' the foremoft Hole of the Share, and entering the Hole *g* in the Sheat; which Nail being bended in the faid Hole (which Hole fhould be at leaft an Inch Diameter) will hold the Share faft to the Sheat ; and, by unbending this Nail, the Share may be eafily taken off, upon Occafion, without damaging the Sheat. *Note,* This Hole in the Share ought to be wider below than above, and the Head of the Nail of the fame Shape; or elfe, as the Share wears thinner, it might come off. The prick'd Line, near the Fore-part of the Sheat, fhews where a Shoulder muft be cut on each Side of it, becaufe otherwife the Sheat, being thicker than the Breadth of the Socket of the Share, could not enter it : But take care, that the Share do not bear againft thefe Shoulders.

Fig. 5. is one Side of the Trunk, being a thin Plate of Iron, and is often made of the Blade of an old Scythe : It is to be riveted on to one Side of the Sheat, to another of the fame on the oppofite Side, by Three Rivets paffing thro' them both, with the Sheat in the Middle of them ; which Holes appear
both

both in the Plate and in the Sheat. Thefe thus riveted on do form the Trunk at the Back of the Sheat.
The whole Breadth of this Plate is an Inch and
Three quarters ; but Three-eighths of an Inch being
riveted on to the Sheat, there remains but an Inch
and Three-eighths for the Trunk. The Length of
the Plate is the fame with the Depth of the Sheat
and Share, except that it fhould not reach to the Bottom of the Share, by about the Thickneſs of a Barley-
corn, to the end that it may not bear againſt the
Ground, as the Share doth. The Notch at the Bottom of the Plate is that which anſwers the Notch in
the Tail of the Share : The Corner of the Plate at
a we make a little roundiſh, that it may not wear
againſt the Ground.

This Plate thus riveted on the Sheat, and another of
the fame Form on the other Side oppofite to it, compofe the Trunk, which is *Fig. 6. a d* is the Edge *a b* of
the Plate *Fig. 5. b c* is the like Edge of the oppofite
Side of the Trunk. A is the Back of the Sheat,
which, together with the Tail of the Share when in its
Place, makes the Fore-part or Length of the Trunk.
The Thickneſs of this Back of the Sheat is the Width
of the Trunk ; and from this Back of the Sheat to
the faid Edges of the Plates, may be call'd the Depth
of the Trunk. The upper Ends of thefe Two Plates
a and *b* we fpread open a quarter of an Inch wider,
for half an Inch down, than the reft of the Trunk,
for the more free Reception of the Seed from the
Hole of the Funnel : We likewife take care, that the
Two lower hinder Concerns of the Trunk do not incline to one another, to make the Trunk narrower
than the Back of the Sheat, left the Earth fhould be
held in by them, and fill the Bottom of the Trunk.

Fig. 7. is one of the hinder Sheats, and appears,
in part, at *c* in *Fig. 1.* It is faftened into one of the
Beams by its Tenon, which, being driven into a Mortife, is pinn'd in by a Pin paffing thro' the Beam, and
the

the Tenon cut off even with the upper Surface of the Beam: This Tenon ftands more oblique than that of the fore Sheat, that there may be the more Wood between its Mortife and the Funnel, its hinder Shoulder being fhort: Its fore Shoulder at *a* muft be very fhort, not above the Eighth of an Inch; but its Shoulder *b* Three quarters of an Inch. The Tenon is alfo fhoulder'd on each Side, as well as before and behind. The Thicknefs of this Sheat fhould be greater than that of the Fore-fheat, becaufe it is much narrower. The Depth of this Sheat, is lefs than the Fore-fheat, by the Depth of the Beam: It is, in all other refpects, the fame with the Fore-fheat, except that it and its Share are fhorter. The Socket of this Share is but an Inch and One-eighth long, its Breadth half an Inch, and from the Fore-part of the Bottom of the Socket to the End of its Tail, but three Inches. Its Point from the Socket at Bottom is but Three quarters of an Inch, whereas the Point of the Fore-fhare is an Inch and Three quarters: There is but one Hole whereby the Share is faftened up to the Sheat. Its Trunk is no wider than the other; for we cut a Rabbet on each Side of the Sheat, that the Plates, which are the Sides of the Trunk, may come within Three quarters of an Inch of one another. Its Tenon, being narrower than the Tenon of the Fore-fheat, muft be thicker than it.

The other Hinder-fheat, and all its Accoutrements, muft be the fame as this of *Fig.* 7.

The Workman muft take care, that the Tenons of the Sheats be not made crofs the Grain of the Wood; and therefore muft make them of crooked Timber.

Fig. 8. fhews how the Share is made of Four Pieces; of which *a* is a Piece of Steel for the Point, its larger End being cut bevel for the Shape of the Fore-end of the Socket. *b* is a Piece of Iron for the other End of the Share, from the Socket to the Tail: The other Two Pieces *c* and *d* are the Iron Sides, which, being

welded

v

welded on to the other Two Pieces, and cut off to
the Length, form the Share, with its Socket, more
exact than it can be made out of one Piece of Iron.

Now we return to the firft Figure ; where the Fore-
sheat being fix'd up at equal Diftance from each End
of the Plank, and as near to the hinder Edges of it
as can be, allowing room for the Funnel C to ftand
with the Fore-fide of its Hole, to make one Surface
with the Back of the Sheat, and for the hinder Part
of the Trunk not to reach the Edge of the Plank,
there muft be alfo room for the Fore-ftandard D to
ftand perpendicular to the Plank, acrofs the Tenon of
the Sheat.

This Standard being clofe to the Fore-fide of the
fore Hopper, there muft be fo much room between
it and the Hole of the Funnel, that the Seed may drop
from the Seed-box into the Middle of this Hole.
Thus much for placing the Fore-fheat.

Next, for the Two hinder Sheats ; they muft be
placed at equal Diftance from the Sides of the Beams,
and fo near to the hinder Ends of the Beams, that
there may be room to make the Funnels in them, and
their Tenons to come up between their refpective
Funnels E and F, and their refpective Standards G and
H, which Standards muft be fet perpendicular to the
Beams.

The Diftance of thefe Sheats from the Plank muft
be fuch, that the Wheels of the hinder Hopper may
not ftrike againft the Plank, nor againft the Spindle
of the fore Hopper ; and the Semidiameters of thefe
Wheels being Eleven Inches, there ought to be a Foot
between the Centre of each Wheel and the Plank ; but
we fometimes cut Notches in the Plank, to prevent
the Circle of the Wheels from coming too near the
Plank.

For the nearer the hinder Sheats ftand to the Plank,
the better ; but thefe Beams may be placed nearer to,
or farther from the Plank, by their Screws and Nuts,
at Pleafure.   Thefe

Thefe Beams muft be fet at fuch a Diftance from one another, that the Shares may be Fifteen Inches afunder from the Infide of one to the Outfide of the other.

To try whether all thefe Sheats and Shares are truly placed, fet the Plough upon a level Surface; and then, if they be right, the Fore-fhare will touch the Surface by its Point and Tail, and likewife the hinder Sheats will do the fame ; except that fome Workmen will have it, that the Plough goes better, when the Tails of the hinder Sheats are a Barley-corn's Thicknefs higher than their Points ; and then their Tails will want fo much of touching the Surface.

The Shares muft be all of them parallel to the Beams, and confequently to one another.

The Chanel made by the fore Share and Sheat for the middle Row, being at equal Diftance between the Two hinder Sheats, is cover'd by them, they raifing the Mould over the Seed from each Side of this Chanel.

The Harrow I is drawn by the Beams, to which it is faftened to their Infides at *d* and *e*, having each a fmall Iron Pin, paffing thro' each End of the Legs of the Harrow, and thro' the Beams ; each having a Nut on the Outfides of the Beams, and being fquare in the Beams, that they may not turn therein to loofen their Nuts ; but are round near their Heads, that the Harrow may eafily move thereon.

The round Ends of the Legs of the Harrow are put thro' its Head I, at the round Holes *f* and *g* ; and pinned in behind it, to the end that either Tine of the Harrow may defcend at the fame time that the other rifes, where the Ground is uneven.

The Two wooden Tines K and L are pinned in above the Head, and have each of them a Shoulder underneath. They ftand floping ; fo that if they take hold of any Clods, they do not drive them before them, but rife over them. They are of a convenient Length,

Length, to give room for the Harrow to fink and rife, without raifing up the Shares ; and to give them the more room to move : The Legs of the Harrow are crook'd downwards in the Middle.

The Diftance of thefe Tines from each other is Twenty-two Inches ; fo that each Tine going Three Inches and an half on the Outfide of each Chanel that is next it, fills it up with Earth upon the Seed, from the Outfides of it ; which caufes the Rows to come up fomething nearer the inner Sides of the Chanels, than to the outer Sides, from whence the Earth is brought into them by the Tines ; and the Two outer Rows by this means come up at Fourteen Inches afunder, tho' the Chanels were Fifteen Inches afunder.

This way of covering adds more Mould to the Top of a Ridge ; whereas, if the Chanels were covered by Tines going within or between them, the Mould would be thrown down from the Top of the Ridge : And thefe Tines ftand with their Edges and Points inclining outwards, by which means they bring in the more Earth to the Chanels.

If we find, that the Harrow is too light, we tie a Stone upon it, to make it heavier ; and fometimes we fix a fmall Box of Board on the Middle of it, to hold Clods of Earth for that Purpofe.

The fore Funnel C has its upper Edges Two Inches high above the Surface of the Plank. It is Five Inches Square at Top ; its Four oppofite Sides being Planes equally inclin'd to each other downwards, until they end at the Hole in the Bottom of the Funnel, which Hole is continued quite thro' the Plank into the Trunk. The Shape of this Hole is fhewn in *Fig.* 9. where the Four Lines $a b$, $b c$, $c d$, and $d a$, each Line being Three quarters of an Inch, make a true Square, and are the upper Edges of the Hole. The Three prick'd Lines $e f$, $f g$, and $g h$, being each of them longer than the former, tho' as little as poffible, make the Three lower Edges of the Hole ; which being

ing thus wider below than above, and having all its Sides true Planes and fmooth, it is impoffible for the Seed to arch therein.   The fore Side of this Hole is perpendicular to the upper and lower Surfaces of the Plank, and, together with the Back of the Sheat, makes one Plane Surface.

When we drill a large Species of Seed, as Peas or Oats, we can make this Hole a full Inch fquare at Top, and of the fame Shape wider at Bottom ; which tho' it be wider than the Trunk, except at its Top, the Seed will not arch there, becaufe there is room behind, the Plates being broader than the Sides of the Hole; for there can be no Arching in the Trunk, unlefs the Seed were confin'd behind as well as on each Side.

The Holes of our Funnels ought to be of the fame Shape with this defcribed; tho', as I am inform'd, the Pretenders to the making of this Plough make the Holes of their Funnels the Reverfe of this; which being wrong-way upwards, the Seed is apt to arch in them, except the Holes are very large.

Of this Plough, *Fig.* 1. the Two hinder Funnels E and F differ from the fore Funnel (which has been defcribed), firft, in Dimenfions ; thefe not being fo deep, becaufe they being made in the very Beams, their upper Edges are in the upper Surface of the Beams, and their Holes at the Bottom, being about the Eighth of an Inch deep.   The Depth of the Funnels muft want the Eighth of an Inch of the Thicknefs of the Beams ; but we make each Funnel an Inch and a quarter broader at Top than its Beam, by adding a Piece of Wood to each Side of its Beam, which reaches down about half-way its Thicknefs ; and thefe Pieces being firmly fix'd on by Nails, to the Sides of each Beam, the Legs of the Harrow take hold of thefe Pieces, which are in the Infide of thefe Beams.   When the Plough is taken up to be turn'd, the Man who turns it takes hold of the

Head of the Harrow with one Hand, and lays the other upon the Hopper, or Spindle, to keep it level, and to prevent either of the fore Wheels from ftriking againft the Ground, whilft the Plough is turning round.

Another Difference there is between the Shape of thefe hinder Funnels from that of the former, to wit, That each fore Side of the hinder Trunks muft not be quite fo oblique as the reft; becaufe then the upper Edge of thefe fore Sides might be too near the Tenons of the Sheats, and there might not be fufficient Wood betwixt them, to prevent the Sheats from being torn out; a thing which has never happen'd, that I know of. We fometimes make thefe hinder Funnels of a roundifh Shape, like a Cone inverted; except that the Part which is next the Sheat, is not fo oblique as the reft, for the Reafon already given.

The only Advantage propofed by this roundifh Shape is, that there is lefs Wood taken out than from the fquare Corners, and therefore more Wood for the added Pieces to be faftened to the Beams, than in the fquare Funnels.

M and N are Two Pieces of Wood, each Eleven Inches long, Two Inches broad, and Two Inches thick: Thefe are fcrew'd on near each End of the Plank, by Two Screws and Nuts each: They ftand parallel to the other Beams, and have each a double Standard or Fork, O and P, in them, perpendicular to the Plank; by which Standards the fore Hopper is drawn and guided, in the manner as is feen in *Fig.* 21.

Thefe Standards ought to be braced (or fpurr'd) before and behind, and on their Outfides; they never being prefs'd inwards, have no occafion of Braces there: Thefe are to be fo placed, that when the Spindle is in their Forks, it may be exactly over the Hole of the Funnel, fo that the Seed may drop into the Middle of it, when the Plough ftands upon an horizontal

6　　　　　　　　　　　Surface,

Surface, the Spindle being alfo exactly parallel to the fore Edge of the Plank.

Fig. 10. is D in the Plough *Fig.* 1. It is Two Feet long, Two Inches broad in its narroweft Part, and half an Inch thick in the thinneft Part, and Two Inches at its Shoulders above the Plank. It is pinn'd thro' the Plank before the Funnel, having one of its Legs on each Side the Tenon of the Sheat : It ftands perpendicular to the Plank : Its only Ufe is to hold the fore Hopper from turning upon the Spindle, being put thro' a thing (*Fig.* 22.) like the Carrier of a Latch, nail'd on to the upper Part of the fore Side of the fore Hopper, in which thing this Standard has room to play, or move fide-ways, to the end that either Wheel may rife up.

Fig. 11. is one of the hinder Standards, which being placed in the Beam, as G or H, perpendicular to it, is driven into a Mortife, and pinn'd into the Beam. It has a Shoulder behind, and another before, and a Third on its Outfide ; which Shoulders ferve inftead of Braces, to keep it from moving backwards, forwards, or outwards : It is Two Feet Four Inches long, Two Inches broad, and an Inch thick : It is placed with its broad or flat Sides towards the Sides of the Beams. It is made fo thin, becaufe it fhould have the more room for the Hopper to play on it ; and therefore muft have its Strength in its Breadth. The Part at *a* muft ftand foremoft.

The Standards G and H are both alike, except as they are oppofite : Their Ufe is to draw, guide, and hold up the hinder Hopper : They are to be placed perpendicular to the Beams, and at equal Diftance from each Side of thofe Beams, and at fuch a Diftance before the Funnels, that when the fore Side of the Hopper by its whole Length bears againft the hinder Surface of the Standards, the Seed may drop into the Middle of both Funnels, the Plough ftanding upon an horizontal Surface.

Be fure to take care, that the Sheats, Funnels, and Standards, be fo placed, that the Spindle of the Hopper may be at right Angles with the Beams.

Q and R Part of the Limbers, which are alfo called Shafts, Sharps, and Thills; from whence the Horfe that goes in them is call'd a Thiller. Thefe Limbers are fcrew'd down to the Plank, by Two Screws and Nuts each. The Limbers are kept at their due Diftance by the Bar S; near each End of which Bar, there is a Staple with a Crook underneath each Limber, to which is hitch'd, or faftened, a Link of each Trace, for drawing the Plough. This Bar is parallel to the Plank, and Seven Inches and an half before its fore Edge.

The Limbers muft be mounted higher or lower at their fore Ends, according to the Height of the Horfe that draws in them; and this may be done by the Screws that hold them to the Plank, and by cutting away the Wood at the Two hinder Screws, or at the Two foremoft Screws, or by Wedges.

Every Workman knows how to team the Limbers; that is, to place them fo on the Plank, that the Path of the Horfe, which goes in the Middle betwixt them, may be parallel to all the Shares, and fo that a Line, drawn in the Middle of this Path, might fall into a ftrait Line with the fore Share, ftanding on the fame even Surface with the Path; for otherwife the Plough will not follow directly after the Horfe, but will incline to one Side.

The Ufe of the Trunks of this Plough is for makeing the Chanels narrow, of whatfoever Depth they are: But, without Trunks, the Chanels muft be made wide by Ground-wrifts, which fpread the Sides of the Chanels wide afunder, to the end that they may lie open for receiving of the Seed; and the deeper they are, the wider they muft be: By this Width of a Chanel, the Seed in it is with more Difficulty cover'd, and the Chanel fill'd with the largeft Clods, and the

Seed

Seed comes up of a great Breadth, perhaps Three or Four Inches wide, so that the Weeds coming therein are hard to be gotten out.

To avoid thefe Inconveniences of wide Chanels, I contrived Trunks like thofe defcribed, except that they were but Five or Six Inches high; and the Tops of their Plates, bending outwards from each other, form'd Two Sides of a Funnel; and the Wood between the Two Plates, being cut bevel at the Top, was as the fore Side of a Funnel to this Trunk: It was open behind from Top to Bottom : The Wheels were low, and the Seed-boxes narrow : The Seed in thefe Chanels was eafily cover'd, efpecially thofe Sorts which were fown in dry Weather; for then the fineft Mould would run in, and cover the Seed, as foon as the Trunks were paft it.

The Seed in fuch a narrow Chanel comes up in a Line, where the Row not being above a Quarter of an Inch broad, fcarce any Weeds come in it; and when the Weather is dry, the Earth of the Chanel not lying open to be dry'd, the Seed comes up the fooner.

I had Two Reafons for making of thefe Trunks higher, as they are now ufed: The one was, to avoid the too great Length of the Shares; and my other Reafon was, that with thofe low Trunks, and long Shares, there could not be Two Ranks of Shares, and their Hoppers in the Plough, which are neceffary for making very narrow Partitions, and abfolutely neceffary for planting this treble Row of Wheat; for if Three Shares for making the Seven-inch Partitions were placed in one Rank, the Mould (which is always moift or wet, when we plant Wheat) would be driven before the Shares, there not being room for it to pafs betwixt them.

Fig. 12. is one End of the hinder Hopper laid open. I call it one End (altho' it be an intire Box by itfelf) becaufe this Hopper is fuppofed to have its middle Part cut out, to have a clearer Sight of the

Plough.

Plough, and fore Hopper; as is feen in *Fig.* 15. which is the whole Hopper in Two Parts.   In this *Fig.* 12, A is the Infide of one End of the Hopper, made with feveral Pieces of half-inch Elm-board nail'd on to the Poft *c a*, on the fore Side; which Poft is a little more than half an Inch fquare, and Seventeen Inches and Three quarters long, being the Depth of that Part of the Hopper which holds the Seed.   B is the fore Side of this Hopper; which muft be nail'd on to the faid Poft, being of the fame Length with it, and Four Inches broad, and half an Inch thick; and this is the Part which on its Outfide goes againft the right-hand Standard of the Plough, when it is at Work.   The other Poft *b d*, of the fame Thicknefs with the former, is nail'd in within half an Inch of the oppofite Edge of this End; to which Poft alfo C being nail'd, makes the hinder Side of this Part of the Hopper.   C is Four Inches broad, and half an Inch thick; and both it, and the Poft to which it is to be nail'd, are fomething longer than its oppofite Side, becaufe the Side B makes right Angles with the Top and Bottom of the Hopper; but the hinder Side C makes oblique Angles with the Top and Bottom of the Hopper; and the Reafon of this is, becaufe when the Hopper is full of Seed, it may be equally pois'd on the Spindle; which it could not be without this Bevel, unlefs the Bottom of the Hopper did come as much behind the Spindle as before it; and that would hinder the Perfon that follows the Drill, from feeing the Seed fall out of the Seed-box into the Funnel; and that Part of the Bottom which is before the Spindle cannot be made fhorter, becaufe that Part of the Seed-box which is before the Spindle, is (upon account of its Tongue) much longer than the Part of it which is behind the Spindle.   'Tis true that when the Hopper is empty of Seed, it cannot be thus pois'd; but then, being fo light, it does not require it.   *e f g b* is a Piece of a Board, nail'd on to that Part of the End

A,

A, which is below the Bottom of the Cavity which holds the Seed, and is commonly plac'd a little crofs the Grain of the Board to which it is nail'd, and ferves to ftrengthen it, and keeps the Hole *i* from fplitting. The upper Edge *e f* of this added Piece of Board is exactly the Length of the Bottom of the Hopper, whereto the Brafs Seed-box is faftened; and this Bottom, together with its Seed-box under it, being put into its Place, bears upon this Piece from *e* to *f*, which holds up the right Side of the Bottom, and keeps it from finking downwards; as the lower Ends of the Two mention'd Pofts, and the fore and hinder Side B and C nail'd to them, prevent its rifing upwards.

The Manner of making the Hole *i* is as follows: Place the Seed-box with its fore End at *e*, and hinder End at *f*, with the Bafe of its Cylinder (or great Hole) againft this added Piece of Board, and its upper Edge exactly the Height of the Edge *e f*; then, with a Pair of Compaffes put thro' the Cylinder of the Seed-box, mark round the inner Edge of its Bafe upon the added Board; then take off the Seed-box, and find the Centre of the mark'd Circle; and then with a Tool call'd a Centre-bit, of the right Size, bore the Hole quite thro' the double Board; and this Hole will be in the right Place, and of the fame Diameter with the Spindle; but in cafe there is to be a Brafs Wreath on that Part of the Spindle which is to turn in this Hole, then the Hole muft be bor'd of the fame Diameter with that Part of the Wreath which is to enter it; and that may be perhaps near a quarter of an Inch longer than the Diameter of the Spindle, upon which it is faftened.

This End A, thus bor'd and fhap'd, is a Pattern for its Oppofite, and for the other Two Oppofites of the other Cavity, which holds the Seed at the other End of the Hopper.

When

When the Oppofite of A (with the Two Pofts whereto the fore Side B, and the hinder Side C, are nail'd, and having a like Piece of Board in its lower Part with a like Hole in it) is added, and when the Bottom (Four Inches broad), with its Seed-box under it, is thruft in at *f* by the prick'd Lines, until it reach *e*, bearing on one Side upon the Piece of Board *e f g h*, and the other Edge of the Bottom bearing in like manner upon the oppofite Piece, then this Cavity of the Hopper, which will contain about Two Gallons of Seeds, will be finifh'd.

Note, The Bottom muft make a right Angle with the Two fore Pofts, having the Side B perpendicular to it.

D is a Part of the Board which comes out farther than the Hopper, in order to hold a Bar at *k*; which being faftened there, and in like manner to the Oppofite of this Board, this Bar bearing againft the fore Part of the Standard, the Hopper and its Wheels are in part drawn by it.

Into the Notch *l* is faftened one End of a long Bar, which paffes the whole Length of the Hopper, and holds the upper Part of its Two Cavities in their Places, as is feen mark'd D, in *Fig.* 15.

E is Part of the Board which comes before the Hopper, and whereto one End of a Piece of Wood is faftened by Nails or Screws, which bearing againft the fore Part of the Standard, and againft its Infide, the Hopper is in part drawn and guided by it, as fhall be fhewn in *Fig.* 15.

Fig. 13. fhews the Outfide of the Figure laft defcrib'd. A is the Standard by which this End of the Hopper is drawn, in the manner as it is here placed. B is one End of the Spindle paffing thro' the Hopper and Seed-box. C the Bottom, having the Seed-box faftened on to it, with one Screw before, and another behind, with their Nuts underneath, and the Heads of their Screws very thin, and the Pins fquare at

Top,

Top, that they may not turn in the Wood; and their Heads muſt either be let into the Wood, even with the Surface, or elſe the Sides B C of the Hopper muſt be cut for theſe Heads of the Screws to paſs in under them.

This bottom Board, which holds the braſs Seed-box, is Four Inches broad, and full half an Inch thick, and at each End a quarter of an Inch longer than the Seed-box : This Piece is firſt thruſt in ſliding upon the Two added Pieces of Board, until its fore End comes under the fore Side of the Hopper, and its hinder End under the hinder Side; then ſetting the Hopper with its Bottom upwards, the Spindle being thro' the Seed-box, and Holes of the Hopper, we hold the Seed-box hard upon the Bottom, at equal Diſtance from each End of it, whilſt the Holes are bored thro' the Bottom, by the Holes at each End of the Seed-box; and then the Screws, being put thro', ſcrew on the Box; and when that is done, we make a Mark upon the bottom Board, with the Compaſſes, on each Side of the Braſs Box, beginning from the Ends of the Axis of the Tongue, reaching as far backwards as is the Length of the Mortiſe : Theſe Two Lines or Marks are a Direction for cutting the Hole in the Bottom of the Hopper, thro' which the Seed deſcends into the Seed-box; then we pull out the Spindle, then draw out the Bottom, take off the Seed-box, and cut the Hole in the Bottom in the manner I will now deſcribe in *Fig.* 14. where the Two pricked Lines *a b* and *c d* are the lower Edges of the Hole, and the ſame with the Two Lines mentioned to be marked by the Sides of the Seed-box. The pricked Line *a d*, being at right Angles with the Two former, is the lower Edge of the fore End of the Hole, and exactly over the Axis of the Tongue, and parallel to it. The pricked Line *b c* is the lower Edge of the hinder End of the Hole, which is juſt over the hinder End of the Mortiſe, and parallel and equal

to

to the laft-mentioned pricked Line: Thefe Four pricked Lines are the lower Edges of this Hole, contiguous to the Seed-box. The Two Lines *e f* and *g h* are the upper Edges of the Sides of the Hole, which, being farther afunder than the lower Edges, make the reverfe Bevel of this Hole ; which may be determined by this, that the Surface between thefe Two upper and lower Edges, being Planes, are inclined to one another downwards, in an Angle of about One hundred and Thirty Degrees. The Two Lines *e h* and *f g*, at right Angles with the Two laft-mentioned Lines, make the upper Edges of the Ends of this Hole ; and, being nearer together, than the pricked Lines under them, the plane Surfaces, betwixt thefe Two Lines and thofe Two pricked Lines, fhew the Bevel of the Ends of thefe, which are inclined to each other upwards in an Angle of about Sixty-five Degrees.

This double Bevel effectually prevents the Seed from arching in the Hole, before it gets into the Mortife of the Seed-box ; and alfo, the Two upper Edges of the Ends of the Hole being nearer together than the lower, there is the more Wood left between thefe Edges and the Screws, which hold the Box to the Bottom, whereby the Board is lefs apt to fplit.

Then the Box being fcrewed on to the Bottom, and thruft again into its Place, the Spindle, paffing thro' both the Hopper and the Box, keeps the Bottom in its Place: Then D, in *Fig.* 13. is the imaginary Plane of the Top or Mouth of the Hopper, being a rectangled Parallelogram, and parallel to the Bottom, to which the fore End is perpendicular, and a rectangled Parallelogram of the fame Breadth.

Fig. 15. fhews the fore Side of the whole hinder Hopper, with its Two Cavities, and all its Accoutrements, except the Wheels ; the Two Ends A and B being exactly alike, having each of them its Seed-box at the Bottom, in the fame manner as in the one has been defcribed. The Bar D holds together the upper

Parts

Parts of this double Hopper at a right Diſtance, which is, when there is Ten Inches clear room betwixt the Two ſingle ones. The Spindle E, paſſing thro' the Whole, holds the Two ſingle Hoppers by Four Wreaths, at the ſame Diſtance below, as they are held by the Bar above.

Theſe Four Wreaths are ſcrewed on to the Spindle, to keep it from moving towards either End, as well as to hold the Hoppers in their Places: Two of which Wreaths are ſeen at *a* and *b*; and the other Two are placed on the Outſides, as theſe Two are on the Inſides. Before we proceed any farther in this Figure, it will be proper to ſhew the Wreaths, which are of Two Sorts.

The one in *Fig.* 16. where A is its Hollow, which is circular, and muſt be of the ſame Diameter with the Spindle; and, being thruſt on upon the Spindle, till it touch the Board, is faſtened to the Spindle by a ſmall Screw thro' each of its oppoſite Holes. *a b* ſhews the Breadth of this Wreath, whether it be made of Braſs or Wood: It is little more than half an Inch. *b c d* is the Part of it that goes againſt the Board: The Thickneſs of the Surface of this End which goes againſt the Board, is a quarter of an Inch, if made with Braſs; but if with Wood, half an Inch; but the Thickneſs of its other End *a e f* is leſs than its End *b c d*, by which means the Screws are the more eaſily turned in.

Fig. 17. ſhews the other Sort of Wreath, which is always made in Braſs: Its Cavity is a hollow Cylinder like the former: When it is on the Spindle, its End *a b c* is thruſt into the Hole of the Board (made wider for the Purpoſe) until *d e f* come cloſe to the Board, and ſtop it from entering any farther; then we ſcrew it on to the Spindle by the Holes, as the other Sort of Wreath is deſcribed to be ſcrewed.

This is the beſt Sort of Wreath; becauſe it keeps the Spindle from wearing againſt the Edges of the

Hole,

Hole, and then the Spindle never has any Friction against the Wood in any Part of it ; but the other Sort are more eafily made (efpecially of Wood), and the Spindle will laft a great while in them; or if it be worn out, the Expence of Three-pence or Four-pence will purchafe a new Spindle.

Now I muft return to *Fig.* 15. where the Spindle E having its Four Wreaths fixt on it, we turn it round with our Hand, to fee whether the Wreaths are put on true ; and when they are fo, neither the Spindle, nor the Hoppers, can move end-ways : Tho' the Spindle be pretty hard to turn round, the Wheels will foon caufe it to turn eafily.   Whilft the Spindle is in this Pofture, we turn the Hopper Bottom upwards, and mark the Spindle for cutting the Notches in the manner before directed ; and then we take off the Spindle, and cut the Notches, and alfo cut each End of the Spindle fquare, up to a Shoulder at each End, fo that the Wheels may come eafily on without knocking or thrufting ; and then we return the Spindle to its Place, and put on the Wheels, pinning them on with each a long Nail, which being crooked at the Ends, prevent it from falling out, but may be very eafily pulled out with the Claws of a Hammer; but we muft take care, that neither the fquare Ends of the Spindle, nor the fquare Holes in the Naves (or Hubs) of the Wheels (into which they enter), be taper; for, if they are taper, the Wheels will be apt to work themfelves off.

The Piece of Wood, *Fig.* 18. is that which goes over the Standard, and, being placed in the Hopper, as F. in *Fig.* 15. draws that Part of the Hopper by its Infide *a b* bearing againft the fore Part of the Standard ; and that Part of it from *b* to *c*, being the Breadth of the Standard, bears againft its inner Infide, to prevent the Hopper from going any farther towards that End.   This Piece of Wood is faftened to the Boards of the Hopper, either by Screws or Nails :
This

This Piece, from *d* to *e*, muft be of fuch a Thicknefs, that the Standard, bearing againft its Infide *b c*, may be equidiftant from each Board, to which this Piece is faftened. The Part, or fore Side of this Piece *f g*, muft be the Length of the Diftance between Board and Board, to which it is faftened; and that is exactly Four Inches. Its Thicknefs and Depth muft be fuch as may make it ftrong enough for the Purpofes intended.

The Piece marked *Fig.* 19. is the Oppofite of the former, and to be placed in the fame manner, and as it is feen marked G in *Fig.* 15. obferving always, that the Part of it, which holds the Hopper from moving end-ways, muft always be on the Infide of the Standard; for, if thefe Pieces fhould bear againft the Outfides of the Standards, the Hopper could have no Play upon them, nor could either of the Wheels rife up without raifing the Share (that was next to it) out of the Ground; but, being thus placed, either Wheel may rife without the other, and without raifing the Share.

I fay more of this, becaufe it is a Point wherein young Workmen are apt to miftake.

Thus having fhewn, in *Fig.* 15. how the Hopper is guided and drawn at the lower Part, I come next to fhew how it is held and drawn at its upper Part; for which the Piece of Wood, *Fig.* 20. being a competent Breadth and Thicknefs, Four Inches long, is fixt in between the Boards with Nails or Screws; and is H in *Fig.* 15. The Standard paffing up betwixt this and the fore Side of the Hopper, its fore Surface bearing againft this Bar, and its hinder Surface againft the Hopper; fo that the Hopper may rife and fink eafily upon the Standard at Top, being in the Middle on the fore Side of the Hopper; there will be an equal Diftance of each Side, for either Wheel to rife, without the Standard ftriking againft the Sides of the Hopper to hinder its rifing. There is another Bar
equal

equal to this, and has the fame Office, at the other End of the Hopper, marked I. Likewife the Bar D is of the fame Ufe with thefe mentioned fhort Bars, and they help to ftrengthen one another.

When the Wheels are put on till they reach near to the Wreaths, they will ftand with their Rings, or Circles, Two Feet Three Inches afunder.

We fet them as near together as conveniently we can; becaufe when they are too wide, they are apt to draw the Plough towards one Side of the Ridge; and fometimes, when the Ridge is high, the Hopper might bear upon the Funnels; and then the Wheels, being carried above the Ground, would not turn to bring out the Seed: And that thefe Wheels may come the nearer together, their Spokes are fet almoft perpendicular; fo that the Wheels are not concave, as other Wheels are. This Hopper is fhewn, put on upon its Standards, in its Place, in *Fig.* 21. where the mentioned Bar D, which holds the Hopper together at Top, is feen, as alfo the Four Wreaths, and likewife the hinder End of the Seed-boxes ftanding over the Funnels, with their Trunks underneath them. Here alfo the back Part of the fore Hopper is feen, with its Seed-box ftanding over the fore Funnel: Its Mouth alfo is feen at A; as alfo the Top of its fore Side held up by the thing *(Fig.* 22.*)* like the Carrier of a Latch, with the Nails in it, which faften it to the Top of the fore Side of the Hopper, and give room for either of its Wheels to rife.

This fore Hopper may eafily be defcribed by the Figure of a Box, like the other already defcribed, at its Ends, which are of the fame Shape with the Infide of the Box, *Fig.* 12. but much lower, being Seven Inches and an half deep, and Sixteen Inches long; and the Breadth of its Bottom is determined by the Length of the Seed-box, and a little wider at Top, on account of the Bevel which poifes it: It carries no more Seed then one End of the hinder Hopper;

but

but it is capable of holding more; but we do not fill it quite, left fome of the Seed fhould fly over in jolting, its Mouth being fo much longer than the other.

This Hopper is kept in its Place, from moving end-ways upon the Spindle, by a Wreath fixed to the Spindle at each End of the Box, in the fame manner as has been defcribed for holding the other Hopper. The Wreaths moft proper for this Purpofe are the Sort defcribed in *Fig.* 17. but the other Sort defcribed in *Fig.* 16. and even made with Wood, will fuffice; but then we muft take care to make the Hole at the End of the Hopper of a confiderable Thicknefs, that it may not wear the Spindle, which, by reafon of its great Length, is the more liable to bend, and be cut by the Edges of the Holes; which Cutting cannot be prevented but by the Thicknefs of the Holes, or by fuch Wreaths as that of *Fig.* 17.

We fometimes make this Hopper exactly like a common Box, without any Part of its Ends defcending below the Bottom; and, in that Cafe, we place a narrower Piece of Board at each End of the Hopper, like that of *Fig.* 23. in which Figure, the Hole A being put on upon the Spindle, the Piece of Board is faftened on by a Screw and Nut thro' the Hole B, near the Top of the End of the Hopper, and by another Screw and Nut thro' the Hole C, near the Bottom of the Hopper. Another fuch a Piece of Board, fixed on in the fame manner to the oppofite End of the Hopper, holds this long Hopper parallel to its Spindle, that paffes thro' the Holes of thefe Two Pieces, and thro' the Brafs Seed-box, which is fixed up to the Bottom, in the Middle betwixt them.

There are Two Methods for letting the Seed pafs from a long Hopper into the Seed-box. The firft is that of cutting the Hole through its Bottom, in the manner that has been fhewn in *Fig.* 14. The other is that which cannot be ufed in a Hopper fo fhort as

the

the Boxes of our hinder Hoppers are; but in the fore Hopper, or any other long Hopper, we can place the Brafs Seed-box to a Bottom made for the Purpofe, like that in *Fig.* 24. where there is a Piece of Board on the fore Part of the Hopper from End to End, as *a b*, and another on the hinder Part of the Hopper, as *c d.*   Then the fore Part of the Brafs Seed-box, being placed under the Piece *a b*, is fcrewed up to it at *e*, and the hinder Part of the Seed-box under *c d* fcrewed up to it at *f*; then the Bottom of the Hopper, being open in the Middle, is fhut by very thin Boards, *g* and *h*, fixed up to the mentioned Pieces: Thefe Boards having their upper Surface even with the upper Edges of the Brafs Box, the Seed can no way arch in coming into the Mortife of the Seed-box. Whichever of thefe Two Methods be made ufe of, in a long Hopper, the Bottom muft be fixed to the Two Sides, by fmall Bars of Wood of about Three quarters of an Inch fquare, to which the Bottom and Sides are faftened by Nails, in the manner that the Ends and Sides of the hinder Hoppers are faftened to their Pofts, which ftand in their Corners.

We take the fame Method for cutting the Notches in this Spindle, as has been defcribed for cutting the Notches in the other Spindle.

But obferve, That the great Length of this Spindle requires it to be the larger; and we make it of an Inch and Three quarters Diameter, the other being only an Inch and an half: We therefore bore the great Hole or Cylinder of its Brafs Seed-box a quarter of an Inch in Diameter larger than of the Brafs Seed-boxes of the hinder Hoppers; and we commonly make a Notch more in the Circumference of this Spindle, becaufe the Semidiameters of its Wheels muft be as much greater than of the hinder Wheels, as is the Thicknefs of the Plank, and the Ends of the Limbers which are betwixt this Spindle and the upper Surface of the Two Beams.

We

We make all our Spindles of clear-quarter'd Aſh, without Knots or Crooks; and when they are well dry'd, and made perfectly round, and of equal Diameter from one End to the other, by the Prong-maker, we pay a Peny *per* Foot for them at the firſt Hand, and they will now-and-then have ſomething more for the largeſt Size; but we are only curious to have the middle Part of this long Spindle exact; for we graft on a Piece at each End, which does not require any Exactneſs: The Graftings are ſeen at *a a* at one End, and *b b* at the other End of the Spindle (in this *Fig.* 21.) by Four flattiſh Iron Rings driven on upon the grafted Parts, as they appear under thoſe Letters in the Middle. Between each Pair of theſe Rings, we drive a ſmall Iron Pin thro' the Joints at *c* and at *d*, to keep the Grafts from ſeparating end-ways; and if they are not tight enough, we make them ſo, by Wedges driven in betwixt them and the Spindle.

This fore Hopper is drawn by the Spindle, and the Spindle is drawn by the Two double Standards B and C, betwixt whoſe Forks it is placed, as appears in this Figure; the Diſtance between each Fork, or double Standard, being exactly the Diameter of the Spindle, ſo that the Spindle may have juſt room to riſe and ſink there, and no more.

The Hopper and Spindle are guided, or kept in their Place, from moving end-ways, by Two Wreaths ſcrew'd on to the Spindle, the one at *e*, and the other at *f*; each of which Wreaths, bearing againſt the Surfaces of both the Legs of each double Standard, on the Sides next to the Hopper, prevent the Spindle and Hopper from moving towards either End: and yet admit the Wheels, or either of them, to riſe and ſink without raiſing either Side of the Plough, contrary to what would happen, if the Wreaths were placed on the Outſides of the Standards next to the Wheels.

We

We make thefe Wreaths a little different from the other Sort of Wreaths, which turn againft the Holes; we make them of a greater Diameter, left they fhould at any time get in betwixt the Legs of the double Standards, in cafe the Standards fhould be loofe, or bend : Therefore we make the Diameter of each of thefe Wreaths, at leaft, Two Inches and Three quarters : We always make them of Wood, and of a pe-culiar Shape, taking off their Edges next the Standards, which Edges would be an Impediment to the Rifing of one End of the Spindle without the other. So that, for making thefe Wreaths, we may form a Piece of Wood of the Shape of a Skittle-bowl (or an ob-late Spheroid) having an Inch and Three-quarter Hole bor'd thro' its Middle, and then cut by its Diameter (which is about Three Inches) in Two Halves, each of which will be one of thefe Wreaths; and they muft be placed on the Spindle, with their convex Sides bearing againft their refpective Standards.

The Diameter of the fore Wheels is about Thirty Inches, as the Diameter of the hinder Wheels is about Twenty-two.

The fore Spindle fhould be of fuch a Length, that its fquare Ends, E and F, may come out Three or Four Inches farther than the Hubs (or Stocks) of the Wheels; fo that there may be room to fhift the Wheels towards either End, for making feveral Sets of Notches, for the Ufe of the Seed-box.

Obferve, Tho' the fore Hopper is drawn by its Spindle, yet the hinder Spindle is drawn by its Hopper.

The Reafon of this great Diftance between the Two fore Wheels is not fo much for their ferving as Marking Wheels to this particular Drill; which be-ing drawn only upon a Ridge, its Top is a fufficient Direction for leading the Horfe to keep the Rows pa-rallel to one another, if the Ridges are fo; but if the Wheels were much nearer together than they are, and

yet

yet more than Six Feet afunder, the Wheels going on the Sides of the next Ridges would be apt to turn the Drill out of the Horfe-path towards one Side, not permitting the Drill to follow directly after the Horfe; and if the Wheels fhould ftand at Six or Seven Feet Diftance from one another, then they muft go in the Furrows which are on each Side of the Six-feet Ridge: This would occafion their Hopper to bear upon the Plank, which would carry the Wheels above the Ground, and no Seed would be turned out of the Hopper, unlefs the Wheels were of an extraordinary Height *(a)*; and the Height requir'd for them would be very uncertain, fome Furrows being much deeper than others; but the Tops of contiguous Ridges are generally of an equal Height, whether the Furrows betwixt them be deep or fhallow; for we feldom make Ridges of an unequal Height in the fame Field: Therefore there can be no need to change the Height of our Wheels, that are to go upon the Middle of the Ridges; but if they went in the Furrows they muft be of a different Height

---

(a) Notwithftanding the Reafons given, and that I have never ufed Wheels of fuch an Height as might be neceffary for going in the Furrows, yet it may not be amifs to try fuch: becaufe with them the Spindle needeth not to be more than half the Length of one that is carried by low Wheels: And high Wheels will allow the Funnel to be much larger, fo that altho' the Spindle go higher from it, no Seed will drop befide a large Funnel; but there is not room for a large one under low Wheels.

J did not think it neceffary to defcribe the Manner of making Drill-wheels any otherways than by fhewing them in the *Plates*; but I will obferve here, that they are to be made very light: One of mine, that is 30 Inches high, weighs Five Pounds and an half; it has a Circle or Ring of Iron, whofe Depth is half an Inch, and its Thicknefs a quarter of an Inch; alfo very thin Iron Stockbands to hold the Nave or Stock from fplitting. The Circle is held on the Spokes by fmall flat Iron Pins on each Side; and each Spoke has a Ring of Iron to fecure its End from being fplit by driving in of the Pins. We alfo make the Drill-wheels lefs concave than other Wheels are.

when ufed for drilling of high Ridges, from what would be required when ufed for drilling low Ridges.

One Reafon why the hinder Shares are fhorter than the fore Share (and confequently the fore Part of their Sheats lefs oblique) is, that they may be fet the nearer to the Plank; and I have had a Drill with Five Shares in the Plank, Fourteen Inches afunder, and Four of thefe hinder Sheats following in another Rank, whofe Shares were lefs than Three Inches long; fo that their Beams were fet fo far forwards, that one Hopper (by a Contrivance that carried the Seed forwards to the fore Rank, and backwards to the other Rank) fupply'd the Seed to both Ranks of Trunks, and planted St. Foin in Rows Seven Inches afunder, when the Ground was too rough to be planted with Rows at that Diftance by one Rank of Shares.

It may be objected, that the fore Part of thefe hinder Sheats might not be oblique enough to raife up the Strings of Roots or Stubble, which might come acrofs them in their Way; but this Inconvenience is remedied by the greater Obliquity of the fore Sheat (or Sheats), which clears the Way for the hinder Sheats, by raifing out of the Ground fuch Strings, &c. which might annoy them; efpecially, in this Wheat-drill, where the fore Share fo clears the way of the hinder Shares, that they can take hold of no String in the Ground, except of the Ends of fuch which the fore Share has loofen'd; and they hanging fafter in the Ground by their other Ends, the hinder Shares flip by them without taking hold of them; and the Harrow-tines, going after fo near to the Chanels of the hinder Sheats, by the fame means efcape alfo from hanging in fuch Strings.

The Reafons for placing the One Share and One Hopper before, and the Two behind, in this Wheat-drill, are fo many, and fo obvious, that it would be but lofing of Time to mention them.

The

The Limbers G and H, we make of Afpen, Pop-lar, or Willow, for Lightnefs; we make them as fmall and light as we can, allowing them convenient Strength; and the fhorter they are, the more exactly the Drill will follow the Horfe, without the Hand of him, that follows the Drill, whofe chief Bufinefs is, with the Paddle to keep all the Shares and Tines from being clogged up by the Dirt fticking to them, and alfo to obferve whether the Seed be delivered equally and juftly to all the Chanels.

Thefe Limbers fhould approach fo near together at their fore Parts, near the Chain, that there may be none or very little room betwixt the Limbers and the Horfe; and therefore muft be nearer together for a very little Horfe than for a great one: The Horfe, which I have ufed in all my Drills for thefe many Years paft, is a little one, about Thirteen Hands high; and the fore Part of my Drill-limbers are Twenty Inches wide afunder at the Chain.

At *g* on the Outfide of the Limber G, is a fmall Staple driven in, having one Link on it, which holds a fmall Hook, which, taking hold of different Links of the very fmall Chain I, raifes or finks the fore Part of the Plough to different Heights. But take care to fet it at fuch a Degree, that the fore and hinder Share may go equally deep in the Ground; and when they do fo, the fore Part of the Limbers ought to be higher than the Traces which draw them.

At *h* in the Limber H, is driven another Staple, which holds the other End of the Chain; or elfe, in-ftead of a Chain, we may make ufe of a Piece of Cord, one End of which put thro' this Staple, and ty'd to the Limber, and a Piece of Chain of half a dozen Links, faften'd to the other End of fuch a Cord, will ferve as well as a whole Chain, for raifing and finking the Limbers.

He who can by thefe Directions make this Wheat-drill, may very eafily make any other Sort of Drill,

B b 3 for

for planting any Sort of Corn, or other Seeds that are near about the Bigness of Seeds of Corn : He may make it with a fingle Row of Sheats, by placing as many of thefe fore Sheats as he pleafes in the Plank, which may be longer or fhorter, as he thinks fit; and he may add a Beam betwixt every Two of them, with a Sheat in it, like thefe hinder Sheats; and then the Drill will be double, having Two Ranks of Shares. But I muft advife him never to make a Drill with more Shares than will be contain'd in Four Feet Breadth, that is, from the outermoft on the right Hand, to the outermoft on the left Hand ; for fhould the Drill be broader, fome of the Shares might pafs over hollow Places of the Ground without reaching them, and then the Seed falling on the Ground would be uncover'd in fuch low Places.

To a Drill that plants upon the Level, Marking-wheels are neceffary, to the End that every Row may be at its due Diftance : As in a Drill with Five Shares, for planting Rows Eight Inches afunder, Four of the Five cannot err, becaufe Four equal Spaces are included betwixt the Five Shares ; but the Fifth (which we call the parting Space) being on the Outfide uncon-fin'd, would fcarce ever be equal, were it not kept equal by the Help of the Marking-wheels. The Rule for fetting of thefe is thus : We compute altogether the Five Spaces belonging to the Five Rows ; which being in all Forty Inches, we fet the Marking-wheels Eighty Inches afunder, that is, double the Diftance of all the Spaces, each Wheel being equidiftant to the Middle of the Drill, which Middle being exactly over the Horfe-path, when the Drill is turn'd, the Horfe goes back upon the Track of one of thefe Wheels, making his Path exactly Forty Inches diftant from his laft Path : By this means alfo the Rows of the whole Field may be kept equidiftant, and parallel to one another ; fo that it would be difficu t for an Eye to diftinguifh the parting Rows from the reft.

But

But when Two different Sorts of Seed are planted, ſuppoſe a Row of St. Foin betwixt every Row of Barley, the Rows of which being Eight Inches aſunder, and the Barley drill'd by the fore Hopper into the Chanels made by the five Shares, and the St. Foin drill'd from the hinder Hopper into the Chanels made by Six Shares, the Marking-wheels muſt be at no greater Diſtance than thoſe above-mention'd, where there are only Five Shares ; becauſe one of the Six, which are for the St. Foin, muſt always return in the ſame Chanel, going twice therein ; for One Row of Barley would be miſſing, in caſe the parting Space ſhould be made by this Sixth Share ; and that parting Space would have no Barley in it. Therefore it is a Rule, that whenſoever Two Sorts of Seeds are drill'd, the Rows of one Sort betwixt the Rows of the other there muſt be an odd Share in the Drill, which muſt go twice in one Chanel, and the Diſtance of the Marking-wheels muſt be accounted from that Rank of Shares which are the feweſt : It muſt alſo be contriv'd in this Caſe, that each outermoſt Seed-box muſt deliver but half the Quantity of Seed that each of the inner Seed-boxes do ; becauſe the outer ones going twice in a Place, their Chanels would otherwiſe have a Quantity of Seed double to the reſt.

In a Drill that has Two Spindles, we place the Marking-wheels on the foremoſt, which upon their Account is the longeſt ; but if we ſhould uſe the Wheels of the hinder Spindle as Marking-wheels, then that muſt be the longeſt, and ſo the fore Wheels (their Semidiameters being much longer than the Semidiameters of the hinder Wheels, and their Spindles ſhorter) would ſtrike againſt the hinder Spindle, unleſs it were ſet farther back than is convenient.

When Ground is harrow'd the laſt time before it is to be drill'd, we contrive that the Harrows may not go directly towards the ſame Point that the Drill is to go, leſt the Track of the Marking-wheel ſhould

be

be exactly parallel with the Track of the Harrow-tines, which might make it difficult to diftinguifh the Track of the Wheel from that of the Harrow-tine.

He that has not a great Quantity of Ground to plant with St. Foin, and does not plant it betwixt Rows of Corn, will have occafion for no other Drill than this Wheat-drill, defcrib'd in *Fig.* 21. He may plant his Rows at Fifteen Inches afunder, by the hinder Hopper, and its Shares, without removing them, the fore Hopper being taken off; or elfe you may plant Three Rows at Sixteen Inches afnnder, by fetting the Beams, and their Seed-boxes and Hoppers, at Thirty-two Inches afunder inftead of Fifteen, equidiftant from the fore Share: and then the Marking-wheels, which are thofe of the fore Spindle, muft be Eight Feet afunder; to wit, double to the Spaces of the Three Shares, which are Three times Sixteen Inches (or Four Feet); or you may fet the Two hinder Beams, &c. at what Diftance you pleafe, fetting the Marking-wheels to correfpond with them; but then the Harrow muft be alter'd, and both its Legs and Tines muft change their Places in the Head, the Legs for guiding it exactly, and the Tines to follow in all the Three Rows, which will require a third Tine to be added in the Middle, between the other Two. But without any other Alteration than that of taking off the fore Hopper, and that of leffening the Seed-paffages of the hinder Hopper by the Setting-fcrews; my Man planted me feveral Acres of St. Foin with my Wheat-drill Two Years ago, the Rows being all Fourteen Inches afunder: It is now an extraordinary good Crop.

In cafe the Shares, being only Three, fhould in fine Ground go fo deep as to endanger the Burying of the Seed, the beft Remedy to prevent this fatal Misfortune is, to place a triangular Piece of Wood, like thofe in *Figures* 25. and 26. the firft of which fhews one Side thereof, with the Nail by which it is

to

to be nail'd into the lower Part of the Trunk, with its moſt acute Angle uppermoſt; the other in *Fig.* 26. ſhews the ſame, and its Back-ſide *a b*, that is to be nail'd to the Back of the Sheat, being of the ſame Breadth with it; its Bottom *b c* being the Breadth of the Plates, on their Inſide, the Angle *c* coming out backwards, juſt as far as the Plates: The Depth of this Piece from *a* to *c* is uncertain, becauſe the Plates of ſome Trunks are broader than of others. The Uſe of this Piece is, to fill up the lower Part of the Trunk; ſo that the Seed, dropping upon the oblique Side of this Piece of Wood, may by it be turn'd into the Chanel, after ſo much Mould is fallen in it, as will ſufficiently leſſen its Depth, whereby the Danger of burying the Seed is avoided: And ſuch a Piece of Wood placed into each Trunk, I think, is preferable to Ground-wriſts, which are commonly uſed for this Purpoſe; becauſe the Ground-wriſts leave the Chanels too wide and open.

But when only the Two hinder Sheats are uſed for St. Foin, we can make their Chanels the ſhallower, by ſinking the Limbers by their Chain, ſo much as that, the Plough bearing moſt upon the fore Share, the hinder Shares will go the ſhallower.

When we drill hilly Ground, both up and down, we cover the hinder Parts of all the Trunks, from their Tops, to within Two or Three Inches of the Ground, to prevent the Seed's falling out far behind the Trunk, in going up Hill; and this we do either by a Piece of Leather nail'd to each Side of a Sheat, the Middle of the Leather bearing againſt the hinder Part of the Plates (or Trunk); or ſometimes, inſtead of Leather, we uſe Tin.

Every Trunk being thus incloſ'd behind, we can drill up and down an hill of a moderate Aſcent; but when it is very ſteep, we never drill any thing but St. Foin on it, and that by a Drill made for the Pur-poſe, ſo very light, that a Man may carry it up the

Hill

Hill on his Back, and draw it down after him : This
Drill has Five or Six Sheats in one Row (with the
Harrow behind them).   Their Shares being extremely
short, the Standards which draw the Hopper muſt be
ſet perpendicular to the Horizon, when the Drill is
coming down, rather than to the Surface of the Side
of the Hill : The Funnels muſt alſo correſpond with
the Standards.

Some, inſtead of theſe Sheats, make uſe of hollow
wooden Harrow-tines, thro' which the Seed deſcends :
But theſe I do not approve of; becauſe where the
Ground is hard, and not fine, they riſe up, and make
no Chanels for the Seed ; and then it lying uncover'd
will be malted.

When a Drill has only one Rank of Shares, we
ſcrew on the Harrow by its Legs, to the Inſide of the
Two outſide Sheats, as near as we can to their fore
Shoulders, leaving ſufficient room for the Harrow to
riſe and ſink, in the ſame manner as when it is drawn
by the Beams.

C H A P. XXII.

Of the Turnep-Drill.

PLATE 5. ſhews the whole Mounting of a
Turnep-drill. *Fig.* 1. is a Plough, but little differing from the Drill-plough laſt mentioned. A, A, are
the Two Limbers, differing in nothing from the other,
except that they are lighter, not being above Two
Inches Diameter, behind the Bar : They are drawn in
the ſame manner as the other.   Their Bar B is diſtant
from the Plank Three Inches, being ſhoulder'd at
each End, with a very thin flat Tenon, paſſing thro'
each Limber, and pinn'd on their Outſides, as at *a a*.
We do not pin in this Bar thro' the Limbers, leſt the
Holes

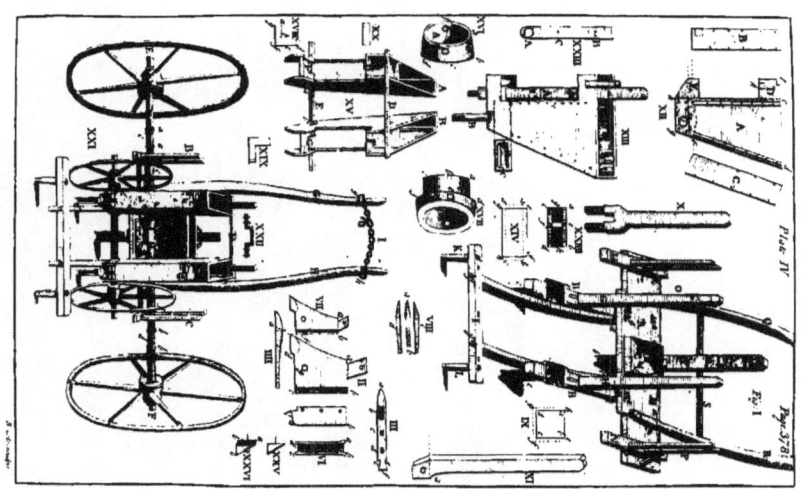

Plate IV

Page 378

Fig. 1

Holes fhould make thefe very fmall Limbers the weaker in that Part. C, the Plank, Two Feet and an Inch long, Five Inches broad, and an Inch and a quarter thick. D, D, the Two double Standards, or Two Pair of Standards, placed into the Plank with Shoulders above, and Tenons pinn'd underneath the Plank, and are Thirteen Inches high above it: Thefe ferve for a Pair of Marking-wheels, when Turneps are drill'd on the Level, to keep the Rows all parallel, and at what Diftance you pleafe, by fetting them according to the Rule already laid down.

Sometimes we place the double Standards into the Plank of the Wheat-drill, in the fame manner that thefe are placed.

We take off the inner Edge of each Standard at the Top, as at *b b* and *b b*, for the more eafy Admiffion of the Spindle of the Marking-wheels into the Forks: This Spindle is kept in its Place by Two of the fame fort of Wreaths, and placed in the fame manner as thofe defcrib'd for the fore Hopper of the Wheat-drill.

Such Marking-wheels are neceffary for drilling upon the Level; but not for drilling upon Ridges.

E is the Beam, Two Feet Two Inches and an half long, Four Inches broad, and Two Inches thick: It is thus broad, that the Screws which hold on the crofs Piece F, may be farther afunder: The Screws muft be placed as near as may be to the Outfides of the Beam, and at equal Diftance from each Side of the crofs Piece; by which means the Standards are kept the firmer from Turning.

The Diftance between the Plank and the crofs Piece is Eleven Inches. The Bteadth of the crofs Piece is Two Inches and a quarter. This crofs Piece is fhewn apart in *Fig.* 2. where its Two Standards A B, are each Seventeen Inches long (or high), and each on its fore Side and hinder Side One Inch and a quarter broad, and nearly Three quarters of an Inch thick: They are

fhoulder'd

fhoulder'd and pinn'd into the crofs Piece at *a b.* The crofs Piece is Thirteen Inches and an half long, and one Inch and a quarter thick in the Middle from *c* to *d*; but for about an Inch on the Infide of each Standard is Two Inches and an half thick, that the Standards may have the more Wood to fupport them, and that the Hopper, bearing upon the thicker Parts of the crofs Piece, may be held up above the Funnel, that the Fork of the brafs Spindle may not ftrike againft it, when the Plough is taken up to be turn'd, there being a little more than a quarter of an Inch of the Breadth of the crofs Piece behind the Standard, for the Hopper to reft on.

The whole Diftance between the Standards is Nine Inches and a quarter. The Standards muft be exactly perpendicular to their crofs Piece: Their Tops are drawn up each to a Point, as at *e* and *f*, by which the Hopper is the more eafily put on upon them.

The Funnel, Sheat, Share, and Trunk, are the fame as thofe in the Wheat-drill, except a few Differences: As G in *Fig.* 1. is the fame as the fore Sheat of the Wheat-drill, with its Accoutrements; only it is lower, being but Eight Inches high from the Bottom of the Share up to the Beam; and the Plates of the Trunk, are fomewhat narrower: Its Tenon paffes thro' the Beam, and comes up above it, betwixt the Funnel and the crofs Piece; and there is pinn'd in thro' its Hole above the Beam. There is no want of Wood behind the Sheat, the Funnel not being cut in the Beam, but placed upon it.

The Funnel is fhewn apart in *Fig.* 3. and is Two Inches deep, Four Inches fquare at Top; its Four Sides terminating at an Hole in the Bottom, half an Inch broad from *a* to *b*, and near an Inch long from *c* to *d*; which Length is divided in the Middle, by the upper Edge of a Brafs Spout, which divides the Hole into Two equal Parts (or Holes), each of which

is

is about half an Inch fquare; this Funnel being
fcrew'd on upon the Beam by Two Wood Screws,
entering at Two oppofite Corners of the Funnel, as
at *c d* in *Fig.* 1. fo that the Seed may drop from the
Seed-box upon the right Side of the Funnel at *e*,
which being about half an Inch diftant from the Partition, and equidiftant from both Holes, the Seed
rebounding is pretty equally diftributed to each of the
Holes.

The fore Part of the foremoft Hole being equal
with the Back of the Sheat, the Beam being cut thro';
fo that the Back of the Sheat, and the fore Part of
the Hole thro' the Beam, and the fore Part of this
Hole, make one plain Surface, whereby the Seed
that falls into this foremoft Hole, defcends to the
Ground, near the Back of the Sheat, thro' the Trunk.

And the Seed which falls into the hinder Hole, is
convey'd obliquely backwards thro' Part of the Beam,
by a fhort thin Brafs Spout, whofe Diameter in the
Infide is fomewhat more than half an Inch; but the
fore Part of it, which divides the Two Holes, defcends firft perpendicularly half an Inch, and then
turns off backwards, and there the Spout begins to
be round: Its joining is on its hinder Part, to the end
that the Seed, never running upon it, cannot be
ftopp'd by it. The lower End of this Spout ends at
the lower Surface of the Beam, a little behind the
Plates of the Trunk, which Hole is feen at *a* in *Fig.* 4.
where this Hole delivers the Seed down into the
Spout A, when it is drawn up into its Place by the
String B drawn thro' the Hole at *b* in the End of the
Beam, and there tied until it ftand in the Pofture in
which it is feen at *f* in *Fig.* 1.

The Shape of this Spout is better feen at *Fig.* 5.
where A is the Spout, Four Inches long, a full Inch
Diameter in the Infide : Its lower End is circular; but
its upper End B is cut at oblique Angles, fo that when
it is drawn up to its Place, its Edges will touch the
lower

lower Surface of the Beam, and inclofe the lower End of the other Spout within it: It is made of thin hammer'd Brafs (as is the other). The Edges of the Piece of Brafs, which make this Spout, are join'd on its hinder Part, for the fame Reafon that they are fo in the other Spout. At *b* there is a Jag cut in one of thefe Edges, and rais'd upwards, by which Jag the String being tied on the Spout juft below, is hindered from flipping upwards.

Joining to the higheft Part, and made with Part of the fame Piece of Brafs, turn'd back from the End of the Spout, is its Hinge C, near Three quarters of an Inch long in its Hollow.

D is a thin Piece of Iron, half an Inch broad, and a little longer than the Top of the Sheat, by which the Spout is held up: This Piece of Iron is riveted by a Rivet paffing thro' an Hole at *c*, and thro' the Sheat, juft before the Trunk, and thro' another Piece of Iron on the oppofite Side; both the Pieces of Iron, with their upper Edges touching the Beam, being thus riveted to the Sheat.

The Spout is pinned in by the Screw E, paffing as by the prick'd Line F thro' the Hole G, and alfo thro' the Hinge C, and fcrew'd into the Hole of the oppofite Piece of Iron, correfponding with the Hole G; and then it will appear as in *Fig.* 4.

Inftead of thefe Pieces of Iron, we fometimes ufe Pieces of Wood, a little broader and thicker, nail'd on the Sheat.

The Ufe of this Spout is for carrying half of the Seed backwards, fo that it may drop upon the Chanel, after the Earth is fallen into it: By this means the Seed lying very fhallow, being only cover'd by a little Earth rais'd by the Harrow, by its Shallownefs comes up in moift Weather, fooner than the other half, which lies deeper in the Ground; but if the Weather be dry when planted, the deeper half, by the Moifture of the Earth from the Dews, will come up

firft,

firſt, and the ſhallow half will not come up till Rain come to moiſten it; ſo that by the ſhallow or deep, the Turnep-fly is generally diſappointed.

Fig. 6. ſhews one of the Tines of a Drill-harrow made of Wood: Its Edge *a b* is made roundiſh at *b*, by which means it raiſes the Earth on its Sides; but does not drive it before: This Edge from *a* to *b* is Six Inches long; from *b* to *c*, being its Bottom, is One Inch and a quarter; from *c* to *d* is the Back, an Inch and an half thick at Top, gradually tapering downwards to *c*, where it is half an Inch thick, being ſhoulder'd all round: It has a flat Tenon A, which paſſes thro' a Mortiſe in the Harrow-head; the Length of which Mortiſe is parallel with the Length of the Harrow-head, into which it is held by a Pin, paſſing thro' the Hole of the Tenon, above the Harrow; as may be ſeen in *Fig.* 7. at *a*; and its Fellow at *b*.

Theſe Two Tines are Eight Inches aſunder at their Points, and Six Inches and a quarter aſunder at their upper Parts, juſt under the Harrow-head. The fore Edge of the Tine A inclines a little to the Left, as the Edge of the Tine B doth to the Right.

Fig. 8. ſhews one of the Legs of the Harrow. At *a* is ſeen the round Tenon, which paſſes thro' the Harrow-head up to its Shoulder, and is pinned in thro' an Hole of the Tenon juſt behind the Harrow-head; upon this Tenon the Harrow-head may turn: The other End has an Hole at *b*, thro' which it is pinned on to the Beam. The Length of the Leg from the Shoulder at *a*, to the Hole at *b*, is Twenty Inches: Its Thickneſs is an Inch and a quarter, and its Breadth an Inch. The Two Legs are ſeen mark'd C, D, in *Fig.* 7. They bend down in the Middle, to give the Harrow the more room for riſing and ſinking; they are parallel to each other. and diſtant a little more than the Breadth of the Beam, that they may have Liberty to move thereon, when one End of the Harrow-head ſinks lower than the other, by the Uneven-neſs of the Ground.   The

The Harrow is pinned on to the Beam by the Iron Pin, *Fig.* 9. paſſing thro' the Hole of the Leg at *g*, and thro' the Beam, and alſo thro' the other Leg on the other Side of the Beam, where the Screw at the End of the Pin has a Nut ſcrew'd on it. This Pin is round from its Head all the Way thro' the firſt Harrow-leg, and thro' the Beam ; but all that Part of the Pin, which is in that Leg againſt which the Nut is ſcrew'd, muſt be ſquare ; whereby that Part being bigger than the round Part of the Pin, and than the Hole in the laſt-mention'd Leg, cannot turn in the Hole of that Leg ; for if it did, the Nut would be ſoon unſcrew'd by the Motion of the Harrow ; but the Pin muſt have room to turn in the other Leg, and in the Beam. This ſquare Part of the Pin is ſeen at *a*, *Fig.* 9. The whole Length of the Pin, from its Head to the End of the ſquare Part at *a*, where the Screw begins, is of the Thickneſs of the Two Legs, and of the Breadth of the Beam.

We ſometimes ſet the Legs of the Harrow Two Inches wider aſunder, by making them each an Inch thicker at their fore Ends in their Inſide, and reaching Five or Six Inches behind their Iron Pin : Theſe thicker Parts, bearing againſt the Beam, keep the hinder Part of each Harrow-leg an Inch diſtant from the Sides of the Beam, whereby the Harrow-legs are Six Inches aſunder, inſtead of Four, by means of theſe added Thickneſſes.

When a Drill is taken up to be turn'd, the Perſon that does it, takes hold of the Harrow-head, and lifts it up : The Legs of the Harrow, bearing againſt the croſs Piece, ſupport the whole Weight of the Drill.

When the Harrow does not go deep enough, we tie a Stone upon the Middle of the Harrow-head, by a String that paſſes thro' the Holes at *h*. All the Wood of this Plough and Harrow is Aſh, except the Limbers.

The

The Hopper of the Turnep-drill is very different from thofe already defcribed · It confifts of a Box placed into the Middle of a Carriage; which Box is defcribed in all its Parts, lying open with their Infides upwards in *Fig.* 10. A is the fore Side of the Box, Five Inches and an half deep, and Six Inches and an half long. B, the hinder Side of the Box, oppofite to the former, and of equal Dimenfions.

Each End of the Box is made with Three Pieces of Board, of which C the uppermoft is Three Inches and a quarter deep, and Five Inches long; which Length is the Breadth of the Infide of the Box. The End of the Piece C, when in its Place, ftands againft the prick'd Line *a b* in the fore Side A; the other End ftanding againft the prick'd Lines in B, which is oppofite to, and correfponds with, the prick'd Line *a b*; the fore Side, and hinder Side, being fcrew'd to the Ends of this Piece by Four Screws.

The Piece D is Two Inches and a quarter broad, and of the fame Length with the Piece C, and fcrew'd up to the Bottom of it with Two Screws, and then its End will bear againft the prick'd Line *b c*, and that which is oppofite to it in the Side B.

E is the lower Piece of this End, and an Inch and a quarter broad: Its End is to ftand againft the prick'd Line *c d*, and its other End at the oppofite prick'd Line in B. The Piece D muft be fcrew'd upon the upper Edge of the Piece E, as the Bottom F muft be fcrew'd up to its under Edge, which will ftand upon the prick'd Line *e f*. The Three Pieces G, H, I, being oppofite to C, D, E, and of the fame Dimenfions with them, placed in the fame manner, make the other End of this Box. At *g* in the Bottom F, appears the Hole which is over the Mortife of the Brafs Seed-box, the Shape and Size of which Hole may be feen by the prick'd Lines upon the Flanches B, C, of *Fig.* 9. in *Plate* 2. The foremoft End of which Hole reaches almoft as far forwards as the

End of the Axis of the Tongue of the Brafs Seed-box, and its hinder End almoft as far as the hinder End of its Cover (*a*). The Bottom F, being of the fame Length, with C, D, E, and their Oppofites, bears againft the prick'd Line *d h* of the fore Side A, and againft the oppofite prick'd Line of B. The Length of this Bottom F is the Breadth of the Infide of the Box, and its Breadth reaches to the outer Edges of the Pieces E and I, being Three Inches and an half.

All the Jointings of thefe Pieces muft be at right Angles, and fo clofe, that no Seed may run out at them. All the Pieces are of Board, full half-inch thick, except the Bottom, which is thinner.

Fig. 11. fhews the Bottom of the Box with its under Side uppermoft, where the light Part A is the Bottom-board, covering the Two End-boards, E and I, in *Fig.* 10. The dark Parts B and C are the under Sides of D and H, in *Fig.* 10. At *a* is the fore End of the Brafs Seed-box fcrew'd up to this Bottom-board. At *b* is the hinder End of the Brafs Seed-box fcrew'd up in like manner, the outer Edge of the Flanch of the Seed-box being even with the Edge of the Bottom-board. The End of the Brafs Spindle, with its Fork, appears at C.

Fig. 12. fhews this Box ftanding upon its Bottom, with its hinder Side laid open. At *a* is the Hole in the Bottom, under which the Brafs Seed-box is faften'd, with fmall Iron Screws, fquare near the Heads, paff-ing thro' the Bottom, and thro' the Holes at each End of the Brafs Box, with their Nuts underneath.

(*a*) Commonly it reaches within half a quarter of an Inch; but if it fhould only reach within a quarter of an Inch of them, it would not have that ill Confequence at that Diftance, as the fame Pofition would have in the large Seed-boxes; for, in them, the Seed would, in fuch Cafe, be apt to bear againft the Bottom of the Hopper, and obftruct the Motion of the Brafs Tongue, which fmall Seeds cannot do in the Turnep-feed Box.

The

The Pins muſt touch all the Sides of the Holes in the Braſs, to prevent the Seed-box from moving any Way.

A is the fore Side of the Box. B the hinder Side lying down. C is the Piece H of *Fig.* 10. which makes a ſort of Shelf in the Box at its left End. D at the right End makes another like Shelf, underneath which, the Fork of the Braſs Spindle is turn'd by the Crank in the End of the wooden (falſe) Spindle. By means of theſe Shelves, there is room for the Two wooden falſe Spindles to come the further into the Carriage, without leſſening the upper Part of the Box. E and F are the Two Ends of the upper Part of the Box, made by the Two Pieces G and C of *Fig.* 10. When the hinder Side B is rais'd up, and ſcrew'd to theſe Ends, the Box is complete.

We put a Lid upon this Box, which is hing'd on to its right or left End. This Box (having the Braſs Seed-box at its Bottom) is to be placed into the Middle of a Frame or Carriage.

Fig. 13. ſhews the Inſide of the Carriage lying down. A is the hinder Side, Eighteen Inches long, Dove-tails and all, and Six Inches broad. B the fore Side of the ſame Length with the hinder Side, and Eleven Inches broad. This Five Inches greater Breadth than the hinder Part is, becauſe a greater Height is required on the fore Side, on account of the Hopper's being drawn, and the Plough held up by that and the Pieces that muſt be fix'd to it. C, D, are its Two Ends, Six Inches long, beſide their Dove-tails, and Six Inches broad. E and F are Two Pieces each Six Inches long, whoſe Ends are to ſtand againſt the prick'd Lines *a b* and *c d* of the hinder Side, and their other Ends againſt the prick'd Lines in the fore Side, which are oppoſite to theſe. The Breadth of each of theſe Pieces is Four Inches : When they are in their Places, their lower Edges come even with the Bottom of the Carriage. Their Uſe is to ſupport the

the Ends of the Spindles which come juft thro' their Holes, after each of them have paffed their Hole at its refpective End of the Carriage.

All this Carriage is made of Board full half-inch thick ; The Ends C and D are made of double Thicknefs by another Piece of Board added to each, that covers all their Infides, except their Dove-tails. Thefe Boards with which they are lin'd, are nail'd to them, with their Grain going a different Way, and croffing the Grain of the Board at the End, either at right or oblique Angles. This prevents the Holes from fplitting out, and makes the Holes of a double Thicknefs ; whereby the Spindle is the lefs worn by them, in cafe there are no Brafs Wreaths to enter them.

The middle Pieces E and F are lin'd by their whole Surfaces, in the fame Manner as the Infides of the Ends are lin'd.

When thefe Ends and middle Pieces are in their Places, a wooden Cylinder, of the exact Diameter of the Holes, is thruft thro' all Four, to hold them exactly true, whilft the Ends and middle Pieces are all fcrew'd faft into their Places.

The prick'd Lines are drawn all round the Carriage, thro' the Centres of the Holes, and at equal Diftance from the Bottom of the Carriage, which is an Inch and Three quarters, and the One-eighth of an Inch. This prick'd Line is a Direction how high to nail on the Ledgers G and H, whereon the Box is to ftand ; and the Diftance the upper Surface of the Ledger muft be above the prick'd Line, is the Semidiameter of the Brafs Spindle ; and the Thicknefs of the Brafs Box above the Spindle, or which is the fame thing, the Diftance between the Centre of the great Hole of the Brafs Seed-box, and the Plane of the Top of its Mortife, being half an Inch and half a quarter, ftrike a Line above the prick'd Line parallel to it, at this Diftance above, and then nail on the Ledger,

with

with its upper Edge at this Line. This, with its oppofite Ledger plac'd in the fame manner, will fupport the Box with the Axis of the Spindle of the S~edbox, at equal Height with the Centres of the Holes of the Carriage; fo that if thofe Holes are parallel to, and equidiftant from the fore Side and hinder Side of the Carriage, and the Axis of the Brafs Spindle be placed in the like manner parallel to, and equidiftant from the fore Side and hinder Side of the Box; then when the Box is thruft down in its Place, upon thefe Ledgers, and the wooden (falfe) Spindles are placed into their Holes, their Axis will fall into a ftrait Line with the Axis of the Brafs Spindle, as they ought.

Fig. 14. fhews the Carriage laid open. A is its back Side lying down. B is its fore Side ftanding up. C is the fquare End of the left (falfe) Spindle, whereon a Wheel is to be put up to the Shoulders of the Spindle, quite clofe to the Ends of the Carriage. This Spindle, being an Inch and an half Diameter, is held in its Place, and kept from moving end-ways, by Two Wreaths; the one at *a*, bearing againft the Infide of the End of the Carriage, the other Wreath at *b*, bearing againft the left Side of the middle Piece; which Wreath keeps the Spindle from moving towards the right Hand, as the other does from moving towards the left. D is the fquare End of the other wooden Spindle, whereon a Wheel muft be placed in the fame manner as the other Wheel. This Spindle is kept from moving end-ways by Two Wreaths, in the fame manner as the other Spindle is; but this righthand Spindle, being that which turns the Brafs Spindle by its Crank, which enters the Fork, fhould have its Wreaths of Brafs, like thofe defcrib'd in *Fig.* 17. *Plate* 4. Part of which Wreaths entering about Three quarters of an Inch into the Hole of the End and middle Part of the Carriage, being firmly fcrew'd on to the Spindle, prevent the Friction that would otherwife be betwixt the Wood of the Spindle, and the

C c 3 Wood

Wood of the Holes; which Friction wearing the Wood of both, would in time cause the Spindle to be loose in its Holes, whereby its Axis would deviate from the strait Line it should make with the Axis of the Brass Spindle, and make an Angle with it ; and then the Crank would change its Place in the Fork at every Revolution of the Wheels; and if the Hole should be worn very wide, and the Spindle worn much less, the Crank might let go the Fork ; but when the Wood is of this Thickness, and each Hole has Wood in it, with its Grains pointing different ways, it would be many Years before the Holes would become large enough for this to happen, tho' only wooden Wreaths were used ; and as to the Two Wreaths of the left Spindle, they may be of Wood, because tho' that Spindle should grow loose, it is no Damage; for it only serves to bear up that End of the Carriage ; but he that has this Sort of Brass Wreaths for the hinder Hopper of a Wheat-drill, may take them thence, and place them upon these Spindles, and remove them again to the Wheat-drill when that is used ; for that and the Turnep-drill are very rarely, or never, used at the same time.

E is the Iron Crank, plac'd into the false Spindle, in the manner shewn at H in *Fig.* 5. of *Plate* 2. for turning the Brass Spindle by its Fork ; but take care that the End of this wooden Spindle do not approach nearer to the End of the Brass Spindle than the Distance of half an Inch, lest, if the inner Wreath should grow loose, the wooden Spindle might bear so hard against the Brass one, as to wrench the Seed-box down from the Wood, and then the Seed might run out betwixt the Seed-box and the Bottom to which it is screw'd,

When the hinder Side A is screw'd up against the Ends and middle Pieces, then the Box describ'd, being thrust down into the Carriage, and standing upon the describ'd Ledgers, and at that Distance from each

End

End of the Carriage, that the Seed may drop on the Side of the Funnel, as is before defcrib'd; the Box is kept in its Place by one Screw paffing thro' its Back, and the back Side of the Carriage.

The Notch F is cut in the Bottom of the hinder Side of the Carriage, up to the Bottom of the Ledger, for the Convenience of feeing the Seed drop into the Funnel.

The round Notch G is made in the Bottom of the fore Side of the Carriage, to make room for one's Hand to go in there, and turn the Setting-fcrew without taking off the Hopper from the Standards.

This Box and Carriage, fo fix'd together, compofe the Turnep-hopper, which is drawn and guided, and alfo holds up the Plough, by Two hollow Pieces of Wood fcrew'd on to the Outfide of the fore Part of the Carriage; their Ends H and I appearing a little above the Carriage.

One of thefe hollow Pieces of Wood is fhewn in *Fig.* 15. The Breadth of its Hollow muft conform to the Breadth of the Standards, which are One Inch and a quarter broad; but we muft allow about a quarter of an Inch more in the Hollow for the Swelling of the Wood. The Depth of the Hollow muft be the Thicknefs of the Standard that is to go in it, allowing about the Eighth of an Inch for the Swelling of the Wood. The Hollow fhould be a little deeper in the Middle than at each End; becaufe the Standard ought not to bear againft any thing, except at or near the upper and lower Part of the Carriage. Altho' the End of thefe Pieces come a little higher than the Carriage in this Hopper, yet I think it is better that thefe hollow Pieces come no higher than even with the Top, nor defcend any lower than even with the Bottom of the Carriage; and then the Length of each of thefe Pieces need be no more than Eleven Inches, which is the whole Depth of the Carriage.

The

The Wood on each Side of the Hollow, sufficient for the Holes *a, a, a, a,* muft be about half an Inch broad. The beft way for fixing them on, is whilft the Standards are in them, placing a fmall Piece of Wood at each Corner of the Hollow, betwixt the Standard and the Wood, to the end that there may be no more room on one Side of a Standard than on the other Side; then fcrew them on (parallel to and equidiftant from their refpective Ends of the Carriage) by Four fmall Screws each, the one at *c, c, c, c,* and the other at *d, d,* with Two below; the Heads of thefe Screws being on the Infide of the Carriage, and their Nuts on the Outfides of the hollow Pieces; then pull out thofe little Pieces of Wood, that were to keep the Standards in the Middle of the Hollows, whilft the Holes for the Screws were bored, and then the Turnep-Hopper is finifhed, and being put on upon the Standards A, B, in *Fig.* 16. is ready to go to Work; and in this Figure the whole Turnep-drill may be feen as in the Profpect of a Perfon following it at Work, except that this Figure has not the double Standard, nor Marking-wheels; becaufe we never ufe them for drilling-Turneps, except it be on the Level, which we very rarely do.

The Circles of the Wheels of this Hopper go Twenty five Inches afunder; were they farther afunder, they would not go fo well upon the Ridges; or were they nearer together, they might not hold up the Plough fo fteadily, but that one Wheel might happen to be rais'd from the Ground, by the defcending of the oppofite Limber; and if it fhould happen to be the Wheel that turns the Crank, no Seed would be deliver'd out whilft the Wheel was rais'd above the Ground; fometimes we ufe Wheels of Twenty-fix Inches Diameter, fometimes Thirty, and at intermediate Diameters, with this Hopper.

The beft Wood for making all Sorts of Hoppers is Walnut-tree or Elm; our Beams and Standards we make of Afh.   What

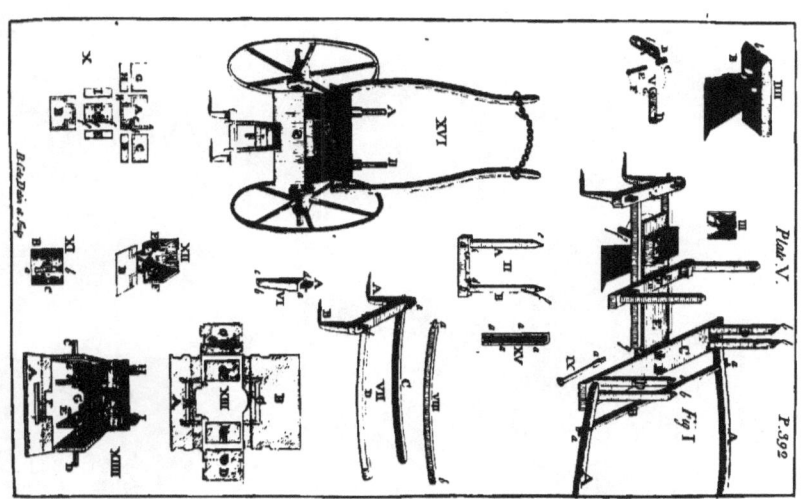

Plate V.

P. 392

What is meant by Wood-fcrews, are taper Screws made with Iron, having very deep Threads, whereby they hold-faft when fcrewed into Wood, and their Points will enter into foft Wood without boring any Hole for them into the Wood they are to take hold of; but near their Heads they are round, and have no Thread, and that Part of them muft always be in a bored Hole thro' that Part of a Board that is to be drawn clofe.

If the Standards fhould be much fwollen by being wet, it may be proper to anoint them with Soap.

In drilling, when the Wind is very ftrong, and the Hopper goes high above the Funnel, the Seed might be blown over it, if we did not take care to guard it from the Force of the Wind; and for doing this there are many Ways: Sometimes we nail a Piece of Linen Cloth round the Ends, and the fore Side of the Hopper; or elfe we nail on a Piece of old Hat, or Shoe-leather, round the Edges of the Funnel, to raife it higher; or if the Hopper go a great deal above the Trunk, we nail up a Pipe of Leather to the wooden Bottom of the Box, which Pipe, being about an Inch wide at Bottom, protects the Seed from the Wind, till it arrives fo near the Funnel, that the Wind cannot blow it over.

If we would have a long Hopper, to plant many Rows at once, of Clover or other fine Seeds, it is eafy to make each of thefe wooden (falfe) Spindles turn Two or Three Brafs or Iron Spindles; but then, as in all other Cafes; where the fame Hopper is to fupply more than one Chanel with Seed, each of its Wheels muft have Liberty to rife without the other, as thofe of the hinder Hopper of the Wheat-drill do.

C H A P.

C H A P. XXIII.

Of the Hoe-Plough, *&c.*

PLATE 6. *Fig.* 1. is the Hoe-Plough in a side
View. A is the Beam and Plough-tail, being
much the same with that of the common Plough described in *Fig.* 1. of *Plate* 1. The Beam of such a
common Plough, being cut off, and screwed up to
this Plank, and its Limbers, might make a Hoe-
Plough. The Share of this, from its Tail to the fore
Part of its Socket, is Two Feet One Inch long, and
from thence to the End of the Point, Ten Inches and
an half: This is the Measure of the under Side of the
Share. B is the Plank, Two Feet Seven Inches and
an half long, Two Inches and an half thick, and
Nine Inches broad. C, D, are the Nuts of the Two
Screw-pins, which hold up the Beam to the Plank.
E is the Nut of the Draw-pin, which Pin has a
Crook underneath, whereto one of the Links of the
short Chain of the Whipper is fastened for drawing
the Plough; the only Use of this Nut is, to hold the
Pin from dropping out by its own Weight, and that
of the Chain and Whipper; but often, to avoid the
Trouble of screwing and unscrewing the Nut, we
supply its Use by a square Pin a little bigger than the
Hole, which we drive up by an Hammer, so tight,
that it may not drop out of itself; but can easily be
driven out by a few Blows of the Hammer, as often
as it is necessary to remove it into another Hole.
F, G, are the Two Limbers; they are screwed on to
the Plank by Four Screws and Nuts: The under Surface of the Limbers by their whole Length are parallel
to the Plank, and to the upper Surface of the fore
End

End of the Beam, contrary to the manner of placing the Limbers of the Drill Ploughs; becaufe their Planks being always parallel to the Bottom of their Shares, if their Limbers were parallel to their Beams, as thefe are, the fore Ends of their Limbers would not be elevated higher than the Plank, but would go within a Foot of the Ground, inftead of being elevated almoft as high as the Horfes that draw them ; and the upper and under Surfaces of this Plank muft not be parallel to the Share, but muft make the fame Angle with it as its Limbers and Beam do.

Thefe Limbers ought to crook outwards from each other all the Way, till they come within about a Foot of the Chain, much more than the Drill-Limbers need to do ; becaufe the Middle of the Plank of the Drill follows directly after the Horfe, but the Middle of the Plank of the Hoe-Plough very feldom does; and therefore there muft be the more room betwixt thefe Limbers. Likewife there muft be the more room betwixt the fore Part of the Limbers, becaufe oftentimes the right Limber muft be raifed, and the left depreffed, in holding the Plough towards the left Side (for if it fhould be held towards the right Side, the Share would go upon the Fin, and its Point be raifed out of the Ground, unlefs it were on a Surface that had a Declivity towards the Right). The Diftance between the fore Ends of thefe Limbers is Two Feet Eight Inches.

The Strength and Stiffnefs of thefe Limbers muft be fuch, that there may be no Bending betwixt their fore Ends and the Tail of the Beam ; for if they be too weak, fo as to yield to the Weight of the Furrow, the Point of the Share will defcend into the Ground, and its Tail will rife up, and then the Plough cannot go well. The fhorter they are, the ftronger and ftiffer will they be, of the fame Thicknefs. We may make them juft of fuch a Length, that there may be room for the Horfe before the Bar H (which holds the Limbers at their due Diftance). Thefe are from
their

their Ends to the Bar, Four Feet Ten Inches long and from thence to the Plank Ten Inches, and Three Inches and an half square at the Bar.

I is the Whipper. K, L, are its Notches, whereunto the Traces both of the Thiller, and of the Horse next before him, are fastened. The Length of the Whipper is uncertain ; but when we hoe betwixt Rows, when the Plants are grown high, we make it as short as it can be, without galling the Horse's Legs by the Traces.

We set this Plough to go deeper or shallower by the Chain of the Limbers ; the changing of whose Links to the Crook M has the same Effect as changeing the Pins to different Holes of the Crow-staves of a common Plough.

Fig. 2. is the Beam with its Mortise and Holes; its Crooking down at the Tail is not very material ; but it causes the hinder Sheat to be a little the shorter below the Beam, whereby it may be something the lighter, and yet of the same Strength as if it were longer. Its whole Length is Four Feet Ten Inches: We make its Breadth and Thickness such, that it may be as light as it can be without Bending. A is the Mortise thro' which the hinder Sheat passes. B is the Mortise for the fore Sheat, upon which it is pinned up. C is a Hole in the Beam, into which the End of the left Handle being driven, holds it from moving, and is the best Manner of fastening this Handle of a Plough. D, E, are the Holes, thro' which the Two Legs of the double Retch pass, and are there held up by their Nuts. F is the Coulter-hole. G is the hinder Hole, by which the Plough is held up to the Plank. H and I are the Two foremost Holes of the Beam, thro' one or the other of which passes the Pin which holds the Beam to the fore Part of the Plank. These Holes must be made as near together as they can be, without Danger of splitting them one into another ; to prevent which there are several Ways: The one is by driving in Two square Pins cross the Beam, under

the

the pricked Line *a b*, before the Holes are bored, which will prevent the Grain of the Wood from being forced out of one Hole into the other; or these Holes may be plated with Iron above and below, which will have the same Effect, and then there need not be more than One Inch between Hole and Hole.

Fig. 3. is the Plank apart, which by its Holes, and pricked Lines, shews the different Manner of placing the Beam. *a, a, a, a,* are the Four Holes for screwing down the Limbers to the Plank.

Supposing the Path of the Horse to be a strait Line, and the pricked Line *h i* (which is at right Angles with the Plank, and equidistant from each Limber) to go exactly over it, without making any Angle on either Side of it; then the Beam must be placed at right Angles with the Plank, to the End that the Share may go parallel to the Horse-path, excepting that very small Inclination that its Point has to the left, shewn by the pricked Lines in *Fig. 1.* of *Plate 1.* But this Plough seldom follows the Horse in that manner. The said pricked Line *h i* generally makes Angles with the Horse-path; else when the Beam stood near the left Limber, and the Draw-pin near the right Limber in the Hole 9. (which it must do to keep the Share parallel to the Horse-path) the Weight of the right End of the Plank and its Limber would be too heavy for the right Hand of the Holder to manage; and if the Draw-pin be removed (suppose) to Hole 7. the Parallelism of the Share with the Horse-path will be lost, and the Point of the Share may be inclined too much towards the Left; and when a Furrow is to be plowed on the right Side of the Horse-path, the Beam must be removed nearer to the Middle of the Plank, and the Draw-pin must be placed on the left Side of the Beam, suppose to the Hole 2. This will bring the greatest Part of the Plank to the right Side of the Horse-path; and then the Share, standing at right Angles with the Plank, will make a very large

Angle

Angle with the Horfe-path, and then the Plough will not perform at all. Therefore it being neceffary, that the Share always go parallel to the Horfe-path, and often as neceffary that the Plank go at oblique Angles to the Horfe-path; it follows then that the Beam ftand at oblique Angles with the Plank, to preferve the Parallelifm to the Horfe-path; and this cannot be done but by the Holes which are fhewn under the pricked Lines which crofs the Plank.

The Holes A, B, C, are thofe to one of which the Beam is fcrewed up by its Hole G, in *Fig.* 2. Thefe Holes are made as near to the hinder Edge of the Plank, as they can fafely be, without Danger of tearing out; which is generally about an Inch diftant from the faid Edge.

Every one of thefe Holes are anfwered by Three others, near the fore Edge of the Plank, as the Hole B has, at the fore Edge of the Plank, the Holes D, E, F. D, E belong to the Hole I of the Beam *Fig.* 2. Thefe Two Holes are made as near together as they can be without breaking into one another. F anfwers the Hole H in *Fig.* 2. and is made between D and E, as near them as fafely it can.

When the Beam is fcrewed up at B and F, and makes the fame Angles with the Plank, as the pricked Line *b c* doth; then the Draw-pin ftanding in the Hole 8 or 9, will bring the Plough fo much to the Left, that the Share will point too much towards the Right; then remove the fore End of the Beam to the Hole D, and then the Beam will make the fame Angle with the Plank as the pricked Line *c d*, which may bring the Share to be parallel to the Horfe-path nearly enough: But if the Draw-pin fhould be placed in the Hole 1. then the Plank would go fo much on the Right of the Horfe-path, that the Share would point vaftly too much towards the Left, ftanding in either of thefe Two Pofitions: Therefore the foremoft Pin muft be removed to the Hole E, and then the Beam

being

being at the fame Angles with the Plank as the pricked Line *f g*, it may be parallel to the Horfe-path, or fo nearly, that by removing the Draw-pin one Hole, it may be made perfectly fo.

Note, That tho' here are but Nine Holes for the Draw-pin ; yet we ufually make many more in our Planks : And fometimes by changing the Draw-pin either Way into another Hole, tho' that Hole be but an Inch diftant from the former, the Share is brought right without any Inconvenience.

The Holes A and C have each of them their oppo-fite Holes, which (when the Beam is placed into either of the Two) have the fame Effect, for keeping the Share parallel to the Horfe-path, as the Hole B and its Three oppofite Holes have ; and if either of the Holes belonging to A, B, or C, fhould not bring the Beam fufficiently oblique to the Plank, for the Share to be parallel to the Horfe-path, when the Draw-pin is in fome one particular Hole, then there may be an-other Hole bored before, on the Right or Left, for the fore Pin to pafs thro' by the Hole H of the Beam *Fig.* 2. which will incline the Beam a little more to the Right or Left, as occafion requires ; and if none of all thefe be fufficient, the Plank may be turned the other Side upwards ; and the Beam being faftened there by the hinder Screw into any one of thofe Holes, which were next to the fore Edge of the Plank before it was reverfed, there may be a new Set of Holes to anfwer the fore Pin, of which that which was an hin-der Hole before the Plank was reverfed, may be one. Thefe may fet the Beam at different Angles from any of the firft Holes ; fo that there may be at one End of the Plank Six Syftems of Holes, Three on the one Side, and Three on the other ; and if we have a mind to make yet more various Pofitions of the Plough, we may turn the Plank, End for End, and there make Six different Syftems of Holes.

But,

But, instead of turning the Plank, it would be better to have a Fourth Hole in the Beam, standing as near to the hinder Hole as H doth to the fore Hole; to answer which Fourth Hole, there may be Two Holes in the Plank, one at each Side of the hinder Hole of every System at proper Distances, to set the Plough still at more different Angles with the Plank; and these, I believe, will be more convenient for the Purpose than the different Holes in the fore Part of the Plank, it being easier to remove the hinder Screw than the fore Screw; because if the Plank and Limbers are not held up by somebody, whilst the fore Pin is out, their Weight will wrench out the hinder Hole of the Plank by that Screw; but whilst the hinder Screw is out, there is no need of holding up the Plank, because its Weight, bearing upon the Beam, cannot injure the foremost Hole, whilst the Limbers bear upon the Horse. Upon this account, I wonder we had not made the Holes, for changing the Position of the Beam, at the hinder Part of the Plank rather than the fore Part; which convinces me, that new Instruments are seldom perfect in the Beginning.

We can also alter the Standing of the Beam, by cutting away the Wood on one Side of an Hole, and placing a Wedge on the opposite Side of the Pin.

The Holder may make some Alteration in the Going of the Plough by the Handles.

The Reason we never set the Beam on the right Half of the Plank is, that the Plough always turns its Furrow towards the Right-hand; and the strait Side of the Share and the Coulter never go so near to a Row on the Right-hand, by the Breadth of Two Furrows, as it does to a Row on the Left-hand.

If by the Drawing of the fore Horse or Horses, the Plough should bear too hard upon the Thiller, it may be helped by making a Row of Holes near the hinder Side of the Plank, for the Draw-pin, instead

of

of thofe in the Middle; for the farther backwards the Draw-pin is plac'd, the lefs will the Limbers bear on the Thiller, efpecially when drawn by more Horfes than one; becaufe the fore Horfes draw the Limbers more downwards than the Thiller doth, as may be feen in *Fig.* 4.

Fig. 4. fhews the manner how the Hoe-plough is drawn, and how the Traces are fix'd to it. The Traces of both Horfes are faftened to the Notches of the Ends of the Whipper at *a* and *b*. The Traces of the Thiller by their fore Part are faftened to an Hook, or Ring, on the Wood of the Collar, as is ufual for other Thillers; and the fore Part of the next Horfe's Traces is faftened to his Collar in like manner; but thefe Traces, being twice as long as thofe of the Thiller, muft be held up in the Middle by a Piece of Cord or Chain, as at *c*, where one End of it is faftened to the Trace, and paffes over the Top of the Collar, behind one of the Hames, and before the other to keep it from flipping backwards or forwards; its other End is faftened to the opofite Trace on the other Side, as this End is at *c*. This prevents the Chain from falling down, and getting under the Horfe's Legs in turning; but beware that this String or Chain be not fo fhort as to hold up the Traces higher than their ftrait Line; for that would prefs upon the Collar, and gall the Thiller, befides occafioning the Plough to be drawn too much upwards; for this drawing of the fore Horfe by a different Line from that of the Thiller, is a great Advantage for keeping the Plough the firmer into the Ground.

If there is another Horfe, his Traces are faftened at the Collar of the Second, in the fame manner as in drawing of a Waggon.

When we hoe betwixt Rows, where the Plants are very high, as thofe of Turnep-feed, which are much higher than the Horfes, to turn a new Furrow up to the Row, when there is a Trench in the Middle of the Interval, where the Horfes muft go, we find it beft

to

to place the Beam by the Holes B and E, in *Fig.* 3. and the Draw-pin near the left Limber, which brings the Tail of the Plough to the Right-hand, and the fore Ends of the Limbers being towards the Left, the End of the right Limber (by turning the Handles a little to the Left) bears against the wooden Saddle at *d*, and cannot hitch into or take hold of any of the Plants to tear them. And that no Part of the Limber may take hold of any Plant, we make it very smooth from one End to the other; and cut off the Corner of the Plank equal with the Limber, that the Plants may slip by it without hanging in it, or being broken by it. The Whipper standing towards the left End of the Plank, its End *b* does not reach so far towards the right as to take hold of the Plants, its End *a* being over the Interval, where no Plants are; and to keep its right End the more out of Danger of hurting the Plants, we place the Hook of its Chain nearer towards this End, by which means the left End, becoming heavier, sinks lower, and raises the right End higher; and the higher it is, the more secure the Plants will be from it; because they are held off by the Limber above.

This way my Turnep-seed has been ho'd, when one would have thought it impossible for a Plough and Horses to go betwixt the Rows without destroying the Crop. Almost in this manner we give our Wheat the last Hoeing, to turn the Furrow a Second time towards the Row. When the Plants of the Rows are very high, the Driver must go in the next Interval, on the Left of the Plough; and the Holder has a Cord, like the Reins of a Bridle, which he lays over the End of the Draw-pin, which keeps it from falling down, until he has occasion to use it for guiding or turning the Thiller.

When we turn the Furrow from the Row (which will then be ever on the left Side of the Plough), the Plough must be set in a very different and contrary

Posture;

Posture; but then the Plants commonly being low, there is no Danger of the Whipper's or Limber's hitching or taking hold of them; but the Driver muſt take care, that he does not tread on them, nor ſuffer any of the Horſes to do ſo; and they of themſelves, when they are not blind, take all the Care they can to avoid it; and I obſerve, that the Plants are oftener injured by the Driver, than by the Horſes.

'Tis in this laſt-mentioned manner of Hoeing, when we go very near to the young Plants, the Firſt or Second time, that we muſt take care of burying them with the Earth, which (eſpecially when dry and fine) is apt to run over to the left Side of the Plough; this we can in great meaſure prevent, when the Ground is clean, by nailing with Three or Four Nails a very thin ſquare Piece of Board to the Sheat, with one Corner bearing at, or below, *a*, in *Fig.* 1. and its other lower Corner bearing on the Back of the Coulter on its left Side at *b*, its upper Corner reaching to *c* or higher; its fore End is ty'd on to the Coulter by a leathern Thong paſſing thro' an Hole very near the End of the Board. The lower Edge of the Board muſt come no lower than the prick'd Line *a*, *b*, which, at *b*, is juſt even with the Surface of the Ground, before it is rais'd by the Share; for if this Board ſhould be ſet down too near the Share, the Plough would not go; but, being ſet in this manner, it prevents the Earth (when never ſo much pulveriz'd in the drieſt Weather) from running over upon the Plants to bury them, tho' the Plough go very near them; except in this caſe, we never uſe a Board, the Earth running over to the left Side, being often advantageous in Hoeing; for it changes more Surface of the Ground, than if it went all to the right; and when in Summer we hoe from the Wheat-rows, not going very near to the grown Plants, this Earth that runs over the Share to the Left, helps to mend ſuch Places where the Furrow

was

was not thrown up clofe enough to the Row by the precedent Hoeing.

The firft time we turn a Furrow towards the Row, the Horfes go in the Trench near to it, and the Plough ftands on the left Side of the Horfe-path, almoft in the fame manner as when the Furrow is turn'd from the Row; but we very often make ufe of a common Plough, for throwing down the Ridge, which has lain all the Winter in the Middle of the Interval. One Wheel, going on each Side of that Ridge, holds that Plough to a great Exactnefs for fplitting this Ridge into Halves, which the Earth-board, being fet out for that Purpofe, throws up to the Row on each Side of the Interval.

We alfo very often make ufe of the Two-wheel'd Plough, for raifing up the Ridges, whereon we drill the Rows; not but that the Hoe-Plough will do every thing that is neceffary to our Hufbandry : Yet the common Ploughs being heavier than we ufually make our Hoe-Ploughs, they by their Weight, and Help of their Wheels go a little fteadier : and befides the Plough-men, being more accuftom'd to them, prefer them before all other, where their Wheels are of no Prejudice.

I never faw neater Ridges rais'd by any Plough, than by the Hoe-Plough, nor finer Plowing; and I believe that were it made as heavy, and as ftrong, it would outdo the Swing-Plough, in plowing miry Clays, where Plough-wheels cannot go; but I, haveing no fuch Land, have never made any Hoe-Plough heavy enough for it. However, I am convinc'd, by the many Trials which I have feen, that no other Plough can be ufed for every Horfe-hoeing Operation, fo effectually as this I have now defcrib'd.

The making the Hoe-plough is not difficult for a good Workman; and a few of the Holes for fetting the Beam are fufficient, provided they are made in their proper Places, which is impoffible for me to defcribe exactly in a Number that is no more than neceffary;

neceſſary ; becauſe the Diſtance the Plough muſt go
from the Horſe-path on either Side, is uncertain, as
the Largeneſs or the Depth of the Furrow is ; and
for that Reaſon, it is as impoſſible for me direct the
Ploughman to the particular Angles, at which his
Beam muſt be ſet with the Plank, to keep the Share
parallel to the Horſe-path, as it is to direct a Fidler,
how far he muſt turn his Pegs to give his Strings their
due Tenſion for bringing them all in Tune, which
without a Peg to each String could never be done;
but when he has his juſt Number of Pegs, his Ear
will direct him in turning them, till his Fiddle is in
Tune ; ſo the Ploughman by his Eyes, his Feeling,
and his Reaſon, muſt be directed in the ſetting his
Plough; but without a competent Number of Holes,
he can no more do it than a Muſician can tune Four
Strings upon one Peg. And I am told, that ſome
Pretenders to making the Hoe-Plough have fix'd its
Beam to the Plank immoveable, which makes it as
uſeleſs for hoeing betwixt Rows, as a Violin with but
one Peg to its Four Strings would be for playing a
Sonata.

Fig. 5. ſhews the Sort of Yoke, that is us'd on
every Ox that draws in a ſingle File, as they always
muſt when they work with the Hoe-plough; but after
they have been accuſtom'd to draw double (*i. e.* Two
abreaſt) they muſt be practis'd for about a Week to
draw ſingle, before they are ſet to Hoeing ; for otherwiſe they will be apt to demoliſh the Rows, one run-
ing off to the right-hand, expecting his Fellow to
come up with him on the Left, and another will run
off on the Left to make room for his Companion to
go abreaſt with him on the Right, endeavouring to
go in the manner in which they us'd to be placed for
drawing in Pairs.

I ſuppoſe I need not give any Caution about muz-
ling the Oxen when they hoe; becauſe they will eat
the Plants as ſoon as they come an Inch above the

Ground, and that will fhew the Neceffity of it; but there is no occafion to muzzle the Horfes until the Plants are grown as high as their Nofes, when rein'd up, as in *Fig.* 4.

Fig. 6. is an Inftrument of Pulveration, which might have been fufficiently defcrib'd by its Matter, Weight and Dimenfions, without any Portrait, were it not to fhew the particular Manner of drawing it, being very different from that of a common Roller, whofe Frame is difficult to make, and coftly; but this, being only Three Feet long, is drawn by a fimple Pair of Limbers, held together, by the Two Bars A and B, firmly pinn'd in at their Ends.

Its Gudgeons muft not come out beyond the outer Surface of the Limbers, left they fhould take hold of the Plants, when drawn in the Intervals; alfo the hinder Ends of the Limbers, behind the Gudgeon, fhould crook a little upwards, for the fame Reafon.

This Stone Cylinder is Two Feet and an half Diameter, and weighs Eleven hundred Weight befides the Limbers. It muft never be us'd but in the drieft Weather, when neither the Plough nor Harrow can break the Clods; and then being fo very ponderous and fhort, it crufhes them to Powder, or into fuch very fmall Pieces, that a very little Rain, or even the Dews (if plentiful), will diffolve them.

I have had great Benefit by this Roller in preparing my Ridges for Turneps. The Weather proving dry at *Midfummer* (which is the beft Seafon for planting them), the Land was in Pieces like Horfe-heads, fo that there was no Hope of reducing them fit for planting with Turneps that Year; the Clods being fo very large, that they would require fo many Viciffitudes of wet and dry Weather to flack them; but this Inftrument crufh'd them fmall, and the Plough following it immediately, the Ridges were harrow'd and drill'd with very good Succefs.

I have also made use of it for the same Purpose in the Middle of a cloddy Field, where it pulveriz'd the Clods so effectually, that the Benefit of it might be plainly distinguish'd by the Colour and Strength of the Two following Crops, different from the other Parts of the Field adjoining on both Sides, whereon the Roller was not drawn.

But crushing has such a contrary Effect from squeezing, that if this Roller should be us'd when the Land is moist, it would be very pernicious, by unpulverizing it; of which I am so cautious, that sometimes I let the Roller lie still for a whole Year together.

There is also a long triangular Harrow, which is sometimes useful in the Intervals when the Earth is of a right Temper betwixt wet and dry; but there is no need to describe it, and I scarce use it once in Two or Three Years.

The Diameters of the wooden and iron Pins and Screws, with their Holes, and the Sizes of the Nails to be made use of in all the describ'd Instruments, I leave to the Discretion of the Workmen, who, if they are Masters of their several Trades, cannot be ignorant of such Matters.

Fig. 7. and *Fig.* 8. shew the Lands of Turneps mention'd at the Beginning of this Work.

AN

AN

APPENDIX

CONCERNING

The making of the DRILL, *and the* HOE-PLOUGH, &c.

O a Workman, who would make thefe Inftruments, I would add the following Directions.

The Firft thing to be done for making the Drill, is to place half a Sheet of Paper to the Back of Plate 2. by pafting it on to its Margin; and likewife another half Sheet to Plate 3. in the fame manner.

Then with a Needle prick through all the Out-lines of A, B, C, and D, in *Fig*. 2. which will mark out both Sides, and both Ends of the Mortife of the Turnep Drill-box. Alfo prick through the Out-lines of the great Hole in the middle of A, and of the elliptical Hole in B. Alfo prick the little Hole at E, in A; and at F, in B. Prick through the prick'd Line *p q*, in B; which is the Line to which the Setting-fcrew *Fig*. 6. or *Fig*. 12. that is to pafs thorough the Hole in C, muft be parallel.

When the Paper is taken off, cut out of it the faid A, B, C, and D, by the Pricks made by the Needle.

Then cut the fame in Paftboard, by laying thefe Pieces of Paper thereon (becaufe Paftboard, being ftiffer than

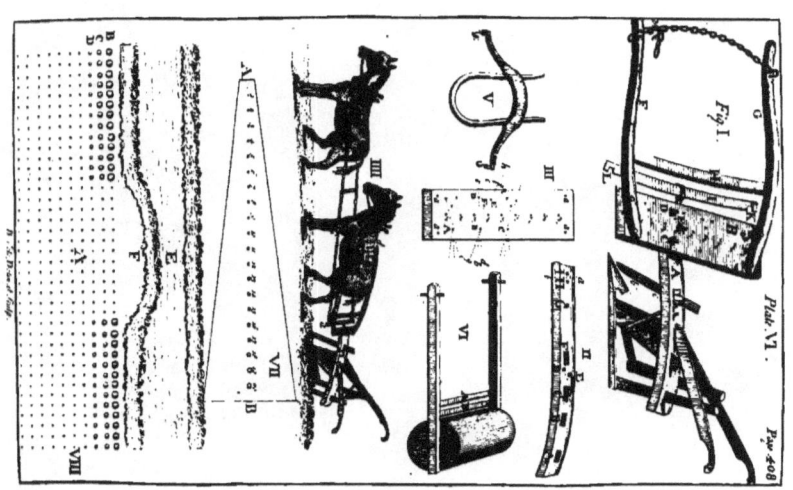

Plate VI.

Pag. 408.

than Paper, will be more fit for the Ufe). Draw a Line with Ink on the pricked Line, *p q.*

The Hole in C muft be fomething larger than in the Cut, becaufe the Setting-fcrew muft be fo, being beft to be of Brafs, which is lefs apt to ruft than Iron, of which Metal it was formerly made; but Brafs, being weaker, requires the more of it to equal the Strength of Iron.

The Wreath, *Fig.* 14. is not neceffary, becaufe the Slider, *Fig.* 15. is fufficient without it; but then care muft be taken, that the Edges of its Claws A B, which rub againft the Cylinder of E, in *Fig.* 9. be taken off, to prevent their cutting it. This Slider is fometimes made of Brafs, and fometimes of Iron.

Thus the Workman will have the Sides and Ends of the Turnep-mortife, which make the Whole of it, whereby he may make it exactly in foft Wood.

Fig. 7. called the inner Cylinder, being put into the Cylinder A, of the Steel Tongue, *Fig.* 4. whereby the Holes for the Axis of the Tongue, being the lower from the Top of the Mortife, do not only fecure the Edges of the Mortife from breaking out, but alfo give room for the Flanches B, C, in *Fig.* 9. to be made to reach as far forwards as the Axis of the Tongue, and farther: Hereby the Hole, in the Bottom of the Hopper, may be as wide at the fore End, as at the pricked Line at the Letter B.

The Notches in the Spindle, *Fig.* 5. feem to appear deeper than is ufual for Turnep-feed; but I remember I have drilled Furze-feed with a Turnep-drill without altering the Notches. As for the Shape of thefe Notches, they are fo fully defcribed in *Fig.* 6. and *Fig.* 8. of *Plate* 3. that I can add nothing to that Defcription; only that thofe being for the Wheat-drill, the Size of Notches for the Turnep-drill muft be leffer in fome proportion to the leffer Size of the Seed.

For making the Wheat-drill do the fame as for the Turnep-drill. The *Fig.* 3. in *Plate* 2. is one Side of of the Mortife, by which muft be made Two in Paft-board. *Fig.* 10. in *Plate* 2. and *Fig.* 9. in *Plate* 3. are the Two Ends of it.

The Cover that prevents the Wheat from falling down on the hinder Side of the Spindle, is one intire Piece of Brafs, which is marked B in *Fig.* 3. of *Plate* 3. but the Shape of it, with its Hole whereby it is held in by a Screw, is only feen in the Side, *Fig.* 3. of *Plate* 2. and there defcribed by pricked Lines; and by pricking through them, the Shape of the End of the Cover may be taken, which Cover is of the fame Shape from End to End.

The Joyner who cannot by thefe Additions, and the Explanations of the *Plates*, make thefe Drills in Wood, doth not deferve the Name of a Workman.

When he has once made them whole, he can eafily make them in Halves like *Fig.* 8. in *Plate* 2.

By thefe Halves the Founder will make his Moulds proper for cafting them in the beft Brafs. But in thefe Halves for Cafting, there muft be no other Holes, but the great Holes, and the Hole for the Setting-fcrew.

The great Hole in the Mould muft be largeft at E, in *Fig.* 9. *Plate* 2. and leffer in the Infide in *Fig.* 8. for as it muft be of a conical Shape for making the Core, if it fhould be caft bigger within, when the Whitefmith bores it (as he muft) to an exact Cylinder, the End E would be in Danger of burfting by the Force of the Boring, as it is much thinner than in the Mortife. And befides this, if there fhould be any little Flaw in the Edges of the Hole within the Mortife (which the Founder muft avoid as much as poffible), it may perhaps be bored out by means of the Hole's being lefs there. The Hole muft be fomething lefs in the Mould than its proper Size, even where it is largeft; elfe it may happen, that in boring it to a true Cylinder it may become too big. And I believe, in the Cooling of the Brafs, the Hole grows bigger as the Spindle grows lefs. For

For the Hole of the Setting-fcrew, lay on upon the dark Part of *Fig.* 8. one of the Paftboard-fides; and from the black Line *p, q,* draw a Line coincident to it as on the Brafs, for making the half Hole A by; and the other Half of it on the oppofite Half-fide.

Thefe Paftboards will be very ufeful to the White-fmith, for directing him to find the Places where the Holes for the Axis of the Tongue, and thofe for fcrewing the Two Halves of the Mortife together, are to be made. I advife againft boring the great Hole with a Tool (a Bit) with more than Four Edges; for it would be apt to tear the Brafs.

The great Hole of the Turnep-drill is bored with Tools like thofe wherewith a Gun is bored. But the Wheat-drill is bored with a Screw-ftock, whofe Edges are made fharp for that Purpofe, and may be fet wider or narrower at Pleafure: It is put into the Hole along with an half-round Piece of Wood, the lower End of the Stock being fet faft in a Vice: The whole Seed-box (for it muft always be fcrewed together before it is bored), being put on the End of the Stock (made taper a little way for entering), is turned round it by a long wooden Spanner, which hath a Notch in the middle of it, to receive the whole Seed-box, in order to bore it by turning it round upon the Stock.

The Brafs ought to be of the beft Sort, which will be eafy to file, and yet not mix with bafer Metal.

The Seed-boxes may be caft whole by thefe Moulds; but I prefer thofe that are fcrewed together, for feveral Reafons, which I have not time now to write.

There is a Turnep Seed-box come to my Hands that was made by Pretenders; I wifh it is the only one made in the fame manner; for it is ufelefs; the Notches in the Spindle are much fhorter than the Breadth of the Mortife; at each End of the Notches is a deep Chanel (as deep as the Bottom of the Notches) quite round the Spindle, inftead of a Mark, which fhould be but juft vifible for cutting the Notches;

3   and

and inftead of a tender Steel Spring, there is a ftrong
Piece of Iron without Elafticity.   By means of this
Iron, the Machine grinds the Seed, inftead of drill-
ing it.

What I fhall here add concerning the Wheat-drill, is
fome Alterations in *Fig.* 21. of *Plate* 4. *viz.* The fore
Share and Sheat muft be left out for drilling Wheat,
no more middle Rows being ufed.   And the Two
Beams B B in the Plough, *Fig.* 1. muft be fet to make
Chanels Ten Inches afunder. And the double Hopper,
Fig. 15. muft be fet nearer together, fo as the Seed
may fall into the middle of the Funnels of the Beams.

Tho' there is no Neceffity of Marking-wheels for
guiding the Drill-horfe upon Ridges ; yet they are
very ufeful for holding the Drill fteady, and to prevent its tottering, which without the Marking-wheels,
and the fore Hopper, it is apt to do, when the Shares
ftand fo near together as Ten Inches ; and on a narrow Ridge one of the hinder Wheels might run off to
the Furrow, and draw the Shares after it, if the Drill
were not kept fteady by the Marking-wheels, and by
their Hopper, which takes hold of the fingle Standard by *Fig.* 22. as is feen in *Fig.* 21. in *Plate* 4.
But there fhould not be fo much room in it on each
Side of the Standard, left the Plough by that means
fhould have too much room to totter, now the
Shares are fo near together.

The Marking-wheels muft be fet at the Diftance
of the Breadth of Two Ridges, which, as we now
make them, is about Nine Feet and an half from
Wheel to Wheel.

The Brafs Box may be taken out of the fore Hopper : And tho' that Hopper be of no Ufe to the double Row, except as is abovefaid ; yet if there fhould
be Occafion to prefs the Marking-wheels deeper into
the Ground for keeping the Plough the more fteady
in its Courfe, it may be ufefully filled with Earth, or
other Matter, fufficient for that Purpofe.   And befides,

fides, it may ferve to plant Three Rows of St. Foin, when the fore Share and Sheat are put in, and the Beams and hinder Hopper fet a Foot or Eighteen Inches wider, and the Marking-wheels at their due Diftance, as is directed in the Effay.   Thus the fame Drill may plant Wheat and St. Foin.

A Drill for the double Rows might be made with a fingle hinder Hopper, inftead of the double one. And there is a Contrivance to fupply the Ufe of the fore Hopper for keeping the Plough fteady, and more eafy to make than that Hopper; but this cannot be defcribed by Words without Cuts.

The Lime wherewith the brined Wheat is dried, receiving fome of the Salts from the Brine, will ftick in the Notches of the Spindle; yet never makes any Stoppage to their Delivery of the Seed; but every Year we clean the Notches from the Lime with a Chiffel, and, if it were done oftener, it would not be amifs.

There is an Accident that may poffibly happen, but never to a careful Driller; viz. a large Clod may fome way be thrown into a Funnel of the Beam of the Plough, either by a Wheel, or by the Paddle that cleanfes the Sheats from the Dirt that fticks to them when the Earth is wet.   This may ftop the Wheat from falling out of the Funnel into the Trunk; and then, fo far as the Plough goes thus ftopped, the Chanel will have no Seed in it; but the Driller that follows may take it out immediately, which if he fhould neglect to do for never fo little a Diftance, he ought to ftop the Plough whilft he fupplies the Chanel with Seed from his Hand as far as it is empty.   When there is any Danger of this, as in very rough cloddy Ground, it is beft to take off the Drill-harrow, to the end that the Chanel may lie open for receiving the Seed from the Hand.   But if the Ends of the Hopper reach below the Funnels, and they are otherwife defended, as they may be, this Accident can never happen.   When

When the Drill-harrow is taken off, the beſt way for taking up the Plough to turn it, is to bore a Hole of about half an Inch Diameter in the End of each Beam behind the Funnels, and faſten a Withe into theſe Holes; by which Withe the Driller very conveniently takes hold with one Hand, and lifts up the Plough, laying his other Hand on the Hopper to keep it ſteady. This Method of taking up the Plough hath been often uſed for the Wheat-drill, and for the Turnep-drill; and in the latter the Hole in the one Beam holds the Withe as well as do the Two Holes in the former.

There are new Editions of ſome of theſe Engines, which cannot be fully deſcribed without more *Plates*; but ſince thoſe already deſcribed are found by Experience to be ſufficient for the Purpoſes they were deſigned for, new Editions of them are not neceſſary, tho' convenient in many reſpects.

Reaſon will eaſily make Additions to the Inſtruments when they are neceſſary; as when more than one Braſs Spindle is to be turned by one or each Wheel for planting Clover amongſt Barley after it is come up. 'Tis done by a very light Plough, drawn by a Man: It plants Four Rows at once Eight Inches aſunder: The Shares are very ſhort and narrow, and ſo are the Sheats and Trunks. 'Tis not difficult to put on a Crank at the other End of the Braſs Spindle, in the ſame manner that the Handle that winds up a Jack is put on, and to faſten it at the Hole at I in *Fig.* 5. of *Plate* 2. This Crank muſt, at its firſt turning, before it turns up towards the Letter H, of the ſame *Fig.* be long enough to reach to within an Inch of the Fork of the Second Spindle. Thus each Wheel may turn ſeveral Spindles, and then this Drill may plant many Rows of Seeds at once.

When you plant Rows nearer together than Eight Inches, it is beſt that the Plough have Two Ranks of Shares and Hoppers, elſe the Earth may be driven

before

before the Shares; but with Two Ranks of them, they will not be more apt to drive the Earth before them in making Rows at Four Inches afunder, than at Eight, when there is only a fingle Rank of Shares.

But I think this near Diftance of Four Inches cannot be proper for any Sort of Seeds, except Flax-feed; and even for that Seed not neceffary. If the Land be made fine, a fingle Rank of Shares will go very well to plant Rows at Seven Inches afunder.

I had formerly a Drill-Plough for drilling acrofs very high round Ridges for Hand-hoeing, where Horfe-hoeing is impracticable : It had no Limbers ; but it had little Ground-wrifts to make open Chanels, and had Handles behind it, whereby the Driller raifed up the Tail of the Plough, when it was paffing the Summit of the Ridge. There were neither Funnels nor Trunks; for thefe would hinder the Seed from falling into the Chanels, both by the Plough's going up and down the Ridge. The Hopper was drawn by the Plough in fuch a manner, that in paffing all Parts of the Ridge the Wheels were not raifed from the Ground : The Chanels were equally fupplied with Seed throughout : It planted Four Rows at once, at a Foot afunder. I ufed this Drill-Plough 30 Years ago in *Oxfordfhire*: I have no fuch Ridges here, nor confequently any Occafion of fuch an Inftrument; and did not make Cuts of it, becaufe it is not ufeful for Horfe-hoeing. I only mention it here for the Benefit of thofe who have a mind to plant fuch Ridges regularly with an Engine : I hope their own Reafon will enable them to contrive fuch a Plough, efpecially now they have the manner of making the Drill, Hopper, &c. fhewn to them.

I have made a very material Addition to the Hoe-Plough, of *Plate* 6. *viz.* At the fore End of the Beam *Fig.* 2. is the Hole I, by which alone let the Plough be drawn, leaving out the Hole H ; inftead of the Hole G make a Mortife, Three or Four Inches long,

long, and as broad as the Thicknefs of the Iron Pin, the End and Nut of which are feen at C, in *Fig.* 1. This Pin fhould be more than half an Inch Diameter, and fquare at that End that goes into the Mortife; let the hinder End of the Mortife juſt appear behind the Plank, when the Beam is at right Angles with it.

By means of this Mortife there may be many more Holes through the Plank without Danger of fplitting into one another the Holes in the Beam, which muſt anfwer thofe in the Plank.

Draw many Lines from the Middle of the foremoſt Hole of the Plank to the hinder Edge of it, at (fuppofe) a quarter of an Inch from one another there; and then bore a Hole in that Part of each Line that is leaſt apt to break into the next Hole to it.

Every Syſtem of Holes in the Plank will have like Benefit of being increafed in their Number by the Convenience of this Mortife; without which it is impoffible to have fo great Variety of turning the Point of the Share to make the Share go parallel to the Horfe-path.

The Board defcribed in *p.* 403. we now ufe very feldom in Hoeing of Wheat.

Explanation of Plate VII.

FIG. 1. fhews the Plank and the Harrow of the lateſt and beſt Drill-plough, moſt fimple, and accommodated to the prefent Practice of planting double Rows.

A is the Plank, with all its Mortifes and Holes; *b* is the Mortife into which the Tenon of the fore Sheat of the Drill-plough, for planting treble Rows, was faſtened; *d* is the fquare Hole for receiving the Seed from a Hole of the fame Shape and Size in the Bottom of the Funnel.

When the Sheat is taken out of the Mortife *b*, and another Sheat is made exactly the fame with that, place them in the Mortifes *a a*, and make the Two
                                                                fquare

square Holes *c c* behind them, for their Funnels to stand on. Make the Mortise *e*, which is to hold the single Standard that is to hold up the fore Hopper in the treble Drill, and in this to guide the Wheels also, instead of Wreaths, that in the treble Drill are put on the Spindle bearing against the Insides of the double Standards; for in this the Shares being but Ten Inches asunder, and at such a Distance from each of the Wheels, that neither of them doth by rising lift up a Share perceptibly; but if the Shares were wide asunder, or there were more of them reaching nearer to the Ends of the Plank, a Wheel might rise up, and lift a Share out of the Ground, if guided by the single Standard and Hopper, as in this. The single Standard is shewn in *Plate* 4. *Fig.* 10. but this has no Fork at its Bottom, as that has. This has only a single Tenon, and is shouldered before, behind, and on each Side, to hold it the more firm and steady, when tightly pinned down by Two Pins underneath the Plank. The Dimensions of this Standard are the same with those of the other; but the Shoulders must not increase the Thickness of the Standard any higher than the Tops of the Funnels.

The Four other square Holes, *viz. f* with another behind it, and *g* with one before it, are for the double Standards, which are to be well shouldered, or braced on the Side of each that is next to the End of the Plank, and on the Outside. There is no need of Shoulder or Brace on the Sides where the Spindle is placed, or on the Side next to the Middle of the Plank.

The Four round Holes *h i k l* are those thro' which the Four Pins pass that hold on the Limbers, and the Piece A, in *Fig.* 2. and the other of the same Sort in *Fig.* 4.

Fig. 2. and 4. shew how the Harrow's Leg B is held to the Piece A, by the Pin C. The Letters *a b* shew the Holes through which the Pins do pass to

E e   screw

screw the Piece A up to the Plank, and the Limbers for guiding the Harrow. This Piece A is somewhat longer than the Breadth of the Plank; it is about Two Inches thick, and Two and an half in Depth. The Pin *Fig.* 3. goes through this Piece near the Bottom of its fore End, whereby the Harrow-tines have the more room to rise up, without being held down by the Legs pressing against the Plank.

Fig. 3. is the Pin C, of *Fig.* 2. *a* is its Head, *b* its round Part, whereon the Harrow moves; *c* is its square Part, that prevents its turning, which by the Motion of the Harrow would unscrew the Nut *d*, and cause it to come off of the Screw *e*, and be lost.

The Harrow is also shewn in *Fig.* 1. as it is guided by the Pieces before described: B is its Head, that holds the Tines D D, drawn by the Legs C C. Tho' these Legs *in Plano* seem in their Middle to crook sideways, yet when out of Perspective, their Middles crook only downwards; which is to give the greater Length to the Tines, and the more room for them to move up.

Fig. 5. is the Spindle in Three Parts. A is the middle Part, wherein are the Notches *b b*. This is best to be of Oak, or some other hard Wood, in which the Edges of the Notches are less apt to wear than in softer Wood; but I have had a Set that have lasted the Drilling of 120 Acres, when made of Ash. B and C are the Two other Parts: D and E are their Ends, whereon the Wheels are put. The Holes *b b b b*, and the same in the other End under the Letter E, are for setting the Wheels at different Distances, in order for making new Notches, or for different-sized Ridges: The Wheels are held in their Places by long Nails put through some of these Holes, and clenched upon the Iron Stock-bonds to prevent their falling out. These Ends B and C need not be cut to a Square; except just enough to prevent the Wheels from turning on the Spindle.

Thefe

These Three Parts are grafted together by Help of the hollow Cylinder *Fig.* 6. which, being put on upon the Joint *f*, of the Spindle *Fig.* 5. holds the Parts A and B together by the Two Pins *a a*, paffing through the Cylinder near its Ends, and through the Holes *k* and *g*.

This Joint may be in another manner; *viz.* One Part of the Spindle may enter into the other by cutting it to a square Peg of an Inch long, and 3-4ths Diameter, entering an Hole that fits it, at the End of the other Part.

These Pins will be beft to have Screws at their Ends with Nuts to them; and then they need not be fo tight in the Holes, and may be the more eafily taken out, when the Part B is to be taken off for avoiding Obftructions in drilling an outfide Ridge.

The Cylinder is a Foot long, and about half an Inch thick, bound with an Iron Ferrel at each End; and if there were another in the Middle, it might be the ftronger.

Place the Cylinder on the Outfide of the Spindle, the Joint *f* being exactly againft the Middle of the Cylinder; and mark at each End of it, in order to fee when it is in its right Place; and after it is put on and pinned, mark likewife on the Spindle the exact Places of the Holes, for the more eafy finding them every Time the Cylinder is put on.

Another Cylinder muft be on the Joint *c*, held together by Pins paffing thro' the Holes *i* and *d*, in the fame manner, and for the fame Purpofe, as the other Joint already defcribed.

The Spindle ought to be of equal Diameter with the Bore of the Seed-boxes, thro' which it is to pafs; but this I find, needs not be quite an Inch and 3-4ths; it may want an 8th of it, even in this long Spindle.

Fig. 7. is one of the Pins which hold the Cylinder in its Place, as has been faid; *a* is its Head; *b* the Stalk, which would be better to be a Screw at its lower End, whereon to fcrew a Nut; but then the Stalk muft be fquare at the Head.

Fig. 8. is a Sheat with its Trunk and Share of the Drill-plough, which has been defcribed in *Plates* 4. and 5. but the Shape of the Share, as it rifes at the Socket, is more plainly feen in this Figure.

Fig. 9. is the whole Wheat-drill, which at prefent I ufe for planting the double Row. A is the Hopper, rifing and finking on the fingle Standard B, which holds it up. C is the thing like the Carrier of a Latch, defcribed by *Fig.* 22. in *Plate* 4. I need fay no more for defcribing this Drill, than to fhew how it differs from that defcribed in *Plate* 4. *viz.* This Hopper has Two of thefe Carriers, the one near its Top, like the other; and another near its Bottom, which keeps the Plough from rifing at either End, without the rifing of either End of the Hopper, which is no Inconvenience here; becaufe the Two Shares, being but Ten Inches afunder, are almoft the fame as one; fo that at the Diftance the Wheels ftand from each other, the rifing of one Wheel doth not lift up the Share that is next to it perceptibly; as it would do if the Shares were farther afunder, or the Wheels nearer together.

This Hopper holds twice as much Seed as the fingle fore Hopper did, *viz.* half a Bufhel; and is divided into Two equal Parts by the Partition *e*, whereby the Driller fees whether the Seed is difcharged equally; and if he perceives that one Part of the Hopper runs out fafter than the other, he muft adjuft them by the Setting-fcrews.

The Funnels *a a*, which receive the Seed from the Hopper, and convey it down into the Trunks *c c*, appear under the Hopper, as doth alfo Part of the Hole *d*, whereon the Funnel ftood when the fore Hopper was fingle. D fhews the Cylinder upon the grafted Spindle at one End, as F fhews where the other End with its Cylinder and Wheel is taken off.

The

The Ends of the Piece A, which guide the Harrow, appear behind the Plank at *f f*. At *g* in the Harrow-head is a Hole exactly in the Middle between the Tines, for tying on a Stone when the Harrow is too light for the Soil. *Note*, This Hole muſt follow exactly after the Middle of the Plank, *i. e.* between the Two Shares at an equal Diſtance from each.

Obſerve, that the Legs of this Harrow go thro' the Head on the Outſides of the Tines, as in the treble Drill they go thro' on the Inſide of the Tines. Inſtead of the wooden Tines, may be put in common Iron Tines of a proper Length.

The Two Hooks whereby the Plough is drawn are at *h h*. 'Tis beſt for the Ends of the Hooks to turn upwards, ſo that the Links of the Chain-traces, that are to be put on them, may not be apt to drop off. Take care that theſe Traces be of an equal Length, which may be eaſily made even by the Links that are put on theſe Hooks.

Note, The Links of the Piece of Chain, whereby the Plough is made to go deeper or ſhallower, may be very ſmall, and by no means in the Proportion they bear to the Limbers in the Cut. There need not be above Four or Five Links. If there be occaſion to raiſe or ſink the Limbers more than that Number will reach, the Cord may be tied longer or ſhorter on the other Limber. And when there is not the Convenience of Chain-traces, they may be ſupplied by a few Iron Links at the Ends of Hempen Traces.

Fig. 10. is the Shape of a wooden Wreath, which (when the Shares ſtand wider aſunder, or when there are more than Two of them, ſo that they come nearer to the Ends of the Plank, this Wreath) is neceſſary to be put on the Spindle, the End *a* bearing againſt the Inſide of the double Standards, and the End *b* being towards the Hopper. 'Tis fixt to the Spindle by the Screw *c*, which ſhould not enter the Spindle above half an Inch deep. There may be another like Screw to enter in the fame manner on the oppofite Side of this Wreath There muft be in this cafe another Wreath the fame of this to bear againft the other double Standards. And when thefe Wreaths are ufed, the Hopper muft have only the upper Carrier C; the lower one muft be taken off. But in this our Drill for planting Wheat, no Wreaths muft be on the Spindle, except thofe at *b b*, which are to hold the Hopper from moving endways. And thefe may be of the Sort above defcribed, the End *a* bearing againft the Hopper.

Fig. 11. is the Beam of the Hoe-plough defcribed in *Plate* VI. *Fig.* 2. with no other Alteration than leaving out the Hole H, and the pricked Line between it and the Hole I; and changing the Hole G into a Mortife. The pricked Line *a b* reprefents the hinder Edge of the Plank, behind which appears a very fmall Part of a Mortife. See *p.* 415, 416.

Fig. 12. is the Plank, which is *Fig.* 3. in *Plate* VI. The Improvement of it in this Figure is defcribed in *p.* 415, 416.

An Appendix *to Chap.* IX. *of* Wheat, *p.* 138. *containing* Memoranda *for the Practifers of this* Hufbandry.

AT the Second Hoeing the Plough goes in the Furrow of the Firft, making it deeper, and nearer to the Wheat. The Third Hoeing fills up this Furrow; and then, at the Fourth Hoeing, the Plough goes in the fame Place as the Second, turning the Mould into the Interval. 'Tis remarkable that though the Furrows of the Second and Fourth Hoeings be deep, and near to the Rows, feeming to deprive the Wheat of the Mould which fhould nourifh it, whereby one would imagine, that thefe Furrows lying long open fhould weaken or ftarve it; yet it is juft the contrary; for it grows the more vigorous: And it is the Obfervation of my Ploughmen, that
they

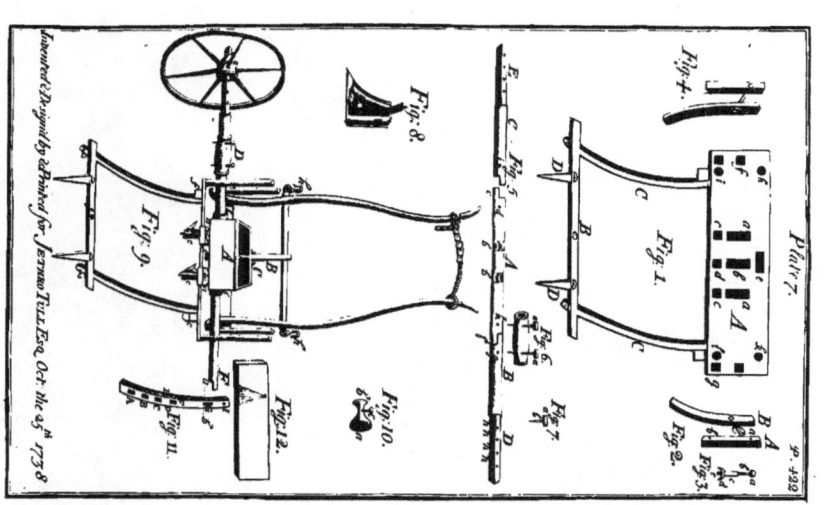

Plate 7.

p. 455

Fig: 4.

Fig: 1.

Fig: 5.

Fig: 6.

Fig: 7.

Fig: 8.

Fig: 9.

Fig: 10.

Fig: 11.

Fig: 12.

Fig: 2.

Fig: 3.

Invented & Designed by & Printed for JETHRO TULL Esq. Oct the 25th 1738

they cannot at thefe Hoeings go too near to the Rows, unlefs the Plough fhould tear out the Plants.

If I may prefume to affign the Caufe of this furprifing Effect, it is, in my Opinion, the following; *viz.* This open Furrow has a double Surface of Earth, which by the *Nitre* of the contiguous *Atmofphere*, is pulverized to a great Degree of Minutenefs near the Row. The Roots that the Plough cuts off on the perpendicular Side of the Furrow, fend out new Fibres to receive the *Pabulum* from this new-made Pafture; and alfo Part of this fuperfine Powder is continually falling down into the Bottom of the Furrow, and there gives a very quick Growth to thofe Roots that are next it, and a quick Paffage through it into the Earth of the Interval, where they take likewife the Benefit of the other Side of this pulverized Furrow. When it is faid, that Air kills Roots, it muft not be underftood, that it kills a Plant, unlefs all, or almoft all, its Root is expofed to it, as it is not in this Cafe. Some think there are Roots that run horizontally below the Plough into the Interval; but of this I am not convinced.

'Tis not often that we hoe above Four times; and then the Furrow is turned towards the Row at the Third time only.

There being no Danger from thefe Furrows lying long open, we are not confined to any precife Diftance between the times of Hoeing, for which we need only regard the Weather, the Weeds, and our own Convenience of Opportunity and Leifure.

'Tis an Advantage when thefe Furrows lie open on each Side of the double Row till Harveft; for then there need only Two Furrows to be plowed on a Ridge to throw down the Partition in order for planting the next Crop; but if at the laft Hoeing the Furrows are turned towards the Row, they muft be plowed back again after Harveft before the Partition can be plowed: This requires double the time of the other ; and the fooner the Partitions are plowed, the more time they will have to be pulverized before they are replanted.   Indeed this Advantage is only when the Rows are to be planted where they were the Year before; for this is rather a Difadvantage when they are to be planted in the Intervals. Whether thefe Furrows lying long open next the Rows in very hot dry Climates may be prejudicial, cannot be known, but by Trials.

As from the external Superficies of an Acre of Pafture on a rich Soil, Animals take more *Pabulum* than of an Acre on a poor Soil ; fo Vegetables take more *Pabulum* from the internal Superficies of a rich Acre than of a poor one ; the Pulveration, or Superficies of Parts, being equal. *See* p. 44, 45. From whence there is no Encouragement for making Trials on very poor Land.

'Tis no great Matter whether the Rows are drilled on the Partitions, or the Intervals; for the Crops of a Field, Four Years fucceffively drilled on the Partitions, were very good.   After the Partitions had been plowed, and lain open till the Weather made them pulverizable by the Harrows, and then turned together by Furrows larger than thofe which opened them, much Earth of the Intervals was mixed with them.   This is the ftrongeft and loweft Ground I have ; and if there fhould be much wet Weather after Harveft, it is fo long in drying, that we take the firft Opportunity the Weather allows for planting the Wheat, which is generally done in the above manner, becaufe it is the fhorteft ; but, without fome fuch Reafon to the contrary, I prefer planting the Rows on the precedent Intervals.

My Field, whereon is now the Thirteenth Crop of Wheat, has fhewn that the Rows may fuccefsfully ftand upon any Part of the Ground.   The Ridges of this Field were for the Twelfth Crop, changed from Six Feet to Four Feet Six Inches : In order for this Alteration,

Alteration, the Ridges were plowed down, and the whole Field was plowed crofs-ways of the Ridges for making them level ; and then the next Ridges were laid out the fame way as the former, but One Foot Four Inches narrower ; and the double Rows drilled on their Tops, whereby of confequence there muft be fome Rows ftanding on every Part of the Ground, both on the former Partitions, and on every Part of the Intervals : Notwithftanding this, there was no manner of Difference in the Goodnefs of the Rows, and the whole Field was in every Part of it equal, and the beft, I believe, that ever grew on it. It has now the Thirteenth Crop, likely to be very good, tho' the Land was not plowed crofs-ways.

The proper Times for Plowings and Hoeings depending upon the Weather, and other Circumftances, cannot be directed but by the Reafon and Experience of the Practifer, as has been faid.

The Number of Ridges being increafed, as their Breadth is now diminifhed, occafions fomewhat the more Plough-work ; we likewife ufe more Handwork than formerly; but the Profit of this increafed Labour is more thán double to the Expence of it.

The Decline of the Woolen Manufacture furnifhes us at this time with Plenty of Hand-hoers and Weeders ; becaufe they can earn much more by working in the Field than by Spinning at home.

'Tis better to make Fifteen Ridges on an Acre, than to leave any Earth unmoved by the Hoe-plough in the Middle of the Intervals ; but when Ploughmen, by Practice, underftand well to ufe the Hoeplough, they will plow the Intervals clean, tho' the Ridges are only Fourteen on an Acre.

Bearded Wheat is in this Country called *Cone*, and that which has no Beard *Lammas*. I obferved formerly the Bread of *White-cone* had a little yellowifh Caft, which I now fufpect was from the Mill-ftones; for I have feen it be very white thefe many Years, fince

the

the Millers know better how to grind this Wheat. Cone-wheat Weftwards yields Six-pence a Bufhel more than *Lammas*; but towards *London* the contrary.

The Reafons why a whole Field of Wheat doth not produce a Crop equal in proportion to a Yard or Perch cut, rubbed out, and weighed immediately upon the Spot, may be, becaufe the Grain of the Field lying to fweat in the Mow, lofes confiderably of its Weight and Meafure. There is alfo fome loft in the Field by Reapers, and by Leafers; and fome is by Threfhers thrown out of the Barn; and fome of them are found to have Contrivances to carry home with them at Night, Part of the Wheat they threfh in the Day. I fay nothing of thofe Thieves, who in Harveft rob the Field in the Dark; tho' they are not very uncommon.

I miffed of making my propofed Experiment of the fingle Row, after I had prepared for it by plowing out one of the double in feveral Places for that Purpofe; but, in the Hurry of Harveft, they were cut together with the reft, without making any Trial; as fhould have been made, if my Illnefs had not prevented my Attendance in the Field at the time of Reaping.

The Practice and Inftruments that are left off for better in their room, as the Quadruple and Treble Rows, &c. are ftill ufeful to be fhewn, in order to deter others from going into an inferior Method that is now exploded; for fome might think it an Improvement of the double Rows, &c. by their own Invention, if they fhould not know it had been already tried.

INDEX.

INDEX.

   The

S *St.*

S

Trans-

F I N I S.

www.ingramcontent.com/pod-product-compliance
Lightning Source LLC
Chambersburg PA
CBHW022015110726
47901CB00006B/1539